"A delightful ode to complicated family relationships, growing up in the theater, and opening your heart to a second chance with your first love. . . . I wish I could move to Bard's Rest immediately!"

—Jen DeLuca, author of *Well Played*

"Reading *For the Love of the Bard* is like entering a fantasy written specifically for bookworms. . . . This is a delight, full of florid language, slow-building tension, groan-inducing puns, loads of food descriptions, and a fun and fleshed-out supporting cast."

—*USA Today*

"Perfect to read on the beach."

—*The Boston Globe*

"The sleepy summer magic of outdoor Shakespeare casts a heady spell that lends the romance a spark of magic."

—*Entertainment Weekly*

"A sizzling second-chance romance full of witty banter, quirky characters, and a sensational Shakespeare-infused setting. . . . For anyone who never got over their high school crush or who adores Shakespeare, this is an absolute must-read!"

—Jenn McKinlay, *New York Times* bestselling author of *Summer Reading*

"Jessica Martin's rollicking and bighearted debut is a love letter to all things Shakespeare, filled with whip-smart banter that would make the Bard himself jealous, a supporting cast I'd love to share an ale with, and best of all, a second-chance romance that's the stuff of sonnets."

—Victoria Schade, *USA Today* bestselling author of *Dog Friendly*

"Sweet and Shakespearean, *For the Love of the Bard* sweeps small-town charm and second-chance swoon up into a delightful rom-com fit for the stage."

—Emily Wibberley and Austin Siegemund-Broka,
authors of *The Roughest Draft*

"Brimming with Shakespeare references to delight the brain and a slow-burn, banter-filled romance to melt the heart, this rom-com captivates. . . . A fabulous, laugh-out-loud experience!"

—India Holton, author of *The League of Gentlewomen Witches*

"This charming romance with its cast of quirky, lovable characters will enchant you. . . . If the question is to read or not to read, the answer is: definitely read."

—Amanda Elliot, author of *Sadie on a Plate*

"Numerous dramas—Shakespearean, familial, publishing related, and more—intersect in Martin's . . . thoroughly enjoyable rom-com debut."

—*Publishers Weekly*

The
DANE
of My
EXISTENCE

JESSICA MARTIN

BERKLEY ROMANCE
NEW YORK

BERKLEY ROMANCE
Published by Berkley
An imprint of Penguin Random House LLC
penguinrandomhouse.com

Library of Congress Cataloging-in-Publication Data

Names: Martin, Jessica, 1981- author.
Title: The dane of my existence / Jessica Martin.
Description: First Edition. | New York: Berkley Romance, 2023. |
Series: A Bard's Rest romance
Identifiers: LCCN 2022044789 (print) | LCCN 2022044790 (ebook) |
ISBN 9780593437452 (trade paperback) | ISBN 9780593437469 (ebook)
Subjects: LCGFT: Romance fiction. | Novels.
Classification: LCC PS3613.A77964 D36 2023 (print) |
LCC PS3613.A77964 (ebook) | DDC 813/.6—dc23/eng/20220926
LC record available at https://lccn.loc.gov/2022044789
LC ebook record available at https://lccn.loc.gov/2022044790

First Edition: July 2023

Printed in the United States of America
1st Printing

For Edna

"*I can no other answer make, but thanks, and thanks, and ever thanks.*"

—*William Shakespeare*

....

The Dane
of My Existence Cast

Portia Barnes ....our no-shit-taking heroine

Benjamin Dane ....real estate developer, potentially redeemable cad

Candace Thornton ....event planner, bestie

Byron Greene..lawyer, Benedick

Gerald W. Cutler the III ....managing partner, mentor

Isabella Barnes ....college professor, bookstore proprietor and matriarch of
   Clan Barnes

Peter Barnes ....college professor, bookstore proprietor and patriarch of
   Clan Barnes

Miranda Barnes .... middle sister of Clan Barnes, bestselling author

Cordelia Barnes.................................youngest sister of Clan Barnes, baking goddess

Emmeline McGandry...battle-ax

Chris Rogers...corporate partner in the trenches

Sam Maeda..real estate developer, complete badass

Tillie Perkins...shoe store proprietor

Ian Grant..lumberjack hipster

Riki Singh...shark in training

The Dane of
My Existence

ACT ONE

June

The Shark Tank

I strode through the shark tank on four-figure heels. All around me, young, hungry, eager heads turned my way. I pressed on, aware of how well my designer dress fit my form like armor and how flawlessly my corona of blond hair shone from this morning's blowout. Everything about my signature look had been carefully designed to exude confidence but not arrogance, taste not flash and, above all, strength not weakness. And I'd been pulling it off since my own stint in the tank years ago.

All the big-name firms had their own nicknames for where they housed their first-years—the bullpen, the cockpit, the boar's den— but I preferred "the shark tank" because it didn't confer gender on the training ground for the future leaders of the firm.

I scanned the ranks of baby predators—they may as well have been wearing signs around their necks that read "Will work all night for your approval" and "Broken by due diligence—can you help?" Well, what had they expected? Our firm's first-year experience functioned like an intro to O-chem—designed to weed out the weak and undisciplined—and only about half of these Brooks Brothers–clad hopefuls would get offers to return next year. If they wanted a touchy-feely experience, they should have gone into I-banking.

"Riki," I called.

The associate in question looked up from her monitor, her dark eyes sharp and her even darker hair swinging out behind her in a silky whip.

"Excellent work on that merger markup. Comments in your inbox. Get them back to me by Monday morning."

"Of course," she answered. No hesitation, even though it was early Friday afternoon and I'd just sunk her weekend.

"I'll forward you the invite for the call with the client scheduled for Tuesday morning. You can take them through the open issues."

"Thank you, Ms. Barnes."

"Portia," I reminded her with a half smile.

"Portia," she echoed firmly.

Several heads swiveled in Riki's direction, their eyes narrowed. I'd singled her out to lead a client call—an opportunity that few of them had been offered in their six-month stint here. Of course, I'd put a target on Riki's back, but I knew she could handle it.

I had plans for Riki. Ample amounts of intelligence and determination—the perfect alchemical formula to be my star associate. Now I just had to convince her to move to Boston. All in good time though.

I proceeded with my swath through the shark tank, blithely ignoring the murmurs springing up in my wake as I pressed the elevator button for the twenty-fifth floor. Even though these heels were modern marvels of foot-cradling wonderment straight out of a woman-owned design house in Florence, that didn't mean I wanted to hike up six flights of stairs in them.

The doors slid open, and the tastefully appointed corporate reception area greeted me like an old friend. I knew every inch of dark cherry furniture and every brushstroke of those neoclassical foxhunts that hung on the wall.

Even though Gerald would be expecting me in exactly eight minutes, I swung by my office one last time. Lingering in the doorway, I surveyed the now sparse room. The walnut desk had only a docking station, and my two diplomas from Harvard hung perfectly straight on the eggshell wall, waiting for facilities to pack them up and ship them to Boston. On the bookshelf where I'd already cleared out several law treatises and publications, a single silver Tiffany frame with a picture of my parents and sisters winked at me in the late-afternoon sun. I hadn't had the heart to take it home with me last night, knowing I'd be back one more time, so I reached for it now, stowing it away in my Stella McCartney vegan leather handbag.

Miranda had insisted we take one this past Christmas, and after fumbling with the timer on her phone and several obscenity-laden retakes because Dad and Cordelia kept closing their eyes, we'd finally managed a mostly normal one of us. Miranda, who looked like one of those Waterhouse maidens—all cascading red hair and milk white skin, deceptively demure and serene but for the slain dragon at her feet—and Cordelia, ever the luscious Botticelli, hogging all the curves and curls our gene pool had to offer, sandwiched Mom in the middle. Dad and I, who shared the same willowy build and coloring—winter-sky blue eyes and pale, straight hair—stood tall in the back. And, of course, because we couldn't have a family photo without him—Miranda's dog, Puck, sitting on her feet and still managing to pull off the best smile of all of us. *Home.* The idea filled me with equal parts longing and dread.

I didn't need to glance at my watch to know I needed to get a move on, so I silently bade goodbye to my home away from home, the corner office that I comfortably occupied up to fourteen hours a day without complaint, and stole one last glance at the sweeping views of Manhattan out my floor-to-ceiling window.

Chris Rogers sat on the other side of the floor in the corner office diagonal from my own. Eons ago, when we'd been summer associates together, we'd shared a tiny, cramped office down on the ninth floor with panoramic views of the alley, our backs nearly touching if we were both in our chairs at the same time. How the mighty and relentless had risen.

Like mine, Chris's present office was spacious and appointed in the same dark walnut, but that's where the similarities ended. His walls were crammed with pictures of a younger version of himself and his friends grinning like loons atop the summits of Denali, Kilimanjaro, Snowdon and Mont Blanc, while his desk and work-table were overflowing with mismatched frames displaying snap-shots of his surgeon wife, Callie, and their adorable but slightly terrifying twins, Alyssa and Kayla, who'd gone off to kindergarten last fall.

Chris himself stood at the window, his back to me. He stretched and yawned loudly, so I knew he'd heard me enter. "I thought you were going to leave by noon to beat the traffic. You know how it picks up in June."

"The best-laid plans. I wanted to finish up the Peterson draft before I left."

"So I don't have to look in on Stu Peterson and his dullard sons this summer?" he asked, a hopeful note in his voice.

"Oh no." I smiled. "You'll be holding their hands through all their ridiculous underbaked deals, but I bought you a week or so. Consider it my going-away gift."

"I'm the one babysitting your clients for the summer. I believe I'm the one gift giving here," he insisted, turning from the window. Coming in somewhere north of six feet, Chris loomed tall and lean, with dark skin and amber eyes. These days, he sported a thin mus-tache, which he insisted he'd grown to look more partner-like, but really, I thought he did it to drive Callie nuts.

He and I had grown up together in the office as freshly minted summer associates and only slighter wiser first-years. We'd both been fast-tracked to senior associates and made partner the same year, two years ahead of our peers. We'd been colleagues and late-night-Thai-in-the-office buddies and occasional rivals. When the opportu-nity for managing partner in Boston's satellite office came up, I assumed it would come down to one of us. But to my surprise, Chris had bowed out early in the process. "Boston does not deserve my Black daughters," he'd told me. "That city has some serious growing up to do." And though I respected his decision, I would miss him, and that was not something I said of most people. Okay, anyone. I didn't say that about anyone.

"Do you have a game plan yet?" Chris demanded. "So you don't go all Annie Wilkes in the backwoods?"

I wrinkled my nose. "I don't live in the backwoods of New Hampshire."

"Portia, there are no Orangetheories or Williams Sonomas within a fifty-mile radius. Face it, you're in the backwoods."

"Says the guy who grew up eating grits and gators," I retorted, crossing my arms over my chest. But not too tight. Wrinkles were unseemly.

"Don't distract me," Chris said with a grin. "I know all your moves. Now, what is the game plan for your sabbatical? You know Gerald will make you take the full three months."

"Sit around in my sweatpants and eat ice cream?"

"You don't own sweatpants and I've never seen you eat ice cream."

"I own yoga pants and have been known to put away my fair share of gelato."

His eyes widened to comedic proportions. "I am in the presence of a rebel."

I sighed. "I've been a little busy closing matters here and making sure the transition team is on top of everything in Boston. I haven't really had time to think of a plan."

"Bullshit. You show up to bagel Fridays with a plan."

While he wasn't wrong (thin-sliced pumpernickel bagels or bust), I didn't think he'd approve much of my paltry plans for the summer, which included little more than brushing up on a couple of management books and TED talks on leadership. I still held out hope that Gerald would drop this whole sabbatical business. This place needed me. He needed me.

"I suppose I'll let my mother put me to work on the festival," I hedged. But even as I said it, my throat tightened with that familiar squeeze of anxiety I felt when I thought of my mother. Well, not specifically my mother per se, but her health. A little more than a year ago, she'd found a lump. A lump that had turned out to be stage two breast cancer and had required surgery and ongoing chemotherapy to treat it. I hadn't told anyone at work about it. Not even Chris. When you shared bad news like this with coworkers, they would go all kid-glove on you, and that could translate to a loss of opportunities. Hard pass.

"Callie and the girls are excited to come to the festival this year," Chris said, slicing through my thoughts. "Thank you for the invite."

"I noticed you didn't include yourself in that list."

He shrugged. "Shakespeare's not my bag."

"Mine either," I told him with a conspiratorial smile. "But home is home, whether that's grits and gators or a bunch of ex–English majors running wild in farthingales and codpieces and sporting bad British accents."

Chris snorted. "So your plan to not succumb to Shakespearean madness is . . ."

"I have hobbies."

"Name one."

"Running."

"That's not a hobby. That's masochistic. Name another."

"Swimming."

"Where are you going to swim in the backwoods?" Chris demanded. "You don't strike me as a skinny-dip-in-the-creek kind of person."

"The creek has eels in it." I shuddered. "Ill-advised skinny-dipping aside, I'll figure something out. On the drive home."

He didn't look convinced, but he let me off the hook all the same. I really admired that about Chris. You could tell he saw everything, but he didn't always feel the need to call you out on it. "Well, I can't say I'll miss you," I said, repeating the exact words we'd exchanged when we'd parted ways after our summer associateship, neither of us knowing at the time whether we'd be invited back to FrancisPearl as first-years.

"I won't miss you in the slightest either," he said, falling into our routine. "I certainly won't be picking up the phone to call or text you."

"Not at all. I've already deleted your number from my contacts. You know how I feel about clutter."

"I won't even say take care of yourself."

"That would be beneath you," I agreed.

He smiled broadly. "See you in August. But if I show up and you're running around in a corset with a decidedly unposh accent . . . I'm not even turning the car off. That's how art house horror flicks start."

"Fair enough. Give my love to Callie and the girls," I called with a blithe smile as I walked out of the office of the only person at FrancisPearl I considered a friend.

When the elevator doors opened, I stood facing the boardroom conference center, which always reminded me of being in a high-rise terrarium: floor-to-ceiling glass windows everywhere that looked out on New York's finest views, with some oversized statement plants thrown in around the tastefully selected furniture for context.

"He ready for me?" I asked, pausing at Marnie's desk. Marnie Symonds, the executive admin to Gerald, was bursting with life and opinions and vibrant auburn curls.

"Head on in. You ready for your summer vacation?"

I snorted. "What did you do with your sabbatical?"

"I took my husband to Santorini and ate my weight in saganaki several times over and drank enough wine to fill the harbor."

"Saganaki?"

"Fried cheese."

"Eating one's weight in fried cheese does sound delightful."

"Honey, I'm willing to wager you've never once eaten your weight in fried cheese."

"I can't say I have," I admitted, then added, "but maybe this is the summer to try it. Wish me luck."

Taking a deep breath and locking my most confident smile into place, I pushed through the doors and was momentarily blinded by the bright afternoon sun streaming in through the windows, hitting the gleaming table where seven suits sat jockeying for airtime.

"Gentlemen," Gerald Cutler said with a magnificent sweep of his hand, "I'd like to introduce Portia Barnes, the jewel of Francis-Pearl's best-in-class corporate department. Portia specializes in mergers and acquisitions, development plays . . ."

As Gerald ticked off my many attributes, I sized up the suits. All men. All dressed like they had something to prove. Good. No surprises, then.

When Gerald had finished, I smiled, showing ruthlessly whitened teeth, and offered my new clients the slightest inclination of my head, making it clear that while collaboration was always on the table, respect would be earned.

While the suit in charge outlined his business model, I listened and nodded attentively, all the while watching Gerald, the managing partner of FrancisPearl and my mentor. Despite being born with a whopper of a silver spoon in his mouth, the man was a grinder, a pugilistic pit bull in a well-tailored suit who had carried the firm on his broad back during the economic downturns and the contentious merger of Francis, Joseph and Cullen LLP with Pearl and Lovejoy LLP that had nearly sunk the firm in the early '90s. He was the man who had plucked me from the obscurity of the shark tank, loaded me down with work and awarded me at the end with a job offer, the highest sign-on bonus ever offered to a first-year and this single comment in my firm recommendation: *Portia does not suffer fools.*

Yet he was saddling me with another client relationship full of them. Was that guy actually talking about structured buyouts? So early 2000s. Still, maybe I could interpret this as some lifting of Gerald's draconian "no work during sabbatical" mandate? After all, he'd asked me to meet this new client, a novel puzzle to take apart and put back together again in much better working order than that in which I'd found it. Maybe Gerald had come to his senses and realized that a summer sabbatical was unnecessary—more of a guideline, rather than a requirement, for a new managing partner.

Managing partner. The words echoed in my head. Not just managing partner. The youngest in firm history. Granted, Boston was a small satellite office focusing on corporate and commercial development plays, but it would no doubt grow quickly under the right leadership. My leadership.

I pulled myself back to the present, making the appropriate noises and saying all the right things. When my new clients had departed with the smoothest of assurances that they would be receiving the best legal treatment that our firm could provide, I turned to Gerald. "Sir?" There were years of working together in that single word.

"They were displeased with their last firm out of Boston. Gladson. Botched diligence on a deal that cost them on the back end."

I wrinkled my nose. "That's what you get for cheaping out on legal counsel."

"I couldn't agree more. I would like you to ensure that they receive the best service we have to offer, which is why I'd like you to personally oversee their relationship."

I tried not to preen; really I did. But I couldn't help but bask in one of his rare compliments. "I'll staff Genevieve as counsel and Riki for associate support and—"

"They will be running out what's left of their retainer with Gladson over the summer and transferring their relationship to the firm as of September," Gerald cut in. "I am serious about the terms of your sabbatical."

"But I—"

"FrancisPearl needs you fresh and rested for September," he said kindly, but firmly. "There can be no missteps, no mistakes, not even the whisper of a hiccup with Boston. We cannot have another Palo Alto on our hands," he said, referencing the last satellite office we'd launched, which had landed us on AboveTheLaw.com when the site broke the story that the managing partners had set up a March Madness–style bracket ranking the associates, taking bets on which ones would advance to the Elite Eight of actually receiving offers. "Tie up the Frederickson merger next week with Riki, look in on email and respond to top-to-top client relationship emails only and leave the rest to your team, but otherwise, you follow firm policy. If I have to send Marnie up there to retrieve your laptop, I will."

"You wouldn't."

"Of course I wouldn't. I'm terrified of that woman. I'd drive to New Hampshire myself."

"Think of the waste of billable hours."

"Portia," Gerald said, rubbing the papery skin around his eyes, steely pitch eyes that had seen thousands of merger agreements and rainmakers and burnouts and closed-door deals. Even though he was approaching the mandatory retirement age for partners, he still seemed godlike, the way Zeus might have been if he'd left Olympus and gone corporate. "You've done all the prep work you can do for the opening. I want you to take the summer and focus on you. Time like this won't come up again for you, not at the rate you continue to rise. Come back well rested and ready to fully devote yourself to FrancisPearl as its newest managing partner."

While I appreciated the sentiment, I also bristled. "Fully devote myself"? How many countless nights, weekends and holidays had I spent here, sometimes sleeping on the floor between turns of the deal drafts, at least until I'd made partner and been awarded an office large enough to accommodate a chaise I could snatch a few hours of sleep on? My career—this firm—was my life.

He touched my arm lightly. I raised an eyebrow. Gerald and I were in the "strictly colleagues who occasionally handshake after big deals" category. We did not hug or high-five or anything beyond that. "Sir?"

"You can't afford another Berlin."

He was referencing the deal, not the city. The sole blemish on my otherwise pristine record.

"I know that," I said, resisting the urge to grind my teeth.

"You need to be at your physical and mental best. Stepping into the role of managing partner at your age will invite scrutiny and criticism. Doubly so because you're a woman."

"If you're having doubts—"

"I have never doubted you, but others will. I don't have to tell you how this game is played. Win at any cost."

"Not at any price," I finished with a small smile. It wouldn't be a meeting with Gerald if he didn't mention his mantra at least once. Winning was the goal, but it was how we won that mattered to Gerald. Having grown my career under his careful watch, I'd understood it to mean we were to win at any cost—that was obvious—but we also had to win smart.

"You know, it's never too early to start thinking about your legacy," he added.

Legacy. Such a tricky word. I wondered if he meant his wife, Gillian, and their four adult children and their children. His biological legacy. Or was he alluding to his legacy at FrancisPearl? Check that box on the second one for me. I'd already made a name for myself in the industry, although I planned to be the stuff of legends one day. It was the first box, that concept of biological legacy, that I found troubling. I hadn't allocated much time to the pursuit of that. Or had any real desire to. Relationships were like store-bought salad dressing: artificial and full of crap that was bad for you. But I wouldn't tell Gerald that. It was the kind of thing married people found upsetting.

Instead, I told him in my best closer voice, "Rest assured, I could begin tomorrow and still be the best managing partner you've ever hired. But I will do what is asked of me. I will take this sabbatical and return ready to lead."

Gerald's ensuing smile, like that of an old winter wolf, flashed in the reflection of the glass. I matched it with one of my own, full of understanding.

Scene Two

....

Bard's Books

I pulled into the empty parking lot of Bard's Books just as my youngest sister, Cordelia, turned the hanging sign to "Closed." Sticking her head out the door, she called, "You planned that!"

"I did not," I protested as I stepped out of my car—even though I had expertly timed the trip so I would arrive as the shop closed. Interacting with my parents' hyper-verbal bookstore clientele, a lot of whom had known me since birth, was not in my social wheelhouse after several hours in the car. "I had to make sure I settled everything at the office and my apartment. Three months is not exactly a weekend getaway."

"Right, because we wouldn't want all your pets and plants to suffer in your absence," Cordelia teased as the sun backlit her shiny black curls and made her eyes glow like robins' eggs. I'd always admired the deep, vibrant blue of her eyes. My own blue looked more like sun-starved winter skies, which Miranda insisted fit my ice maiden aesthetic.

"Plants and pets are emotional crutches," I tossed back.

"Don't let Miranda hear you say that," she warned. "Oh hey, did you give Geoffrey my love before you left?"

"I promised him I'd return with no less than a dozen of your handcrafted desserts." Geoffrey was my building's concierge, an old-school French gentleman who would have given the Anthony Hopkins butler character in *The Remains of the Day* a run for his money in the decorum department. I'd always appreciated Geoffrey's professionalism and ability to procure late-night pho at a moment's notice, but when Cordelia had come to visit me in March and I'd been half an hour late getting back from a client meeting, the two had bonded in the foyer over the finer points of macaron making, and now they exchanged holiday cards. Cordelia was like that, picking up friends wherever she went.

"I'll make it two dozen. How was the vibe at work? Were people wearing all black? Tearing their hair out?"

"That would be different from a normal Friday how, exactly?"

Cordelia snickered. "I still can't believe they sent you away."

"Stop making it sound like I'm some unwed teen being shipped off to a convent. It's a firm-mandated sabbatical, Cordelia. Everyone is required to take one after the fifth year of employment and, in my case, before assuming the role of managing partner."

"Yeah, yeah, corporate ass kicker. Well, come on in, you can say hi to Dad and Mom—they're both here."

"I thought Mom agreed to take some time off this summer? That's why they hired a full-time manager to oversee the store."

"Cool your tits," Cordelia said with a careless wave of her hand. "Mom's not working in the store or teaching any summer classes, per Dr. Wu's orders, but she's still doing committee stuff, of course. Because otherwise the Shakespeareverse might cease to exist as we know it. She stopped in for some tea after her committee meeting. You know how many meetings there are during the first two weeks of June to get things up and running. I'll get you an espresso. Although it seems weirdly counterintuitive, I think it will calm you down."

"Do you have any of your fruit tarts left?" I asked.

"Portia Barnes," she tsked, "hitting the hard stuff."

"Long drive," I admitted as I followed her in. I didn't eat many sweets or refined sugars these days. But Cordelia's agave-glazed fruit tarts were a notable exception, the perfect bite of summer fruit and pastry crust.

To my left, our parents' bookstore loomed large and homey, full of comfy chairs and quiet nooks and stained-glass windows that transformed the sun into brilliant shards of color. I didn't have much time for reading anything other than contracts, but I'd grown up a reader, and the shop reminded me of church, only for people who worshipped the written word.

But the real prize lay before me in the form of an inviting bistro-style café with gleaming espresso machines and impressive glass cases that showcased my sister's virtuosity with a pastry brush. Cordelia had added photos of her travels to the brick walls, demonstrating that her talents extended beyond her skills with the whisk. The blues of Santorini, the twinkling lights of Paris, sunbaked Florence, misty Edinburgh and mysterious Prague all demanded to be noticed and admired. Oh, how I wanted to check off all of those destinations. Sure, I'd been to Paris a few times to FrancisPearl's office there, but I never seemed to have the time to partake of any of the fine art or dining.

My mother sat at a table in the corner, sipping from a steaming mug and poring over a binder I assumed had to be chock-full of her plans for the summer Shakespearean festival. A wisp of auburn hair had escaped the elegant twist gathered at the nape of her neck, and the sinking sun's rays had caught it and turned it to spun red gold. The chemotherapy hadn't robbed her of hair. A small thing, I knew, but an important one. At least for me anyway.

She lifted her eyes, catching sight of me. Her smile stretched wide and welcoming. Even so, she looked thinner to me, a little more tired around those green-glass eyes she shared with Miranda. "Portia," she said, rising and holding her arms open to me.

I crossed the room into her waiting arms. She smelled like the gardenias in her garden, subtly sweet and graceful in a way that even the most expensive perfume could never mimic. "How are you feeling?"

She drew back, her lips quirked. "I thought we agreed you wouldn't lead off every conversation with that."

"I think we agreed that I would only lead off every *other* conversation with that. I'm due." She'd definitely lost some more weight; her fine bone structure, so elegant and classic, had felt a bit sharp when she'd hugged me.

"I'm fine," she assured me. "Cordelia, can you slip some of that CBD oil you think I don't know you take into Portia's coffee?"

"Do not put mood-altering substances in my coffee," I warned my baby sister. "You'll regret it. I know where you sleep." I turned back to Mom even as Cordelia's cackle drifted over my shoulder. "Don't encourage her."

"I make my own fun." My mother gave a shrug that reminded me so much of Miranda. I might have gotten Mom's killer bone structure, but my middle sister had inherited her irreverent sense of humor and dry-as-Muscadet wit. "Speaking of fun, what do you have planned while you're here with us for the summer?"

"I thought I'd call Candace and see if she wanted to meet up for drinks."

My mother hummed approvingly. "And tomorrow and the next day?"

A faint smile crossed my lips. "Something tells me you have something in mind for me."

"Well, now that you've asked"—she pointed to the three-ring binder on the table—"I could use some help with the negotiation of the vendor contracts and the annual plague of permitting and zoning issues."

"Petting zoo proximity to the food vendors again?"

"Every year, a new hoop to jump through." She hefted the binder and pressed it into my waiting hands. "Wouldn't want your mind to go dull while you're home."

"Perish the thought." Gerald might have banished me from the office, but I could still be useful. The thought—like the weight of the binder now in my arms—felt comforting somehow. "Where's Dad?"

"Finishing up training our newest manager on inventory. He'll be here any minute. So excited to have all his girls home for the summer." Mom smiled in that dreamy way she always did when she talked about Dad, which was only matched by the equally moony expression he made while talking about her. On paper, they shouldn't have worked—she the ultra-elegant but fiery-when-crossed Isabella Beaulieu, French by birth and attitude; and he, Peter Barnes, whip-smart but never showy about it and as midwestern American as cherry pie. During Dad's senior semester abroad in Paris, they'd met at a lecture and bonded over—what else—the Bard. Mom liked to joke that she'd followed him home to the States. They had settled in Bard's Rest to build a life and their careers as professors in their respective Shakespeare-focused fields. Along the way they'd become bookshop proprietors and parents, raising the three of us. I was a damn delight, but Miranda and Cordelia had been downright unpredictable and—in the case of Cordelia—unruly. It couldn't have been easy, but somehow they had made it look so.

Until last year, anyway, when life had thrown Mom a curveball and she had tried to duck rather than swing at it as she did everything else. Mom's unwillingness to face her cancer head-on had shaken our whole family, but especially Dad. We'd all been sort of lost until Miranda stepped in and took charge of the situation the only way she knew how—snark-based bribery, plain and simple. Miranda, a bestselling author, had offered Mom first crack at reading her latest book before anyone else, and Mom had fallen on it, begrudgingly going to her biopsy, only to learn she had cancer. Cancer that had first required surgery and later several rounds of chemotherapy. We were all still anxiously waiting to hear whether it had been vanquished into remission or not.

We all pitched in throughout Mom's treatment, but Cordelia and Dad bore the emotional brunt of it, as I lived in New York and Miranda called Boston home. Yes, I drove up for holidays and faithfully Zoomed once a week, but the day-to-day cancer battle had been left to them—something I felt heaps of guilt over.

"Lambkin," Dad exclaimed from the doorway, snapping me out of my descent into the doldrums. "Come give your old man a hug."

Embarrassing Elizabethan endearment aside, I loved my Dad, this steady, constant rock of love and support. I squeezed him tight. Whereas Mom smelled of her beloved garden, Dad smelled of fresh-cut wood and sap, a byproduct of the time he spent in the theater workshop. "I missed you," I whispered into his shoulder. Did he seem thinner as well? Was the strain of watching the love of his life go through chemo robbing him of his vitality? *Stop*, I admonished myself. *Stop this narrative.* The words of Kim, my therapist, came floating back to me. *Stop assuming that the universe is going to obliterate everything you hold dear.* Okay, I was paraphrasing. She would have said something more along the lines of "Don't assume the worst." Because Kim was very much to the point. I liked that about her.

"I've missed you too. Now we just need Miranda and we'll have the whole clan back together." He rubbed his hands together.

"Yeah, in what alternative reality does Portia beat Miranda home?" Cordelia teased, giving me the slightest jerk of her head— Cordelia-speak for "come hither and I shall spill some tea."

I sauntered over casually, so as to not alert either of my parents that a game was afoot. I leaned over the glass, pretending to admire the pastry. "Is that a new pate a choux technique you've used?" I asked, a shade louder than necessary.

"You like? If you dare to lift your carb embargo, come behind the counter and I'll let you have one," Cordelia answered. Risky, I thought, since my parents knew I didn't have a sweet tooth. Growing up, I'd always been the most health conscious one in a family of gourmands, but these days that decision felt more like a necessity than a personal choice.

Quick as silver, I slipped behind the counter and stepped squarely into Cordelia's space. I wondered if she felt the same high back here that I did in my office. Probably.

"Miranda texted me. Said she had news." She absently handed me a plate with one of those pastries that looked like a finger. I'd never quite understood the appeal of that. I looked longingly at the fruit tarts.

"News?" I hissed. "What kind of news? Book news or Adam news?"

"Too cryptic to tell."

To say Miranda was cryptic was an understatement. In addition to working as a literary agent, she also wrote *New York Times* bestselling young adult novels, and until fairly recently, she'd been writing said bestselling books under the pen name Hathaway Smith. For years, Miranda had been protective about her privacy to the point that instead of enabling her life, it had been hindering her from living the life she wanted to. Of course, that had all changed when she rekindled an old relationship with Adam Winters, this guy we'd both known in high school and I'd dated and sort of stolen from Miranda when I'd found myself in need of a prom date—admittedly not my finest moment. While home in Bard's last summer, Miranda had embraced this whole "live your truth and damn the consequences" mentality. And she'd shed the Hathaway Smith name. Just like that.

"Well, what do we think?" I demanded.

"I dunno." She shrugged. "New book? Engaged? Pregnant with Adam's adorable hipster baby? Adopted another dog?"

The animal count had climbed to four, which made for two humans, three dogs and a rescue pig—yes, a pig—living out of Adam and Miranda's place in Arlington, Massachusetts. Thankfully they owned an actual house with a yard; otherwise that would have gotten messy. I was actually surprised they weren't in the double digits in terms of pets, considering that Adam was a vet with a big moosh of a heart and my sister loved animals.

But their restraint seemed to end there, given they'd moved in together after a scant six months of dating. An engagement wasn't out of the question. Selfishly, I rooted against the baby thing. Babies were gross, and I was really bad at faking any enthusiasm for them.

Truth be told, I was a little hurt that Miranda hadn't texted me. I mean, prior to last summer, things had been a little frosty between us, but I thought we'd grown closer, and I'd been trying to be better about calling and texting and—my phone buzzed once and then about a dozen times. I looked down to see an influx of texts. Well, apparently, I now had Wi-Fi, tragically slow as it was. Ah, and there in the midst of several from Candace was one from Miranda, as cryptic as the one she'd sent Cordelia.

"I need to call Candace," I told Cordelia, "but text me the minute Miranda shows up."

Cordelia gave me a little salute as I ducked out into the hallway between the pastry shop and the bookstore. "Please pick up, Candace," I breathed as it rang once and then twice. "I am in need of some sparkling conversation and an excuse to—"

"So, how's the first few hours of your sabbatical?" a familiar voice on the other end of the line asked. "Scouting an escape route yet?"

"I'm thirty seconds from booking a flight to Madrid," I groaned. "You're coming."

Candace's ensuing laugh rippled through the line over the clink of glasses and general merriment. "Attractive proposition but a logistical nightmare. Why don't you slip into cocktail attire and get over here? I've missed you, and there's so much to catch you up on, including"—her voice cut away—"What did I say? Only mignonette, no cocktail sauce. It mutes the oyster." An indistinct voice clapped back at Candace. "When I want to be mansplained, Oliver, I'll find someone who graduated in the top ten percent of their culinary class," she said icily.

I snickered, but mostly covered it. Because I was a lady.

"Sorry, my new executive chef is a pain in the ass. Thinks he owns the kitchen or something."

"I'm sure you'll disabuse him of that notion in no time."

"Of course I will. Now get over here. I've missed you."

The Bower After Hours

I slipped into The Bower after Hours, the music thrumming in the low-lit space and the smell of expensive leather mingling with rum and mint. I had to hand it to Candace. She'd transformed this latest expansion of Titania's Bower from the slightly stuffy restaurant you frequented for graduation dinners and other stilted special occasions to an all-out scene. Want to get married somewhere gorgeous and tasteful in the woods? Try the gardens of Titania's. In the mood for quirky dinner theater? Try special events at Titania's. Chef's tasting table for two or twenty-two? Titania's fine-dining experience. And now, The Bower after Hours, Bard's Rest's only speakeasy-style establishment. No menus. No Shakespearean kitsch. No social media presence. Just A-list bartenders with ink and signature drinks for days.

Sidling up to the gleaming hardwood bar, I scanned the shelves of glistening bottles in search of the right drink. A bartender with an impressive gingery man bun and even more impressive forearms set down the lemon he'd been zesting and offered me a dazzling smile. "What can I get you?" he asked in an Irish accent that was sure to earn him a slew of fervent admirers in short order.

"Oban neat, please."

"I have the fourteen- and eighteen-year."

"Eighteen, please."

"That's a big-kid drink," said an admiring voice to my left.

Without turning, I used the bar mirror to size up the owner of the voice. Tall and dark-haired with a strong jaw rising out of a five-o'clock shadow. Sporting standard-issue charcoal slacks and a white button-down open at the neck and rolled up at the elbows, signaling he was all business but off duty for the day.

"What can I say? I like my drinks like I like my men," I replied to his reflection. "Adult." I offered him what Chris called my ice-pick smile. As the name suggested, it was not an inviting smile, but one that threatened highly creative malevolence if provoked.

To my surprise though, the guy only chuckled, the sound low and rich, like those wrapped caramels swirled with bourbon, one of my rare but favorite indulgences. I couldn't quite make out the color of his eyes and found that I wanted to know to complete my assessment of him. Pivoting ever so slightly, I turned to regard him with an open curiosity that had caused many a male specimen to break eye contact.

But this guy didn't flinch; he stared back with an expression as frank as my own. Those eyes were a dark and textured gray—something my sister the writer might have described as rain-soaked granite or something swoony like that—and they had a magnetic pull all their own. Which likely served him well in whatever line of work he was in. All in all, handsome, but not obnoxiously so.

"I appreciate someone who knows her way around a scotch," he said as the bartender returned with my drink. "Any chance you're a bourbon drinker as well?"

"Not really." I'd picked up my affinity for scotch from Gerald, who liked to offer his team a pour of the good stuff he kept in his office after we'd closed a particularly big deal. Potential HR nightmare aside, I enjoyed this little ritual, associating that delicious complex smell and the burn of the liquor on the back of the tongue with a job well done.

"Nobody's perfect," he said with a mischievous grin. "Can I

convince you to try the Barrell Bourbon Gray Label 15?" He raised his own glass for my inspection.

"All right, I'll bite. Pitch me on why I might like to opt for some trendy, overhyped bourbon swill instead of my classic scotch?"

Behind me, the bartender let out a surprised snort.

The guy didn't back down though. If anything, his grin intensified at the challenge. "It presents with notes of blood orange, lychee and damson plum, but it checks its own sweetness with paraffin and scorched earth."

"So it drinks like waxy fruit?" I leaned a little closer so he could see me widen my eyes. "And you thought scorched earth would be a selling point?"

Those gray eyes shone with sly merriment. "With you? Yes. You strike me as a woman who goes unapologetically scorched-earth when the mood strikes her."

"It's more like when the situation warrants it," I corrected. "But I think I'll pass on your trendy, overhyped bourbon."

"What if I told you I know the crew that makes it and they're a scrappy bunch that founded the company with nothing but a few barrels and money begged and borrowed from friends? When I drink it, it reminds me of the need to be gritty to produce something so smooth. It's like I can taste the effort that I know went into it."

For the first time, I offered him a real smile. "An intoxicating medley of exotic fruits, paraffin, scorched earth and determination?"

"Exactly."

"Maybe I'll consider it." I let a slow smile spread across my mouth before pushing off from the bar and sauntering off toward the spiral staircase without a backward glance.

I found Candace, head event planner and the undisputed monarch of Titania's, perched on a plush chaise in the presently-closed-to-the-public VIP lounge. Lean, leggy and occasionally prone to tossing her honey-blond hair when pissed, Candace Thornton was the only person I'd ever met who I thought actually embodied the term *coltish*. She waved at me, rolling her oceanic eyes and pointing toward her phone with an apologetic grimace.

I nodded and strode to the railing to survey the scene below—and what a scene it was. In addition to the inviting leather chairs and couches that Candace had expertly placed around the room, there was a motley array of steamer trunks serving as tables and gilded maps covering the walls with places I was certain didn't exist. Fillory, anyone?

Allowing my eyes to wander over Candace's gorgeous table lights—glass pots of amber that reminded me of honeycombs—I caught sight of TDP—tall, dark and presumptuous—with a pair of equally attractive men in bespoke after-work attire. They'd attracted an orbit of young women in body-con dresses who were laughing too loudly and bringing down Candace's carefully cultivated class factor. TDP's expression remained polite but a little bored as he sipped his bourbon. Interesting.

"Hey, sorry about the interruption. How was your drive, twinsie?" Candace joined me at the railing.

"Uneventful," I answered, smiling at the joke. While we certainly didn't look enough alike to pass as twins, our similar builds and men's general inability to distinguish between cool-tone and warm-tone blonds provoked the question enough while we were out together that it had become our inside joke. I wouldn't have minded if Candace had been my biological twin; it would have evened out the Barnes household. She and I could have balanced out Miranda and Cordelia's general weirdness with our level-headed, ordered approach to life.

"I admire the aesthetic."

"I know it's not your darling Empire city." Candace drummed her mint manicured fingertips on the balcony railing. "But we make do."

"If we were in the city, you'd have a quarter of the space and lower ceilings." I swept my arm toward our private lounge. "You wouldn't get a people-watching spot like this. I'm enjoying the vibe tonight and the fact that I could actually get a decent drink at the bar instead of being jostled seven bodies deep."

"Did Rowan take care of you?" Candace asked, nodding to the bartender. "He's still getting his legs beneath him before the summer starts picking up with the influx of Bardolators. Before you know it they'll be in here trying to order ale in their bad British accents." She cocked her head at me. "Come to think of it, I've never heard yours."

"That's because I don't have a library of bad British accents to pull from," I assured her. "Just because I grew up here doesn't mean I'm enamored of the Bard like everyone else. Present company included."

"I admire Shakespeare," Candace said primly, "but you know I'm not slavish about him. Particularly the way he wrote women: virgins, villains or bust." She wrinkled her pert nose. "But it's the theater life for me. Give me some Treadwell, a little Beckett and a Miller chaser."

"I'm not sure *Death of a Salesman* would appeal to your dinner theater clientele."

"Oh, of course not," she scoffed. "Which is why I've taken great pains to update *Much Ado About Nothing* for a modern crowd. Everybody loves some Beatrice and Benedick, but wait until they see them as two maladjusted therapists vying for clients."

"That could be fun," I hedged.

"Come try out for Beatrice. You'd be perfect."

"Are you implying I'm maladjusted?"

"I could swap out the word 'therapist' for 'attorney' and nobody would bat an eye."

"Hurtful," I sniffed.

"You were great as Lady Capulet. C'mon, step up this year. Take a bigger role."

"I can't," I demurred, sipping on my scotch.

"Why, because your calendar is packed?"

"Still hurtful." I shot her a wry smile. "It has more to do with my general abhorrence of all things theater and—oh yes—my crippling stage fright, of which you're well aware."

"But you were able to master it last summer. You're such a no-shit-taking badass that way."

"Well, of course I am. But when I get on the stage and there's all the lights and the inability to see people, it sets off my fight or flight. I only played Lady Capulet because you blackmailed me into doing it."

"More like extortion," she pointed out. "You're the lawyer—aren't you supposed to know that?"

The sound of a booming male laugh rose above the strains of Charlie Parker. It was a million-dollar laugh, the laugh of a closer. My eyes followed the sound, and somehow I knew who I'd be looking at. And there he was, granite eyes and all, laughing at something his companion must have said.

"Leave it to you to find the biggest shark in this room," Candace noted.

"What are you talking about? I'm the biggest shark in the room. You're a close second. That guy is like a lemon shark, at best."

"More like a tiger shark," she murmured, sipping her drink. "That's Benjamin Dane."

"Is that supposed to mean something?"

Her lips quirked. "He's a developer out of Boston. I'm surprised you don't have a dossier or something on him already."

"Because I'm Carmen Sandiego in this scenario?" I snorted. "So, of all the gin joints in the deep dark woods, what's he doing in yours? Too early for Bardolators, and he doesn't look the part. Wedding? No, wait, D3 lacrosse reunion?"

"Rumor has it he's in town scouting some property."

"For development? Please. Walmart and Target can't get a foothold here, what with all the zoning regulations designed to keep big-box out. What's this guy think his angle is?"

"Why don't you ask him? Since he seems to be staring at you."

Against my better judgment, I glanced over to where, indeed,

Benjamin Dane was watching me. I lifted my scotch and the corner of my mouth a little to mock toast him. He inclined his head.

"I'm not sure I like the look of him," I muttered.

"I like his looks just fine," Candace drawled, a smidge of her Southern roots showing.

Watching the soft light play across his strong jaw, I silently agreed. "You said he's out of Boston, right?"

"You wouldn't be scoping potential clients in my place of business? While on sabbatical?" Candace demanded, clutching at her imaginary pearls.

"I'm a managing partner now. If his shop is big enough, maybe Mr. Dane is in need of local legal counsel. Never hurts to keep one's finger on the pulse. Let me know if you hear anything else on him?"

"Does this mean I can count on you to try out for Beatrice, then?"

"Is that the going rate for favors among friends these days?" I frowned.

But before she could respond, we were interrupted by a now familiar Irish accent. Rowan stood at the top of the stairs, a serving tray in one hand. Looking at me, he said, "The guy trying to sell you on scorched earth at the bar sent these up." He gestured down to the two generous pours of bourbon.

"That wouldn't be the Gray Label 15, would it?" I asked.

Rowan nodded solemnly. "At least it's not that cosmo swill."

Candace rolled her eyes. "Rowan thinks drinks should not taste like Jolly Ranchers."

"Good man," I agreed. "Please give our thanks to the Bostonian holding court in your bar."

Rowan nodded gamely, deposited the drinks with a flourish and clomped back down the stairs.

"Care to explain?" Candace said, inspecting her drink.

I took an experimental sip and was surprised at the sweet and smoky balance that filled my mouth. When I looked up, I saw Benjamin Dane staring at me with one eyebrow raised. I held up a hand in the gladiator thumbs-up/thumbs-down position and waggled it back and forth, coming to rest on thumbs-up. His ensuing grin was as rich as the caramel notes in the bourbon. With a low chuckle, I murmured, "The game is up."

"What now?" Candace asked. "Portia Livingston Barnes—"

"I should never have told you my middle name," I sighed, sipping the bourbon again and finding that elusive note that Benjamin Dane had described as scorched earth.

"Did you quote Shakespeare?"

"Of course not," I said, taking another sip for posterity. Miranda might have been able to recite entire monologues on command, while Cordelia had memorized every innuendo and insult the Bard had to offer, but what resonated for me were the lines whose meaning people got wrong—like this little gem that everyone thought meant all was lost. But it didn't mean that at all. In Shakespeare's time, "the game is up" would have meant that the hunt was off and running.

I eyed Benjamin Dane and sipped the bourbon. Something definitely felt like it was off and running, though I couldn't have said what exactly.

Two Gentlemen of Daytona

Someone was touching my thigh. What in the actual hell? Startling out of the uneasy state that happened when sleeping somewhere unfamiliar—and while my childhood bed wasn't technically unfamiliar, it felt like it had been a few millennia since I'd bunked down here—I whipped off the covers to find an unrepentant mutt. Drooling on my leg.

"Damn it, Miranda," I huffed at the elfin redhead perched at the foot of my bed. "You know I don't like"—I glanced down at her lab mix, not wanting to hurt his canine pride (because what was a little drool between friends)—"surprises," I finished.

"We missed you too," she said airily. "Brought you something." She leaned down out of view and reappeared with a plated Pop-Tart. My stomach lurched at the sight of it and tried to scramble up into my rib cage in an attempt to shield itself from whatever GMO horror lurked in that pastry. "I even bought the fruit ones just for you because I know you think the fudge ones don't have any nutritional value."

I wanted to point out that the violently red ooze leaking out of the pastry likely didn't qualify as either fruit or nutrition. Instead, I smiled wanly. "Thanks. You can put it on the dresser, and I'll have a nibble in a bit, when I've worked up an appetite."

Miranda guffawed, reaching down once more and coming up with what looked like a fresh green smoothie. "The Pop-Tart is for me. This is for you," she said, offering me the cool glass. "But you should have seen your face. You were really going to nibble on it, weren't you?"

"I considered crumbling one of the corners to look like I'd taken a bite, yes. This is much better though, thank you." I took a sip of the smoothie, reveling in the bright notes of apple and mint. The sun streamed in through the windows of the turret, which Miranda had dubbed my bedroom because of its circular nature and similarly shaped top. I'd always secretly liked the nickname. "What are you doing up so early, bringing me breakfast and stashing a furry stowaway in my sheets?"

"Hate to break it to you, but it's almost nine, Porsche. Mom thought maybe you'd stroked out in your sleep and wanted me to check on you."

"I thought we agreed you wouldn't call me that anymore since I traded in my actual Porsche for an environmentally responsible Tesla?"

"That's adorable you think I'd give that up," she chirped.

I stared at her. Hard. "Wait, nine o'clock? In the morning?"

"Rough first night back? Bedhead looks good on you—makes you look all human and stuff."

"I do not have bedhead," I said, smoothing my hair down. As I dropped my hand to my side, a furry black head slipped into position beneath it, so really, I had no choice but to pet Puck. Clever mutt. Little-known fact: I actually liked dogs. I just didn't have time for one. "To what do I owe the pleasure of your company this morning?" I asked pointedly.

"I need a favor."

"Interesting. Looking to break another contract?" I teased.

"I think we can all agree the world is better off with one less Elf

Shot book," she insisted. "But this is sort of related. Remember when my contract said I could substitute a new project subject to Susannah's approval?"

"Of course. Did you land on one?"

She nodded. "I'm doing an adult contemporary fantasy series."

I sat up a little straighter. "Intriguing." Miranda had previously published only young adult fiction. "Tell me more."

"It's set in modern-day Boston. The protagonist is an ice maiden of Jotunheim banished to the body of a mortal until such time as she retrieves a magical artifact that belongs to Odin."

I looked at her blankly.

Sighing, she said, "Jotunheim is the realm of ice and giants. Have you never seen a Marvel movie? Or read a single Norse myth?"

"Is that a serious question?"

"You are missing out on Hemsworthian abs and I'm sorry for it," Miranda clucked, shaking her head. "Anyway, my protagonist angers Odin, god of Asgard, and she gets banished to Boston to track down Gungnir, Odin's missing spear—"

I held up a hand. "Is there a favor in here somewhere, or are you trying to intimidate me with your vast knowledge of mythology?"

"I'm getting to the good part," she promised. "Anyway, Inga, our ice maiden turned mortal, wakes up in the body of a Boston-based attorney."

"Why an attorney?"

"Plot twist involving the spear." Miranda shrugged. "I was hoping to pick your brain on some lawyerly things."

I wrinkled my nose. "What? Why? It's fiction."

"I need to be accurate."

"You're writing about a mythological creature magically banished to a human body in search of some god's spear and you're worrying about making it realistic?"

"Well, certain parts of it need to be realistic."

"The lawyerly parts?" I clarified

"Exactly. I don't need much; just for you to weigh in if I have questions that cannot be answered by the Internet."

"You should not consult the Internet for legal advice." I shuddered. "Here, try a question on me."

"What's the most ethically iffy attorney thing you've ever done?"

I stared at her. "That's what you lead off with?"

"I need scenarios."

"Maybe you should use the Internet."

"Porsche!"

"Hate to disappoint you, but I worked my tail off to get my license, and I've never been near that ethical line."

"Not even once?" She eyed me doubtfully.

"Not even close."

Miranda flopped down beside me. "Well, that's thoroughly disappointing."

"Such is the life of a big law firm partner," I said, elbowing her. "How goes the whole cohabitation experiment?"

"You know that Adam and I are not pandas in a zoo, right?"

"I meant, how is it living with another person and all those pets?" I asked, absently stroking Puck's head.

"Ninety percent of the time it's the best thing ever." She sighed moonily.

"And the other ten percent?"

"Adam and I have a fight that resolves faster than most stomach bugs. Or sometimes somebody takes an unauthorized poop in the house."

I raised an eyebrow.

"Loki, our latest rescue, is still working on his indoor manners." I looked down at Puck, who I swear rolled his doggy eyes.

"But in general, things are going well?" Other than college, I'd never had to share a bathroom or a fridge with someone else in my adult life. The thought made me queasy.

"I was a little nervous sharing space with someone else, especially a guy. But I love waking up next to Adam, feeding and walking the brood together, coming home after work and making dinner. Okay, I mean, he makes dinner. I set the table and pick out wine. Ian's over a lot, which always makes for an entertaining evening. But he's pretty good at making himself scarce before . . ." She trailed off, blushing furiously.

"Before the best sex of your life?" I teased.

"Stop!" Miranda swatted me with a pillow.

I loved my sister, but she was a private person, particularly when it came to sex. I considered myself more liberal in this respect, but I was a rank amateur compared to our baby sister, whose sexcapades were the stuff of legend. "I'm not looking for details. I'm just glad you're happy." I patted her hands. "Doing grown-up things."

"I really am." She gave me a bright smile. "So, what's on your agenda today? I assume you're fully calendared."

"Umm," I said, not wanting to think about the gaping hole of nothing that lay before me, "I told Mom I'd stop in at the festival meeting. She said it might be helpful if I listen in to get a sense of some of the issues."

Miranda cackled. "Have you learned nothing? That's Mom code for she's going to assign you a role."

"I'm not a pushover like you are," I said, "and besides, I don't have any talents she can leverage except the review of the contracts, and those I can look at in my sleep. Half of them are Legal Zoom templates anyway." I rolled my eyes.

"I'm just saying, I've already been drafted into directing another mainstage. Tread carefully, sis."

"Thanks for the warning," I scoffed. "But I won't be needing it."

"CODE RED?" AARON, coproprietor of Two Gentlemen of Daytona, the most tasteful cookware shop I'd ever been in, asked.

"Yes, please," I said, my mouth watering at the thought of his signature coffee drink. Although I had what one might describe as a less than ideal gastrointestinal system these days, it still held up well against coffee. And for that, I counted myself lucky.

While I'd been in cookware shops packed to the brim with every gadget out there, Aaron had gone for a more streamlined approach, with three thoughtful displays: cookbooks to the left, cookware in the middle and on the right a rotating seasonal table, this one featuring all things blueberry—pie tins, bread mixes and jams. I loved it. I didn't cook much, unless you counted the raw fruit and veggie smoothies I made every morning, but I loved everything about this place.

"You're a god among mortals, Aaron," I told him, gratefully accepting the cornflower blue mug with two jaunty lords in white and a blazing orange sun between them—a nod to Aaron and his husband Dan's Floridian roots. I drew in a deep sip, basking in the perfectly prepared one and a half espresso shot. "That's so smooth."

"I figured you'd want to be on your toes today," he said with a covert nod in the direction of my mother.

I'd vanquished the titans of Wall Street and tamed the top investment banks so many times, I'd lost count. I wasn't worried about my mother, even if she'd been asked to chair the festival committee again. Well, actually, she had been asked to chair the committee, but had only agreed to do it if Dan agreed to cochair it with her, graciously maintaining that it was a role best suited for two people.

"Noted with thanks," I said smiling at him. Aaron had one of those faces you wanted to smile back at. With his neat, dark hair, just starting to silver, and mischievous eyes, he served as the laid-back, easygoing yin to his husband's intense, all-in yang. "How's Dan doing with his new cohosting responsibilities?"

Aaron leaned in, dropping his voice to a conspiratorial whisper. "All poise on the outside, complete wreck at home. At this rate I may need to start ordering bulk wine for the shop *and* Chez Townsend. He's going through pinot blanc like the second coming of Prohibition is upon us. I don't know what I'll do if Iz steps down next summer and he has to chair the festival alone," he clucked. "Will probably have to sell a kidney or something."

"Or you could invest in a vineyard. Less scarring."

"That's debatable." But he gave me one more of those warming smiles before heading back to his espresso machine. God bless Aaron and his expertly prepared beverages and kind heart.

It had been a strange morning to say the least—even without a sisterly wake-up call. I wasn't sure what to do with myself. I'd gone to check my email, and other than that markup from Riki I'd asked for, I'd had precious few emails. The out-of-office message reminder at the top of my account was jarring. "Returning in September." Months away. Sure, the committee meeting would serve as a decent distraction this morning. But what about tomorrow and the next day?

The smell of bergamot wafted toward me and I turned to find my mother, her Much Ado About Pastry travel mug in one hand and a determined expression on her face as she worked the room.

Wanting no part of that, I made a beeline to a handsomely carved table that I suspected had been cleared of coordinated place settings for this meeting and sank into the most advantageous people-watching spot. It afforded me a perfect view of my mother saying hello to our hosts, chatting with Stan Hobbs, long-standing committee member and the third-generation owner of Measure for Measure Hardware, and embracing Kitty McMahon, florist and owner of Candace's favorite local shop, Sweet Williams. Mom reminded me a little of Gerald that way, weaving her way through a room and greeting everyone, whereas I gave more of a "come find me when you're ready to talk shop" vibe—something Gerald constantly reminded me that I needed to balance with more glad-handing of the clients when I took over as managing partner.

"This seat taken?" Byron Greene, former classmate, current local flirt and a mostly respectable attorney, asked as he claimed the seat next to me. "I'd heard a rumor you might be here today but had to see it for myself."

"Of course she's here," Candace said, sliding into the seat next to him. "Byron's afraid you're not going to take over looking at the contracts for him."

"Shirker," I teased.

"I'm hoping to land a role in both the mainstages and the dinner theater," Byron said, with a sidelong glance at Candace. "If she'll have me."

"I suspect he's doing dinner theater for the perks," Candace said with a wave of her hand.

I raised an eyebrow at her.

"The chef makes a family-style meal for Sunday night rehearsals," she said quickly.

"Titania's gourmet cuisine means I don't have to eat all my meals at the Tavern." Byron ran a hair through his coal-black hair.

I wrinkled my nose. "That can't be good for you."

He patted his chest, which, even constrained behind a work polo, was still impressive. "I do okay."

"He's a gym rat," Candace confided. "It's all the mirrors at The Gym's the Thing."

"Byron," I groaned. "Are you still that creepy guy at the gym?"

"You mean, am I the guy who courteously wipes the weights when he's finished using them and listens to ABA podcasts as he does leg presses? Then yes."

"Do I even want to know what an ABA is?" Adam asked. Tall and lanky with blond hair and hazel eyes, Adam also hadn't changed much since our high school days. He was basically the human equivalent of a golden retriever—big goofy grin and even bigger heart. I expected that punch of guilt when I saw him, the uncomfortable reminder of how much I'd hurt Miranda by stealing Adam away when I needed a prom date. But it didn't come this time. Huh. Maybe it was because I'd apologized, truly apologized, to my sister last summer for it. Whatever it was, I finally felt able to return his open grin.

"American Bar Association," Byron and I said at exactly the same time, causing Candace and Adam to laugh at us.

"I'm thinking that somewhere these two have 'ABA' tattooed on their person," Miranda chimed in, sitting down beside me. "But Portia's pretty tight-lipped about it."

"Did you go for the tasteful ankle tat, Portia," Byron asked with comically wide brown eyes, "or a regrettable tramp stamp, like I did?"

I snickered as Adam's face crinkled in disgust. But he recovered quickly enough. "So, you joining the ranks, Portia?" Adam asked. "The few, the proud, the batshit crazy?"

"I'm pretty sure that's not the expression," Tillie Perkins, arguably my favorite person in this entire town, deadpanned. Her shop, The Taming of the Shoe, had been my high school stepping stone to designer heels, while Tillie had been a role model for me—a successful businesswoman who didn't mince words. She'd not only bestowed on me the "If the Shoe Fits" scholarship my senior year, her way of giving back to local students going off to college or trade school, but she'd given me all the confidence I needed to try—and win—one of the few cases I'd ever brought in court. Granted, it had been family court, but I still remembered it vividly—standing up in front of the judge and demanding that Tillie be allowed sole legal and physical custody of Opal, her then-middle-school-aged niece, after Opal's deadbeat father attempted to extort Tillie for money in exchange for relinquishing his custody rights. The judge had been unimpressed by this less than altruistic behavior and had given Tillie full custody. My career had taken a more corporate focus thereafter, but I'd forever remember that hot summer afternoon in the poorly air-conditioned courtroom with its faded yellow walls when I felt the whole world was on the line.

"Hello, Tillie," I said warmly.

"Don't give me any of that hello crap—you come in for a hug, chicken wing," she said, nearly upsetting the table in an effort to reach me. I leaned into her hug, scented with violets and expensive shoe leather, and even ignored the old high school nickname she had given me on account of my slender build.

"How's Alice?" I asked.

"Like a pig in clover," she said, patting her salt-and-pepper braid and smiling. "Just kicked off the summer reading program. You know how she loves connecting kids with books." I nodded. If Tillie had been my introduction to fine shoes, her wife, Alice, had been my introduction to Agatha Christie and Dorothy L. Sayers. I didn't have much time for reading these days, but I liked to listen to audiobooks while I worked out, and my tastes ran to isolated islands, a cast of shady suspects and a dead body or two.

"And Opal?"

"In love with Boston, her internship and Jazz," Tillie crowed. "All thanks to Miranda."

"She's so hardworking, Til. Great eye for talent. And I hear Jazz is killing it at Berklee in the summer theater program," Miranda gushed. "Though I'm afraid Ian's had a bit of influence on both of them. Sorry in advance for whatever hipster obscenity comes out of their mouths."

"A small price to pay for her happiness. Besides, she's no stranger to proper cussing when the situation calls for it"—she grinned wickedly—"like when Alice cheats at mini-golf." .

"And cards," Aaron and Dan called in unison.

"I do miss Opal something fierce. The house has been quiet without her, but we'll see her and Jazz in August for the main-stages," Tillie said, with all the heartbreaking pride and restraint of a parent.

The table soon filled out with Dan and my mother at the head and the other members of the committee along the sides. Once she set her travel mug down, my mother wasted no time getting down to her agenda and timelines. I was struck at how similar we were, her running this festival the way I ran my deals—ruthlessly efficient and planning for every contingency. I particularly enjoyed watching her sharing her space with Dan, who was still trying to work out his style of leadership. Miranda had mentioned once that she thought he looked and sounded like Vincent Price, and now I couldn't get that out of my head.

"I'd also like to welcome two of our newest members: Candace Thornton, who will be stepping into the newly created dinner the-ater liaison role; and my daughter, Portia, who will be our festival lawyer—reviewing contracts and permits and mediating any dis-putes that may arise."

I choked on my Code Red. "Since when does the festival need its own lawyer?"

"Since we were sued by the petting zoo vendor last year over a breach of contract, claiming his proximity to the food booths drove his goats into a mating frenzy," Dan said dryly.

I closed my eyes. "Please tell me you didn't pay him."

"It's still in mediation," Dan sniffed. "It should be one of the first things you make go away as festival lawyer."

"I dodged a bullet, huh?" Byron whispered, elbowing Candace.

"I don't understand," I spluttered, looking over to my mother for help.

But my own flesh and blood only nodded sagely. "Last year a fistfight broke out between Betty Tilney and Mabel Higgins over who secured the spot closest to the gazebo. It would be good to get out in front of these situations."

"Right. It's important we don't have septuagenarians fighting in the streets and riling up the goats," Miranda added, her voice appropriately serious, but her eyes dancing with gleeful malice. She leaned over, her curling red hair obscuring her face, and whispered, "Welcome to the show, sis. Don't say I didn't warn you."

The Town Hall

The Bard's Rest Town Hall was one of those fairy-tale-style ginger-bread affairs, buttercup yellow with stunning white trim that the town refreshed every year. And like in every good fairy tale, a witch lurked within.

Squaring my shoulders and settling my blond braid into place, I took three deep, cleansing breaths. *Festival lawyer.* I shuddered. Nope, it still sounded wrong. Maybe I should call Chris. But I decided against it; it was too early on a Monday to be laughed at more than I already had. As much as I loved this new iteration of Miranda—more confident, more settled—she was also a hell of a lot smarmier with the "I told you so."

I hefted the binder of contracts that Dan had handed me, almost apologetically, after the meeting. I needed to prioritize the petting zoo thing, he'd added. It was unseemly. Seven years at Harvard and two degrees later and I would be spending my summer wading through frivolous lawsuits and making sure the cotton candy booth remained properly distanced from the porta potties. On the other hand, working through the binder and coming up with a plan of action would give me something to do. But before I could dive into any contracts, I had to get a list of permits.

My fingers brushed the cool brass of the knob. Maybe it wouldn't be so bad, I reasoned. A summer of pro bono. For a bunch of half-crazy, Shakespeare-worshipping cultists.

Despite a childhood steeped in Shakespeare, I didn't get the hype. He was prolific, sure, assuming one believed he'd written everything attributed to him, but c'mon, he wrote the equivalent of romantic comedies and melodramas with plot twists that would make a teenager roll their eyes.

I stepped into the foyer. On my left curved a dizzy rotunda of Shakespearean scenes painted in gilt frames. On the right stretched the hall of notable New Hampshirites—faded portraits of Daniel Webster; Josiah Bartlett, the chief justice of the NH Supreme Court (not to be confused with beloved President Josiah "Jed" Bartlet on *The West Wing*, a longtime crush of mine); and Mary Baker Eddy, giving way to more recent and eyebrow-raising entries like Steven Tyler and Mandy Moore.

Maybe Emmeline wouldn't remember me from last summer. Or the altercation we'd had over a last-minute permitting issue that had held up the entire centennial and, as a result, my mother's happiness and general decrease of stress during a time when she needed to calm her nervous system down. Maybe Emmeline was too senile to remember me, or she'd retired, or some enterprising ingenue in gingham had dropped a house on her.

"Do you have an appointment, Ms. Barnes?" Her voice was a wintry scrape like a shovel dragged over frozen pavement.

So that would be a no, then. Did one need to schedule an appointment with the devil? Or would snapping your fingers suffice? "Ms. McGandry, so nice to see you again," I said with even more frost than Emmeline had used.

"I thought I made it clear you weren't welcome in my town hall." Emmeline McGandry, unbent and unshrunk by age, glowered at me, her immaculate silvery white bob and stark black rims completing the portrait of someone completely unimpressed.

Ignoring the "my" town hall comment, I asked with an even smile, "Well then, how could I have an appointment?"

"What can I do for you, Ms. Barnes?" Emmeline asked, pursing her impressively painted red lips—no bleed, no feathering, just a stunning red pucker. I wasn't sure they made women like this anymore, grade A battle-ax, but if so, this is what I wanted to be when I was pushing eighty. Except less of a pain in the ass.

"I'm here to pull a list of zoning permits from last year to get a sense of what's needed this year." When she raised an arctic brow, I added, "In my official capacity as the festival attorney."

"The festival needs an attorney?"

"My mother seems to think so."

"Ahh, nepotism." Emmeline gave me a dour smile.

I ignored this, pretending I hadn't heard her. Instead I stared at her expectantly, which, after a decent amount of time, unnerved most people. But not Emmeline.

"You'll have to come back another time. When you have the common decency to make an appointment."

"So my ban is lifted, then? Excellent, thanks so much." I couldn't help it. I could needle with the best of them. I swept my arms around the empty office. "Any chance I could make an appointment for three minutes from now?"

"I have another appointment. With a young man who had the common sense to make one." She smirked.

I thought about calling her on that bit of bull. But as if on cue, the door opened and in stepped Benjamin Dane, a polished smile on his face that paired nicely with his dark wash jeans and a white button-down that gave the town hall's recently refreshed trim a run for its money in the brightness department. His face didn't register surprise as he took in the sight of me squaring off with a woman old enough to have taught Moses in the third grade, but his granite eyes flashed in recognition—a small tell, but a tell all the same.

"Ms. McGandry," he said, the smooth caramel of his voice filling the room, "my apologies for my early arrival. I'm happy to wait outside until my appointment."

"Of course not, Mr. Dane. Five minutes early is right on time, I always say," she murmured, her only slightly watery blue eyes glittering with admiration. "Let me retrieve those maps you requested and I'll be right with you. Ms. Barnes was just leaving." She gave me a look that communicated I should make myself scarce.

"How about nine tomorrow morning?" I called after her.

"I'll see you at seven sharp next Thursday," she clapped back before disappearing into her office.

"Wow, next week, huh? What did you step in?" Benjamin Dane whispered.

"She and I didn't see eye to eye on some permitting issues last year," I said dryly. "Call it a draw."

"Doesn't feel like a draw."

"You're right; I won," I said with a mirthless smile.

"Scorched earth, then?" His mouth lifted at the corners, and even I had to admit it was a sexy mouth.

"Something like that."

"May I make an observation?"

"You don't strike me as the type to hold back. By all means," I said with a sweep of my hands.

"This town, this place, that keeper of the permits back there," he said, gesturing in the direction Emmeline had gone, "they all fit. But you don't."

"On the contrary, I was born here."

"But you don't live here anymore?"

"No."

"Thought so."

"What is that supposed to mean?" I asked, arching a brow.

"You give off this vibe that is distinctly clashing with the laid-back vibe here. Like you have somewhere to be and someone's ass to hand to them. I am really enjoying it."

"I'm delighted. But speaking of things that don't fit—what brings you to my laid-back hometown?" I asked. If Emmeline could claim the town hall, I could claim the town. Go big or go home.

"I'm a huge Shakespeare fan, of course."

"But the festival isn't for two months," I said, letting my eyes go a little wide. "You must really love Shakespeare."

He gave an easy laugh. "You got me. I'm in town looking at some property."

I quelled the urge to pepper him with questions. "Well, it's a beautiful spot to buy a vacation home."

"Do you have one here?"

"I'm not much for vacations." Because saying your hometown made you feel like all the walls were closing in around you was not something you admitted to a complete stranger. "I never know what to do with myself on them."

"Me neither," he said with a rueful shake of his head. "I can't seem to find that right balance of adventure and relaxation."

"Exactly," I agreed. "If I'm well rested by the end of it, did I win or fail?"

"Most people wouldn't characterize vacations as win or fail," he said, his upper lip curving into a delicious smile.

"I'm not most people."

"No, I'm beginning to think not," he said, his tone appreciative.

From Emmeline's office, I heard a scuffling of orthopedic shoes and the clang of those old metal filing cabinets that never close right.

"Would you have dinner with me this evening?" Benjamin asked.

"Why?"

"Because we all need to eat and I think you'd provide sparkling dinner conversation?" When he saw my unimpressed look, he added, "You could give me a download on Bard's Rest. An insider's perspective."

So he wanted to milk me for local insight. I considered that. How many countless networking dinners, mixers, golf events and conferences had I attended in the name of FrancisPearl? How many listless glasses of chardonnay had I downed in the name of client development? Surely, this couldn't be half as bad as listless chardonnay. Besides, Benjamin Dane, in addition to being rather attractive to look at, was turning out to be a bit of a banterist. I liked a man who could banter.

"Where are my manners? I'm Benjamin Dane," he said hurriedly, offering me his hand. "Please call me Ben."

His hand was warm and a little bit calloused—not at all like the majority of my clients, whose hands were smooth from manicures or disuse. This man used his hands. Maybe on his sailboat or something. "Portia Barnes. She of the scorched-earth fame."

"I've always wanted to dine with someone of scorched-earth fame."

"Yes, I will have dinner with you," I said, a small laugh escaping me in the wake of his heavy-handed hint and hopeful expression.

"Excellent, there's this place I've been dying to try. How about seven o'clock at—"

"The Merchant of Venison," I interjected with a knowing smile.

"How did you—"

"You strike me as a carnivore," I tossed over my shoulder, turning and striding to the door before Emmeline could lob another conversational grenade my way.

....

The Merchant of Venison

W hat are you wearing?" Candace's voice rose above a cacoph-
ony of clattering dishes and clinking silverware.

"Did you morph into the low-rent best friend of early nineties
rom-coms since I last saw you? Do you have curly red hair now and
a winning smile?"

"Of course not," she snorted, "but I am splattered with honey
plum sauce after a server dropped an hors d'oeuvre platter, and that
was still better than being chewed out by the father of the groom
for not adequately warning him that the state of New Hampshire is
home to winged insects. I need to live vicariously through you for a
few minutes. So tell me, are you wearing something hot to dinner
with the developer?"

"It's not like it's a date. We're both on fishing expeditions. He
wants the inside line on the town and I want to know what he has
planned for Bard's."

Candace groaned. "You're such a mercenary."

"How many grown men on your payroll have you reduced to
tears?" There was a lengthy pause where I thought Candace might
actually be tallying that number up. "Don't answer that. Remember
that Monique Lhuillier?"

"The noir bandeau with the floral pattern?" she breathed.

"The same."

"Love it." She paused. "Wait, you're not putting some sort of jacket over it, are you?"

"The black lace bolero. It's practically a business dinner. Bare arms are for interns and influencers."

I could almost hear her pouting over the line. "That dress deserves better."

"You're impossible."

"I prefer 'hard to please.' Now give me the dirt—how did this go down, exactly?"

"I ran into him at the town hall, where he had shown up to retrieve previously requested property plans from Emmeline McGandry."

"The woman who banned you from the town hall?"

"How many Emmeline McGandrys do you know?"

"Fair point. Which property plans?"

"No idea, but I'm hoping to find out. But in case I strike out, if you get any intel, let me know."

"So, I'll see you Sunday for auditions then?" she chirped.

"You're incorrigible."

"I thought we agreed I was hard to please?" There were muffled voices in the background, and Candace barked something back I couldn't make out. "I have to run. Apparently, the size of the sustainably sourced sea scallops is now displeasing the groom's father. Do you ever dabble in justifiable homicide representation?"

"That's not a thing," I said solemnly. "So please don't kill anyone."

"Fine," she grumped. "Have some of Marty's prawns for me."

I promised I would and hung up. Fifteen minutes later, I arrived at the Merchant of Venison exactly five minutes before seven o'clock. Smoothing my dress, I strode across the pea gravel parking lot, never missing a step. The trick in stilettos, which I'd learned over years of chasing down partners and clients in tiled restaurants and over the turf of golf courses, was to position the weight in your toes and never lock your knees.

The Merchant of Venison, done in the French farmhouse style, reclined effortlessly against a backdrop of the lake and trees, its painted brick and shutter-flanked windows understated and utterly charming as the sun sank low behind it.

The MOV's interior was equally low-key. Slightly uneven floorboards, unassuming brick walls and exposed wooden beam ceilings greeted the diner with a reassuring and calming smile. In the back corner, Ben sat at a thoughtfully laid table with a vase of daisies in the middle, perusing the menu. As I traversed the floorboards, he lifted his eyes, catching sight of me, his appraisal of my dress subtle but appreciative, as was the smile on his face as he rose from the table.

For his part, Ben wore dark suit pants and a crisp white shirt open at the collar, revealing bare, tan skin beneath. I was starting to think of it as his signature look. No five-o'clock shadow tonight; he'd touched up for the occasion. Several heads turned in his direction when he stood, and I had to admit that even without the incredibly flattering lighting, he cut a dashing figure. "Ms. Barnes."

"Mr. Dane," I replied, trying not to smile at the obvious pleasure he was taking with formalities. "I see you made it out of the town hall intact," I said, settling into my seat and admiring the exposed wooden beams of the ceiling and the iron chandelier with its flickering tapered candles.

"Manners and shameless flirting with small-town bureaucrats will only get you so far. It's important to have another body there to draw fire."

"Words to live by. Did you find what you were looking for?" I asked.

His eyes, dark as shale, lingered on mine, his mouth quirking up at the corners. "Too early to tell."

A decent bullshitter, then. Well, I'd have been disappointed if he'd been anything less.

"What's good here?" he asked.

"Marty will kill me for saying this, but I'm not much for the deer or duck, which I know are the signature dishes. The wild-caught trout is my favorite."

"You're on a first-name basis with the James Beard Award–winning chef and owner?" He raised an eyebrow.

"Home turf has its perks."

Our server, a serious-looking young woman with neat braids and a shy smile, appeared to fill our glasses with ice water, and we both voiced our thanks. Point for Ben. I'd served as a hostess in Bard's as a teenager and graduated to waitress in several fine-dining establishments in Harvard Square. The old adage that if you wanted to understand people, you waited tables still rang true for me, but as a constant fixture on the business dinner circuit, I'd learned you could also tell a lot about a person by the way they treated their waitstaff.

"When I asked you to dinner, I didn't realize I'd be dining with the future managing partner of FrancisPearl's newly established Boston office," he said. "You could have said something."

"Like what?"

"Like 'Dream on, upstart.'"

"That would have been a very awkward thing to say." I smiled, taking a sip of water. "Besides, I like to network." That wasn't exactly the truth, but it was what one was expected to say. I didn't love the song and dance of business courtship. But I understood the need to appear at endless dinners, mixers and events to give clients a glimpse of what they'd be getting for a four-figure hourly billing rate. Besides, Benjamin Dane was easier on the eyes and ears than most of the Wall Street stiffs vying for my attention.

"Well, thank you," Ben said. "I'm clearly outclassed and in the presence of greatness. I wasn't aware you could make managing partner in your early thirties." At my raised eyebrows, he added smoothly, "Yes, I can do the math on LinkedIn."

"What a coincidence," I said, without missing a beat. "Me too. You've built quite an impressive résumé in your short tenure. Boston's not exactly an easy market."

"No, it isn't," he said, with a gleam in his eyes.

"How did you get into development?"

"I worked construction to put myself through school. Eventually graduated from the back of the truck to the front of house. I like the moving pieces."

Now, that I hadn't expected. But it would help explain the visible muscles beneath that dress shirt. I was a little disappointed though when he didn't say more. I could sense there was a story behind that perfectly manufactured sound bite.

"What brings you home to Bard's Rest?" Ben asked. "Besides settling old scores with town officials."

"I'm on sabbatical," I said with as much enthusiasm as I could muster. "The firm requires new managing partners to take time prior to assuming the role."

"Not loving that, huh?"

"Sabbaticals are even worse than vacations. I have no idea what to do with myself until September," I admitted.

"What about traveling? Seems like the natural choice."

"I'd love to travel," I said, my voice uncharacteristically wistful. "But I need to be close to home right now." Seeing his expression, his mouth poised for the question, I added, "My mother is going through some medical stuff."

"That can't be easy."

"It isn't," I agreed, but didn't elaborate, because my voice always quavered when I talked about Mom's cancer.

"There must be something to do in Bard's to pass your time?"

"Well, in addition to settling old scores with town officials, I'm moonlighting as the festival attorney, if you can believe it. I'm thinking of it as extended pro bono that doesn't violate the terms of my sabbatical. Even Gerald, my partner mentor, wouldn't be able to find fault with this."

"Gerald Cutler?" Ben asked, his eyes suddenly sharp.

"How much time did you spend on LinkedIn this afternoon?" I teased.

"He's your mentor?" he asked, his tone shaded with something I couldn't quite place.

I wanted to ask how he knew Gerald, but our server reappeared to relay the specials, all the while her gaze darting to Ben. I couldn't blame her. There was something about the way he carried himself, the way he spoke, the way he smiled. A pleasing package that drew the eye. And for the most part, it rang more authentic than practiced.

Ben listened politely, asking the server what she liked best among the appetizer specials, and then inquired if I'd be up for the prawns she'd recommended. She beamed when I agreed and suggested a sparkling wine out of California to pair. I looked at Ben, who cocked his head at me. "I'm up for it, unless you want to go straight to scotch?"

"I thought this was a quasi-business dinner," I reminded him.

"Later, then."

"Presumptuous."

"More like hopeful," he said with a grin.

After our server disappeared, I steered the conversation back to Ben. "Rising star in the Boston market. Having met you, this makes sense. But how does Bard's Rest fit in?"

"You seem very focused on Bard's Rest."

"Please don't mistake my interest for hometown sentimentality," I said, pinning him with my eyes. "I don't understand the angle. When something seems out of place, I want to understand it. So why here?"

"In the aftermath of the pandemic, the demand for secondary space distinct from the primary home has increased exponentially. This town's highly commutable location makes it ripe for development. Throw in the established summer tourist following and the picturesque location and it's a no-brainer."

"Try draconian zoning laws and passionate locals with a history of theatrics—and I'm not just talking about Shakespeare. Who wants to tangle with that?"

"Winning over the locals is part of the fun."

"I don't think you'll win over these locals. Last year, they chased out an all-day brunch place because the owner had another location in Portland and that was too close to a chain restaurant for them. The guy made his own kefir."

"I think the opportunities I'm looking at are sufficiently out of the way of the town proper that locals wouldn't mind a few luxury condos."

"Unless you're in the town over, I highly doubt it."

He smiled at this. "Well, Bard's is one of a handful of towns I'm considering based on their potential and commutability to Boston."

"Bard's isn't a done deal, then?"

"Hardly. Tomorrow I'll be driving over to Sherburne to look at some property as well."

Our server came back with our appetizers, and we both ordered the trout and an additional wine pairing.

"Tell me more about relocating from New York to Boston in the fall," Ben asked.

"It puts me closer to my family, which is important because of my mother. My middle sister, Miranda, lives in Arlington, so that will be a shorter commute to visit her and her—" I stumbled on the verbiage. Calling Adam a boyfriend seemed inadequate. He and Miranda lived together and shared custody of all sorts of pets. "Partner," I finished.

"Are you uprooting any partners of your own in this move?"

I shook my head.

"Pets, houseplants?"

"Just my Hydrow rower."

"The Charles River workout is a delight," he said.

"Though it does lack the verisimilitude of still-drunk undergrads bracing themselves against the boathouse in their attempts to stumble home."

"Are you speaking from personal experience?" Ben asked, arching an eyebrow. I'd never considered men's eyebrows sexy. But I was willing to make an exception for Ben.

"Oh, you don't know me well enough to guess at what I might or might not have done during my undergrad years," I said, waggling my fingers at him.

"But I'd like to." His eyes tracked the movement of my fingers and came to rest on my lips. "I bet you were a fearsome undergrad."

"You don't know the half of it." Smiling, I took a sip of wine. "How about you? Do you have a partner?"

"Unmarried and unrepentantly so."

I liked that. More than that, I found myself starting to like Ben. I appreciated his smoothness, his polish, but I was even more intrigued by what was beneath that granite exterior. He had this way of giving me his full attention when I spoke, leaning forward in his chair, his posture alert and his eyes intent. As if what I was saying was the most interesting thing he'd ever heard.

"Don't get me wrong," Ben continued. "I'm not saying never. But my business is everything for me right now. Not in this sad, 'Oh, I don't have anything else to sustain me' kind of way, but as an 'It's the reason I get up every morning and it drives me' thing. I love that every day brings a new insurmountable challenge begging to be solved." His mouth curved into a self-deprecating smile. "I'm rambling."

"You're hardly rambling," I said. "What you said resonates. I know the knee jerk is to pity people like us, consumed by the job, with nothing else to distract them. But I enjoy being consumed by my work. I like that I care enough about something to be consumed by it."

He raised his glass. "To being consumed by the things we love." He winced.

"I bet that sounded better in your head." I smirked, clinking my glass against his.

"It really did," he admitted. He dug into the prawns, a look of absolute delight spreading across his face. "Oh, wow."

"The Merchant of Venison does not disappoint."

"I'm going to have a tough time containing my excitement for the trout." He sipped his wine. "So, I have been trying to figure it out since I met you: ENTJ?"

"Is this, like, the corporate equivalent of 'Hey, baby, what's your sign?'" I scoffed. "Of all the things that I thought would follow a statement about trout, this was not it."

"C'mon, humor me."

"Fine." I heaved a sigh. "You're very close. I'm an INTJ."

"The architect," he said, shaking his head. "I should have known. One of the rarest of personality types. Introverted. Intuitive. Thinking. Judging." He ticked them off on his fingers.

"You have the Myers-Briggs personality types memorized, just like that?"

"Of course. I'm an ESTP. Extroverted—"

"Sensing. Thinking. Perceiving," I finished for him. "I don't live under a rock."

"But you don't buy into the concept of personality types?" he asked, leaning forward in his seat.

"Every time I get promoted at the firm, I have to take the test again. Never changes. You would think in all the times I've taken these, I'd have moved the needle once in the last decade."

"Where would you move the needle if you could?"

It was an interesting question, not one I'd given much thought to. I didn't actually believe we were predestined creatures who would default into their personality types. What mattered to me was how a person behaved when the chips were down. Would you fold like a cheap card table or rise up and face the challenge at hand? I'd made FrancisPearl a ton of money off the first category and seen so few of the second category that they'd become unicorns in my mind.

"I suppose the correct answer is to be less judgmental. But in truth, I'd like to be less introverted. I wish I could draw energy from social gatherings like you E types. It would serve me better at work."

"Don't like selling work?" he guessed.

"I could do with a better ratio of substantive practice to galas and symposia," I admitted as I sliced into a prawn. Seafood was generally a safe bet for me. "What about you? If you could move the needle?"

"More perceiving."

"Is that the one that clues you in that bringing up personality types is an odd topic of conversation at dinner?"

"I like to know who I'm dealing with."

My smile was sharper than one of Marty's steak knives. "I'm the person who gets the deal done."

"Noted," he said with a curving smile of his own.

"And you?"

"Let's go with . . . I'm your intrigued dinner companion." He pointed his fork at me. "I get the sense you don't have any interest in taking Dane Development on as a client, which I can respect, but you're definitely interested in my plans for Bard's." He weighed me with his eyes. "Yet you don't seem the sentimental type."

"I'm not," I assured him. "But I'm curious. What makes you think you can make it here when no one else has managed to get a foothold?" I took another sip of wine. "Or that you should? That you think this would be a valuable commercial play that outweighs the high risk of failure here makes me doubt your judgment."

"Call it a hunch." He smiled. "I have a sense for these things."

I snorted. "Of course you do." I was certain Gerald would have preferred that I push the FrancisPearl agenda. Locked this guy and his company down as a client. But then again, I was not some junior partner; I had more than enough clients and a bursting book of business. I could be selective. Gerald might have quibbled that I should have considered passing Ben on to a junior partner to weave him into the firm's income pipeline.

But strangely, I found I didn't want that for Ben. I wanted him to be someone's top priority, and the best way for him at this life stage for Dane Development was to go the boutique-law-firm route, not paying top dollar for our rates.

As if reading my thoughts he said, "You know, if you took me on as a client, I'd happily divulge all my secrets."

Was it wrong that when he said "secrets," my mind wandered to expensive sheets and champagne in the chiller, indecently expensive shirts rumpled on the floor and discarded heels? My heels? His shirts? Probably.

"You do realize that I don't need to take you on as a client to find out what you're doing? It's a small town. I'll figure it out soon enough. Why keep me guessing?"

"Because I get the sense that you don't spend a lot of your time guessing." He smiled. "It's good for you."

"That's very paternalistic."

"And annoying," he added. "Can I amend to say it keeps you interested in what I'm up to?"

"I'll allow it. I'll even provide you a list of firms you may want to consider in the area."

"Is that your way of letting me down easy?"

"Can I level with you?"

"I'd expect nothing less."

"You don't need a FrancisPearl right now. You want to be at a top boutique firm that specializes in development. Somewhere you'll be a big client for them and get your money's worth out of the rates."

"I appreciate your candor." He sipped his wine thoughtfully. "Now, can we take it for a spin and you tell me about Bard's?"

I laughed. "Well, if I were considering development in Bard's, which I wouldn't because it's a fool's errand, I would think about proximity to What's in a Main Street. Most of the action in Bard's centers around the shops and eateries there, as does the Shakespearean festival. You can't discount that. Then I'd factor in waterfront considerations, as one might want to putt around the lake in a pontoon boat or tie up at the docks for the mainstages."

"The mainstages?"

"Bard's puts on one of Shakespeare's comedies and tragedies each year, the highlight of the two-week festival. They're staged at the amphitheater on Will's Island. Boat ownership or boat access is important, unless you want to take the ferry over, which a lot of people do."

"Say more on the festival."

"It's the town's moneymaker—two weeks of bad British accents and questionable period costumes. Food booths, minstrels, people hawking jewelry that looks like it came straight out of the Shire."

"You're really selling it," Ben observed wryly.

"If sonnets and swoon are your thing, then I think the festival is a fun way to spend a chunk of change and time."

"But that's not your thing."

"Work's my thing."

"Mine too."

When our server returned with our entrées, Ben wasted no time cutting into the trout. "This," he said, putting his fork down, "is the best trout I've ever had. As a kid, I used to go fishing with my uncle and we'd catch them fresh. He'd do them up on the grill, best thing I'd ever tasted. But I'm sorry, Uncle Rob, some guy named Marty has usurped your fish scale throne."

"My deepest apologies to Uncle Rob," I said as I sliced into my own trout, appreciating that Marty never oversalted it, never retreated to butter to hide the flaws. Just perfectly cooked fish every time.

"He had a good run." He chewed thoughtfully. "Why did you really agree to have dinner with me this evening?"

"I wanted to know more about you and your plans for Bard's."

"And now?"

"And now I know you've underestimated the lack of appetite in this place for development." I seasoned my words with a smirk. "It doesn't make you a bad person. I just hope for your sake you end up in one of these other towns, where you'll meet less resistance from the locals."

"Is that it then? No other interest in me?"

"I didn't say that. You do have interesting taste in bourbon."

He laughed, and the sound of it—the confidence and ease of it—rolled over my bare skin, bringing my body to delicious attention. I wondered if his hands were as confident as his laugh. It was an odd thought to have at a quasi-business dinner, but I liked a man who was as good with his hands as he was with his words.

I ate another experimental bite of the trout and then another, realizing I had been braced for disappointment, certain that something would taste off the way that everything had after Berlin, when even my favorite foods had tasted dull, muffled, wrong. Much to my relief, the fish tasted just like I'd remembered from last summer: an enticing balance of maple and sage that didn't overpower the fish itself.

When I looked up, I found Ben watching me, his expression one of careful evaluation, his curiosity there but at bay. But he didn't say anything, and I appreciated that. Berlin had left me with a complicated relationship with food, but that was not a topic for a dinner like this. Or, really, a topic I ever discussed with anyone.

"Tell me what it was really like growing up here?" Ben asked, his tone conspiratorial.

"Like growing up in any small town—small school, tight-knit families, everyone intimately acquainted with the goings-on of everyone else."

Ben narrowed his eyes, and it did interesting things to his top lip, giving it an almost pouty cast. "Oh, come, pull back the curtain for me. Let me have a look."

"So you can use that information to profit off my town?"

"No, because I want to understand you better."

"My four-letter Myers-Briggs code is insufficient to unlocking the secrets of my personality?"

"I deserved that," he said solemnly. "C'mon, give me something you don't share with the rich and famous you represent."

"Like what?" I asked.

"Your first job. Managing partners have to start somewhere."

"Aide to the reference librarian at our local library."

"Riveting," he teased.

"It was, actually. But it had nothing to do with the job itself."

Ben cocked his head. "Dazzle me."

"Ms. Audrey Mayfair was well into her seventies by the time I made her acquaintance. She helped me cultivate a love of order and systems."

"I thought you said this was riveting?"

"She may have been a septuagenarian reference librarian by day, but she was an amateur taxidermist by night. Ms. Mayfair would drive around town collecting recently deceased specimens and stuff them."

Ben choked on his wine. "What do you mean 'recently deceased specimens'?"

"Gently hit roadkill. Victims of falls from trees. That kind of thing. When she finished a project, she'd bring it to the reference room and display it. Ms. Mayfair was very passionate about her hobby. There were over fifty specimens adorning the shelves, walls and tables by the time I moved on to a hostess gig."

"I can see why you moved on to hostessing," Ben said mildly.

"Even if they'd had a gentle demise, in death they were fierce. Teeth bared, wings and talons outstretched. That kind of thing. I think it cut down on the amount of people using the reference room, actually."

"I bet no one dared lift reference materials under her watch, huh?"

"Who would steal reference materials?" I said, wrinkling my nose.

"You're right. That's the real oddity in this story," Ben deadpanned.

"Okay, tell me about your first job."

"Golf ball collector."

"Excuse me?"

"You ever been to a driving range and seen some poor sucker driving up and down the range in a souped-up golf cart enclosed in a cage?"

"I can't say that I have," I admitted. "Why is the cart enclosed in a cage?"

"Because entitled rich kids like to use a slow-moving vehicle and the kid stuck inside as target practice."

"That's horrible."

"It wasn't so bad. Most of them were horrendous golfers and usually drunk. But every once in a while somebody would drill the cart, and as it let out this godawful clang against the cart I'd think, 'This is it. This is the time the cage is going to come down around my head and I'm going to wind up with a cracked skull.'"

"That seems like a rather traumatic first job."

Ben shrugged. "Paid well. It's shocking how many people will turn up their nose at being a moving target. Plus, I got to drive what amounted to an armored golf cart at fifteen."

"Is that legal?"

"I don't know, counselor," he said, his voice a silky challenge. "Why don't you tell me?"

I snickered into my wine. "Can I take it from your disdain of entitled rich kids that you didn't grow up an entitled rich kid?"

"Far from it," Ben said, his voice casual, but his posture stiffening into what I'd have called locked-and-loaded mode. Our server turned toward the table. "How about that bourbon now?"

"Alas, I didn't save any room for your very pretentious after-dinner drink," I teased. As pleasant as dinner had been, I demurred, as I'd already had two glasses of wine, the maximum number of drinks I'd ever allowed myself at a work dinner—even if that wasn't quite what this felt like.

"The check then, please."

"We're splitting it," I told him firmly.

"Business expense," he shot back.

"Client development," I countered.

"This hardly qualifies as either since I failed to interest you in my business or convince you to take me on as a client," Ben said dryly.

"The conversation really was sparkling though," I said, unable to hide my smile.

"Actually, there is no check," the server piped in. "Marty says your money is no good here, Ms. Barnes. He says it's the dinner rush and he's too busy to come out of the kitchen right now to argue with you."

"Coward," I gasped. "I'm a delight."

Both Ben and the server looked dubious.

"When I want to be," I clarified. "All right. Will you please tell him I am so appreciative of his generosity and that as usual, his food and waitstaff are unmatched? Better than any of the fine dining in New York."

Our server nodded brightly, looking more than a little bit relieved that I hadn't pressed the issue.

"Care to explain?" Ben asked as he extracted his wallet and plucked a bill out to leave our server a generous tip.

With the smile that my sisters called the Cheshire, I added my own contribution to the tip pile. "Can't a woman keep a bit of mystery about her?"

He regarded me thoughtfully, sitting back in his chair to take me in. I liked the way his shirt stretched, but not strained, across his chest. The man had exceptional posture, which gave him an air of ease that even I envied. "Color me intrigued, Ms. Barnes." His tone was teasing, but there was heat in his eyes when he said it.

When dinner ended, Ben insisted on walking me to my car. "What if you turn an ankle in the parking lot?" he asked, and I assured him I'd ice it down with a scotch when I got home, but I let him walk me anyway because his blinding white shirt was nearly as good as a flashlight in the dimly lit parking lot.

"An enchanting and surprising evening," he remarked. "I think this is the most entertaining rejection I've ever had."

"Try not to take it too hard. I'll send you that list of boutique firms. I think you'd be served best in a smaller shop that focuses on development plays like yours." We exchanged numbers, me giving him my work contact rather than my personal cell. It was a reflex, and one I instantly regretted, but it was too late now to backpedal.

"Yeah, yeah. I get it," he said as he saved my number into his contacts. "Not a big enough fish for the likes of FrancisPearl."

"It's not like I'm personally rejecting you. Just your business." I winked.

"That does leave open a rather wide range of possibilities," he agreed. He leaned in and opened my car door for me. In doing so, he nearly brushed his cheek against mine and I felt the sliver of air between us shift.

For one thrilling moment, I allowed myself to envision pulling his mouth to mine for a hot, searing kiss. Nothing about this man seemed half-assed. I was willing to bet he was one of those all-consuming, urgent kissers but would take his time and tease between the sheets.

But even though there was zero chance I'd be taking him on as a client, I wasn't in the habit of kissing professional contacts. All the more so, given his interest in Bard's Rest. Whether or not a development project materialized, something like that would definitely complicate things. I sighed. Kissing him was definitely off the table. As was standing here, staring at his lips. "Good night, Mr. Dane," I said, harking back to Ben's earlier formality as I slid into the car.

"Goodnight, Ms. Barnes," he said in a voice as smooth as whiskey stones. He closed my door and stepped back, watching me drive off with a faint smile.

Scene Seven

··········

Peaseblossom's

I awoke sweaty and cocooned in twisted sheets. My left calf screamed as it contorted and tightened. Through gritted teeth, I reached down to massage the area through the agony of the spasm. I cursed silently, kicking myself for not having drunk more water before falling asleep last night. My charley horses always arrived on the heels of insufficient hydration.

Now here I was. Wide-awake. With absolutely nothing to do and nothing to get up for. There were no committee meetings today. No email to check. No appointments until my meeting with Emmeline later that week. I lay there utterly still, staring up at the ceiling of the turret and wondering what to do with myself. Now that there was . . . nothing. Nothing.

Get up, I told myself. *Get up before it starts. Get moving.*

I reached for my phone. I would check the news. Play a logic puzzle. Maybe Chris had texted. But in my haste, I knocked the phone to the floor.

With a curse, I thunked my head against the pillow, ignoring the soreness still pulsing in my calf. I should get up. If I wasn't doing something, I wasn't useful. I might as well—the stinging prickle started in my fingers and worked its way up and down my arms.

Swallowing hard, I closed my eyes tight against the insistent and increasing beat of my heart that followed the prickle. *It's okay; you're okay.* Kim's words floated through me, and I latched onto them like a kite struggling to lift. *This is your body's way of dumping excess anxiety.*

That's all this was. My body wasn't broken—it was trying to right itself. *This isn't Berlin,* I reminded myself, willing it to be true.

I swung my legs out of bed and set about the comfort of my morning routine—my complicated skin regimen, the satisfaction of a luxurious brush and floss of the teeth and attending to my hair until it gleamed. Doing something would make me calm.

Next, I selected a casual, weather-appropriate cerulean summer dress unlikely to be dismissed by Miranda as overly fussy and slipped on a pair of sandals. Once I looked presentable, I wound my way downstairs to find . . . an empty kitchen.

Of course. My parents had lives and jobs and things to keep them busy in the summer. Dad had no doubt already headed over to the high school to work on the sets for this year's mainstages, and Mom would be off doing a myriad of festival things.

I fixed myself some tea, liberally raiding Mom's English breakfast stash—none of that overly flowery Earl Grey that Dad and Miranda liked. As I boiled the water in the ancient teakettle, only then did I think of last night's dinner with Ben. Ben, who was handsome in a way that wasn't flashy and whose intensity vibrated at just the right frequency. Ben, whose dark eyes and expressive mouth were the last things I'd thought of before drifting off last night.

Mug in hand, I slipped out the side door to the back gardens. While I'd taken these for granted when I was a kid, I had a deep appreciation for them now that I lived in a city with little green space. In our backyard, Dad had built this circular patio of tiles and added a patio set, and centered around that Mom had added layer upon circular layer of flower beds emanating out in a riot of colors and varying heights. There were birdbaths and sundials scattered about in a way that made me think of planets orbiting around the sun— deliberate and balanced and yet somehow still pleasingly random.

Closing my eyes, I took several deep breaths, trying to recall that mindful minute meditation that Candace and I learned at our yoga retreat last year, something about cutting off one of your senses to heighten others. I inhaled the scents of Mom's flowers. I couldn't pick out anything specific, but the overall perfume of florals smelled lovely, the morning air warmed my skin and . . . something snapped to my left. My eyes flew open.

"Mom?" I yelped.

"Portia?" She looked as surprised to see me as I did her.

"I was meditating," I said quickly. "Well, I was trying to, anyway. I'm not very good at it."

"I've found with meditation, it's practice that makes you better. It's hard to turn the mind off at first. But you get there eventually."

"You meditate?" It was hard to picture my elegant, sophisticated and always on-the-go and in-the-middle-of-things mother meditating.

"We started right around when you girls became teenagers. Your father and I found it helped during those"—she paused for a delicate second—"challenging years."

"Huh."

"I also find gardening meditative. There's an extra pair of gloves in my bench over there," she said, inclining her head toward one of those outdoor storage affairs. "You can help me deadhead."

I opened my mouth to protest that I didn't have time to garden, I needed to—I needed to do what, exactly? I had no job responsibilities. No plans. I could . . . garden. I could garden. The idea was oddly appealing. "I'd like that," I said, standing and retrieving a pair of surprisingly comfortable gardening gloves from Mom's ruthlessly organized storage bin.

Although I hadn't deadheaded anything in years, it was a simple enough thing to remember. Find spent blooms and pinch them off, thereby channeling the energy away from seed production and into further flower production. It proved satisfying as hell, the snap of the bloom, that release that you knew would enable the plant to move forward, to generate a new flower, to—

My mother cleared her throat. "I said, how's it been so far? Stir-crazy yet?"

I declined to tell her about my most recent paralyzing moment of doubt this morning in the turret. "Great," I said in a voice too bright and cheery for even the garden. "So great."

"Glad to hear that," Mom said, her head bent in concentration over a hot pink geranium, but I could see the twitch of her lips. "I had no doubts my high-powered daughter would seamlessly transition into the life of leisure."

"Liar."

"Right back at you, darling." She smiled.

"I need to find my rhythm," I insisted. "I have the festival to keep me busy . . ." I trailed off. "I'm working on the first pass of most of the contracts. I should be able to get them out next week to the vendors for review. I have a meeting scheduled with Emmeline to discuss permits. But if there's anything else you'd like me to do, I'd be happy to—"

"While I'd love to leverage your talents further on the festival committee, the less mercenary, more motherly parts of my being think you need to find non-work-related pursuits to fill your time. Discover new hobbies. Forge new relationships."

"Spoilsport," I grumbled.

"Well, if you insist, maybe a few more festival tasks, if you don't mind."

"Now we're talking," I said gleefully, moving on to the petunias. "Load me up."

She ticked off a dizzying list of items, all of which I mentally catalogued into level of difficulty. I'd add these to the spreadsheet I'd started when she wasn't looking.

"One more thing. I would love if you could run these flyers over to Peaseblossom's later. They're under new management—William Douglas passed this spring—but I'm hoping his nephew will continue the mini-golf tie-ins for the festival. Put in a good word for the festival?"

"Sure, happy to do that."

"Maybe you could take me to my treatment next week, if you're up for it."

My hands stilled. I hadn't gone to one of Mom's chemo appointments yet. At first, she'd only allowed Dad to drive her, gradually allowing Cordelia into the mix. Even Miranda had made the trip up once or twice, but I'd been exempted. I'd told myself it was because I lived in New York. But it still hurt she hadn't even asked. "I'd like that very much."

"But I get to pick the music," she added firmly.

"Oh come on, no Wagner," I pleaded.

"Musical troglodytes, all of you."

A few hours later, when not a wilted bloom remained, I showered and dressed for the early June weather in a tea-length white skirt with bold orange poppies on it, a black top with capped short sleeves and sandals. Slipping a pair of sunglasses into my purse, I gathered up the flyers for Peaseblossom's and drove into town.

Peaseblossom's was a quintessential New England mini-golf establishment, green and well-manicured and complete with a driving range, batting cages and, most important, a dairy barn with happy cows and homemade frozen yogurt and ice cream offerings. Like a lot of mini-golf establishments, it had a theme, and that theme was all Shakespeare, all the time. There were two courses—thespians and playwrights. The thespians was the more accessible, family-friendly course, complete with the works-of-Shakespeare-themed holes, while the playwrights was the more challenging course. It was still Shakespeare themed, and after five o'clock, it transformed into an adults-only course where ale and mead could be purchased and consumed out of novelty goblets.

I headed down a winding path to a small cottage with a hand-carved office sign and knocked softly.

"C'mon in," a voice called.

Ducking my head and entering the tiny space, I found a lanky man in faded jeans and a wrinkled polo at the desk, or rather, with his legs propped up on the desk as he reclined at a precarious angle in his chair. If *True Detective* Matthew McConaughey and *Dazed and Confused* Matthew McConaughey had a time warp love child, this would be the result. Frankly, it was very blond and more than a little off-putting. As was the way his watered-down blue eyes raked me up and down. "What can I do you for?"

After mentally adding that to the list of expressions I thought should be wiped from humanity's collective consciousness, I smiled brightly. "Are you Mr. Douglas?"

"Depends on who's asking," he said with a cockeyed grin that fell far short of whatever look he thought he was going for.

"I'm Portia Barnes with the festival committee, and I wanted to leave these flyers with Mr. Douglas and confirm Peaseblossom's generous support again this year."

"People call me Archie." He eyed the flyers suspiciously. "What kind of generous support are you sniffing around for?"

"Peaseblossom's typically offers a daily special promotion during the festival. Sometimes, it's a 'bring your one true love for two-for-one mini-golf.' Or 'all the little Hamnets and Judiths get a free ice cream cone with the purchase of a sundae.' That kind of thing. It's all noted there on the cover page." I smiled sweetly. Though I now sold my professional advice to the tune of four figures an hour, I'd cut my teeth at the ripe old age of seven hawking Girl Scout cookies. It had been a lucrative venture, teaching me not only the value of bulk sales but immunizing me to the gross stares of greasy man Muppets.

Archie stood and came around the desk in an attempt to get closer or loom over me or both. He smelled of stale tobacco, unwashed socks and bad decisions. I subtly shifted away from him. "That seems like a lot of work," he said, resignation in his voice. "Look, I don't know if you know this, but I inherited this place from my uncle, and every time I turn around there's a busted sprinkler or the damn lights on hole eight have stopped working or the high school drama kids want to host a fundraiser."

"That must be so hard for you," I said, trying to make my tone sympathetic. "Running a business can be challenging, especially when you take it over from a beloved member of the community and want to maintain your current client base." Here my smile grew a little sharper than it absolutely needed to. "Luckily, local businesses that participate in the annual festival in a highly visible way see a marked return for their efforts." I'd read Mom's spreadsheet where the committee tracked such things in a rudimentary way that would have an accountant fretting. Still, there was definitely an uptick in business come August.

I pointedly looked past Archie, who was still violating the "If I can see your nose hairs, you're too close to me" policy, my gaze flitting to the walls, where William Douglas, who had been a handsome man with neatly combed white hair and a gregarious smile, stared back from photos snapped at various holes around the course, where he posed with patrons in costumes and gap-toothed kids. That man looked as wholesome as oat bran—whereas his nephew reminded me of soggy cornflakes.

My eyes traveled over Archie's desk, where I saw several property maps strewn haphazardly on top of one another, at least one of them sporting a crescent-moon coffee stain. Either Archie was an amateur cartographer, which I doubted, or he was considering offloading his uncle's holdings. I couldn't blame him. It would be difficult to maintain this place without a spine.

"I'm evaluating my options. This wasn't exactly what I had in mind when I heard I'd received an inheritance," Archie sniffed when he saw where my gaze had landed.

Well, if that wasn't the most entitled thing I'd heard today, I wasn't sure what would top it.

"Well, I for one hope Peaseblossom's remains an establishment here in town for years to come," I said cheerfully. "The kids love this place." Okay, I was laying it on a bit thick, but this man's eyes had slid so far down my chest, I felt like I'd be picking them out of my belly button.

"Oh yes, the kids. Of course, that's who we do it for," Archie said absently, his eyes still on my breasts. Gross.

Pointedly clearing my throat, I stood up, careful to swing my body well out of Archie's reach. "Thank you so much for your time,

Mr. Douglas. I'll follow up in a few days to see what you've decided to contribute." Then I slipped out of his office, feeling like I needed another shower even though I'd had one less than two hours ago.

Mission accomplished, I headed for the parking lot. Maybe I'd go for a run and then see if Mom would let me deadhead the flowers over at the gardens at Bard's Books.

"Portia?"

Frowning, I turned around to find Ben standing by the entrance to the driving range. He sported a burgundy golf shirt, which I approved of, and navy golf pants, which I did not. But honestly, golf pants were a lost cause on everyone. At least he wasn't wearing one of those tacky visors.

"Hey, what are you doing here?" I asked.

"Out enjoying the driving range. Beautiful view over that pond. How about you?"

"I came to drop off some flyers for the festival."

"Festival business, then. That makes sense. Didn't figure you for an avid mini-golfer."

I cocked my head at him. "What's that supposed to mean?"

"Nothing," he said. "Mini-golf is kitschy. Didn't seem your speed."

That rankled me because I was, in fact, a scratch mini-golfer. Growing up, Peaseblossom's had been a Friday night tradition. Miranda had loved the fairy gardens, Cordelia the ice cream barn and me, the competition that seesawed back and forth until the final hole, a treacherous narrow ski jump with an opportunity for a hole in one that could make or break your game.

"Is mini-golf your speed?" I countered.

"I've been known to play my fair share of golf," he replied, his grin sly.

He hadn't said *mini-golf* though, and in my experience from watching my dad and uncle John square off at Peaseblossom's, golf skills didn't necessarily translate to mini-golf proficiency. "Do a lot of mini-golfing, do you?" I asked in an arch tone.

"Are you calling my golf prowess into question?"

"I believe I am."

"I have an appointment in a bit, but I'm early. Don't suppose you'd be up for a round?"

"Despite the fact that you don't think mini-golf is my speed?"

The corners of Ben's mouth twitched. "Care to put a wager on it?"

"What do you have in mind?"

"Well, since our first dinner was so enjoyable, shall we say winner picks the time and place and loser picks up the tab?"

"You're on." I grinned, gesturing to the mini-golf hut, where a bored-looking teenager stood replenishing the red mini pencils.

"Now, very important question. What color ball are you?"

"Blue," I answered without hesitation.

"What if I want blue?"

"I'm blue," I insisted. "You can have red. That's the next-best color."

Before he could say another word, I slid my credit card to the girl at the window. "Two, please. One blue ball, one red."

The girl ran my card and sized us up for battered putters. I smiled, amused, as she snuck furtive glances at Ben. I couldn't blame her. But for the whole unfortunate golf pants decision, Ben was Henry Cavill hot. *Tudors* Henry Cavill. Not *Witcher*.

We walked toward hole one, a jaunty crimson toadstool with Peaseblossom herself sitting cross-legged atop it, her pink-petaled dress and thistle hat freshly painted. At least Archie had gotten that right. "Would you like to shoot first or second?" I asked.

"Please show me how it's done," Ben said with a mock sweep of his hand.

Stepping past him, I dropped my ball on the mat and toed it into place. Squaring my shoulders, I adjusted my grip, sighted the hole and swung. The ball shot forward with a satisfying crack, straight between the tunnel in the toadstool and into the cup with a resounding plunk for a hole in one. Ben stared at the hole and then back at me. "I guess mini-golf is your speed."

"I guess so," I said with a sardonic smile, stepping back to let him play.

"Home field advantage. I should have known," he said ruefully, shaking his dark hair.

"But you have your golf prowess," I reminded him. "I'd say we're evenly matched."

And we were, the two of us battling back and forth over the next few holes, at least until we got to hole six, a mischievous ode to Puck from *A Midsummer Night's Dream* with a harrowing shot up an incline bedecked in twinkle lights and vegetation onto a mounded hill ringed by fairies. As Ben evaluated his shot, I leaned slightly forward—not touching his shoulder, but close enough to smell the crisp note of birch in his aftershave—and murmured, "I think I'll choose the tasting menu at Titania's when I win."

He swung his head around to look at me, his face so near to mine, I could see flecks of ore in the granite quarry of his eyes. "Are you trying to trash-talk in my backswing?"

"I never trash-talk," I said solemnly, easing away from him. "It's beneath me. I just know you're not going to make this hole in fewer than five strokes."

"You know, I've always been the type of person that people underestimate," he remarked. I doubted that, but let it pass, standing transfixed as he zeroed in, his attention fully on his shot with an intensity that made me wonder what else he might accomplish with those hands, given the chance. And though my thoughts were a bit sexed-up for Peaseblossom's, there weren't any kids around this early. I now felt a certain amount of freedom since deciding I wouldn't take Ben or Dane Development on as a client. At least this way I could appreciate Ben's attractiveness and confidence. Not every man out there could pull off such swagger with a neon green putter in hand.

Ben swung, and the ball shot up the ramp, weaving between the matchstick legs of a fairy and circling the hole in dramatic fashion before settling into the cup. I'd never seen someone sink a hole in one on Puck's.

He flashed me a dazzling smile. "I'm full of surprises," he murmured as he pivoted on the mat to glide past me, close enough that I imagined the ions in the air between us, charged and crackling against the bare skin of my arms.

A mortifying thought struck me. What if it was just me experiencing this attraction and this just happened to be Ben's normal banter? I decided to see what happened if I turned the conversation in a different direction. "How goes the property search?"

"Eh, I'm not seeing anything I like in Sherburne," Ben said gamely. "Pellsworth is next, plus one or two places here I'm still interested in seeing."

"Pellsworth does have that lovely winery. No Shakespeare—just grapes and unforgiving New England soil."

"Why do I feel like you're trying to throw me off my game here by throwing in shoptalk?"

"Because you're a smart man."

"You'll do anything to beat me at mini-golf, won't you?" he teased. "Even stoop to shoptalk. Wait, is that a bear?"

Ben stepped around me so he could get a better look at the next hole. Still unsatisfied, he walked over to the hole and crouched down to get a better look. "Am I supposed to hit the ball into the mouth? Would that mean the ball comes out of the bear's—"

"It's best not to think through the mechanics of it," I said breezily, glad that there was no one around to watch me ogle the way Ben's pants stretched tight across his quads.

"What's with the bear?" he asked, straightening up.

"In *The Winter's Tale*, a character with, let's say, less than virtuous intentions, is eaten by a bear. His demise is precipitated by Shakespeare's most famous stage direction."

"Which is?"

"'Exit, pursued by a bear.'"

Ben snickered. "That seems expedient, if a little harsh. Not unlike the angle on this hole."

"You could skip the gullet shot and go between the bear's legs."

"Why would I do that? It will cost me an extra shot to get to the hole."

"It will cost you an extra shot when you bounce it off the bear's teeth and it rolls past us. And then I mock you."

"You don't think I can hit it?" He raised an eyebrow and leaned in ever so slightly.

"I know you can't hit it," I said smugly, reciprocating both the eyebrow raise and the lean in. Our faces were close again—close enough that I could see a faint trace of stubble and imagine the sandpaper scrape of it against my own cheek, the shiver it would send down my spine.

"What if I do hit it?"

"What if you don't?" I countered.

"Side wager?"

"Okay," I said, nodding slowly while I thought. "I want to hear something about you that's not on the approved menu you serve to your clients."

He drew back, a broad challenge of a grin on his face. "I'm an open book."

"No, you're not," I said primly.

"You're right, I'm not." He looked from me to the bear and back again. "You're on."

Ben's shot was decent enough, but still a beat too hard. It bounced off the bear's yellowed canines and rolled down the slope until I stopped it with my foot, my rather fabulous pedicure glinting in the morning sun. "You were saying?"

Ben tapped his chin thoughtfully. "I despise golf."

I frowned at him. "Really?" I snatched his ball up from under my foot, and instead of offering it to him, I closed my fist around it. "You're going to have to do better than that if you want this ball back."

"No, really, I despise the sport. I know it's bad for business to say it, but I hate the pace, and I hate the concept of mulligans. Life seldom offers you one; why should a sport?"

"Are you sure you're not traumatized from your days as a ball collector?"

"I suppose being drilled for sport by entitled rich kids might have left a lasting impression on me," he conceded. "Okay, how about this? My favorite beach activity is bocce, and I've been known to indulge in a game of curling. With a hot toddy in hand, of course."

"Are you pitching a guest column for *Men's Health*?" I shook my head. "This is my unimpressed face."

"That's how your face always looks," Ben pointed out.

I narrowed my eyes at him.

"Okay, fine." His eyes darted furtively around. Dropping his voice, he admitted, "When I'm stressed-out, I listen to Christmas carols. Doesn't matter if it's two in the morning on a hot July evening or a rainy afternoon in April. When I start to sweat, I want to hear 'Silver Bells.'"

"Stop it," I said, unable to keep a surprised laugh from slipping out. "That's monstrous."

"No, I swear. When I can't get something to line up or I'm bumping up against a deadline, there's something about Bing crooning 'White Christmas.'"

"Yes. That 'something' you're referring to is just plain wrongness."

"Hey, some of my only good memories from childhood were set to the backdrop of Christmas carols. They make me peaceful and warm inside, like for that one night, nothing bad will happen to me. How can you not smile when Nat King Cole is singing 'The Christmas Song'?"

"Good taste?" I offered. "A general sense of propriety?" I teased gently, weighing whether I wanted to ask him what had made him think something bad would happen to him, but hesitant to tread somewhere I wasn't wanted.

"Uh-huh." He nodded to the bear. "Your turn. When you miss the mouth, you can tell me something not on the approved list for your clients."

"Joke's on you. I'm going between the legs."

"Never figured you to back down from a challenge."

I whipped around to stare daggers at him. "You're on." I returned my concentration to the hole, lining up slightly to the left to compensate for the curve, and shot the ball straight through the bear's mouth. It plopped out the back of the bear a few scant inches from the hole. I tossed Ben a triumphant look.

"No fair," he protested, catching my hand in his. "I saw you compensate for the lip. That's hardly sporting."

"Fine. How about—I'm exceptionally good at mini-golf?" I offered.

"Something better," he insisted, still holding my hand, his fingers warm on my skin. I didn't want him to let go, so I stood there, enjoying the press of his thumb and making a show of mulling it over.

Soon, the smile that Chris described as my "game, set, match, sucker" spread across my face. "How about you're currently man-handling a former Mermaid Queen of Webster's Cove?"

Ben looked down at our joined hands in surprise. He didn't drop them right away, not before letting his thumb trail down my wrist anyway. "Sorry, did you say 'Mermaid Queen'?"

"Seashell crown, scaled tail and everything."

"You have to say more," Ben pressed. "You can't drop a Mermaid Queen reference and not explain it."

"My freshman-year roommate, Sasha, lived in a small New England fishing town, and the summer after our freshman year, we both landed internships at a botany research institute there."

"Botany?"

I shrugged. "They were doing interesting things with vaccine research and I wanted to keep my options open. That and I really didn't want to be in Bard's for the summer."

He nodded. "That checks out."

"Sasha's parents owned a houseboat they usually rented out to summer tourists, but they gave it to us at a discount. The stipend from the institute covered rent and groceries, a little into savings and the rest into a 401(k)."

"Tell me, did you emerge from the womb knowing the difference between pre-tax and after-tax IRA contributions, or did that come in your toddler years?"

I snorted. "Keep it up and I won't finish the story."

"I'm not mocking you," he said, pressing his hand over his heart. "I'm in awe of you. I had to figure out how to adult at an early age as well. Only I had to do it out of necessity. You did it to set yourself up for success later in life."

I studied his face, trying to match his words with his expression, but his eyes and his mouth gave nothing away. He'd offered another glimpse at something in his past. Like he was testing the waters, not sure if the temperature was right yet or not. I knew that feeling. I also knew how much I didn't like being nudged under the surface when I wasn't ready. I held his eyes for a beat, trying to convey to him that I clocked it.

"Sasha insisted on introducing me to everyone in town that she was related to by blood or marriage, which accounted for about eighty percent of the Webster's Cove inhabitants. When I met Nan, Sasha's aunt and the local business magnate, she told me I should audition to be that year's Mermaid Queen. Since Sasha had already achieved the honor of Mermaid Queen the prior year, she was only too happy to nag me until I relented and allowed her to coach me."

"I think I'd like to meet Sasha," Ben said. "Anyone who can get you to give an inch on anything is worth meeting."

I laughed. "She's the managing partner of Carr and Martin's Milan office. She always did have a knack for the romance languages. Somehow she married that with her love of mergers."

"Now I definitely want to meet her," Ben insisted.

"I'm afraid that in addition to being married to her job, she met a local Italian wine wunderkind and they now live on a vineyard with a pack of poorly behaved dogs."

Ben's lips quirked. "It was more I wanted to meet the person who got that note of admiration to creep into your voice."

"Are you saying I'm hard on people?"

"I'm saying I'd like to earn that note of admiration," he said, his eyes pinning mine.

"Not with that mini-golf game," I teased as we meandered down to the next hole, where Ophelia knelt by the water's edge. I'd never liked this one, not only because it had a water hazard and I despised fishing my ball out of slimy water that was likely harboring all sorts of antibiotic-resistant bacteria, but because I'd always felt that Ophelia had deserved more. If anyone deserved the Nick Carraway treatment, it was the woman who'd had to put up with the forever-complaining Hamlet.

Ben nudged my shoulder. "In case you were wondering, this would be the perfect time to regale me with the tale of your reign as the Mermaid Queen."

Snorting at his none-too-subtle hint, I relented. "Webster's Cove is a bit like Bard's in that it draws a summer crowd, but to a much lesser, contained extent. Think steady beach traffic on the weekends and one big festival, the Blessing of the Catch. It somehow manages to skirt any particular religious affiliation and instead is akin to an all-encompassing 'bless the boats and everyone on them so nobody drowns' tradition involving swimming events and a food festival downtown."

"So you traded in Shakespearean festivals for a nautical-themed one?"

"I abhor Shakespeare," I pointed out, giving Ophelia the side-eye as I took my shot, carefully avoiding the water. "But I do enjoy swimming, which is part of the reason I tried out for the Mermaid Queen. Anyone living in Webster's Cove could compete for the title, and since I lived with Sasha on the houseboat, this earned me a screening interview with the chamber of commerce."

"The interview is conducted by the chamber of commerce?"

"The Blessing of the Catch is a huge income generator for the town. There's a lot riding on the Mermaid Queen and the Pirate King. There was an hour-long interview to weed out anyone who wouldn't take their duties as a nautical monarch seriously."

"What kinds of questions did they ask you?" Ben asked, lining up his ball.

"Well, there were some basic questions about the feeding and swimming habits of mermaids. I had to scour the first-person accounts of mermaid sightings at the local museum archives. I wanted my answers to be as historically accurate as possible."

"What?" Ben sputtered as he whiffed the ball and drove his putter into the mat.

"That counts as a stroke."

"You did that on purpose," Ben fumed.

"They asked me about the town's history and what I liked best about Webster's Cove."

"What did you tell them?" Ben asked, still looking put out.

"I told them I respected how salty they were to the tourists even though they needed that income for schools and infrastructure."

"Of course you did."

"You're just mad I had you going on the mermaid thing." I grinned. "Once I passed the interview, there was a swim race out to Kip's Island, a little under a mile in the early-summer, decidedly still-chilly waters of June. The first ten contestants to make it to the island competed in a secret event for the title of Mermaid Queen."

"Good god, woman," Ben groaned. "Don't stop now. What was the event?"

I shrugged. "It changes year to year. But the year I won, I had to tie a man in knots."

"Excuse me?"

It was wrong to enjoy the fact that I'd literally made Ben's mouth fall open, right? "I had to tie the head of the chamber of commerce, who also happened to be the owner of the local drinking establishment, to a chair. I had ninety seconds to secure him with boat knots I'd learned from Sasha. Apparently, I had a deft hand at tying them, since he was unable to so much as move the chair when I'd finished."

"That's how you became the Mermaid Queen? You tied a man up?"

"Sure did. Then I got to ride around on a float in a clamshell bra and swim out to a makeshift grotto in the harbor and everything."

"Please tell me there are social media pictures of this."

"The town website posts a few pictures every year, but that was after my time. Good luck finding anything."

"You had them scrubbed from the Internet, didn't you?"

I smiled evenly. "A girl's got to have some secrets."

"I see that you never got over tying men up in knots, huh?"

I didn't bother dignifying that with a response.

When we reached the eighteenth hole we were dead even. Honor dictated that one should stand back at a polite distance for this one, but since we'd previously dispensed with honor in favor of trash talk and one-upmanship, I wasn't surprised—or particularly dismayed—when Ben stepped up behind me.

"Excuse me, sir," I said, "what do you think you're doing?"

"You're the one who talked in my backswing earlier. I am now standing at an impolite distance from the tee pad."

"You mean an impolite distance from me," I corrected. "You're standing too close to me."

"Am I?" he asked innocently. I felt him nudge a step closer. "How about now? Is it distracting you?" he murmured in my ear.

"Not a bit," I replied softly, fully aware that if I turned around right now, we'd be nose to nose. There would be nothing to do then but kiss him, a prospect that both thrilled me and sent me spiraling down a dizzy path of want.

Instead, I took a half step of my own back so that my skirt brushed against his pants. "I'm unflappable." Even with the heat from his thighs radiating against the back of mine and the frosty tickle of wintergreen on his breath. A breath, I noted, that had hitched when I'd stepped closer.

With a determined smile, I put my head down, sipped in a breath, sighted the hole and swung, the motion sending me back against Ben, whose hands shot out to either side of my hips to steady us.

Together, we watched the ball traverse the narrow, twinkle-lit path where Peaseblossom, Cobweb, Moth and Mustardseed peeked out from behind the trees. I knew from experience that if you hit one of those winged creeps, your ball would bounce into the water below. But this time, my ball struck true and disappeared into a hole made up to look like a giant sunflower. A trumpet started to play, and a blinking "Thou art a winner! Please proceed to ye olde clubhouse for your free game" sign popped up from behind the hole.

"Guess I'm the winner," I said, lingering a moment longer in Ben's hold before easing away from him and turning around to catch his grin. The one that practically dared me to step closer and see where it got me.

Behind Ben, a family of four stepped onto the first hole, their voices and laughter drifting toward us. Right—Peaseblossom's was picking up, and I didn't want to add "making out at a children's establishment" to my list of idle summertime pursuits. I was Portia. Complete and utter master of my emotions. I did not kiss random men on mini-golf courses.

"When am I buying you victory dinner?" Ben asked.

"Titania's only offers the tasting menu on Friday and Saturday," I teased, not actually expecting him to take me out for a pricey tasting menu just because I'd beaten him at mini-golf.

"The tasting menu sounds perfect. Let's do Friday evening."

"Looking forward to it," I said. We both stood there a moment, staring at each other.

"Until then," Ben said. He hesitated a moment before deciding against whatever he'd been thinking of saying or doing and walked off in the direction of the parking lot.

I watched him go, admiring his exit and aware that I was ogling a man in golf pants. But when he stepped out of sight, my thoughts turned to his mention of appointments. Mini-golf-based flirting aside, Ben still had the eye of a developer, and there was the matter of the greasy man Muppet who now owned Peaseblossom's and seemed eager to sell it.

I sighed, staring out over the expansive driving range, and tried to calculate how many condos could go up here. Would whomever eventually bought the place tear down the mini-golf courses as well? Staring back at the chattering children and their parents, I sincerely hoped not. Peaseblossom's was as much a part of the town as any of the storefronts on Main Street. It deserved its place in Bard's.

Realizing that I was still standing there by the last hole with a dumb expression on my face and no putter, I straightened and headed for home. Bard's was starting to rub off on me in strange ways, and I couldn't say the overall effect was necessarily a flattering one.

The Black Box

"I don't see how this is an improvement over the basement of Titania's." I sniffed. "It smells like fungal infections and broken dreams."

"Well, they say you can never go home again," Candace cracked as we made our way down the long stretch of hallway between the cafeteria and the gym where trophies, ribbons and photos of students past reigned supreme. She paused at the 2009 glass case. "I'm adding unfortunate hairstyles to the mix. How could you have committed to sideswept bangs like that?" She leaned closer, inspecting the contents. After a beat, she asked, "Were there any academic awards you didn't win?"

"She lost the spelling bee in seventh grade," Byron offered as he drew up beside us, his shoes squeaking on the freshly polished floor. "My god, it smells like feet in here."

I shot Candace a triumphant look. To Byron, I said, "First, that was middle school, not high school, and second, I was hopped up on pain pills because I'd had my wisdom teeth out. That doesn't count."

"Now that we've established Portia has a scary amount of prom crowns and academic trophies to her name, can we get back to how important tonight is? I know Miranda pulled serious strings to put dinner theater on equal footing with the mainstages. Drawing from the general audition pool is a big deal, and she gave us the black box instead of the gym," she added as we headed for the theater space in question. "That's a mark of respect, right there."

"Still smells like fungal infection," I muttered under my breath as we stepped into the black box.

"What was that?" Candace demanded.

"I said, if you have such a deep talent pool to pull from, why did you insist on making me try out? You know how I feel about acting."

"Because a deal is a deal," she insisted. "You struck out at the Merchant of Venison with the developer. Admit it. You still need info."

"You had dinner with Benjamin Dane?" Byron asked, a note of mild curiosity in his voice.

"I wanted to feel him out." I held up a hand when he opened his mouth. "Don't be juvenile."

"Why must you stifle all my fun?" Byron pouted.

"It was just dinner," I said, leaving out the small detail that I'd scheduled a second dinner with Ben. Well, *scheduled* was the wrong word. I'd won a wager fair and square. "I was curious about him."

"I bet," Byron snorted.

"He's looking at developing condos up this way, while still keeping his hand in the game in Boston. I would think you'd want to know as well, since this could affect your beloved Bard's Rest."

"Condos?" Byron echoed. "That never works here."

"I know. What did you find about him?" I asked Candace.

"After you audition," Candace said firmly as she handed me a sheet of paper.

"What is it?"

"Lines from *Much Ado About Nothing*?" she said dryly.

"I can see that," I said. "What's going on here?"

"Portia Barnes, are you asking what your motivation is?" Byron teased.

I leveled him with a look that had the smile running off his face and fleeing the building.

"Beatrice and Benedick are dancing. He's in a mask and she pretends not to recognize him."

"Why?" I asked although it seemed on par for the sort of pointless drivel Shakespearean nuts liked.

"Because she's making fun of him, but she pretends she has no idea it's him behind the mask."

"Oh," I said, my tone brightening. "Gamesmanship. I can do that in my sleep."

"Excellent. Why don't each of you take two minutes, read over the lines and we'll try it?"

Byron and I retreated with our scripts, reading over the lines. I couldn't really remember *Much Ado About Nothing*, other than that Miranda had played the supporting character in it. What had her name been? Hero? Hero, yes, that was it. A misnomer if I'd ever heard one. I spent the entire show squirming in the audience, wanting Miranda as the wronged Hero to stand up for herself, leave her fickle lover at the altar and ride off with Don something, the only guy who had an ounce of common sense. But no, silly Hero had gone back to her fickle lover.

The moment I stepped onto the stage, the lights blinding and bright, my palms began to sweat and my resting heart rate, a steady seventy-five that my physician assured me was perfect for someone in my rather stressful line of work, began to stutter and speed up. Even though I knew it was only Candace sitting there, I couldn't see her. I couldn't see anything coming at me, just the glare of the lights against the darkness, and I didn't like it one bit.

I relaxed as Byron stepped up beside me and began reading from the script, and we began to exchange verbal blows. He was an excellent reading partner that way. Actually, Byron was excellent in a lot of ways. It sometimes got lost in the way he presented himself—the cocksure local lothario—but Byron was really a stand-up guy. We'd been friends since the first week of middle school, when a pre—growth spurt, braces-wearing Byron had thrown down for a fellow undersized sixth grader who some eighth-grade Neanderthals had decided to make their bullying target for the year. Byron had walked away from that encounter with a split lip and my utmost respect. We'd been friends all through high school—Byron had been a bit of a closet academic—and he was one of the few classmates I actually kept in touch with over the years, as we pinged each other over notable legal developments and lambasted the current Supreme Court.

"Satisfied?" I asked. Candace regarded the two of us with a thoughtful expression that made me nervous. "You will keep in mind that I have no interest in being in the dinner theater, yes?"

"Because your schedule is so packed these days?" Candace asked, her tone wry.

"Because I'm already doing my part by negotiating each and every contract for the festival and wresting permits from the iron-clad fist of Emmeline McGandry."

"The lady doth protest too much," Byron snickered beside me.

"Keep it up and I will kill you and leave your body for the crows. That's very Shakespearean, right?"

"She'll do it," Candace said mildly. "I'll be honest, I'll probably help her."

"Hey, what did I do?" Byron demanded.

"You're breathing," Candace shot back, but her tone was playful. In fact, the banter between Byron and Candace seemed to be pretty playful and plentiful these days. I evaluated Candace with a calculating eye. Had my friend bedded one of Bard's best-kept secrets and failed to tell me about it? I was so bringing that up over scotch.

An hour later, after auditions ended, the three of us were nestled into a booth at the Tavern of Ill Repute, a surprisingly decent eatery despite dressing itself down as a dive bar. Byron and Candace were plowing through a plate of wings while I happily decimated the meze plate. I know that might sound lame, but the garlic hummus and pita were homemade. So what if I liked my protein spreadable? Besides, hummus had proved a safe source of protein for me amidst my stomach turmoil; I wouldn't desert it now.

"I read the Shakespeare. Now spill," I said, pointing a celery stalk at my companions. "I want to know what you know about him."

"Well, Benjamin Dane had a quick rise to success. He's done several major projects in Boston, all of them winners. He's not in the big leagues yet, but well on his way."

"Tell me something Google can't," I said, faking a yawn. "I read verse for you. You know how I feel about that."

"I bet a search engine can't tell you which properties he's looking at." She ticked off three locations in Bard's and others I didn't recognize in Sherburne, Pellsworth and other surrounding towns. "I'll send you an email," she promised. "I can already tell from the look in your eyes what you'll be googling later."

"None of the ones in Bard's are viable for condos," I noted, with a strange twinge of relief. Did I actually care whether Ben built condos in Bard's or not? I mean, other than the epic ranting about change and sullying the Shakespearean nirvana that would inevitably surface at a family dinner or two, what did it matter? "I'm sure he's already figured that out. Any other properties coming up for sale?"

"Not that I'm aware of," Byron said.

"Frankly, I'm all for the way Bard's resists big-box stores and chain restaurants," Candace added. "It's better for the health of our local businesses. I'm not an economist, but I do worry about the slippery slope of bringing in high-end condos, creating that need for the überconvenience of Starbucks and Whole Foods, and then Bard's isn't really Bard's anymore."

"From the woman who used to scorn living here," Byron noted mildly, but he was smiling—looking rather pleased, actually.

"What can I say? I came for the job and fell in love with the town." Candace comically batted her eyelashes.

For a moment, I envied her conviction. The ease with which she'd found her place here. Bard's wasn't my place. I wasn't even sure the city was my place. FrancisPearl had always been my place. That was fine. I didn't necessarily need a home base. My work was my home base.

But something stirred in the back of my mind. Something in Candace's words. I turned to Byron. "Just curious. Who would be most likely to bring an action to keep the condos out? The town?"

Byron tipped his hand back and forth. "Potentially. But more likely the Bard's Merchant Association. They'd be in the best position to make a claim that they would suffer irreparable harm."

"Interesting," I noted.

Byron and I locked eyes. Representing a town could be messy, but a merchant association would be like taking on any other client. He gave a small nod of understanding at the same moment I did.

We both looked at Candace.

"Why do I feel like the last gazelle caught drinking at the watering hole?" she asked, sipping her wine.

"How would you like to take a purely preventative measure to keep condos out of Bard's on a more permanent basis? A contingency plan, if you will," I added.

"Why does this feel like a black op?" she demanded.

"More like a black box op," Byron quipped.

Candace and I gave Byron equal looks of disdain.

"Miranda would have laughed," Byron muttered, which earned him a smile from Candace. "What did you have in mind?"

I waited until Candace's headlights disappeared from the Tavern's parking lot, a beat later than Byron's. I wasn't doing anything wrong, I reminded myself. But I still felt like one of the Tavern's storied villains. Lady MacBeth, maybe. I'm not saying I liked her murderous tendencies or anything, but the woman had been a master-class planner. I was doing the same thing—just for less homicidal-based ends.

Extracting my phone, I dialed Riki.

She picked up on the second ring. "Ms.—err, Portia."

I smiled at her course correction. "Hello, Riki. I'm sorry to bother you this late."

"I'm still at the office," Riki admitted.

I glanced at my watch, tamping down the urge to tell her to go home. That there was something more interesting out there. Because for some of us, the deal—the draft, the deadline—was the thing.

"I'm wondering if you can help me with something. I know this is well below your capabilities, but I'm hoping you can initiate a conflicts check and open a new matter for me?"

There was a pause on the line. "A conflicts check and a new matter request. While you're on sabbatical." Riki wasn't exactly throwing shade, but I appreciated her healthy skepticism.

"That's exactly why I'm asking you to initiate it for me. I need it done quickly and quietly." Great, it sounded like I'd just asked her to whack someone.

"Understood. Do you have the parties?"

"I have one party. The Town of Bard's Rest Merchant Association. Potential property or zoning disputes. Actually, please open it under general matters."

Another long pause.

"Riki, are you there?"

"Yes, I am. FrancisPearl would represent the town's local business interest against who, exactly? A potential developer?"

I admired how quickly she put it all together. "It would be a high-profile pro bono matter."

"That has to remain a secret from Gerald Cutler?" I could hear the scathing smile in her voice. God, I adored this young woman. "That's some pro bono matter."

"I'm building my reputation as a managing partner," I said with all the airy blasé I could muster. "Can you submit that into conflicts checks immediately and let me know if anything comes back?"

"I'm on it."

"Thank you, I appreciate it," I told her before I hung up. I thunked my head against the seat. I wasn't doing anything wrong, so why did I feel like I'd entered into some irrevocable course of action?

Something Gerald had said to me early on came floating back to me in eerie clarity in the stillness of my car, his words prickling on my skin. "It's chess, Portia. That's all there is to it. Plan your moves well ahead. Play the long game."

That's right. I was playing the long game, laying the foundation so that if something ever came of this, I'd be in an ideal position to help my friends and family.

Win at any cost, not at any price. Another of Gerald's favorite pearls of wisdom floated back to me. The price. There was always a price. Would the price here be Ben? It didn't seem likely that he'd nibble at any of the properties here in town, but if not Ben, then someone else? I could easily see a scenario where Archie or someone equally slimy wised up and sold a commercially zoned parcel of land like Peaseblossom's. That driving range could be converted into condos, couldn't it?

Ben. I'd turned him down for any type of representation at our first dinner. But taking this action would block him from using anyone at FrancisPearl. I grimaced. He was the wrong kind of client for FrancisPearl. I knew that. I knew he would be better elsewhere. But had I wandered into an ethically gray area?

I looked at the clock. Too late for a call, but a text would do.

A minute later my phone rang.

"Is this the part where I review the finer points of what a sabbatical entails?" Chris asked.

"Is your door shut?"

"Nice to hear from you too, you weirdo. I'm at home, where Callie and I are engaging in a rousing debate as to which Netflix series we're starting next. Do I need to initiate cone-of-silence protocol?"

"You tell me. I find myself in a gray area."

There was a beat of silence. Followed by the sound of footsteps and the closing of a door. "Is there a body?"

"Why do people always ask that?"

A loaded pause ensued. "If you have to ask . . ."

"No, there's not a body. Like I would even need your help getting rid of one." It was an old game we'd played back in our associate days. One of us would propose a hypothetical situation in which a hypothetical murder occurred and the other person had to cover up the crime. It helped pass the long nights spent in an office, waiting for drafts to come back from the financial printer and avoiding contemplating one's bad life decisions that had led to firm life.

"All you need is a boat and some gators."

"Pigs are more pragmatic and prevalent," I countered. "Okay, so we've established we both could dispose of a body. I need real help." I walked him through meeting Ben, the dinner, the little I knew about Archie and urging Candace to request that I represent the merchant association. "What do you think?"

"I think Gerald is going to veto it."

"Choosing my own pro bono work is one of the perks of being management."

"He'll still find a way to kill it. You know how he is. Appearance is everything. How's it going to look if we take on a developer? We represent developers. A lot of developers."

"We have no idea it's going to come to that." But I considered my friend's words. Still, I remained confident that Gerald would respect my decision.

"You declined to represent this Ben guy. You offered additional resources. He's not an adverse party here. He doesn't have a vested interest; he's looking at property in your area and several others. In the interim, your longtime friend has asked you to represent your hometown's interest in a potential matter. I think you're in the clear from a conflict-of-interest perspective and ethical obligations. You can sleep with this guy if you want."

"Sleep with him?" I sputtered. "What? No. Where did you get that? I just need to know if I'm in a gray area representing the merchant association."

"No you didn't," Chris countered. "Because you wouldn't have needed me to make that call. You already know you're in the clear, ethically speaking. You want to know if it's all right to sleep with this guy. I can hear it in your voice. You're intrigued by him, which means you're thinking of sleeping with him. My answer is, you have no way of knowing if he'll be an adverse party down the road. Sleep away. One-woman tear through the backwoods of New Hampshire."

"You're the absolute worst. You should know I'm contemplating where to hide your body."

"Burn me in a fireplace and scatter my ashes out at sea," he laughed. "You're a cutthroat attorney, but in the decade we've worked together, I've never known you to get within sight of that line. You're fine here."

"I know." I let out a sigh of relief. "Thanks, Chris."

We chatted for a few minutes about Callie and summer camps for the girls. I assured him I hadn't gone all local yet or acquired any regrettable tattoos and I hung up.

As I washed my face, brushed my teeth and applied my nightly regimen of skin care, I thought about what Chris had said about the Ben thing. *The Ben thing.* Was Chris right, did I want to sleep with Ben? I mean sure, objectively speaking, Ben was handsome, smart and equipped with a personality I liked. There'd been undeniable physical chemistry on the golf course. His banter game was certainly next-level. I was betting his bedroom game was even better.

But did I actually want to sleep with him?

It wasn't that I thought I was in any danger of being hurt by Ben, romantically speaking. That wasn't my style and didn't seem like his either. Ben seemed like a bona fide adult who would be up for something hot but short-lived. Perfect in every way that I wanted for a fling.

Except for the development angle.

Ethically speaking, I might have been in the clear, but I was still prepared to do battle if Ben decided to try to erect condos here. Not only that, I'd taken steps to ensure I'd be on the front lines if he did. That was not a conversation I wanted to have with someone who had seen my sex faces.

That potential Ben angle (the development thing, not the sex faces) smacked of complications, and historically, I didn't do complications. I had neither the time nor the temperament for them. Even my longest-standing relationship—with David, a fellow corporate attorney I'd met on a panel a while back—hadn't been complicated. The most complicated thing about David had been figuring out the flight schedules back and forth to his place in Chicago and mine in New York. And when I'd tired of airport lounges and the way he occasionally disparaged his junior associates, servers, housekeepers and generally anyone he considered beneath his regard, I'd ended it, citing an uptick in my caseload at work. David had understood and we were still connected on LinkedIn and sent each other articles and invitations to conferences we thought the other might enjoy. No complications to speak of.

I slipped into soft sleep pants and a breathable tank and slid between the sheets.

This Ben thing . . . well, I was starting to think this whole situation was getting too complicated. I was supposed to be getting my head in a place to be managing partner, not rolling around in the sheets with a real estate developer I planned to run out of town if he became a problem.

Your problems and possible solutions to them are not like other people's, I thought as I reached for Agatha Christie's *The Thirteen Problems* on my bedside table.

It still felt strange not to be reaching for my work laptop at night; the lack of its weight on my abdomen as I answered emails and reviewed contracts left me somehow bereft. However, there was something equally delicious about knowing I could read late into the night, even finish all thirteen of these individual stories if I wanted to, and sleep until the unthinkably luxurious hour of eight forty-five. Nobody would mind, because nobody would need me.

It was both a freeing and a concerning thought.

....

Much Ado About Pastry

I rolled my neck and shoulders and rubbed at my temples. This morning I'd claimed a bistro table in the back of the café, where I'd set up camp with my laptop, the binder full of festival contracts and one of my sister's fruit salads. The fruit was long gone, as was the cortado with the words *Sabbatical Fail* swirled into the foam—Cordelia really did have a deft hand with that sort of thing. I'd been at the contracts for hours, striking out penalty clauses and replacing them with more customer-friendly language and cleaning up the invoicing processing. I may have given them more attention than they realistically needed, but whether it was a seventeen-thousand-dollar contract for a weeklong true-to-period Elizabethan jousting demonstration or a seventeen-billion-dollar healthcare takeover for FrancisPearl, there was no excuse for sloppy language.

I'd probably have sat like that all day if Cordelia hadn't kicked me out for the lunch rush. After assurances my laptop and binder would be returned to me in the condition in which I left them, I'd gone for an early afternoon run, notching a solid three miles before the heat smacked into me like an indifferent subway rider with its hefty, humid hip. At that point, I'd retreated home to shower.

Dad had come home to retrieve something for lunch, and together we'd built a charcuterie board and eaten it together in the garden. Along with the figs and fresh blueberries, I popped a few slices of cheese into my mouth and waited. Not only did they taste good, but my insides didn't spontaneously combust like they used to when I ate dairy. I kept that particular revelation to myself, as I didn't want to upset Dad. He had enough on his plate with Mom's cancer care. I didn't need to pile on.

While we ate, I peppered him with questions about the set building and his reunion with Adam, his favorite summer set-building buddy. Their friendship was an odd one in some ways, given that Adam was living in domestic, unmarried bliss with Miranda. One might expect a father to take umbrage to such a thing, but Dad was pretty mellow. I imagined he took comfort in the fact that he and Mom had raised us to respect and take care of ourselves. That, and I was pretty sure Adam sweetened the pot by plying Dad with his famous homemade lox.

When he'd left after lunch, I'd sat alone at the kitchen counter sipping iced tea, a bottle of antacids on the island in front of me, waiting for some sort of latent intestinal reckoning. But to my utter relief and surprise, it hadn't come.

Eventually, I'd headed back to the café and settled in for a late-afternoon contract review session. After a few hours and a seemingly endless supply of jokes about charging me rent, Cordelia set down a steaming mug of green tea in front of me, wiping at her "Beignet, Done That" T-shirt. Though I'd never admit it aloud, I enjoyed my sister's punny T-shirts, so much so that while on a scouting trip to the new Boston office, I'd picked up a "Claw and Order" lavender heather tee from the New England Aquarium. I sometimes wore it around my condo on the weekends as I worked.

"Thanks," I smiled, taking a small sip of tea. "How goes the annual courting dance over at Titania's? What did they offer you this year?"

"At last count, four weeks of vacation, full benefits, 401(k) match, company car, a clothing allowance and carte blanche to hire my own team."

Marla Crawford, owner of Titania's Bower and one of my first business clients, had had her sights on adding my sister to her award-winning culinary team for years now. But Cordelia always turned her down. Miranda thought Cordelia wanted to break out on her own but hadn't figured out a way to tell our parents yet that she didn't want to continue on at Much Ado About Pastry.

"What could they offer you to make you move? If anything?" I asked, keeping my tone level. This was my bread and butter. Yes, it was important for attorneys to keep abreast of the legal landscape, but this was where true transactional attorneys earned their keep: the ability to distill it all down to what someone truly wanted. Not what they said they wanted. Not what they thought they wanted. But what they actually wanted.

Cordelia paused, her hand on the glass case. She looked past me, out the window, her dark curls gleaming in the warm lights of her café. "Nothing. There's nothing Marla could offer me. Because I—I want an adventure. I'm not ready to settle down in Bard's for the long haul. At least not yet."

Our eyes met, hers full of determination and a heavy dose of reluctance.

"But I'm not ready to tell anyone that. Not until Mom's health is a little more squared away. Maybe next year."

That familiar twinge of guilt over leaving the bulk of Mom's care to Cordelia and Miranda twisted in my throat.

"Anyway, Marla will have to keep her treasure trove of perks. As fun as it would be to team up with Candace more, we'll have to stick to weddings and the dinner theater for now." She nodded to the binder. "Does it hurt your soul that Mom still collects these as hard copies as opposed to all electronic?"

"More than you know," I sighed. "Electronic documents are searchable and kill fewer trees. But this year's binder came with a drive," I said, holding up a USB key that Mom had clipped to the binder with one of those spiral rings. "Some of the more progressive vendors have converted. But I already did those ones."

"There's hope, then," Cordelia snickered as she closed the glass case.

While Cordelia readied the café for closing, I opened the binder to the last contract I'd resolved to work on today. The damn petting zoo contract for the new vendor, since we were in a dispute with the prior one. Why did it have to be the petting zoo? Sighing, I settled into the familiar rhythm of a contract: the parties, the recitals that previewed what the parties intended to do, the services, the fees and the rest of it designed to govern expectations and behavior while providing for the worst if shit did hit the fan. Contracts were comforting that way, providing answers for worst-case scenarios. This one, for example, had a dizzying laundry list of situations where the petting zoo vendor would not be liable for what I deemed "goat-based mayhem." As in, if the goats broke free and ravaged the town, even if due to negligence on the part of the vendor, the petting zoo wouldn't pay a dime. I smiled, clicking my pen and boldly striking through that language. Not on my watch.

About five minutes before close, the door opened. Cordelia muttered, "There's always one," and in a much brighter voice called out, "I'm afraid we're closing up for the day. Not much in the way of pastry left, but if it's coffee you want, happy to fix one."

"I'd very much like a black coffee, though I hear your pastry is legendary."

I looked up sharply at the familiar voice. "Ben," I said, my face breaking into a smile. "How are you?"

But Ben didn't return my smile. He stared at me, his expression a little wary, a little distant. "I'm well. Yourself?"

If we had been in one of those nature specials, this would have been the moment the collective herd of gazelles all lifted their heads in the direction of the predator sneaking through the underbrush.

"Did you have a nice trip out of town?"

"They were fine," he said, and I saw the tell, a tensing of his jaw. "Just fine."

I closed my laptop cover. Never one to beat around the bush, I met his gaze head-on. "What's wrong?"

Ben's eyes flicked to where Cordelia was pretending to be fascinated with pouring a single-drip coffee. I gave the barest of nods.

We both waited as my sister added a lid to the recyclable cup and handed it to Ben. "On the house. Beginner's luck." She winked. "That and I've already closed the register."

"Thank you very much," Ben said, appreciatively accepting the coffee and slipping a five into the tip jar.

"I can show him out," I offered, slipping my laptop and binder into my bag.

"Thanks, sis," Cordelia called as she disappeared into the kitchen.

Ben followed me out without a word.

"Out with it," I said once we'd cleared the door and made our way down the path and into the gardens. To our left, the bookstore still had lights on—it kept later hours than the café—so I maneuvered us out of eyeshot. I dropped my bag in the grass and crossed my arms over my chest, my back to the side of the café.

"Were you going to tell me FrancisPearl can't represent Dane Development? Or were you going to keep pumping me for information?"

Oh, right. I'd received the text from Riki last night that conflicts had cleared. But I still bristled at the implication lurking behind Ben's words. "I planned to discuss that with you at our dinner on Friday."

Ben snorted. "I'm sure."

"Who I choose to represent and not to represent is my business," I noted, my tone terse. "I told you I wasn't going to take Dane Development on as a client. Consider my surprise that you called my firm anyway."

"I called FrancisPearl for a consult to get a sense of what the rates were. If you're the top of the market there, I wanted to compare your rates against those on the list of firms and contacts you gave me. When I noted the potential property might be in Bard's Rest, I was informed of the conflict. It's called doing one's due diligence. Perhaps you've heard of it?"

"I sincerely hope you're not implying I have crossed some sort of professional or ethical line," I said frostily. "Because you would be mistaken. Unless something has changed in the last twenty-four hours that I'm unaware of, you're not an adverse party. Instead, you're someone who called my firm after I declined to take you on as a client. So at best, you're someone who can't take a hint, and at worst, you're unscrupulous."

"I am not an adverse party," he said through gritted teeth. "Yet. I am not an adverse party yet, nor am I sure I plan to be."

"Excellent, glad we've cleared that up," I said icily.

"But I thought you'd have done me the courtesy of a heads-up. I don't like your gamesmanship here, Portia," he spat, an angry light in his eyes turning the gray molten.

"As I already told you, I planned to discuss it with you in a way that didn't violate client confidentiality at our dinner, Ben." I didn't appreciate the implication that I had acted unethically or unprofessionally, because I hadn't. If I was being honest and all self-reflective like my therapist wanted me to be, I was a little hurt.

"When you asked me to dinner, I was unaware of the potential property at issue. Later, a member of the local merchant association requested representation on a potential matter of which you are not the adverse party. So let's be precise. I didn't violate my professional or ethical obligations here, and I deeply resent the implication I did."

"And I deeply resent that you would do this to me," Ben said, his fingers drumming on his pants. "I thought—"

"You thought what?"

"I thought that maybe we"—his eyes burned into mine—"that we had a connection."

Now, the word *connection* is not what I would ever term a particularly sexy word without context, but my god, the way he said *connection*, it actually sent a full, racking shiver down my spine. The rather robust self-preservation part of my brain pointed out that we needed to deny this connection. This connection made things complicated. Even if Ben wasn't an adverse party now, he could be down the road—or he could be the guy buying a piece of property in Rockwell right now and I'd be missing out for no reason. "A professional connection? I don't think so. I made it clear I wouldn't offer you representation."

"A personal connection," Ben corrected. He took a step closer. "Or was it just me who felt it?" His eyes were churning now, like gray ocean waters before the storm blew in.

I moistened my lips, which felt suddenly so dry, despite the generous application of balm I'd applied this morning. "There could be complications with a personal connection."

"What if I said the likelihood of Dane buying any property in Bard's Rest is less than a ten percent chance right now?" he continued. "Would that change the complication?"

Slowly, I nodded, almost afraid to meet his gaze. Afraid as to what I might see reflected there. Disgust? Desire? Which would be easier to weather? "I believe it would nearly negate the complication," I all but whispered. Still, I applauded myself for being able to string words together in a decidedly coherent manner while standing so close to Ben—whose scent reminded me of silent winter woods growing up. I really needed to stop staring at his lips like that.

"Nearly?" he echoed as he closed the narrow gap between us. "Not entirely?"

"I don't deal in absolutes," I informed him.

"That's too bad," he said, his voice deceptively quiet, "because I would absolutely, unequivocally like to kiss you right now."

My eyes flicked up to his, a moment of open challenge and delicious invitation shimmering in the humid air between us. I seized the moment and shattered it, grabbing a fistful of shirt and pulling him toward me, our mouths crushing against each other.

His lips landed rough on mine, brushing hard against my mouth. No tentativeness, no shyness. No room for it here. I wanted him to devour me.

I braced myself against the side of the café, yanking Ben down against me. He never missed a beat, working my mouth with hungry determination—no politeness, or slyness—just steady, deliberate strokes of his tongue. Ben kissed me like a man who'd made up his mind. Direct, no bullshit and utterly intoxicating.

But somehow that all-consuming kiss wasn't enough. I wanted

him closer. Now. Right now. Surging up against him, I molded my body to his, reveling in how our angles and curves fused together as the heat of his body melded with mine.

His hands caressed my cheeks, surprisingly gentle, before he sank them into my hair. My own hands, fingers splayed, responded in kind, working their way up Ben's taut back, coming to rest in that thick hair of his. Still, I needed him closer. Maybe if I—

"Ahem." A throat cleared behind us, and if anyone could infuse amusement into a throat clearing, it was my sister. Ben and I broke apart, breathing hard. "You do know you are within fifty feet of the bookstore owned by our parents and Dad's car is in the lot, yes?"

I thunked my head against the bricks. "Yes," I managed.

"Perhaps you would like to move your conversation elsewhere?"

What I wanted to do was keep kissing Ben, maybe rip his shirt open and run my hands over the tan skin of his chest. What I said was "Thanks, Cordelia. That's not a terrible idea" in a nonplussed tone, as if being caught ravaging the mouth of a potential rival out in public and fifty feet from my parents' place of business was par for the course.

"Lovely, I'll see you for dinner this week," Cordelia said, her raven curls swinging behind her as she turned, her step jaunty as she trekked down Main Street.

"Well, that was . . ." Ben looked at me sheepishly. A sheepish Ben was still a surprisingly kissable Ben.

"Awkward. The word you're looking for is 'awkward.'"

"The aftermath, sure. I'll grant you that. But . . ." He leaned in and swept a long, lingering kiss across my mouth, finishing with the slightest graze of teeth across my bottom lip. Now, that was teasing. "There was nothing awkward about that. Or do I need to do it again to convince you?"

"More of that," I breathed, tilting my face up to his. "I need convincing."

Ben worried my lip between his teeth, making heat pool between my legs.

"Perhaps we should take your sister's advice and adjourn to somewhere more private?"

"I would like that very much."

Ben stepped back and gallantly pulled me up off the wall. "Shall we—"

Of all the inopportune times for a phone to ring. And, irony of ironies, it wasn't even mine. Ben and I stared in the direction of the ringtone. "Do you need to get that?"

"God, I hope not." But Ben looked at the screen and grimaced. "Shit, I do. That's my partner, Sam. She prefers texts and only calls when something is wrong."

"Right." I let go of his hand and stepped far enough away to give him privacy. I looked around for my phone and, realizing it was in my bag, I cut a wider berth around Ben so I could retrieve it from where I had dropped it. I focused on texting Cordelia. Your subtlety never ceases to amaze me.

Says the woman making out against my place of business. A pause and then another reply. Wait, why are you texting me? Why aren't you making out with that fine specimen? Does he taste as good as he looks? Can I have a lick?

"Portia," Ben called, his voice filled with regret interrupting the typing of my scathing retort to my sister that I don't like sharing. "I am so sorry, but something's come up that I need to take care of. Immediately, I'm afraid. I need to drive back to Boston."

It was like someone had sprayed me with an outdoor hose, the water brutally cold and clarifying. "Of course."

"I'll call you," he mouthed. But I was already moving away. Away from Ben. What in the actual hell had come over me? Had I actually just made out like a horny teenager against a brick wall outside? Apparently, Ben was my personal social kryptonite, sending all my vestiges of decorum out the window when he was around.

Well, I didn't believe in karma the way my sisters did, but I was pretty sure karma had just done me a solid. What had I been thinking, exactly? Making out with the guy who'd accused me of professional chicanery? I shook my head. I hadn't missed out on an opportunity. I'd dodged a bullet.

ACT TWO

July

What's in a Main Street

The first week of July arrived in Bard's, and with it came that hot, slinky humidity that settled on your body like a wet suit. As a general rule, the heat didn't exactly improve my disposition. I tried to keep this in mind as I approached the town hall for my twice-rescheduled meeting with Emmeline McGandry. She'd had to go out of town, she said, to tend to a sick relative. But the thought of Emmeline crouched by the sickbed of a loved one and offering tender ministrations did not compute. More likely, she'd taken a few days off to harvest the souls of the innocent or however else she got her jollies, or maybe she'd been here the whole time and was screwing with me. Either way, I could respect that.

I'd spent the last few days finishing up vendor contracts, methodically working through payment schedules and termination clauses and generally saving the town a boatload of money and potential headaches in the process. I definitely had not spent the last few days thinking about Ben and that kiss. Or the way his mouth fit over mine. Nope.

Keeping the white bakery box in my hands level, I stopped mid-step on my way into the town hall. *To hell with this,* I thought, squaring my shoulders and readjusting the angle of the box in my hands. I was Portia Livingston Barnes, damn it. I did not sit around wondering whether a man liked me or not. I had places to be and people to cajole.

With that firmly fixed in my mind, I crossed over into the crisp air-conditioning of the town hall foyer, noting that it had accumulated more evidence of the upcoming Shakespearean festival—flyers, posters and even a meticulously detailed diorama of *A Midsummer Night's Dream*. Even I could spot that one. The donkey was a dead giveaway. I bent down, giving it a closer examination. Fairy queens and sprites and silly mortals—how had this held up all these centuries? I wondered.

Still ten minutes early and not wanting to surprise the dragon in her lair just yet, I loitered in the corridor that led to the bathroom, following the progress of old black-and-white photos around town—the town hall in its infancy, What's in a Main Street from the 1920s (at least according to the neat handwritten label beneath the picture), an early Shakespearean performance on Will's Island, the audience in full 1940s regalia—the women in curve-loving hourglass dresses, complete with nipped-in waistlines and peep toe heels, their male counterparts in big suit jackets and even bigger pants.

At the sound of approaching footsteps, I glanced up to find a gentleman clutching a newspaper striding purposefully down the corridor toward me. I quickly pivoted to the other side of the hallway so he could access the bathroom.

The photos on this side were even older, maybe the mid- to late 1800s. I may have been an unrepentant skeptic of Shakespeare, but I was an unabashed history buff, and I secretly loved the way Bard's celebrated its roots as one of New Hampshire's oldest colonial settlements.

Despite my nerdery, I didn't recognize any of the images, but luckily those handy labels informed me that I was looking at the First National Bank of Bard, complete with a gleaming vault with one of those handles that looked like a ship's wheel, and that next to it was the second early meeting house of Bard's. I squinted at the label to make sure I'd read it right. What had happened to the first? A fire? Was it morbid that my mind went there—or was it just a logical conclusion that the combination of the all-wooden structure and the lack of modern firefighting equipment had done it in?

Frankly, the second early meeting house wasn't much to look at: a white-walled room with a solid-looking wooden table and shelves containing clothbound books, their spines sagging and decomposing. I did, however, clock a portrait of Josiah Bartlett over a particularly handsome writing desk. I recognized him straightaway because I'd written a high school paper on him for our "New Hampshire Notables" class in AP history. He'd been a signer of the Declaration of Independence, a delegate to the New Hampshire Continental Congress and, eventually, chief justice of the New Hampshire Supreme Court, and the cornerstone of my argument to my fellow classmates that there were famous people from the granite state besides Triple H the wrestler.

As much as I was enjoying this historical, non-Shakespearean trip down Bard's Rest's memory lane, I didn't want to be late to my meeting with Emmeline. Heading back down the corridor, I made my way to Emmeline's office and knocked politely on the door, making it a point not to peer through the privacy glass, which would have been pointless and gauche. Also, I'm pretty sure Emmeline would have seen my shadow and arrived at the same conclusion.

"Come in," Emmeline said. She sat at her desk, her silvery hair expertly pulled away from her face and neck, an absolutely perfect response to the humidity, as was her ecru summer-weight cardigan over a caramel shift dress.

"Cordelia says you like the lemon scones." I set the bakery box on her desk. An immaculate desk, I might add. The whole office was like that, actually. The walls were flanked by filing cabinets with impossibly neat labels on them, and despite their age, they were gleaming and undented. She even had a lovely view of Main Street through a large window, her windowsill sporting three vining plants of some sort, all shiny and healthy looking, in the prime of their lives.

"We're a little past bribes, dear. Don't you think?" She smiled sourly.

"I'm not a scone person myself," I said, blithely soldiering on. "But I love that icing. My sister makes it with real lemon, none of that artificial poison in the plastic lemon. Anyway, I wanted you to have these," I said, gesturing to the box. "Because they're tart like you are, and I like tart things."

Emmeline stared at me, her glasses sliding down her nose. "Did you have a stroke in the parking lot?"

"Of the two of us, I'd be far less likely to have one. So I'll ignore that."

The teeniest, tiniest—not even a crinkle; more like a crease—of her lips told me she found that funny.

I hadn't come here to apologize to Emmeline McGandry for last summer, because I hadn't been in the wrong. I'd reached a point in life where I'd tired of apologizing for things I wasn't actually sorry for. But I did admire this woman's saltiness and commitment to running this place like her own personal fiefdom and I wanted to honor and acknowledge that. Hence, the offering of scones. Something in her expression, austere as it was, indicated she understood that and appreciated it.

She gestured to the chair in front of her desk with her chin, and I took it without further comment. Emmeline handed me a manila folder. "Every permit you requested and some you didn't." Her mouth quirked. "Your mother is very thorough, but that binder could use some updating. I made some annotations."

"Thank you, I'll certainly incorporate those," I said as I paged through the first few, nodding here and humming there. Unsurprisingly, Emmeline had a keen eye for details. Not wanting to be impolite, I closed the binder and looked up to find Emmeline watching me, as still and as stealthy as an alligator pretending to be a sunken log. "May I ask you something?"

Her nod was as sharp as her little ski jump nose. "You may."

"If I wanted to ensure a smooth festival, what should I be concerned with?"

"For starters, that jackass who runs the petting zoo."

"Why?" Though I was pretty sure I already knew the answer.

"He parks his animals too close to the food booths. He's a lawsuit waiting to happen."

I didn't mention that the jackass in question, one Rufus Andrews, was currently suing us and threatening drastic action. Confidentiality and all that.

"What else?"

"I'd make sure you put Betty Tilney and Mabel Higgins as far away from each other as possible. That way it's less likely a fistfight breaks out. Last year, a cotton candy machine was overturned in their scuffle. Nobody wants to scrape burning liquid sugar off Main Street again."

The idea of brawling septuagenarians was not a comforting one. Particularly if the brawl involved a liquefied substance of any kind. "Maybe we can erect a moat between them. It would be very period. You'd grant me a permit for that, wouldn't you?"

She snorted. "I'd certainly consider it if it kept those two twits from trying to gouge each other's eyes out."

"I'll keep that in mind." I stood, gathering the permits. "Thank you for the time today."

"Ask me what else I'm worried about."

I looked down at the steely-spined Emmeline, the only person I'd ever seen make a swivel chair look like a throne. "What else are you worried about?"

"The preservation of long-standing traditions."

I squinted at her. "What do you mean by that?"

"Some traditions are worth preserving, don't you think?" Her eyes flicked left to a black-and-white framed photograph on the wall of some sort of production—the rest of my family would have known which one—on the island. Below the photograph was that label with the neat handwriting again. In fact, I noted as I panned her office, that handwriting matched those on the filing cabinet labels. Our Emmeline was a town history buff too. Not exactly surprising, given her line of work, but yet another thing I found myself admiring her for. "I would hate to see the festival diminished in any way, wouldn't you agree?"

"I would agree," I said slowly, not quite catching her drift, but certainly aware there was something in her words I should be paying attention to. Like being handed a precious gift wrapped in thorns. Proceed with caution.

I clutched the binder protectively to my chest. Maybe she'd left me something a bit more illuminating in her notes.

"Sometimes it's up to us tart individuals to make sure that doesn't happen. There are traditions here worth preserving, Ms. Barnes. Things and places worth fighting for."

"I hear you loud and clear," I said solemnly as my mind flashed to those property maps Ben had requested. But by that same token, Ben had said recently it was unlikely he'd be buying anything in Bard's, and that was information that Emmeline didn't have. Maybe she meant development and change in general. Or maybe she meant Archie and his inheritance. He was certainly a weasel worth keeping an eye on. "Thank you again for your time, Ms. McGandry."

"Call me Emmeline." She offered me a thin-lipped smile, meager but genuine.

"Thank you, Emmeline," I replied, extending a quiet smile of my own.

GLANCING AT MY watch and deciding it was a perfect time to drop into Bard's Books and make sure my mother wasn't working, per doctor's orders, I was heading down Main Street when my phone rang. When I saw who it was, I hastily hit accept.

"Hello, this is Portia," I said, confident but formal, as I always was with Gerald.

"Portia, how are you?"

"Very well. And yourself?"

"The same."

"How's Gillian?" I liked Gerald's wife, Gillian, who worked as a medieval archivist at the Cloisters and had insisted on keeping her maiden name, Dumonde—a fact I'd learned when she'd hosted the corporate summer associates at their palatial home in Battery Park. Maybe it had stuck with me because so many of the partners' wives I'd met had seemed to shrink and morph into their husbands' looming shadows, whereas Gillian burned bright all on her own.

"She's wonderful. Hard at work on a new exhibit opening. How is your sabbatical going?"

"Couldn't be better," I said.

"That's wonderful," he said, his voice dropping, and I could practically see his brows furrowing on the other end of the line as he readied himself for what he actually wanted to talk about. "Listen, did you recently authorize a conflicts check on a new matter?" The "in violation of the terms of your sabbatical" was implied.

"I requested one, yes."

"Portia, we talked about this."

"It's a pro bono matter," I replied. "Opening one does not violate the terms and conditions of my sabbatical." The "I checked" was equally implied.

"I agree that it doesn't violate the technical terms of your agreement, but it certainly skirts the intent and spirit of it."

Gerald and I had never seen eye to eye on this kind of thing. I frankly didn't give a shit about the intent and spirit of anything. You couldn't take that to court or an arbitrator with a straight face.

Moreover, I was a named managing partner. Gerald and I were theoretically on somewhat equal ground now, so why did it seem like I was being called on the carpet like an associate who'd colored outside the lines? "Agree to disagree."

"But more importantly," Gerald forged on, "why would you agree to represent a merchant association in the first place? Knowing that the likely adverse party would be a developer or other business interest?"

Because it's a pro bono matter and it would hardly do for us to represent the developer, I thought, but left that one unsaid. "Unless you think this needs to go to the board, I don't see how this is problematic for me as a managing partner to establish a new pro bono client." Occasionally, management voted on certain matters and whether we should take them on, but normally they involved headline cases like whether we'd represent a law-breaking disgraced commander in chief (no) or the latest hedge fund manager caught with his hand in the proverbial insider trading cookie jar (generally yes). But to my knowledge, a pro bono matter didn't require board approval.

"I want to ensure you're not letting your personal ties to your hometown cloud your judgment."

"I appreciate your concern, Gerald," I said, trying to assume positive intent on his part and not bare my teeth at him in response. "I would hope you'd know by now that I'm more strategic than that. This is an opportunity to garner some goodwill, potentially some fantastic press if a development company does attempt to establish a foothold in Bard's Rest and take a run at the long-standing zoning regulations. Need I remind you that the Shakespearean festival that's held here has garnered national attention and rivals the tourism numbers enjoyed by the Cape, the Vineyard and P-Town? Could paint FrancisPearl in a very favorable light. That's where my head is at. I couldn't care less about the festival itself."

"Of course you don't." Gerald let out a dry chuckle. "I'm not questioning your judgment. I trust you."

Charming. Except he'd just come right out and asked if my judgment was clouded.

"I'm only looking out for you, Portia. It's my responsibility to provide the guidance and counsel you need to be the most successful managing partner you can be."

"Of course, Gerald. I appreciate that."

"Nothing may come of it anyway."

"Agreed. Nothing may come of it," I echoed.

"Things are good otherwise? You're finding ways to fill your time?"

"Yes, I'm thoroughly enjoying this time to clear my head and gain perspective."

"Very good. Talk soon," he said and hung up.

I stared at the phone. Why had that call been so grating? Sure, Gerald trended toward the paternalistic, mansplaining side of the spectrum, but that was true of a lot of older men. He meant well— or, at least, our goals had always aligned. Were our goals misaligned now, or was I chafing at the thought of his continued oversight when I was ready to step up and manage on my own?

I was mulling that over when my phone buzzed again, only this time it was a text, so I knew it was unlikely to be Gerald, who despised electronic paper trails of any kind.

I glanced at the picture of the Boston Harbor, the sun hitting the water, splintering its reflection into hundreds of glittering diamonds. The text read: Stuck here for a few days. Thought you might like a preview of your new stomping grounds.

Despite my prior resolution to forget Ben, I couldn't help but smile at the picture. How did you get this number? I asked. I gave you my work number. This is my personal number.

I contacted the official email address of the Bard's Rest Shakespearean Festival Committee looking for the contact email of the festival lawyer. An Isabella Barnes sent me your number instead. Any relation?

I sighed, rubbing my temples. Mom and I were so going to dialogue this. My mother. My new stomping grounds are lovely, by the way. Thanks for sharing.

Want to meet some of your neighbors?

Sure, I responded, intrigued to see what he'd send back.

I was hoping you'd say that.

I burst out laughing at the selfie of Ben next to a half-submerged seal in the water, eyes shut and looking like the world's most content living sausage. Ben, for his part, looked all rugged and handsome in a black Dane Development performance fleece, his hair slightly windblown and his cheeks flushed with color.

Say hello to the New England Aquarium's resident harbor seals. I don't know this guy's name, but he looks like an Edmund. You agree?

I squinted at the heavily whiskered seal. Looks more like an Alphonse to me.

You're right, that's more cosmopolitan.

I bit my lip. This was a perfect time to end the text exchange, and yet . . . So, you and Alphonse? What's the backstory there? I thought you were unattached. I hit send before I could consider the consequences of text-based flirting.

Why, you interested? came the immediate reply.

Are you saying Alphonse is on the market?

I think you may have to fight a cadre of little girls vying for his affection. But don't worry, they were easy enough to elbow out of the way for this selfie. You should have no trouble.

My fingers hesitated for a second before typing. The hell with it. On second thought, Alphonse sounds a little high-maintenance for my tastes. A world traveler with a coterie of adoring fans? I need something more low-key.

I hear ESTPs are very low-key.

I snickered, my hands flying over the keys. ESTPs are most certainly not low-key.

My phone buzzed. Another picture of Ben, crouched down among a small gaggle of girls all making puppy dog eyes at the camera and making heart shapes with their hands. Ben's puppy dog eyes were particularly sad. I laughed out loud. Alphonse's coterie disagrees with you and thinks you should give me a chance. So do their mothers. It has absolutely nothing to do with me offering to buy them all ice cream while they wait in line.

I laughed out loud. Well, how could I refuse Alphonse's fan club? Maybe an ice cream when you're back in Bard's? I wanted to ask when that would be but didn't want to come off desperate about it. Bantering was one thing; pining was another.

Of course. I still owe you dinner. Ice cream for dessert. What's your flavor?

You're an ESTP. Use your powers of perception to figure it out ☺ Oh god, had I just used a wink emoji?

Challenge accepted.

I knew I should end this exchange before any additional emojis were employed. Of course, that self-preserving thought would have been more impressive if I hadn't been grinning like an idiot. Slipping my phone back into my purse, I continued on to the bookstore, the events of the morning—Emmeline's veiled warning, Gerald's not-so-veiled advice and my texts with Ben—tumbling around in my head like a delicates cycle. Is this what people did when they had a spare minute to think about something other than work? Arranging for carb-based peace offerings and engaging in highly entertaining text conversations? I had to admit it wasn't the worst thing ever.

Nor, I thought later that night when the doorbell rang, were surprise deliveries. A courier from Mercutio's Mercantile, Bard's local market, dropped off a gallon of mint chip ice cream. The note read, *To hold you over until I can buy you a scoop of your very favorite ice cream in person in a few days. In case this isn't it. But I'm pretty sure it is.*

I reached for the kitchen drawer and extracted a spoon. How had he even known I loved mint chip, so subtle and cool with that bite of chocolate to finish it all off? I took a shaky selfie of myself with the ice cream lifted to my lips. Not a suggestive picture by any means and not as cute as, say, posing with blubber-based sea life, but it only took me six takes to get a halfway decent one. I hit send. Your powers of deduction are spot-on, sir.

The Scarborough Campus of Maine Medical

Mom slid the cloth bag of tiles across the table to me. "Your turn."

I stared down at my tiles. "Really? You're not going to add a red ten to that string or anything?"

"I am not," she said, smiling.

"How about an orange five? Are you holding out on me? You can't add to those three fives?" I said, nodding to the row of blue, red and black fives.

"I cannot," she said, smiling more broadly.

I rolled my eyes and reached into the bag. A red thirteen. Thirteen represented the highest possible value—and therefore the worst tile to draw—in Rummikub. "Oh come on," I exclaimed and then dropped my voice. Even though we were in a treatment suite by ourselves, I was pretty sure yelling in the chemo wing was frowned upon.

Although Scarborough was a bit of a drive, I liked this outpatient facility of Maine Medical. The state-of-the-art facility had instantly relaxed me as we'd walked in, and everything about it screamed, "We are competent. Give us your loved ones and we will treat them right."

Mom had asked me to wait outside while they'd started her IV line, which was probably for the best. I'd been known to faint when getting my blood drawn. Needles were not my thing. But Mom was made of much sterner, non-needle-averse stock, and she looked pretty sanguine and maybe even a little bit smug—although that was probably due to the fact that she'd be notching another Rummikub victory shortly.

"How are you—"

She lifted an imperious brow.

"—coming along with the festival?" I finished, determined not to ask how she was feeling. Even though I desperately wanted to know if the chemo made her nauseated as she sat there. But Cordelia had been pretty clear that Mom was tight-lipped about whatever side effects she experienced after a treatment, and Dad had only offered that she would be tired and likely sleep in the following day.

"Oh, things are coming together so much more easily than last year. For one thing, it's not a centennial, so there's less work. Second, I have Dan as a cochair, and he's so willing to jump in anywhere. It's good practice for him. He doesn't know it yet, but he'll be doing it solo next year."

My fingers skittered over the tiles. "Why?"

Taking in my expression, she leaned over to pat my hand. "Darling, it's nothing like that. Your father and I are planning a trip to Scotland for July next summer. We can't do that if we're here on committees or building sets. We'll be back in time for the festival itself. But it's time to pass the torch."

"Wow," I said, my mouth sort of hanging open. "Wow." In my thirty-plus years on this earth, my parents had never missed the festival. "That sounds incredible. Will you get a place in Edinburgh?"

"We'll spend a few days there to start," she said, "but we're also looking at rentals in Isle of Skye. Do a little hiking. See some hairy coos. Explore some fairy pools and glens."

"That all sounds wonderful." Especially the implication there that Mom thought she would be well enough to travel internationally next summer.

"Portia, have you thought about taking a few weeks this summer? Go somewhere new. Prague? Paris? Portugal?"

"Any other destinations that start with *P* you want to throw in there?" I teased.

"You love your work. I know that. You've always expressed an interest in traveling, but say you have no time. What better time to travel than a sabbatical?"

What better time indeed, I thought. I certainly wasn't going to tell her that if things had been different, if she hadn't been mid-treatment, I'd have considered it. But therein lay the beauty of the sabbatical: I had this time to spend with her, to slow down, to sit with her, to listen to her. To me, that was so much more valuable than traveling. Hell if I was going to tell her that though. She might smack me with her IV pole or something.

"It's hard to argue with you when you're mid–chemo drip. You get that, right?"

Mom smiled wickedly. "My opportunities to dispense unsolicited motherly advice are rare indeed. Let me have this one."

"Fine. I'll consider it. Maybe I'll take the week after the festival and put my passport to good use. That will still give me a week to settle into my condo and get ready for my new role."

I could tell from the pinch of her lips that she wanted to say more. But I didn't give her the chance. Gerald might like to think he'd been the one to teach all his prized associates how to negotiate, but I learned the dance from my mother. I took my opening to change the subject. "I'll plan something spectacular. Besides, how could I miss out on this rich career development opportunity? When else will I get to negotiate funnel cake contracts? Did you know the vendor is digging his heels in over equipment maintenance?"

"Equipment maintenance? On funnel cakes?"

"On the funnel cake fryers. Did you know they have no distinct sediment zones? So it's critical to clean regularly not only to prevent the sediment from burning the funnel cake but to make sure you can pass a health inspection. Like the one that will be occurring twenty-four hours before the festival opening."

"Sediment zones?" My mother arched a brow.

"I took the liberty of educating myself on the common issues that can arise with food booth vendors. Sediment buildup is a real concern in the funnel cake community."

She said nothing, but gave me such a look of maternal pride that I felt my chest expand a bit. Maybe I was going a bit over the top on these contracts, but an ounce of prevention up front could potentially stave off a larger grease fire down the road.

"I appreciate all you're doing for the festival," she continued, pressing her lips together as if she was trying to hold back a smile.

"Well, someone needs to safeguard the interests of the town."

"I know that. I'm just delighted it's you. Safeguarding us from sediment buildup."

Okay, she was definitely mocking my sediment concerns. No way was I going to let that stand. I smiled sweetly. "Would you rather talk about safeguarding personal information? Like how you gave my personal phone number to a complete stranger who cold-emailed you at the festival address?"

My mother's smile mirrored my own. "Oh, are we pretending the developer you made out with outside the café is a complete stranger?"

I choked on my surprise, jostling my Rummikub tray. "What are you talking about?"

"Darling, you do know Cordy is about as discreet as assless chaps, yes?"

"Mom!" I would have words with Cordelia about that one.

"Oh, it's nothing to be embarrassed about. You're on sabbatical. It's important to fill your days. It can't be all about sediment zones all of the time."

I put my face in my hands. "I don't want to talk about this."

"You're the one who brought it up," she said mildly.

"Oh, I am not sharing any details with you."

"Why not?"

"Because you said 'assless chaps' and mocked my sediment zones concerns."

She gave me one of her classic "I am your mother, I know all" smiles. But she didn't push me. Which I loved her for. She could verbally spar with the best of them, but still respected my boundaries. Even when I'd been a teenager and I was sure she could sense my unhappiness, that unsatisfied urge that I needed to be doing more, I needed to *be* more, she hadn't pushed me. She'd made it so clear the door was open for me to walk through, but never dragged me through it or demanded things of me I couldn't give her. God, I loved my mother. And yet . . . she loved to banter as much as I did. She'd given up way too easily here. "You want something, don't you?" I teased, a challenge in my voice.

"Well, since you're offering," she said, playing a particularly upsetting run.

"You had the orange seven?" I sputtered indignantly. "How long have you been sitting on that?"

My mother preened. "Since you're so invested in the success of the festival, maybe you could assist me in avoiding last year's fiasco with the petting zoo—"

"You mean, the frivolous lawsuit I'm wrestling to the ground and out of existence?" I said dryly.

"Yes, that one. As you know, because you reviewed the contract, we have to vet the new vendor. He's coming Monday for a site visit to see if his current setup will work. If you could oversee that, I'd appreciate it."

I drew back. "What do you mean by current setup?"

"He's going to set up in town and do a demo to ensure that the environment works for him and his animals."

I rubbed my temples. "Did the Elizabethans even have petting zoos? Or did William Shakespeare own a heretofore undisclosed herd of llamas I'm unaware of?"

"I don't think there were petting zoos in the Bard's times," my mother said dryly. "But the kids love it. I'm not going to be the co-chair that sounds the death knell on it."

"What if I do it as your festival attorney? I have no problem sounding the death knell. I'll be your enforcer. I love being bad cop."

Mom chuckled. "If only it were that simple."

"You do know that the 'do it for the children' approach isn't going to have much impact on me. Petting zoos are gross. As are children."

"Then do it for me."

"Curse you," I muttered. "You know my weakness."

Her face lit up. "I'll send you everything I have. He has this website you're going to love. Every animal has its own bio." She launched into the details and once again I was struck by her poise, her ability to sit there hooked up to an IV drip and recall festival planning minutiae with such stunning clarity while simultaneously destroying me at Rummikub. I watched her, taking in the way she talked so elegantly with her hands, the assurance in her tone, the way her eyes seemed to be smiling even when her lips weren't. She was right. I should get out there and travel. But there would be time for travel— I would find time. For now, this was everything.

Scene Twelve

....

The Petting Zoo

Monday arrived, another heavy-lidded morning sky hinting at the humidity to come. Rethinking the wisdom of hot tea in my travel mug, I opted for the pitcher of unsweetened iced tea and doubled down on ice cubes. Despite the weather, I'd managed morning runs on Saturday and Sunday, attended two family dinners that ended in hotly contested Trivial Pursuit victories (mine), chipped away at a few more vendor contracts, deadheaded the gardens over at Bard's Books, snoozed in the hammock and burned through all of Christie's *Cat Among the Pigeons*. It was still strange being in no particular rush to do anything, but it was no longer panic inducing. Even better, Sunday night had brought a text from Ben that he'd be back in Bard's Monday and wanted to make good on that offer to take me to dinner and buy me a scoop of mint chip for dessert.

Armed with iced tea and attired in a sporty but breathable sundress, I headed off to Main Street. Bob Callow and Sons, though there were no sons in sight, showed up right on time driving an enormous shiny trailer and proceeded to construct a petting zoo in the middle of Main Street. Soon, there were spring-heeled goats and snowy white ducks and tall, slightly goofy-looking alpacas milling about and tucking into the alfalfa with gusto. Chickens strutted and velvety rabbits lounged in the shade and one particularly adorable pony swished her tail and tossed her caramel-colored mane for all she was worth.

Despite choosing a livelihood that involved driving around with a veritable metal ark of animals, Bob Callow seemed to be a reasonable human being, answering all my questions about process and contingencies while making nice with the children of Bard's, whose parents had been warned—err, invited—in advance by Tillie to the dry run of the petting zoo. I could see in the wide smiles and soft giggles of the kids as they stepped into the enclosure and latched the gate behind them why this was a cornerstone for the festival.

All in all, the morning chugged along swimmingly well, I thought, as I stood in the shade with Tillie and Alice, listening as Alice recapped the summer reading program so far. But her words died abruptly as another giant trailer—which, from the sound and smell, appeared to be carrying even more animals—squealed to a stop alongside Bob's trailer.

"What is he doing here?" Tillie demanded, pointing to the new trailer, which had the words "Andrews and Sons—Petting Zoo for Your Petting Pleasure" emblazoned along the side. Someone should talk to Rufus Andrews about that. Or his sons, of which there didn't seem to be any either.

"I'm not sure," I said, still frowning at the slogan. I'd been emailing back and forth with his lawyer, but no meeting time for mediation had been set yet, and even if it had, it was not going to occur in Bard's with a trailer full of animals in tow. "Let me go find out what he wants."

"Give him hell, honey." Tillie clapped me on the back.

"Oh, Til." Alice rolled her eyes. "Settle down. I'm sure it's nothing."

But I wasn't so sure as I watched Rufus, or at least the beefy guy in overalls I presumed was Rufus or one of his sons, slide out of his truck. "Well, well, well," he spat in the direction of a now scowling Bob. "My sources were correct. You're snaking the festival out from under us, Callow."

"Mr. Andrews," I interjected in my most reasonable and professional tone. "You no longer have a contract with the town of Bard's

Rest. We served you a notice of contractual breach, and when you failed to respond in a timely manner, we terminated your services."

"But you didn't pay me," Rufus complained, running a hand through a spectacular mullet.

"Actually, the town paid you what was owed under the contract. It will not be paying any kind of special damages for—as you describe it—the 'agitation resulting in the procreation' of your goats." Well, that was a new professional low for me.

"But your festival caused my goats to go into heat and then we had a bunch of baby goats when we weren't planning to. You owe me pain and suffering."

"That's not how that works. Ask your attorney. But for now, I am going to need you to vacate the premises, Mr. Andrews."

"Better do what she says, Rufus," Bob crowed. "She chose us. We're the best petting zoo in fifty miles."

"My petting zoo is twice the size of yours," Rufus barked.

"Ain't a matter of size, but quality," Bob shot back.

I closed my eyes. Middle-aged man taunting was so not what I needed at this delicate juncture. But it would hardly do to tell Bob to put a lid on it in front of Rufus. So instead, I maneuvered into their line of sight to each other and glowered at Rufus Andrews— which I'm sure was intimidating in this sundress-and-sandals ensemble. "Mr. Andrews, I'm going to ask you one more time. You need to leave immediately."

"Is there a problem here?" a smooth voice asked from my right. From out of nowhere, Ben appeared at my side. I noted—not without some satisfaction and familial pride—that he'd invested in a Much Ado About Pastry travel mug and was sipping from it now, looking for all the world like an unconcerned corporate version of a deputy, not trying to take control of the situation, but offering some backup if I wanted it. God, that was so hot.

"Did you just get into town?" I asked conversationally, hoping to further defuse this situation by signaling to Rufus that I had this locked down enough to make side conversation.

"Yes, and made a beeline for your sister's pastries." He frowned. "That sounds wrong."

I hid a smile.

"Mister, are you in charge here?" Rufus demanded.

"No, she's in charge here." Ben smiled, his tone still easy, but something in his posture had changed, a rigidity in his spine that communicated his alertness. "So I'd suggest you do as she says."

"If I don't?" he sneered.

"Then I'm going to enjoy quite the show with my morning coffee." He inclined his head in my direction. "Because you have no idea who you're dealing with. You ever seen those MMA fighters?" He gestured to me. "That times ten."

"Mr. Andrews, I'm afraid I'm going to have to call your lawyer and explain that we won't be entering into mediation talks after all unless you get in your vehicle right now and I'll forget this unfortunate incident happened and—"

"You heard her, Rufus. Take your horny goats and go home," Bob called over my shoulder.

"What did you say to me?" Rufus yelled.

"You heard me fine," Bob hollered back. "Something unnatural with your goats, Rufus."

"Don't you talk about my goats like that." Rufus's face had turned the color of expired beets. He made as if to walk off in the direction of his trailer, but then put his head down and charged Bob Callow like a bull.

That's when the morning transformed from an idyllic picture of children snuggling animals with wide-eyed wonderment to a surreal tableau of two overall-clad men shoving each other in the middle of Main Street.

"The hell?" Ben muttered. "Want to call the sheriff and I'll see if I can pull them off each other, or do you want the honor of—" But before Ben could finish, Bob landed a blow that sent Rufus over a makeshift fence, sending it crashing to the ground. Within seconds, a half dozen baby goats were bounding all over

Main Street, followed by some exuberant piglets and one very sassy donkey.

"Get the animals," I yelped at Ben as I scrambled toward the two men grappling on the ground and—if I wasn't mistaken—slapping at each other like Real Housewives. Ben took off at a run in the direction of the now very free-range animals.

But before I could reach the two men, a goat slammed into me. I whirled on the gray and black specimen and stared it down. It bleated plaintively and stepped aside. "That's what I thought," I said sternly, rubbing my shin.

Out of the corner of my eye, I saw Dan and Aaron step out of Two Gentlemen of Daytona, twin expressions of horror dawning on their faces. I shouted, "Grab whatever you can and put them in that trailer," as Tillie, Alice and about a dozen other residents joined the scramble. Even the kids were getting in on the action—I watched a girl in pigtails snatch a duck from beneath trampling hooves and cradle it against her chest protectively.

Gritting my teeth, I pushed away a hay bale and some ruined fencing that lashed at my bare ankle. Somewhere in the fray I'd lost a rather expensive sandal and my dignity, but that was a future Portia problem. Now I was just a few feet away from the squabbling pair when something hard smacked into me from behind. I spun around to find a wide-eyed alpaca with flared nostrils rearing up. I leapt out of the way of its hooves and tried to grab the frightened animal's halter. I missed, and it bolted toward a man pushing a baby stroller. "Not on my watch," I muttered as I took off after the alpaca and tackled it from behind, dragging down its momentum moments before it crashed into the man and his stroller, which coincidentally contained not a child, but a pug.

Realizing that holding the back end of an alpaca was not a winning strategy, I quickly let go and grasped the halter before the dazed animal had a chance to think. Handing the alpaca off to the man as best I could, I stomped back to the two still-quarreling men, promptly reached in and separated them. "Get up!" The two men, panting, stared at the ground. "Get your animals and get out. Both of you." When they didn't move, I yelled, "NOW."

Properly chastened, Rufus began to help Bob collect his animals as I directed townsfolk with animals toward the trailer and those who were empty-handed toward overturned trash cans and benches. When the chaos had finally settled and every single animal was (miraculously) safe and accounted for, I whirled on the pair of shamefaced men still unable to make eye contact with me. "You will each be receiving an invoice for your share of the damages you've caused today, do you understand me?" The two men nodded meekly. "Now kindly leave the premises immediately."

Once both trailers had pulled away, I turned to the crowd. "Is everyone all right?"

"If not, I know a good lawyer," Tillie crowed.

I shot her an exasperated look.

The other townsfolk waited until the two trucks were actually out of sight before breaking into cheers and applause.

Shaking my head, I brushed at my now ruined sundress, wincing at my scraped knee and ankle.

"Here, let me help with that," Ben said, pulling up beside me with a first aid kit and crouching down before me in a manner reminiscent of a proposal.

"Where did you get that?" I asked.

"I keep one in my car," he said matter-of-factly.

If Ben wasn't careful, I might reconsider my stance on matrimony and marry him.

I opened my mouth to tell him I didn't need him to do that, but he was already dabbing at my ankle with an antiseptic wipe. I watched as he ripped open a travel-sized packet of Neosporin, managing to apply it without actually touching the cut. Yeah, I was definitely going to marry this guy, I thought, as he expertly positioned a Band-Aid and moved on to my knee.

"Well, that was something," Ben said, rising and wiping mud— at least I hoped it was mud—off his general person.

"I'm so sorry," I said and resisted the urge to help him wipe his pants. Because that would be weird.

We both stared at each other and burst out laughing, loud, racking peals of laughter. "Let me make it up to you," I said, trying to stifle the tail end of a giggle. But then I looked at him again and lost it. When my sides were still aching with laughter, but I could draw breath again, I wheezed, "Dinner tonight at Titania's? My treat."

Ben reached over and plucked alfalfa from my hair. "Nah, I owe you dinner there. So rain-check that, because I always make good on my bets. But for now, because I'm covered in what I think is a mixture of goat crap and hay, I think that warrants me something more spontaneous than mere dinner. You're a local. Tell me what this place has to offer."

"Besides fine dining?"

"Besides fine dining," Ben said firmly. "C'mon, dazzle me."

"I would have said Peaseblossom's, but we've checked that box. There's bowling over at The Two Noble Pinsmen."

"I've already had my cardio for the day, thank you."

Again with the uncontrollable laughter. Maybe it was some sort of adrenaline response to having survived a farm animal invasion. "Well, there's cooking classes over at Dan and Aaron's, a paint place, the drive-in," I said, ticking each one off on my fingers.

"A drive-in?"

"Yes, Midsummer Night's Screen. It's an old one on the outskirts of Bard's. It shows a double feature every night in the summer. One Shakespearean flick and one classic film like *Raiders of the Lost Ark*, *Jurassic Park*, *Jaws*—"

"You had me at *Jaws*," Ben said solemnly. "*Jaws* is a masterpiece."

"I love *Jaws*," I agreed.

"Really?" Ben levied a skeptical brow.

"I appreciate Quint's fatalism and Brody's dogged determination."

"No love for Hooper?"

"His beard bugs me," I admitted. "When he's in the cage, I root for the shark."

"Of course you do."

I pulled out my phone and located the calendar for the drive-in. "You're not going to believe this." I looked up at Ben's expectant face. "*Jaws* is playing tonight. Well, *Jaws*, with *Midsummer*—the one with Michelle Pfeiffer—playing first. *Jaws* is the second movie. We could go late if you want?"

Ben looked offended. "That's like showing up at the baseball game midway through the fourth. Who does that?"

"Posers," I offered. "I just wanted to offer you an option. Two movies is a long time in a car with a near stranger."

"We're hardly strangers at this point," Ben scoffed. "I think once you wind up covered in goat shit in front of a person, that materially changes your relationship."

"Not going to let that drop, huh?"

"No, but if you're very lucky, I won't wear this to our date."

"A true gentleman. Where should I pick you up?"

"I'll text you the address. I was tired of not having a kitchen and upgraded to a rental. This place has a fancy name and everything. Falstaff's Folly."

I snickered. I was well aware of Falstaff's. "Classy."

"It's a little over-the-top for my tastes," he conceded. "But I'm getting the immersive Bard's experience. And they rent by the week."

"Of course they do."

He glanced at his phone. "My apologies. I have an appointment in an hour or so and need to change my pants." He shook his dark hair ruefully. "Filing that under 'things I'd never thought I'd say until I was in my later years.'"

"To be fair, this was not exactly the way I saw the morning going either."

"No, I suppose not even the great and powerful Portia Barnes could have foreseen an animal jailbreak." Ben gave me a dazzling smile. "Looking forward to seeing you tonight."

"Me too," I said, watching him retreat down Main Street, head high and looking effortlessly unperturbed despite the fact he was covered in crap.

"Oh man, Miranda is going to be so mad to have missed this," Cordelia chirped.

I jumped, snapping out of admiring Ben's ass. "Where did you come from?"

"Well, when an unattended pony trots into one's open doorway, it's a sign that one should put the biscuits down and investigate. On an unrelated note, ponies are apparently huge fans of apple tarts."

I suppressed the urge to scrub my hands over my face, because they were filthy from animal wrangling. "I would say I feel bad for Bob and whatever gastrointestinal horrors await him in that pony's stable later . . . but he engaged in some low-blow goat shaming of Rufus. That and he unleashed a plague of farm animals on the town. He deserves it."

Cordelia's gaze followed mine, landing on Ben as he climbed into his car. "I saw your make-out partner put a llama in a headlock, by the way." She waggled her eyebrows. "I didn't think Ivy League had it in him."

Eyes on Ben's car, I murmured, "He's not my make-out partner."

"All signs to the contrary."

"I'm also willing to bet he's not Ivy League–issue. He's not an insufferable ass."

"Says the Ivy League issue," Cordelia said, knocking my shoulder playfully with hers. "You like him."

"I'm intrigued by him," I admitted.

"Is that what we're calling it now?"

"Oh, shut it," I told her, trying not to think of how sexy it had been when he'd shown up to back me up earlier. He hadn't tried to defend my honor either, but had stepped up beside me like a partner.

My stomach grumbled. "Do you have any fruit tarts? Maybe some hand sanitizer? I need to pick your culinary brain. Nobody does snacks like you do."

"Go on." My sister made a "keep going" gesture with her hand. "I'm listening."

Midsummer Night's Screen

I thought you said you were taking me to the drive-in," Ben noted as we drove by the entrance to Midsummer Night's Screen, where cars were already lined up and people were spreading out their chairs and blankets, settling in for the double-feature long haul.

"That's the tourist entrance," I said dismissively as we crested the hill. I failed to mention to Ben we were heading to the Look Out, a notorious teen make-out spot. That wasn't the point of this exercise, I reasoned, even as I hit the brakes and took a sharp right, nearly missing the pull-off. Ben grabbed at the handle over the window but didn't cry out. Good man.

"Am I going to end up on *Dateline*?" Ben asked mildly as my car ambled down the unlit, unpaved road. "I'd have worn something nicer if I'd known I was going to be found in a shallow grave three weeks from now."

"'John Doe in Tom Ford' has a nice ring to it, don't you think?" I deftly maneuvered us onto the grassy ledge that had room for a single car and provided an unobstructed view of the screen. "Best seat in the house. Except for the lack of restrooms. But we can walk down the hill between movies to use the facilities. Or sooner, if you have a child-sized bladder."

"Challenge accepted." He grinned. "The view is spectacular up here, but how will we hear the movie?"

I reached behind me and plunked a Bluetooth speaker on the dash. "There's an app."

"Still, that's impressive range."

"A couple of years ago, Hen Gonzalez, a former classmate of mine, bought the drive-in. They're this interesting mix of tech meets nostalgia. After rehoming the racoon family that had taken up residence in the snack shack, Hen modernized the screens and sound system."

"Sounds expensive."

"It was. But Hen had the support of Bard's in preserving a much-beloved landmark. The merchant association rallied around them and kicked off a fundraising drive."

"Shakespearean-themed?"

"Is that a serious question?"

"I suppose not in this town."

"I believe one event was called 'Sonnet Slam for Screens' and another was called 'Horatio's Hundos for Hen.'"

"Wow." Ben's face was equal parts fascination and horror. "So, you have kept in touch with Bard's despite moving to New York and dominating the legal scene in your rise to managing partner."

"I've kept in touch here and there," I hedged. Hen had reached out for help in preparing their small business loans paperwork, and I'd been all too happy to help. They'd been my project partner on *Ulysses* in AP English. It was the kind of scarring reading experience that bonded people for life. I wouldn't have made it through the talking soap chapter if it weren't for Hen.

"Mmm-hmm." Ben eyed me with that unsettling and seemingly casual but actually very probing curiosity.

I swiveled my head to meet his gaze. "Yes?"

"I think you do more here than you let on."

"Right, between my domination of the cutthroat New York legal scene and rise to managing partner glory, I side hustle as a town philanthropist."

He squinted at me, not sure whether to believe me or not. I suspected he was leaning toward not. Time for a subject change.

"Hungry?" I asked.

"I could go for some popcorn," Ben said amiably. "Shall we walk down to the now-uninhabited-by-woodland-foes snack shack?"

"What do you think this is? Amateur hour? Wait here, please," I said, getting out of the car and popping the trunk. I reappeared with two insulated bags. "Here," I said, handing him one while I opened the other. "I have beer, bubbly, Polar Seltzer, Dr Pepper and root beer." When he raised an eyebrow, I said, "Cordelia let me raid her fridge."

He unlatched the other bag, where two fragrant, still-warm bags of movie popcorn waited. "There's real butter in the bottom in two little containers. I figured you'd want to dress your own popcorn."

"Marry me," Ben blurted.

I laughed, even if the idea itself sort of gave me pause.

Below us the screen lit up with instructions on how to use the app, followed by tantalizing ads for the concessions.

"So, are we aligned that we talk through *Midsummer* and settle in hardcore for *Jaws*?" Ben asked. "Because I seem to remember this movie having a shirtless, horned Stanley Tucci in it."

I giggled. "We are perfectly aligned in that regard."

"Good, because speaking of horned creatures, I wanted to reiterate how impressive you were today. I literally saw you stare down a goat."

"I don't know what you're talking about," I said airily.

"That goat slunk away, clearly defeated by whatever you said to it. And don't think I didn't see your takedown of that alpaca."

"I'll never look at those mittens Miranda gave me last Christmas the same way again, that's for sure," I laughed. "Let's not forget what a deft hand with that first aid kit you were. Thanks for staving off what I'm sure would have been an alfalfa-based infection."

"Working in construction, you learn a thing or two in the first aid department."

"I bet you have some interesting scars, huh?" I bit my lip. "That was not an invitation."

Ben's ensuing smile, which I watched out of the corner of my eye, was equal parts devastating and inviting. I had this urge to crawl into his lap and nibble on his bottom lip. I needed a subject change. Something safe.

"Did you get everything under control in Boston?"

Ben opened a can of Liquid Sunshine and sipped, eyes momentarily closing in pleasure. "It was nightmarish. My partner, Sam, and I had to deal with a zoning board on an issue we thought we had locked down months ago. Of course, the board found something last-minute that had to be addressed or construction would be delayed, and in this supply chain climate, any delay means you lose your spot for production, and then, well, you may as well call yourself the Big Dig."

"Sounds intense."

"Yes, but enormously satisfying when we resolved it in record time."

"Because you felt like you were the only person who could have closed it?" I asked.

"Well, Sam and me working together and harnessing the powers of the universe. But yes, only the two of us could have pulled that off."

"Sounds like you have quite the partner in Sam."

"I do. We found each other at the right time in our lives. There's no one I trust more than Sam." He dug into his popcorn bag with gusto. "Can we go back to the Bard's thing?"

Instead of answering, I opted to ignore him as the movie started to play and hoped he'd just drop it. That and I was bracing myself for a bunch of half-naked fairy folk.

"A few weeks ago, I meet this intriguing woman in Titania's. Excellent taste in scotch, terrible taste in bourbon." He shrugs. "But nobody's perfect, right?"

"Clearly," I agreed, treating Ben to some well-deserved side-eye.

"Come to find out she's a local girl who left town for more cosmopolitan digs. A successful New York corporate lawyer with an impressive track record, she's back in Bard's for a firm-imposed sabbatical. She has an ailing mother, although now having met the formidable Isabella Barnes at Bard's Books, it's difficult to characterize your mother as ailing."

"You got that right." I snorted. "You stopped into Bard's Books today?"

"After I changed my pants, yes. I was looking for a book on the history of the town. Your mother was lovely. Met your father too, a very nice man. But back to my conundrum. You claim to have no attachment to Bard's. Yet at every turn, there's something to suggest otherwise."

"Name one."

"You're the festival attorney."

"That's easy," I scoffed. "I was cajoled into that by said ailing mother."

"You're on a first-name basis with the owner of the Merchant of Venison to the point where he comped our meals."

"I've known Marty Cabot a long time."

Ben arched a brow.

"I helped him with a liquor board license in the early days of MOV."

"Why?"

"He's a nice guy and he needed help."

"I also heard from Candace Thornton, the head event planner at Titania's Bower and arguably the most connected woman in town, that you acted in the dinner theater last summer?"

"It's true. I played Lady Capulet as a favor to my sister. It's a long story."

"I heard you're taking the stage again this year?"

"Yes," I grumbled. "Candace strong-armed me into taking the role of Don John, who helps broker peace amidst the chaos. Except that Candace rewrote it as Dame Jan. She's the only level-headed character in the entire play. Is this line of questioning going somewhere?"

"Admit it. You're a closet do-gooder."

"Nope." I didn't think helping my friends and people who needed it qualified me as a do-gooder.

"Agree to disagree," he said, his smile mischievous. "Okay, riddle me this. You claim you've moved on from your hometown, but at every turn, I find you still have a foothold here."

"Helping out a couple of friends from time to time isn't exactly fortifying a stronghold. Besides, lots of people keep ties to their hometown." I laughed uneasily. "That's hardly a conundrum."

"I get that. But you don't seem all nostalgic about Bard's. Can I ask what made you leave in the first place?"

"College. Harvard for undergrad and law school. When I sat for the bar exam, I took Massachusetts and New York. I interviewed for half a dozen firms and settled on FrancisPearl because it had the most robust corporate program. That meant I came home less." I took a sharp breath, determined that my voice would not waver on the next part. "Until last summer, when my mom got sick, and then again this summer, because it coincided with my sabbatical and Mom's chemotherapy treatments."

"You told me that first night at dinner that you weren't attached to this place."

"So?"

"But why?"

"Why is it important for you to know?" I asked.

"Because I like you," Ben said. "And I'm trying to figure you out. You said it yourself—when something doesn't fit, you want to understand it better. I want to understand you better. Is that okay? I'm happy to drop it if you prefer."

I looked at Ben for a long moment. Internal wobbles were rare for me. But here I was, still experiencing one. "You ever read 'The Ugly Duckling' in school?"

"Yes, I attended kindergarten," Ben said dryly. "It was required story time reading, if I remember."

"You know how initially all that duck wants to do is to fit in, but he sticks out like a sore thumb until he transforms into another creature?"

"I am familiar with the plot," Ben said, trying and failing miserably at hiding his smile.

"I'm the duck in this scenario."

"It would be a little weird if you weren't."

"I am pretty sure that I'm the only person born and raised in this town who actively dislikes Shakespeare. I don't get it. I don't get the fascination with him and the hero-worshipping. I find his plays contrived, his sonnets overly flowery and the fact that nobody actually knows much about his life to be highly suspect."

"A fair assessment."

"Not in Bard's Rest. I grew up in a town of artists, people who cultivated creativity and diversity, yet worshipped slavishly at the altar of this hack."

"You should probably keep your voice down," Ben murmured. "You're still within town limits."

"Don't you think it's a little twee that people in this town name their businesses after bad Shakespearean puns?"

"I'm not entirely sure how to answer that, because I don't know what 'twee' means."

"Overly quaint; precious," I supplied. "Like, if someone were reading a book about our town and didn't go in for the whole Shakespeare thing, that's how they'd describe us. Twee."

"Mmm," Ben hummed.

"I used to think there was something wrong with me growing up," I admitted. "Like I was missing something that everybody else had figured out. I struggled with Shakespeare in school—unable to find the deeper messages and meanings my classmates did—it was the closest I'd ever come to making a C in anything. I didn't, by the way; I managed to pull out a B-minus in Shakespearean Studies my sophomore year and the same in Sonnets my junior year. But in our house, a B-minus might as well have been an F.

"I constantly felt like an outsider. At home, in school. Every year

I'd dread August and the arrival of the Bardolators. It drove home how very much I didn't belong here, that there were a bunch of strange tourists crawling all over the place who had a deeper connection to this place than I did. I wanted something more, something different."

"Is this the part where you transformed into a beautiful swan?" Ben quipped. He flashed me what I'm sure he thought was a winning grin.

"If by transforming into a beautiful swan, you mean I became highly involved in academics and sports, eschewing all things Shakespearean and theater based in favor of pushing myself to win each and every non-Shakespearean accolade my town had to offer without stopping to ever consider why I wanted to win and whether the cost to do so was worth it, then yes."

Ben blinked. "I think you've surpassed what 'The Ugly Duckling' has to offer in terms of the moral of the story."

I snorted in the darkness. "If I couldn't fit in with everyone else, then I would forge an identity where I stood out. Academics and sports got me there, and I liked the attention I received from my parents and classmates every time I won something. I don't want to put too fine a point on it, but let's just say that if it's possible to be addicted to winning, I was. It didn't matter what it was. When I wasn't winning, I felt hollow."

I squeezed my eyes shut. I hated this next part. "As a result, I did some shitty things in high school, including stealing Miranda's prom date to ensure I wouldn't be dateless and would still win prom queen. That was a low point. But there were others. By the time I started junior year, I didn't like myself much. I knew I needed to get far away from Bard's. Enter Harvard. Then FrancisPearl. I found a way to channel my need to win into my love of the law. And here we are. You listening to me complain about my completely normal upbringing that I somehow twisted into a tragedy worthy of Shakespeare."

For a long while, the only sound in the car was my breathing and Ben's.

"Say something," I said finally. "Anything."

"It must have been so hard for you finding out your mother had cancer last summer and deciding you had to come back here. That must have brought up a lot of stuff for you."

I bit down so hard on my lip, it bled, stinging and salty. He'd said it so gently and yet it had cut right through to the core of me. Ben had seen me. Not only that; he'd distilled my fear down and put his finger right on what had scared me most.

"I'm not good with death." God, that was such an understatement. I prided myself on the ability to keep my calm when deals were going down faster than the *Titanic*. The level-headed problem solver, the rock in the storm, the one you could count on. But when it came to death and what might be beyond, I fell apart.

Swallowing hard, I continued. "My grandma Bea had breast cancer, just like my mother, and she died from it. So yes, I came home last summer but was too much of a basket case to be much help. At least now I've had time to adjust and I can take her to her treatments, since I felt like I'd been mailing it in from New York and had left my Dad and my sisters to shoulder the burden." I didn't add that my mother's diagnosis had come on the heels of Project Berlin. I wasn't ready to talk about Berlin with anyone other than Kim.

"I can see why it's hard being back in Bard's."

"My mom has a good prognosis. She's responding well to chemo and her oncologist is very optimistic. I think it's a matter of giving myself permission to believe that, you know?"

Ben nodded. "Makes sense."

"I just dropped a lot of heavy," I pointed out. "If you'd like to go back to watching this ridiculous movie, I would understand."

"I'd rather sit through a sales pitch on the various grades of concrete than watch this movie," he snorted. "Look at these Muppets in the woods. Are they looking for water or shelter? Thinking about weather exposure while prancing around in nightgowns? Of course not."

"Well, it is an enchanted forest," I pointed out, grateful he'd picked up on my need for a subject change.

"Ridiculous." Ben snorted. "If I had to wind up lost in the woods, I'd plan ahead to make sure I had good company." He grinned over at me. "Like you. Quick thinking. Task oriented. You wouldn't be running around wringing your hands."

I laughed. "I'll admit you wouldn't be the worst lost-in-the-woods companion either. With your construction background, I bet we'd be fine in the shelter department."

"You'd better believe it." He grinned. "Though I'm sure you'd be full of all sorts of surprises out in the woods. I bet you can start a fire with nothing but a rock, some sticks and a bobby pin."

I appreciated that Ben didn't pity me or think I was somehow less for having confessed a major chink in my armor. There was something surprisingly hot in that. I squirmed in my seat. Why was I so hot and bothered at this juncture? It surely had nothing to do with these Muppets in nightgowns. Was it because I'd let Ben see a less-than-flattering side of me and he hadn't shied away from it? That seemed more on point than a bunch of Darwin Award candidates lost in the enchanted wood.

Before I could think about it anymore, I carefully set down my popcorn. In a feat of agility and flexibility, thanks to the yoga practice that Candace had helped me cultivate, I sort of crawled into his lap, straddling him in the passenger seat. "How's this for a surprise?" I asked, staring down at him.

"Consider me surprised," he murmured as I leaned in to kiss him.

Unlike our first kiss, which had been all tangled up in the aftermath of our verbal throwdown, this kiss was unhurried and exploratory. I leisurely ran my lips over his, tasting the salt from the popcorn and the tang of the beer. Planting soft kisses along the line of his upper lip, I lingered on his bottom one, nipping playfully at it.

Ben responded by leaning forward to claim my mouth and deepening the kiss, his tongue finding mine and settling us into that steady, confident rhythm. His hands tightened on my back, at first helping to steady me on his lap, then they slipped under my shirt to do far more interesting things, like stroking up my rib cage to find the delicate silk of my bra and winding their way around my back to deftly undo my bra clasp.

That's when I heard the crunch of something outside, followed by the ocular onslaught of glaring lights. I scrambled off Ben's lap, launching myself into the driver's seat. Ben tossed me my bra and I quickly dropped it in the side pocket of the door before the cruiser lights flicked on. A moment later, a knock on the windows. Great, I'd be facing law enforcement braless. But that didn't mean I was unarmed. Despite Ben kissing me senseless, I still had my wits about me. Some of my wits.

Sheriff Eddie Knight looked perplexed as he stared through my steamed windows. If you called up central casting and asked for a sheriff, you'd have gotten Eddie Knight—a little owl-eyed, a little jowly, a little weathered and supporting a generous, genre-defining mustache.

"Hello, Sheriff Knight," I said as evenly as I could manage. I was an adult, damn it. Despite this being the Look Out, I was not some horny teenager sneaking around. So what if Ben and I had been making out like we were? We were consenting adults.

"Ms. Barnes." He looked past me to the passenger seat.

"This is Benjamin Dane," I offered. "He's in town scouting some properties. I asked Hen if we could use the Look Out tonight. We're big *Jaws* fans."

"My apologies, Portia. I sometimes swing through here, making sure there aren't any teenagers doing what teenagers do best up this way."

"Mocking their parents and unleashing unfortunate fashion trends on society?" Ben offered.

"More like smoking weed and littering the woods with beer bottles," Eddie said dryly. "I get it. I was a teenage boy once. But I thought this generation was supposed to be the 'there's no Planet B' generation. Wouldn't that suggest they'd take their recycling with them? Is that too much to ask? I'm tired of sending my deputies up here to clean up the place, and I know Hen is too. Anyway, I'm sorry to have disturbed you folks. But you know how it is. We gotta run patrols." He peered down at me, and I prayed that this upstanding pillar of the community and forward-thinking recycler had not noticed my free-swinging state. "Portia, I've been meaning to email you, but it's been so busy these last few weeks."

"Not a problem at all," I assured him. "Miranda mentioned she'd cast you in her mainstage."

His chest puffed up with pride. "It's an honor to be cast in one of your sister's plays. But that's no excuse. I've been meaning to thank you for all your help with Marnie."

I could feel Ben's eyes on me.

"Happy to help," I told him, and I meant it.

"If there's anything I can ever do for you, you let me know."

"You could forget the petting zoo incident that rocked Main Street?"

He chuckled. "Already forgotten—no lasting damage done. Besides, that was hardly your fault." The radio on his hip came to life, the voice static and indistinct. "All right, you two enjoy *Jaws*. Never did care much for Hooper."

"Right?" I pointed a finger at Ben. "I told you."

"I didn't say I liked Hooper. I just draw the line at rooting for him to be eaten," Ben said dryly.

Eddie shook his head. "I'm with Portia, son."

When he'd gone, I couldn't help but glance over at Ben, my expression triumphant. "Admit it. Hooper is the most annoying character in the *Jaws* canon."

"Sure you're not trying to distract me from another example of hometown girl makes good?"

"You mean 'hometown girl makes out like a teenager in the woods.'"

We both dissolved into laughter, the motion making a dimple appear on the right side of Ben's face. God, I loved laughing with this man. I seemed to do it a lot more with him too—something I'd have to ruminate on later.

"Who's Marnie?"

"Eddie's daughter."

"Are you going to elaborate on that, or should I assume you discreetly busted her out of her jail some weekend while Eddie was away fishing?"

"I wrote her a recommendation for Harvard and did a mock interview with her to prepare for the admissions process. I still volunteer as the alumni interviewer for both the undergrad and grad school," I admitted, rubbing at my arms. "I'm going to grab a blanket from the trunk. I have some pastry in a cooler. Want anything?" As much as I wanted to continue climbing Ben like a particularly fetching tree, I didn't want Eddie to swing back on his rounds because he'd forgotten to tell me something and find me braless and/or pantless.

"You have pastry too?" he said, his voice hopeful. "Any brownies?"

"Cordelia only makes fancy desserts, but there's a mousse cake that reads like a fudgy brownie."

"In."

I discreetly grabbed my bra and opened the car door. Popping the trunk, I righted the girls and reached for the blanket and cooler. Shutting the trunk again, I whirled at the sound behind me as a high-pitched scream erupted from the trees.

A moment later, Ben stepped out of the car. "What was that?"

"Easy, city boy," I teased. "Your roots are showing."

"Because it's a regular occurrence out here in the country for people to get murdered in the woods?" he asked, his eyes scanning the underbrush.

I snorted. "It's a fox or maybe a fisher cat. Though the verdict is out as to whether fishers can actually scream or not. It's more like a hiss or low chuckle—"

"That is most definitely not a low chuckle," Ben insisted. He'd tried for nonchalant, but the way his eyes were flicking across the trees told me the noise had spooked him.

Something crashed in the bushes off to our left. Before thinking too much about it, I reached into the trunk and pulled out the elegant long-handled umbrella from a Chihuly gallery I'd visited and turned toward the noise, makeshift weapon in hand.

Just then something stumbled out of the woods, illuminated and indistinct in the headlights. It made a whimpering noise and staggered a few more feet before collapsing in the dirt. Umbrella still in hand, I crept closer for a better look, Ben on my heels.

It was neither fox nor fisher, but a small, filthy dog. As I crouched down beside it, I could see its ribs poking out painfully from its rapidly rising and falling belly.

"Whatever made that noise was likely after it," I said to Ben.

At the sound of my voice, the dog lifted his head and made a hopeful sound in his throat, thumping his tail a little. Making soft cooing sounds, I scooped him up, noting that he hardly weighed anything at all. I pressed him against my chest, stroking his crusty fur. "We have to do something," I said, looking up at Ben. "We can't leave him out here to get picked off. Maybe somebody is looking for him, maybe he's lost."

"Or feral," Ben said. "Either way, we have to help him."

"We can call Adam. He's Miranda's boyfriend and a vet. He's in town for the summer and will know what to do."

I walked toward the car, carefully cradling the shivering dog. I stopped at the driver's side door, staring dumbly at it.

"You want me to take him?" Ben called. I found I didn't. For whatever reason, I couldn't have handed over this dirty creature, who I'm sure was infested with fleas and god knows what else. "Can you drive?"

"You're trusting me to drive your car?"

"You unhooked my bra with one hand. I'm confident you can back out and drive us into town without injuring us." With one hand still cradling the pup, I reached for my phone with the other.

Fifteen minutes later, we met Adam and Miranda on the porch of The Winters' Tail, and even then I still couldn't even hand the dog over to Adam, a licensed medical professional, choosing instead to follow him inside to an exam room.

Eventually, I did set him down on the exam table, where the puppy commenced making indignant yips as Adam gently checked him over. "Malnourished, dehydrated, covered in ticks, but otherwise appears to be in good spirits. I'll start a fluids IV and we can sedate him so he can rest and I can take some blood and remove those ticks. Some of them are pretty embedded. No need to put the little guy through that while he's awake though. You said you found him in the woods?"

"We found him at the Look Out."

"The Look Out, huh?" Miranda grinned, her sea-glass-green eyes darting between me and Ben.

"Hen told us we could watch the movie from there."

"The Look Out?" Ben asked. He turned to me. "It has a name? So you did take me to a notorious make-out spot," he crowed.

"Oh, shut it," I said, certain that I'd just flushed the color of raspberry compote.

"I hope she at least bought you dinner first," Miranda teased.

"There were light snacks." Ben smiled.

I squeezed my eyes tight, as if that might drive away the embarrassment. "Can we focus on the dog, please? Did you see any bites on him?" I asked Adam. "Fox or fisher?"

"Now you've done it," Miranda said under her breath. "You know he has a fisher cat phobia."

"They're four-legged nightmares with teeth," Adam insisted, returning to the puppy and rechecking him. "I'm not even sure what color his coat is, this little guy is so crusty, but I definitely don't see any open wounds on him."

"That's a relief," I said, letting out a gush of breath I hadn't known I'd been holding.

"Did you see a fisher cat in the vicinity?" Adam asked, even as Miranda hid her "here we go again" smile.

"No, but if we had, Portia would have had the situation well in hand," Ben said proudly. "She had an umbrella and was brandishing it like the boom stick from—"

I interrupted him with a groan as Miranda burst into a hooting laugh.

"*Army of Darkness*," she finished for him. "Portia's a big fan of the Chin."

Ben turned to me, his mouth adorably hanging open. "You're a fan of low-rent, highly entertaining zombie films starring men with impressive bone structures?"

"No," Miranda singsonged. "But Portia had a massive crush on Bruce Campbell. Ask her about the time she waited in line for two hours at a comic con to meet him."

"You met Bruce Campbell? The B-movie legend?" Ben demanded. "How have we been to a notorious local make-out spot, but I didn't know this about you? It's like I don't even know you."

Even as I felt my face flame, I kept my gaze set to unimpressed and held Ben's eyes. I would not look at his well-sculpted chin in this moment. I would not.

"Children," Adam said mildly, "if you could continue your good-natured ribbing in the waiting room, I'd like to start sedation. Of the puppy, not Portia," he added with a sly grin.

"You too?" I groaned.

"I can't let Miranda have all the fun," he insisted as he pulled over a metal table on wheels that had a stark white paper towel and a plastic bag of what could only hold . . . needles. I hated needles. The sting, the press of the tourniquet and the sharp smell of antiseptic—but I looked down at the little dog, so small on that table. "I want to stay," I heard myself say. "If that's okay."

Ben stepped up beside me and slipped his hand into mine. "Then let's stay. As long as it's cool with Adam."

Adam nodded. "Of course."

"Can I help hold him while you do the IV?" I asked, my voice tentative.

"Sure," he said, his voice kind. "I'm good. Really quick."

Adam was true to his word. The puppy let out one indignant yelp and then he commenced furiously licking my fingers with a very dry tongue. I felt the moment his body relaxed, his little head falling forward into my hand as he started snoring. Rather loudly, actually.

"Now what?" I asked into the silence of the room. The four of us looked at one another.

"Now I go to work. I'll remove general pests from his person, check his blood, double-check him for any signs of fisher cat violence and scan him for a chip. He might be lost, though I suspect it's more likely he's feral and has been fending for himself in the woods."

I looked down at the little sleeping body, and that made me inextricably sad.

"Hey," Adam said, touching my arm, "you two did a great thing bringing him. I'll get him fixed up and we'll find him a good home. I promise."

I nodded, my throat suspiciously tight.

"Good night, sweet prince," Miranda whispered, gently stroking his head.

"Don't jinx him," I cried. Three heads swiveled in my direction. "Hamlet dies at the end," I insisted. "Oh come on, I was a straight A student," I added dryly in the face of Miranda's astonished expression. "I did all of the reading for AP Shakespeare, you know."

Ben cocked his head. "Tragic end aside, he kind of looks like a Hamlet."

I stroked the dog's fur gently. "He does, doesn't he?"

"He's certainly not an Alphonse," Ben added.

"Or an Edmund," I agreed, a secret smile passing between us at the shared joke. "Let's call him Hamlet." I swear, the little dog smiled in his sleep.

"Excellent. Now that that's settled," Miranda said, clapping her hands together, "I'll get some brews. I have Del's blackberry summer ale in the fridge upstairs." She headed for the door, and in a few moments, I heard her tread on the stairs to the apartment where Adam and Miranda were staying for the summer while Dr. Winters the elder and his wife, Bunny, were away in Colorado.

"You're in for a treat," I told Ben. "Our former classmate, Del, is the best brewmaster in a fifty-mile radius. Her beer is the stuff of legend."

"More legendary than Bruce Campbell's chin dimple?" Ben teased.

"You're going to have to let that go," I grumped.

"I'm gonna make nachos," Miranda called down.

I must have looked alarmed, because Adam patted my arm. "I'll be forsaking the brew until after I've taken his blood and removed the ticks. But if either of you wanted to supervise some nacho-making upstairs, I wouldn't say no." He looked at me quickly. "I love your sister beyond reason, but the last time she used the broiler . . ."

"Say no more," I said, pressing my lips together in an attempt not to laugh out of sisterly solidarity, even if she had brought up my unfortunate crush on the Chin. In any event, Miranda was a disaster in the kitchen. And around tools of any kind.

I looked at Ben.

"I'm in," he said. "I have strong opinions on cheese-to-chip ratios."

As we turned to head off in the direction of the stairs, Adam called over his shoulder, "Before you head up, do you mind grabbing my cell charger from my bag? It should be in the waiting area." Adam smiled apologetically. "I don't want to leave the room when there's a patient under anesthesia."

"No problem," I said, walking Ben to the stairs and explaining in a whisper that Adam hadn't been joking about the potential for mayhem when Miranda was in the kitchen. With wide eyes, Ben wasted no time hurrying up the stairs, though I'll admit that I lingered a moment, admiring the view.

I headed for the waiting area and easily located Adam's messenger bag, with a black button that proclaimed him a "theater nerd" with the words "Broadway, NY" below it. Miranda had a matching one on her bag from their now quarterly tradition of going to Broadway and giving me less than twenty-four hours to move my schedule around so I could meet them for dinner.

I carried it back to the exam room, where Adam stood bent over a sleeping Hamlet. "I'll leave this right here for you," I said quietly, hoping not to startle him.

"Can you fish it out for me and plug it in? I don't want to lose my place."

"Your place?" I echoed, a note of distress in my voice. "He's hardly a book, Adam."

"I don't want to have to stop, sterilize and glove up again. I'm in a groove here. C'mon," he cajoled me. "My bag is not the cave of wonders. I don't mind you rooting around my cache of protein bars. There's nothing incriminating in there, if that's what you're worried about."

I exhaled loudly to let him know that just because he wasn't worried about it, that didn't mean I wasn't. What if I accidentally touched a dirty gym sock or something? I stared hard at Adam's back and begrudgingly admitted to myself that since he was diligently attending to Hamlet, I could manage a little social discomfort on my part. "Fine," I muttered.

I opened the bag, and to my utter relief, the contents were sparse and not particularly noteworthy. I spotted the cord and pulled it out, but I pricked my finger on what I suspected was an uncapped pen, and my hand jostled the little interior side pocket of the bag and . . . a velvet jewelry box tumbled out and onto the floor.

"Shit," I yelped, fumbling for the box.

But it was too late, because Adam had turned around to investigate, and his eyes widened when he saw what had landed on the floor between us.

"You said there was nothing incriminating in there," I accused him as I snatched up the box and wiped at it, hoping I hadn't covered it in . . . antibiotic-resistant pet germs? Was that a thing?

"Shit, sorry," Adam said, his brown eyes still wide, "I thought it was in my gym bag."

"You've been carrying this around in a gym bag?" I demanded. "What is wrong with you?"

"I don't know. I keep transferring it from bag to bag, in case the perfect opportunity presents itself. I don't want to be without it."

I stared down at the little blue box in my hand. "So this is—"

"Yeah," he said. "Surprise." He made little jazz hands. "What do you think?"

"I think I'm just going to put this back in here," I said, sliding the ring box back into the interior pocket.

"Portia." Adam fixed me with pleading eyes. "C'mon. What do you think?"

Licking my lips, I considered the box, the vet and my sister. "I think she loves you."

"Do you think it's too soon?"

"I'm hardly an expert here," I said, shaking my head, trying to find the right words. God, Cordelia was so much better at this kind of thing. She'd be hugging Adam right now and giving him pointers on the best way to propose to our sister.

Here I was, freezing up like I always did when the emotional table stakes were high. Screw it—I didn't have to be perfect. I just had to be honest with an old friend. "I think you two spent so long apart mourning your lost connection that when you finally did make the decision to be together, you moved quickly because you were that much more confident in your decision."

"Cryptic, thy name is Portia," Adam sighed, but he smiled a little.

"I don't believe in fate or any of that overhyped drivel, but what I do believe in is how well matched you two are and how lockstep you are as a couple. If you're thinking it's the right time, then she likely is too."

An honest expression of delight slid across Adam's face. "You're right. You're absolutely right."

"I usually am," I said slipping into more smugly comfortable territory.

"You won't say anything?"

"I'm an attorney," I assured him. "Ninety percent of my job occurs in the cone of silence." I gave him a sly smile of my own. "Besides, can you imagine the squealing and the hugging and general emotional fallout if I dropped a bomb like that? Do you think I'd risk that?"

"Good point," Adam said.

"Since I'm apparently in advice-dispensing mode, might I recommend you keep that box somewhere where an innocent bystander, or more likely Miranda, won't stumble upon it?"

"I'll stash it somewhere more subtle," he agreed. "Until I'm ready."

"Excellent. Let's pretend we never had this conversation," I said brightly, clapping my hands together. I headed for the stairs. "For the record, I'm happy for you," I said over my shoulder before disappearing up the stairs to intervene in whatever sheet pan–based atrocities were occurring in the kitchen.

Ben and I ended up staying late into the night, munching on non-incinerated nachos while Miranda regaled us with Mom's mainstage shenanigans. This year Miranda had chosen *The Taming of the Shrew*, only she'd gender-flipped all the roles, and Mom of course had all sorts of opinions about that. Adam occasionally chimed in with funny stories about working with our father in the theater shop. Apparently, even good-natured Adam had his limits, as he admitted he'd had to have an intervention with our father after he had asked to listen to the audio version of *The Hobbit* for the third time that summer. "Heat and hobbits were making for unproductive afternoons," he noted grimly. "I feared one of us was going to pass out while using the table saw."

As I sat there listening to Miranda and Adam, I realized I was hearing their banter through different ears. They were so truly in tune with each other, right down to the way their laughter rose and fell at the same times, that the ring box in Adam's bag seemed like a mere formality in the face of something so settled.

For his part, Ben seemed to be enjoying this, making himself right at home with my sister and Adam by recounting some of his encounters with the locals, which had culminated in Tillie interrogating him about his intentions for the town, deeming him a lost cause and handing him a coupon to Comedy of Eros, the town's only sex shop.

It might have been the way he looked so engaged by Miranda and Adam, or, admittedly, it could have been the intense make-out session in the Tesla earlier, but either way, I found myself wondering for one idle moment if maybe someday, Ben and I might find ourselves in a rhythm like Miranda and Adam had found. I pushed that thought away. Maybe I was suffering some sort of proximity-based emotional high from being around that ring earlier.

Still, when eventually the conversation slowed and a covert yawn erupted into a chain reaction, I was reluctant to leave the cozy den. There was no work email demanding to be answered. No early meeting to get up for. Nothing to do except be here in the moment. And to my surprise, it didn't feel like some kind of indulgence. It felt like the way things should be.

....

The Merry Wines of Windsor

C an we go back to the part where you tackled an alpaca and later rescued a feral dog?" Byron asked, peering down at the chalk-scrawled explanations of the wines he'd selected for his tasting flight.

"He was hardly feral," I insisted, sticking up for the little puppy. "Hamlet was a total gentleman in the Tesla." I didn't admit to my friends that during our rehearsals for dinner theater today, I'd been texting Adam regularly for updates, or that once I'd gotten them, I'd been passing them on to Ben, who'd offered to pay for any of the pup's expenses. But I'd already beat him to that punch, and we settled on splitting them. I'd even sprung for DNA testing, not because it mattered to me what Hamlet was, but because I thought it might entice people to adopt him if he had a fun DNA profile to go with his sparkling personality.

"Hamlet?" Candace raised an eyebrow.

"He can't go nameless while waiting to be adopted."

"Mmm-hmm," Candace noted, but she let it go. "Now can we go back to the part where you took Ben to the Look Out? Did you do the deed in the Tesla?"

"Of course not," I sniffed. "We made out in the Tesla. There's hardly enough room to have sex in there. Comfortably, anyway."

Byron bobbled his wineglass. "I thought we were doing a post-rehearsals classy night out. Sex in a Tesla is hardly classy." He gestured around to the clientele, who were predominantly women and couples. "If I knew we were going to discuss something fun, I'd have pushed for beers at the Tavern."

"Sssh," Candace said, half laughing, half shushing.

Byron was right though. This was a classy establishment. One part adorable wine shop and one part wine cave, the Merry Wines of Windsor had charm to spare, with its freshly swept stone floor and real wax candle lighting and scarred wine barrels, although to be honest it reminded me a little of "The Cask of Amontillado," where somebody ends up buried alive behind a brick wall.

Byron elbowed Candace. "She's not going to tell us whether she actually scored in a Tesla or not. Get on with it."

Candace put on her serious face.

"Oh no, I hate that face," I said. "It's like you're going to tell me that my favorite trainers have been proven to cause knee injuries or quinoa is bad for you."

"Quinoa is bad for your soul," Byron said solemnly. "It chips away at your will to live."

Candace shot Byron an exasperated look. "Can we focus here?" She knocked back the rest of her viognier and folded her hands on the table. "We have an emerging development, no pun intended, we wanted to talk to you about. As in, I found out a few hours ago."

"You found out about an emerging development I'd want to know about and you waited until after rehearsal to tell me?" I demanded.

"You were in such a groove tonight." Candace winced, her expression a little sheepish. "I didn't want to lose that momentum."

"She thought we should get some wine into you first," Byron said hurriedly. "For the good of everybody. Me. Candace. Innocent bystanders."

I smacked him. "I do not have poor impulse control."

He glanced pointedly at his arm as he rubbed it. To Candace he said, "Just get it over with."

"It's Will's Island," Candace said. "Will's Island is going up for sale."

I choked on my chilled pinot noir. Recovering, I said, "I thought Will's Island was owned by the town. Where they hold their biggest moneymaker every year?"

"I think you mean 'where the town holds its annual cherished tradition of staging the Bard in the round'?" Byron helpfully supplied.

"How do you find this out?" I demanded.

"One of the Realtors in town had a bit too much merlot and told my mom about it at their Rotary Club lunch today. So I texted Candace, and we thought you'd want to know as soon as possible."

"Byron didn't want to tell you himself," Candace said, rolling her eyes.

"But only because you're scary, and I respect that about you," Byron protested.

"Shit," I breathed. "How does the town not own the island? Wait, who owns it, then?"

"Until recently, William Douglas."

"The guy who owned Peaseblossom's?" I asked.

"You mean the big-deal Broadway producer who retired here and invested heavily in the theater program? He also happened to be the mini-golf guy," Byron deadpanned.

"Huh. I thought Will's Island was named after the Bard."

"Well, William always maintained he was happy to share the island with the immortal Bard, so you're half-right," Candace said.

"People in this town are so damn weird about Shakespeare," I muttered under my breath.

"When William Douglas passed away this spring in his sleep at age eighty-six, he left all his worldly possessions to his sole living relative, a nephew," Byron continued.

"Oh, it's Archie," I groaned.

Byron frowned at me. "You know Archie?"

"Yep, I ran into him a few weeks ago, actually. Dropping off flyers for the festival. Stared at my breasts the entire time while pointing out that running the place was a lot of work. Kind of a creep."

"A full-blown creep, if you ask me," Byron added. "I thought he was just looking to sell Peaseblossom's. But maybe he hadn't gotten around to getting an appraisal or something for Will's. Shit."

"What are we going to do?" Candace asked. "If we know about it, I'm sure Ben knows about it, or soon will. That's probably going to be a hot piece of property. If not Ben, I mean, why not some other developer?"

I nodded slowly. "We have to buy Will's Island."

"Do you have two point four million lying around? Because that's what he wants for it," Byron said. "Allegedly. According to my sort of tipsy mother."

"Two point four for an undeveloped hill of rocks and crabgrass?" I scoffed. "I mean, I have investments and savings. But not that kind of flush. Could the town swing it?"

Byron shook his head. "I'm on the town finance board. We don't have that kind of cash lying around that isn't earmarked for something else."

"Shit," I muttered.

"What if the merchant association went in on it with the town?" Candace asked slowly.

"Now there's an idea," I said thoughtfully. "Maybe the association could take a small percentage of the funds raised from the festival each year and the town could pay back the investment until it's bought out the association. Or something like that."

"It could work," Byron said. "Depending on what the association can raise. But I'm thinking we should move quickly. See if we can get it off the market fast."

"Agreed. What's the best way to do that?" I pressed.

"We call a clandestine meeting of the merchant association," Candace said, matter-of-factly. "Leave that part to me. Then you two can pitch the idea."

"Portia, are you sure you're on board with this?" Byron asked, exchanging a glance with Candace.

"Why wouldn't I be?"

Candace stared at me. "If Ben's interested in Will's, this could put the two of you in a very awkward position."

"A more awkward position than, say, making out in a Tesla," Byron added.

We both turned twin glares on him.

"Oh come on, it was right there," he complained. "I'm not a saint."

"Ben doesn't seem the type to overpay for something. I'm no appraiser, but I think what Archie is asking for has to be on the high side. But then again, the island might be a waterfront play too good to pass up. Even if it is basically a hill of rocks."

I swallowed hard, thinking about making out with Ben in the Tesla and sitting next to him in the den last night, our knees bumping up against each other. How I'd wanted to take him up on his invitation to join him for some coffee back at his place, but how I'd begged off because I had hit a wall of fatigue so hard I wasn't sure even the almighty bean would keep me awake. But I'd countered admirably, I thought. Now we had another date—I could call it a date—tomorrow night. Our competitive natures had won out over our general disgust for bowling shoes, and so we were meeting up at the Pinsmen to test our mettle on the lanes. And then we'd go back to his place.

I didn't want it getting complicated when things were just getting good. On the other hand, my family would freak out, along with the rest of the town, if something happened to Will's Island and their beloved mainstages. "Why don't we cross that bridge when we have to, if we have to?" I said. "For now, count me in."

"Good, because I don't have the stones to do this myself," Byron said. "She does," he added, nodding to Candace, "but I don't."

This latest development—no pun intended—had the potential to complicate things, but I stopped myself, trying to think positively. Kim had counseled me on not borrowing trouble when there wasn't any. There was still a possibility here that I was worrying about nothing. I swirled the wine in my glass, staring down into its red-purple contents, looking for answers and coming up empty.

....

The Two Noble Pinsmen

I eyed the bowling shoes doubtfully, mentally calculating the likelihood of foot fungus being able to penetrate my socks. I didn't like my odds.

"Having second thoughts?" Ben, sporting a T-shirt and jeans, asked, his gray eyes wide and guileless.

"About beating you a second time? Of course not." I jammed my feet into the shoes and laced them up before I could stop and think about it too hard.

"I'm better at bowling than mini-golf," Ben warned.

I gave him a cool smile. "What a coincidence. Me too."

He groaned. "I'm going to get my ass handed to me a second time, huh?"

"Looking that way."

"How's the patient doing this afternoon?"

I swiveled my phone around to show him the latest video of Hamlet from a few hours ago, this one shot by Miranda. He turned out to be a black dog under all that mud and was frolicking in the back of The Winters' Tail with Puck. Puck had apparently taken it upon himself to show Hamlet how to dog while Adam's pig, Lucille, looked on from the porch.

"Is that a pig?" Ben asked.

"Oh, you think he stopped at dogs? That's cute. No, Adam rescued Lucille from a couple of college kids keeping her in a dorm room."

Ben's eyes widened. "That couldn't have been hygienic."

I shuddered. "No, it could not."

"Hamlet looks great though. Any word on the DNA yet?"

"Not yet. Whatever breed he turns out to be, I'm sure Adam and Miranda will find him a good home," I said, but my throat sort of tightened when I thought about that. But what could I do? It would hardly be fair to keep a puppy in my new condo. He'd be bored all day. Hamlet deserved someone who could take him for long walks, sleep in late with him on the weekends and spoil him rotten. He needed a Miranda. Not a Portia.

Shuffling that singularly depressing thought along, another random thought took its place. "Remember when I told you I stole my sister's prom date in my quest to win everything ever in high school? That was Adam. We used to date, but we're just friends now."

Ben nodded. "Thanks for telling me." He frowned. "You and Adam? I'm having trouble picturing that."

"We were a complete mismatch."

"He and Miranda seem well-suited for each other," he settled on. "You seem like you might need someone who understands your murderous feelings toward Hooper. Somebody who excels in the sports of mini-golf and bowling." Then, as if remembering his mini-golf loss to me, he added, "Or at the very least doesn't embarrass themself."

"I'd probably settle for someone well versed in the management of escaped farm animals," I said, trying to suppress a smile.

Ben leaned over and brushed a lingering kiss across my lips.

"You should know if I win," he whispered in my ear as he pulled away, "I'm getting a giant burger, wings and some more of that Del miracle beer. I don't want to throw your game off, but I do have a full gallon of mint chip ice cream back at my place to sweeten the deal."

"How could a girl say no to all that?" I said, my eyes wide. "But first, we bowl."

"We bowl."

Lucky for Ben, he turned out to be a much better bowler than he was a mini-golfer. Unlucky for Ben, I was a much better bowler than a mini-golfer. I wasn't sure where that had come from, other than to note that bowling had a rhythm and windup that reminded me of my tennis serve. And I'd been a decent tennis player through high school. Whatever it was, I beat him soundly in two strings, notching several strikes and spares to add insult to injury.

Despite his defeat, Ben still ordered a giant burger and a mess of wings and asked Del, who took our order, to bring him whatever beer she recommended that would go with the shrimp and pineapple skewers I'd ordered.

"Well, I don't know about the shrimp pairing," she deadpanned, "but I do have something I'm calling True Apothecary. It might help with that burn my girl here laid on you on the lanes."

"I would take umbrage to that," Ben said mildly, "but you make an excellent point and even better beer. I'll take whatever you give me."

She returned a few minutes later, depositing two beers that were amber-orange and smelled of citrus. "Give it a whirl. Be back in a bit with your food."

Ben and I clinked our beers and sipped experimentally.

"Oh shit," he said. "That is smooth. What is that?"

"Mandarin," I guessed. "Wait, no, it's scorched earth. I'll swear to it."

Ben's mouth quirked up at the corner. "Not ever going to let me live that down, huh?"

"If it ever stops being funny, I'll stop," I promised. "Until then, you said it."

"In the pursuit of trying to get a stunningly beautiful, incredibly intimidating woman to speak to me in a bar."

"Oh please, don't pretend you don't have great game."

"Oh, I have topflight game," he assured me. "But I could tell straight off you were not going to be impressed with even topflight game. I had to be memorable. Did it work?"

"We're here, aren't we?" I said with a smile. Not for the first time, I wondered at what exact moment I had decided I cared for Ben. Had it been our dog rescue? No, earlier than that. Even before the way we'd laughed together covered in mud and crap after the petting zoo incident. That kiss outside the café? Dinner at Merchant? No, I thought, with conviction. It was when we'd first squared off at the town hall. I'd felt challenged by an equal. By someone who wasn't going to let me steamroll him. "Memorable for sure," I told him, taking another pull of the beer. "But also mysterious. I still feel like I know so little about you."

Ben sat forward. "What do you want to know?"

I steepled my fingers. "When we had dinner at Merchant, you gave me the highly sanitized version of how you ended up in construction. I want the real one. If you're willing," I added, thinking of how careful he'd been with me that night at the Look Out.

Ben's friendly expression dimmed. "Oh, that's a heavy one. Like your Tesla confession." He pointed to the caricature of the Bard in a bowling shirt above our table. "Sure he's ready for it?"

I shook my head. "You don't have to, if you don't want to."

"No, I want to," Ben said. "I don't tell a lot of people this story. And by that I mean, I've told Sam. That's it."

"Okay," I said, nodding.

"You have to promise you're not going to go all slack-jawed pity on me."

"Deal," I said, schooling my face into a polite mask.

"Okay, not that face. That's the listening-to-clients-talk-crazy face."

"This is my listening face," I insisted.

"When you asked me how I got into construction, I didn't lie to you. I just left a bunch of stuff out."

Del dropped Ben's heart attack on a bun—her words—and my arugula salad—slight eye roll from Del—on our table and, sensing something had shifted in the mood between us, promptly strode off.

"My parents were alcoholics," Ben said, his eyes on his plate. "Lots of fighting and lost jobs when I was a kid. I learned to make myself small and quiet, that kind of thing. My father took off when I was twelve after an epic bender, and my mother, who was usually the better of the two at holding it together, started in on oxy. And things went down from there over the next couple of years. My life before that wasn't a Hallmark card, but at least we'd consistently had a roof over our heads and the utilities were paid.

"On half-day Wednesdays from school, she would send me down to a construction site in Southie with most of our grocery money in a plastic bag to see Sully. He would swap me the plastic bag for a paper one I never opened, even though I knew what had to be in there. Sully wasn't a bad guy for a drug dealer. Sometimes, he'd even slip me a sandwich or a Coke. I think he knew that when I didn't get free lunch at school, I didn't eat. Like I said, not a bad guy, all things considered.

"One Wednesday though, when I showed up, instead of Sully, it was the owner, Danny, who told me he'd figured out what Sully was up to and let him go. Danny bought me a sub and asked me a lot of questions about the drugs, and I think he quickly figured out I wasn't the one using them or dealing them. He asked me if I had a place to go. I had found us Section 8 housing that even my mother couldn't get us bounced out of, so we were covered there. Danny wanted to know if I attended school, I told him I was a straight A student. Then he offered me a job and an opportunity to learn a trade."

"At fifteen?" I frowned.

"It was an after-school thing, a couple of hours each day. I looked forward to it—it kept me out of our bug-infested apartment and away from my mother, who was spiraling out of control by that point. That job helped me earn money, which Danny kept for me in a savings account that only I had access to."

"He set up a custodial account for you?" I asked.

Ben shrugged. "He set up an account he was sure my mother couldn't touch. It was in his name, but I was the only person who made withdrawals from it. I used it to buy food, pay the heating bill, splurge on the occasional luxury item like toothpaste or sneakers without holes in them. That kind of thing."

He sucked in a breath. "When I was sixteen, I came home after school one day to find that my mother had died of an overdose. Danny offered me a place to live. He was a widower who'd lost his wife to cancer early in his marriage. Never remarried, never had any kids, just the business. If you could picture that tough-talking, R-dropping guy from Southie who ate the same Dunkin's cruller every day of his life and worshipped at the altars of Jim Rice and Carl Yastrzemski, that was Danny."

"He sounds wonderful."

"The best," Ben said, the admiration in his voice warring with a tougher emotion that lay beneath. "I'm sure you already know what a corrupt scene construction is, particularly in Boston. But Danny always played fair and followed the rules. He was one of those guys willing to give you the benefit of the doubt or the shirt off his back. A shit businessman, but I helped him with the books. But as far as actual construction went, well, one would have been lucky to live or work in anything built by Danny Dane."

"Danny Dane," I repeated. Then cocked my head at him and said slowly, "You took his name."

He nodded proudly. "I legally changed it when I was eighteen. Right as I left for Babson, which he covered—everything that my scholarships didn't. Benji Coombs was a poor kid from the projects whose parents each ran out on him in different ways. But Benjamin Dane had a dad who loved him, even if he was late to the game."

Unexpected tears welled in my eyes.

"Hey, hey, you promised," Ben said gently, covering my hand with his.

"It's the hot sauce," I protested weakly.

"You haven't even touched the wings."

"They're potent," I insisted.

"It's okay," he said. "I'm not sure I want to tell you the next part though."

I wiped discreetly at my eyes. "I can take it."

"You sure?" he asked with a smile that was profoundly sad, and even though I knew where the ending of this story was going, it was still like someone had kicked me in the stomach.

"Oh no," I said.

Ben nodded gently. "I worked construction all through my time at Babson, undergrad and B-school, learning the family business, such that it was. I had these big plans for Danny and myself after graduation. We'd agreed that I should take over the business so he could retire, go fishing in Ipswich, visit some old buddies of his in Key West and eat some mahi-mahi. I think he would have done all of those things and I would've helped him, except that a week or so after I graduated B-school, Danny had a massive heart attack in his sleep. Doctors said it was quick. I'm sure if he was here now, he'd tell you it was the way he wanted to go. But I really miss him."

I nodded, my voice too thick to say anything.

"I had some great years with Danny, and I don't regret any of it," he said. "But when I tell you that work is my whole life . . . Work is my whole life, Portia. I don't have a family. I have work. And I have Sam. That's what got me through losing Danny. But please don't ruin this incredible Thomas Crown persona I've cultivated."

"McQueen or Brosnan?" I asked, trying hard not to sniffle.

"I do love the King of Cool, but Brosnan was a better Crown. I'll fight the room on that one."

"I don't think either incarnation listened to Christmas carols year-round when stressed."

"No?"

"No, but I bet Danny was a fan of them."

Our eyes met.

"Danny loved Christmas. The day after Thanksgiving we'd go out on the lawn. In Southie all the lawns are about this big," he said, measuring out something roughly the size of a pizza box with his hands. "We would first risk death by electrocution as we covered every square inch of grass with light-up elves, carolers and snowmen that tripped the circuit breakers every few days. Then we'd double down, climbing up the world's most rickety ladder to the roof, where we'd assemble a tiny sleigh with nine little reindeer and old Saint Nick himself, adding a lovely dash of potential death by falling to the list of inadvisable holiday activities. Every single night in December, Danny would play Christmas carols—Bing, Nat, Frank, Ella, Dean and the entire soundtrack to *A Charlie Brown Christmas*."

I sank back in the booth. "And when you were with Danny, you were safe."

He nodded. "The best years of my life after some pretty rough ones." Ben looked up at me from beneath his lashes. "Sometimes when I'm listening to carols, I can hear him humming along. He had a terrible falsetto, especially during the Jackson Five's version of 'Santa Claus Is Coming to Town.'"

I reached for his hand, not saying anything.

"That old life of mine is light-years away. But I'm always going to miss Danny, and I'm proud of all I've accomplished." He bit into his burger. "Who knows what the future may bring. Maybe I'll adopt Hamlet."

"Oh, then I'll definitely look you up when we're both back in Boston," I joked.

"You should just sign the papers now and make him a Barnes," Ben said, his eyes twinkling.

"Then what excuse would I have to come see you?" I said, feeling a little less bold than my words suggested.

"You need an excuse to come see me?"

"Well, I suspect that after your adventures here and my new duties in Boston . . ." I trailed off. "You know how it is."

"I'm definitely adopting Hamlet, so you'll have to make time for me."

"That's not a good reason to adopt Hamlet," I sputtered, laughing into my beer.

"Portia, let's leave it at: you're the kind of woman a guy makes time for."

And you're the kind of guy a woman makes time for, I wanted to say back. But right at that moment, my phone buzzed. "Excuse me," I said.

I glanced down at my phone. I had a text from Candace. 8 tonight at the Shoe.

"Shit," I muttered. I loved Candace, but did she have to rally the troops so quickly? My heart sank. Why did it have to be when I was sitting here with Ben and he was finally opening up to me?

Ben frowned. "You okay? Oh no, is it Hamlet?" When I shook my head, he asked, "Is it your Mom?"

I looked up into Ben's gray eyes and hated myself for taking the out he'd just offered me up on a platter, for being so disingenuous about what I was going to do. Years of excuses and platitudes at Francis-Pearl had made me an effortless liar. Even still though. After all of what Ben had just told me about his life. Could I actually do this?

Sadly, I found I could. Because I too had people I loved, and the reptilian part of my brain slithered into compartmentalization mode. I didn't *technically* owe Ben an explanation. I represented the merchant association, and this was *technically* confidential information I wasn't authorized to be sharing. "She's having a rough time tonight and wanted to know if I could pick up a few things for her. My dad's night vision isn't what it used to be." Even as the words uncoiled and slipped out, I held fast against my rising regret. *I wasn't technically in the wrong here.*

But it wasn't like I was in the right here either.

"I get it. Do you want some company? My night vision is significantly better than my lane vision, I promise."

Lizard brain or not, it hurt to see Ben's decidedly earnest face and hear his matching offer.

"I appreciate it," I forced myself to say, "but I think that might be weird for her. I'll pick up what she needs at the pharmacy and settle in for a long evening of losing at Rummikub."

"So you do lose at something?" he said, his eyes sparkling.

"Only to my mother," I assured him. "Don't get your hopes up."

He stood. "Can I walk you to your car?"

I nodded, swallowing hard.

"Let me settle up our tab first," he said. "Del strikes me as the kind of woman you don't walk out on."

"We'll split," I said, but then we reached the bar and, much to my horror, Del waved me off. "On the house," she said. "Cordy said you know stuff about trademarks?"

"Call me tomorrow," I told her. "I'll walk you through it."

Ben turned to me, waggling his eyebrows in a decidedly "I told you so" manner. Once we'd cleared the door he said, "I can see why you can't come back here too often. You're the town's lawyer."

"Don't let Byron Greene hear you say that." The words were out of my mouth before I could stop and wonder what the hell I was thinking.

"Who?"

"Another old classmate of mine. He's the guy you go to for real estate and trusts and estates around here," I said weakly, not adding that he was also the guy to go to when you needed a legal partner for clandestine matters. Like thwarting would-be developers.

Outside, Ben pulled me in for a kiss and I curled against him, his arms going around me. It was so cozy and also—shit, why did I need to leave, again? Oh right. Helping the town avoid economic disaster and a potential blow to its history and way of life.

I pulled away from the kiss far too soon and pressed my forehead to Ben's. He kissed the top of my nose, and it was all I could do not to blurt out everything right there. The lie. The meeting. The plan to swipe Will's Island out from under him or any development company that might want it.

I grabbed Ben and leaned into him, pressing against him and kissing him like it was the last time, because as much as I wanted to believe otherwise, I was starting to believe it would be the last time we were on the same side of things.

....

The Taming of the Shoe

When looking for a clandestine location to plan some skulduggery, you couldn't go wrong with Tillie's place. There were always enough wine and comfy chairs to go around and the whole place smelled like very expensive leather.

I watched as all the usual suspects filtered in: Dan and Aaron, Stan Hobbs, Kitty McMahon, Marty Cabot, Cat Jackson and my parents, as well as some new faces I didn't recognize. "When I said to call a meeting," I whispered to Candace, "I didn't think you'd schedule it so damn fast."

"Did you send out a 'Merchants, assemble' call?" Byron asked.

We stared at him blankly.

"You know, at some point you both are going to need to watch a Marvel movie. You can't keep putting it off forever," he grumbled.

Ignoring that nugget of cinematic wisdom, I turned back to Candace. "I'm just saying a little heads-up next time would have been nice instead of a twenty-eight-minute warning."

"Next time I'll shoot for forty," she said dryly.

"What's the problem anyway? Did you have a hot date or something?" Byron teased.

Answering that question was a no-win situation, so I ignored him, trying not to focus on the night's events with Ben. Ben, who'd gotten authentic and vulnerable with me. And to whom I had lied in favor of a secret town meeting that might impact his business if he was thinking of throwing his hat in the ring. I was a terrible human being. I could only hope that this wouldn't blow up in my face and I'd find a way to make it up to Ben somehow. But for now, I schooled my face into the picture of calm, because in my experience, when you bring a bunch of people together for a potentially heated discussion, a game face was key. Like knowing where the bathroom and exits were.

As more people filed into the shop and wineglasses were handed out like those foil blankets they give to people who've just finished a marathon, I elbowed Byron. "You should kick things off."

"Why me?" he asked. "You're the festival lawyer."

"This isn't a festival matter. You're their local lawyer. Earn your keep, Greene."

Byron rolled his eyes. "Damn you, Portia, for playing on my town pride like that."

Candace snickered but covered it with her hand as Byron strode off to find Tillie. A few minutes later, Tillie let out a shrill whistle that stunned the room into silence.

"That's one way to do it," I murmured.

"Byron Greene would like to say a few words," she announced.

"Well, it certainly looks like he's going to his own funeral," Candace stage-whispered.

I tried and failed not to laugh at that. Byron glared in our direction, but otherwise put his own game face on.

"Will's Island, previously thought to be owned by the town, was actually owned by William Douglas." There were some murmurs of sympathy in the small crowd. William Douglas seemed to have been a well-loved man around town. "Upon William's passing, the property passed to his nephew, one Archibald 'Archie' Douglas. Who is kind of an ass."

I cleared my throat, staring at Byron, who shrugged and said, "Well, he is. Anyway, I have it on good authority—i.e., the

Bard's Rest Rotary Club gossip circuit—that Archie just had the property appraised. He'll be asking for at least two point four million."

Dan's face twisted into somewhere between "accidentally licked a persimmon" and "received undesirable correspondence from the IRS." Alice's brows knit together. Tillie dropped the F-bomb. And my mother, no doubt pulling on her French heritage, looked non-plussed, even as my father looked like he might pass out beside her.

Byron glanced at me, and in a moment of attorney solidarity, I stepped into the line of fire. "The good news is, because Byron discovered this so early, we likely have the jump on any other prospective buyers." I wasn't sure if that was actually true or not, but I had to believe we were the only clandestine meeting going on in town right now. At least, I hoped we were the only clandestine meeting in town right now. "Now the question becomes what can we do about it?"

"Can the town afford it?" Stan Hobbs, the owner of Measure for Measure Hardware, asked hopefully.

Byron shook his head. "As many of you know because you sit on the finance board with me, the town cannot afford an unearmarked, out-of-budget-cycle purchase like this. But if anybody has two point four lying around and thinks it's a good time to invest in real estate, now would be the time to step forward," Byron added, earning him a few nervous laughs.

"Or," I added, "the association could pool its resources along with potential individual contributions. We could work out an arrangement with the town whereby the town could buy back the property from the association over a two- to three-year period." I looked at Byron for confirmation that might work, and he gave a small nod.

"We'd need to talk amongst ourselves," Aaron said, "but we could probably put together some sort of offer."

"This is not part of my sales pitch," Byron said, his tone apologetic, "but if we're going to do something, we're going to have to do something fast. There's already one developer in town who we know from some selfless and diligent reconnaissance on the part of one of our own"—he paused to let Candace's snort abate—"has been scouting opportunities here in Bard's, so let's not leave the door open too long, yeah?" He looked around. "Talk amongst yourselves. Dan, you're in charge of math."

Dan preened.

"Not bad," I told Byron as he joined Candace and me.

"Not bad at all," Candace agreed, looking at Byron with admiration in her eyes.

We joined the larger group as people ran numbers on their phones and rattled things off to my father, who was furiously scribbling down notes as Tillie drained several wine bottles into people's glasses.

I sat quietly listening as the merchant association talked themselves in and out of canceling vacations, putting off renovations and dental work they'd been meaning to get around to and cutting off their grandchildren for a while. Nobody had asked me if I wanted to contribute, which was sort of a relief on one hand, but also a little surprising. I had socked away savings and invested well, but maybe people thought I didn't like Bard's enough to contribute. Even Candace, Byron and Cat Jackson, the proprietor of the sex shop and star of Miranda's *Twelfth Night* production last summer, the younger members of the association by a decade or so, were talking about putting up impressive contributions.

The conversation eventually wound down, and people refilled their glasses as Dan did math. "Two point five million, give or take a couple of hundred," he said, his face flushed.

"Just over ask," Dan noted.

"But is it enough of an ask for Archie to take without wanting to shop it around?" Alice wondered.

"It's not like we can offer more than that," Tillie responded glumly.

While they'd been deliberating, my mind had been going through different cost-structure scenarios. "We could sweeten the deal and add a profit-sharing component," I said, "if the town is up for it. We could offer the two point five million with a small percentage of the festival proceeds going to Archie for the next three years or so. I'm not sure how the town board approves something like that, but since more than half of that board is in this room, you can figure it out and then make it all official."

There was even more conferring, but eventually we settled on a two-point-five-million-dollar cash offer with an opportunity for Archie to earn an additional two hundred fifty thousand dollars over the next four years—pending town board approval, of course. Which I was assured we'd have by midmorning tomorrow. Plenty of time before Byron and I had to take the offer to Archie.

"What do you think?" Candace whispered as the town meeting broke up.

"I think it's worth a shot," I said.

As I slipped into my car, I saw I had two texts from Ben. The first, How's your Mom? and the second, You need anything? I'm around if you need help. Both of them were like little Shakespearean daggers to the heart, reminding me that I was a terrible person. I ignored them, knowing that soon enough, Ben would know it too.

"ICEMAN, WE'RE A GO," Byron said as I met him in the driveway. "We have all the approvals we need."

"Did you just make a *Top Gun* reference?"

"Yeah, of course. You're Iceman and I'm Maverick and—"

"We are not the kind of friends who make *Top Gun* references."

"I really need some more guy friends," Byron muttered.

"You really do," I agreed.

"Ready to do this?"

I nodded mutely. After I'd returned home last night, I'd texted Ben to let him know everything was fine. He hadn't texted back, making me wonder if somehow he'd gotten wind of the impromptu town meeting, my involvement or both. I tried to reassure myself that I was being paranoid, but that sour taste of bile that slicked down the back of my throat said otherwise. Sliding into the front seat of Byron's car, I debated whether I should text Ben again to test the waters, but decided against it. Once this business with Archie was done, I needed to face Ben in person.

For his part, Archie was in high spirits for our meeting, and by that I mean he'd slicked his hair back and put on something that could pass as a polo shirt. I mean, it was a baffling pink shirt patterned with red macaws and purple palm trees. But it had a collar. He'd also acquired an attorney, a balding man in his late fifties who introduced himself as Ted Stinson and remarked to Byron that it had been real smart of him to bring along his assistant. I was welcome to take all the notes I wanted as long as I remained quiet, he'd added magnanimously. Better yet, when Byron explained that I was an attorney, Ted Stinson smiled broadly and said I could still take all the notes I wanted.

What I wanted to do was remove Ted's pea-sized brain through his nose with a fishhook and chuck it at Archie for funsies. But instead, I returned his insincere smile with an acidic one of my own.

Byron cleared his throat, looking at Ted as if he were a lump of graying sirloin on rush sale, and forged ahead. "Archie, we're here to make an offer on behalf of the merchant association to purchase Will's Island."

"You don't have to take the offer," Ted added.

Byron stared at Archie's lawyer for a long moment before slowly saying, "That's right, Archie. I'm not sure that needed saying, but yes, you can turn it down. Because that's what an offer is. Please note though that we are going to need you to sign a confidentiality agreement before we can proceed."

"I object," Ted said.

"It's not a courtroom," I said dryly.

"I object on the grounds that I told my client we weren't going to be signing anything today."

"Mr. Stinson," I said in my "talking to first-year associates on the verge of a nervous breakdown" voice. "This is a one-page confidentiality agreement that states neither party will disclose the existence of, or any details concerning, the offer we're about to make." I handed over the file with the agreement in it. "Now, if you'd like us to wait outside while you discuss with your client, we'd be happy to oblige. But we're not going to talk shop until you sign it."

Forty-three minutes. It took forty-three minutes for Archie and Ted to read our three-paragraph confidentiality agreement, and even then Ted indicated that his client signed under great personal duress, which I ignored because I'm pretty sure Ted didn't know what the word *duress* meant and I couldn't envision a scenario where any judge, jury or arbiter would think being asked to sign a three-paragraph agreement that bound both parties to be particularly duress inducing.

That settled, I launched into my explanation of the mechanics. "The offer is two point five million up front with the ability to earn an additional two hundred fifty thousand dollars over the next four years." I explained the profit-sharing piece since I was the deal lawyer. And because Byron claimed in the car he was too pretty to do math.

"I don't know," Archie said, a greedy gleam in his eyes. "I'm happy to consider it, but I'm a little disappointed it's not higher."

Years of negotiations kept me from issuing a pithy retort that involved an island that amounted to a pile of rocks. Instead, I tried another tactic I'd learned: flattery. "I can see what a discerning businessman you are. Of course you can understand why we didn't put our best and final on the offer right away." Archie and Ted glanced at each other, smirking for all they were worth.

"You drive a hard bargain, Mr. Douglas, but we'd be willing to go up to two point eight with the two-hundred-fifty-thousand-dollar kicker to put you up over three million."

Years of negotiations apparently kept Byron's eyes from bugging out. But it was a near thing. "Anyway, we'll leave the paperwork with you and your counsel. Talk it over with your lawyer and let us know," Byron said.

"The offer is good for twenty-four hours," I added. "You'll see that noted in the offer letter. In bold," I added for the benefit of Ted Stinson. I turned to Archie. "It's a smart play, and you're a smart man, Archie," I said without even the hint of a smirk. Seriously, where was Candace when I was actually delivering my best acting performance to date? "Take the deal."

When we cleared the parking lot and were sure we were out of sight, Byron said, "I know I said I'm too pretty to do math, but where did that extra three hundred thousand come from?"

"An anonymous investor."

"An anonymous investor who is you?" he demanded.

I leveled him with my gaze. "If you tell anyone, I'll deny it."

Byron grinned. "I knew you were a marshmallow on the inside. On the outside you're like Ben Grimm from the Fantastic Four, all hardened like—"

"You do realize when you make any kind of comic book or superhero movie reference, I tune you out and speculate how it is you passed the bar exam?" I slipped my phone out of my bag. No text messages. "I guess it's a waiting game now." Though I wasn't sure if I was strictly referring to Archie, Ben or some combination of the two.

"I'm great at the waiting game," Byron assured me. "I'll go to the gym."

"You'll go to the gym for the next twenty-three hours of your life?"

"It won't take that long for him to get back. You'll see. We'll be signing this deal by lunchtime."

Titania's Basement

The waiting is killing me," Byron grumped later that night as he flopped down on the red leather chaise that Candace was using for one of the scenes in the therapist's office. Byron was still in his Benedick costume, a houndstooth blazer with suede elbow patches, and I was still in mine, a charcoal sheath dress from my own collection, because in Candace's retelling, my character was an attorney. That, and Candace trusted me to dress myself.

"What happened to your twenty-three-hour gym bender?" I teased.

"I was certain he'd have called by now."

"Well, the offer letter was two pages—maybe they're still reviewing it," I snarked. I didn't tell Byron that I hadn't had much of a productive day either. Taking a play from his playbook, I'd gone for a run, showered and quizzed myself on my lines for rehearsal. I definitely did not check my phone frequently to see if Ben had texted. The feeling that he knew something now felt more like a certainty than ever. And still, I didn't text him. Not until this mess was over and I could explain my actions in person.

"I was total crap tonight," Byron wailed. "I kept dropping lines during rehearsal and Cat kept laying into me."

"Isn't that kind of her role as Beatrice?"

"Well yeah," he agreed, "but more so."

"Is it weird to be acting opposite against Cat?" I asked. "After last summer?"

"Not really," Byron said. "To be honest, what we had was stage chemistry. When the play was over, we didn't work. We attempted one spectacularly bad date before agreeing we were better off as friends and colleagues in the same small-town ecosystem who do not see each other's sex faces anymore."

"I definitely didn't need that level of detail."

"You asked." He swiveled his head in my direction. "Wait, why did you ask? You never talk about feelings if you can help it."

"Why does everyone always say that?"

"Because you hate feelings."

"I really do," I said, nodding slowly. "I feel so seen. It's like you're a real therapist."

Byron snorted. "Uh-huh, out with it."

"For what it's worth, I could get behind you and Candace." I frowned. "In a completely platonic manner."

Byron barked out a surprised laugh. But after a few moments, it was replaced by something more uncertain. "I'd be lying if I said I hadn't thought about it. Candace is the total package: smart, creative, caring. And in a zombie apocalypse scenario, she'd be the last one standing atop a pile of rotting undead carcasses."

Looking down at his hands, he added, "I know she's your worldwide bestie and all, I lay no claim to that, but she's my best friend in Bard's. I share more meals and texts with her than all of my family and friends combined. I'm afraid of blowing that up for a chance at something that may or may not pan out in the long run."

I blew out a long breath. "I hear you."

"You're not going to chastise me for being a total coward?"

"No."

"Or give me a pep talk about why I should go for it? 'Tis better to have loved and lost and all."

"Again, no."

"Why?"

"Because I think the risk-reward analysis is spot-on. I see the way you look at Candace and she looks at you. But I also see that effortless camaraderie you two have in a town full of weirdos. I wouldn't want to give that up either without some careful consideration."

Byron sighed heavily. "I thought you were going to tell me to go for it."

"Is that what you want me to tell you?" I countered.

He looked thoughtful. "I suppose not." Scavenging for his phone, he checked it again, and I could tell from the downward turn of his mouth that there were still no developments. "In what I'm sure is equally depressing news, do you want to tell me what's going on with Ben?"

"It's complicated. I'm not sure where we're going to be after this Will's Island thing. It's going to come out that I was involved. I think it will depend on whether he was considering making a run at it."

"I feel like healthy relationships should not rise or fall based on the potential purchase of property," he said.

"I agree. I think that's part of the problem. If something tangential to your relationship can have that big of a disruption to it, it makes you question the foundation of that relationship."

"That's one way of looking at it. But the Portia Barnes I know would look at something like this as an opportunity."

"An opportunity?" I echoed.

"Even when we were kids, it didn't matter if it was Mock UN or hawking Pop Warner swag, you'd think through every angle to see if there was a better play to be had. Maybe you should talk to Ben instead of assuming it's dead in the water," Byron said.

"And maybe you should talk to your lady love," I fired back.

We were saved further mutual interrogation by the sound of heels on stairs. Candace swept into the room, her blond hair a whipping corona around her. "Sorry," she cried. "Total disaster in the kitchen. Any word from Archie yet?"

"Not yet," I said.

"Shall we go to the Tavern, then? I could use a change of scenery."

I shook my head. "You two go. I committed to dinner with my parents. I was hoping to have good news on the Archie front." I turned to Byron. "Call me if you hear anything?"

"Will do." He stood up, giving a bow to Candace. "My lady."

"Byron, go change out of your costume. I don't want to have to explain to Tillie how you got wing sauce on it."

"But I look so professorial," he protested. "I am rocking this blazer." He looked at me for help, but I just shook my head, laughing.

Byron shrugged out of his jacket and disappeared backstage.

"You should have seen him earlier with Archie," I said to Candace. "He's a great attorney."

"He's great at a lot of things," Candace said, her gaze uncharacteristically unfocused.

I stood. "I bet he'd be surprisingly good at other things too, given the chance." I tossed her a meaningful look. "Anyway, I'm off to field a million island-based questions that I don't have answers to yet."

I was wrong though. I had my answers about halfway through my drive home.

Byron's text was to the point. Call me. Archie turned down our offer. He's accepted an all-cash offer for three million from Dane Development.

Without thinking, I changed course to Falstaff's Folly.

THERE WAS SHAKESPEAREAN tacky. And then there was Falstaff's Folly, an over-the-top Tudor, decked out in bright white paint and dark wood lattice and a hand-carved sign above the door that proclaimed the place "Falstaff's Folly." Because, you know, houses needed names.

The yard was littered with a stone bacchanal of satyrs, fauns, centaurs and nymphs, all toting some sort of wine jug or grape-based accessory. I scowled down at a cross-eyed satyr specimen on the porch and lifted the brass knocker.

"Portia?" Ben answered the call of the outdated door accessory in navy sweatpants and a white T-shirt that hugged him all too well. I had to drag my eyes up to his face.

"I need to talk to you," I told him.

He stepped out onto the porch, his arms crossed over his chest. "That's funny, I need to talk to you as well. How's your mom?" he said pointedly.

I winced, but even as I did, I was grateful for the opening. "I shouldn't have lied to you."

"No, you shouldn't have. Here I was legitimately worried about your mother, then I hear she's at the secret town meeting you ran out on me for."

"I'm sorry," I said, meeting his gaze. "I made a poor decision in the moment."

"No, you didn't. You made a calculated decision. If it wasn't me on the other end of it, I might have admired it."

"I'm sorry, Ben."

"No, you're sorry you got caught," he said, and in the light of ridiculously over-the-top lamps made to look like torches, I could see how angry Ben really was. His face, normally so handsome, was remote and marble-like, his eyes were cold and his mouth—that beautiful, generous mouth—had shuttered into a tight line.

"No, I'm sorry I hurt you," I said, correcting him, because damn it, I was not going to allow him to control the narrative like that.

"And now you're here because you've heard the news."

"Regardless of what's going on between us, you can't do this. It's going to cripple Bard's."

"A couple of luxury condos aren't going to cripple Bard's," he shot back, exasperated.

I cocked my head at him. "Will's Island is the site of the main-stages and the heart of the festival. That's going to affect the town financially. You know it is."

"I hear Peaseblossom's is still up for sale. The town could build an open-air theater there."

"Or, conversely, how about some condos?" I said, squaring my hands on my hips. "Why do they have to be on that island? It's basically a heap of rocks. The amount of work you're going to have to do to make it level . . . C'mon, Ben. It's good for one thing."

"Should you even be here right now?" Ben asked coldly. "You represent the merchant association, remember? The losing bidder, if I recall."

You know how some people see stars when they're dizzy or in love or shit like that? I saw thunderclouds gathering at the corners of my eyes when I squeezed them shut and could taste the ozone of lightning. "There's no need to be a jackass about it."

"I'm not being a jackass. You're the one making this uncomfortably personal. It's just business."

"Really? It's just business? You're threatening the happiness and arguably the livelihood of the town's residents, which include my parents, my sisters and my friends. Of course it's personal. You don't need the island the way the town needs the island. I'll help you find other lakefront property. Hell, I'll represent you for free in the closing of it. But not this island," I said, enunciating every word, not to be pedantic, but in an effort to slow things down. My blood was pounding in my head, my throat, my heart.

"This is an incredible opportunity for Dane Development, to get in on a piece of property like this. You know, you're the only person on this planet I thought would understand."

"And I thought you would understand the concept of family," I shot back.

Now it was Ben who recoiled. "That's low."

"I meant Danny," I said, exasperated. "You had Danny. What wouldn't you have done for him? That's me, Ben. Right here, right now. My family, that island means something to them. It's irreplaceable to them."

"Are you sure it isn't something else?"

I stared at him. "I have no idea what you're talking about." Then I stopped, realizing what he was driving at. "Wait, you think this is some sort of weird competition? I can assure you it's not. I'm not trying to beat you here. I'm trying to preserve something that's important to the town."

"That's not what I'm talking about." Ben met my eyes, his gaze unyielding. "Cut the shit, Portia. He told you to kill the deal, didn't he?"

I looked at him, bewildered. "Huh?" *Brilliant counterpoint, Portia.*

"Gerald Cutler. He saw an opportunity here and asked you to ensure we won't get a foothold. He doesn't want us increasing our presence, whether it's in Boston or elsewhere."

"What are you talking about?" I said, genuinely confused. "Gerald couldn't care less about Bard's Rest. Other than he thinks it's distracting me from my duties as managing partner."

"You're more right than you know. What he cares about is squashing anyone who doesn't get in line with his interests. Dane Development and other smaller shops looking to make a name for themselves. And now you."

I shook my head, like I was trying to shake some logic loose. Nothing Ben was saying was making any sense. "I don't know what your deal is with Gerald, but I can tell you what my deal is with him. He told me to drop this because it's a bad look for us since a healthy portion of our clientele are developers."

"I'm sure that's exactly how he told you to position it."

"I don't know what kind of history you have with Gerald, but I don't like what you're insinuating. I'm not anyone's pawn."

"That's not what I'm saying."

"Then what are you saying, Ben?"

"I'm saying there might be a larger game going on here that you're unaware of."

"Do you hear yourself right now?" I crossed my arms over my chest, suddenly feeling chilled despite the summer heat. "Let me tell you what's going on right now, right here, at this moment in time. This is about you, me and development in Bard's Rest. I wish I didn't give a shit about this town or anybody in it. But it's the truth. It's the messy, very inconvenient, not at all advantageous truth. Believe me, I wish I could get out of your way and let you build a bunch of tacky condos because that's the smart play, but I can't. I can't, and I won't let you do it. I am going to the mat on this."

"I'm not building a bunch of tacky, cheap condos," he spat. "You think I do cheap work?"

"I shouldn't have said that," I said, instantly regretting the words and how they must have landed for Ben. I hadn't met Danny, but I'd heard enough to know how much of who Ben was today was because of Danny. And Danny hadn't been the tacky condo type. I needed to pull back. I was angry, but Ben was not some counter-party in a deal. I cared about Ben. And I needed to act like it. "I'm sorry."

"Thank you," he said, his tone softening. "Would you just look at the initial drawings with me? So you'll believe me when I say I'm not planning tacky, cheap condos for Bard's Rest?"

I'd rather have stuck my hand into a garbage disposal than look at the blueprints of the demise of my family's collective happiness, but I reminded myself this was Ben and he was trying to offer an olive branch. Maybe they weren't so bad.

Ben pulled out his phone, and after a few clicks, he offered it to me. I gamely swiped through the drawings. They weren't bad. If we were talking new construction in the West Village, these would have fit right into the landscape. But this was Bard's Rest. Not only were locals going to hate them on principle, but the actual condos themselves, although tasteful and expensive looking, struck a dis-cordant note with the way they protruded over the lake, like a beer gut straining the limits of a belt.

"Well?" Ben demanded.

Lucky for me, I possessed an ironclad poker face forged in the fires of C-suite corporate bullshit. Unlucky for Ben, I wasn't going to use it, because I didn't want to lie to him again. "They're lovely, Ben. But wrong for Bard's." I handed him his phone.

"What?" He sputtered and ticked off various attributes of the waterfront accommodations—the private docks, the placement of windows to maximize the water views—but the more he spoke, the less convinced I grew.

"Local commerce isn't well positioned to service the demand of your target audience."

"They'd fall in love with the charm of Bard's."

"Then why not build housing that incorporates the charm of Bard's or, better yet, respect the traditions of Will's Island and its importance to local commerce and build elsewhere?"

Ben shook his head. "You're wrong."

"I'm not. Bard's will never forgive you for razing the amphitheater."

"Portia, I know what I'm doing. You have to think bigger and remember this is my livelihood, this is my purpose, this is what drives me and why I get up in the morning."

"So, for you to have purpose, you have to chip away at my family, my friends and all the people I grew up with? Their purpose doesn't matter?" I fired back. To hell with apologies. I hated feeling patronized.

"You can hardly afford to play the wide-eyed ingenue," he snorted. "How many of the deals you've done have had similar consequences for who knows how many people? It's different here because it's your town, it's your people."

He had a point there, though I'd never thought of Bard as my town. When had that changed? "Fine, I'm going to do what's right for Bard's. You do you."

"What gave you the right to decide what's right for Bard's?"

"I'm not deciding what's right for Bard's. I'm choosing to represent the people who will decide what's best for Bard's. Those people are my family and my friends and the merchants of this town. It's their voice I'm interested in here. Not thwarting yours personally. I'm not doing it to hurt you, Ben."

"I'm not doing it to hurt you either." Beneath the anger I could hear the note of utter miserableness. Or maybe it was that I was so desperately looking for it.

"So that's it, then."

"That's it," I agreed.

"You and I are going to be on opposing sides here."

"We are."

He nodded. "I can respect that."

"Thanks," I said, though it was still cold comfort. "See you around, Ben."

"See you around, Portia," he said as he stepped through the doorway and slammed the door behind him. The cross-eyed satyr wobbled at my feet.

I stormed down the porch steps, stalking across the lawn of drunken garden statues. I was late to what I was sure was going to be my own execution. Complete with side dishes.

The Kitchen Table

There are two kinds of people in this world. There are those who agonize by degree, digging into their own flesh with their nails in the hopes of loosening the seal of the bandage. As if that has ever worked in the history of adhesives. Then there are those who find the weakest edge, take a deep breath and rip. I am, of course, the latter. Though I do suppose there's a third category of people who just ignore the griminess of the situation until it all falls away. But I digress.

I surveyed the cozy domestic scene—my sisters carrying side dishes to the table while Mom added a serving fork to the chicken marsala and Dad expertly uncorked a bottle of white and commenced filling the waiting wineglasses—and mentally decided he should make mine a double. One by one they dropped into their seats, and with a soft sigh, I sank into my chair. *Rip the bandage, Portia.* Clearing my throat, I said, "We lost Will's Island. Outbid by a developer."

My mother was still putting her napkin in her lap as I said this. She looked up sharply, while my father froze mid-reach for the salad bowl. Miranda's mouth formed an O of surprise, while Cordelia, probably most true to form, dropped an F-bomb.

"By how much?" Mom demanded.

"By whom?" Dad asked.

"Three million cash offer," I said glumly, noting that other than Dad's half-hearted attempt, no one had reached for food. "Dane Development."

Cordelia dropped another F-bomb. I glanced over at her, and she shrugged.

Mom abruptly pushed back from the table with a flourish and marched into the kitchen, muttering under her breath. I could practically see the moment when Dad did the mental math and then, reaching out swiftly, grabbed the wine bottle and doubled the amount in her glass.

"Who does this upstart think he is?" Mom called out from the kitchen. I wasn't sure if she was talking about Archie or Ben, but I wasn't going to be the one to clarify. "Is there no consideration or respect for the town's history?" That was rhetorical, obviously. But the next question was not. "How did it happen?" she asked as she reappeared. With a knife in her hand. Yes, it was one of those long, serrated affairs used for slicing bread, but it was doing nothing to make me feel good about this situation.

I cleared my throat, not wanting to state the obvious, but rather to set the record straight. "When Archie saw how much Dane Development was offering up front, he took it."

"He sold out in style, huh?" Miranda remarked, her eyes flicking to the various exit points around the kitchen. My money was on her bolting to the garden. My sister liked confrontation about as much as I liked small talk.

"What a cream-faced loon. Absolutely no respect for tradition or what his uncle would have wanted." Mom glowered, retaking her seat. "That's it then? It's a done deal?"

"I don't know for sure if the deal is inked yet or not, but unless we're going to counter with an offer that beats Dane, I'd say it's a done deal."

"What are we going to do about the mainstages?" she demanded.

Four heads swiveled in my direction.

Fronting with more equanimity in my tone than I actually felt, I said, "I can't see how it can affect this year's schedule. Dane Development won't be able to get the purchase and sale completed before August." Dane Development, not Ben. It hurt to even think his name right now. "It would be hard to imagine they could begin construction before then. The permitting process alone is going to take months. But I would presume that, given the actual square footage of buildable property on the island, future mainstages will need to be staged . . . elsewhere," I said, trailing off.

"If they think giving us one last season of mainstages is going to placate us, they have another thing coming," Mom said, a flickering flare of revolt in her tone.

Dad's eyes widened, and for one more brief moment, I wondered if he was envisioning Mom leading an angry mob of Shakespearean enthusiasts brandishing period-appropriate weapons at a bunch of construction guys in hard hats, like I was.

"Iz," Dad said, taking Mom's hand. "The festival is more than the mainstages."

"I know that, you know that, they know that," she said, exasperated, "but that's a huge draw for the Bardolators, a one-of-a-kind experience that keeps them coming back year after year. It could financially impact future festivals."

"I agree with Mom," I said.

"But haven't you always taught us to embrace change?" Cordelia asked, looking pointedly at our parents.

"Right," said Miranda quickly. "This town is full of some of the smartest, most creative and most dynamic minds out there. We'll figure this out."

My stomach hurt. I hated being on the back foot. I was built for the offensive line. When we'd left his office, I thought we'd sold Archie on our offer, scraping the cash together we could and promising an additional payout. It was maddening. But more than maddening, it was crushing to watch Mom looking so defeated and the rest of my family trying so valiantly to rally her.

You should have done more, I told myself. *You should have done a better job of closing Archie. You're the closer. You didn't close him.* My throat tightened uncomfortably and that inevitable burn in the back started bubbling, so much so that I reached for my water, sloshing it onto the table in my haste, and knocked it back.

I'd had the best shot at closing Archie, and I'd failed. Instead I'd lost Ben and my family was going to have to give up one of their greatest sources of joy.

Mom fixed her gaze on me. "Is there anything that can be done?" In that question, I could hear her bewilderment, the desperate need for me to reassure her. Instead I looked the woman who had raised me, soothed me and gotten me through my darkest moments straight in the eyes. This woman I wouldn't do the dishonor of a sugarcoat. "It's as good as done."

She closed her eyes and nodded, the only sign of her distress in the slight flare of her nostrils. Opening her eyes once more, she pushed back from the table and swept from the room without a word. I sat there in the silence, staring at the paralyzed expressions around the table. It might have been less jarring if she had actually slammed a door.

HOURS LATER, WHEN I was nose-deep in *Crooked House*, a soft knock sounded at the door to the turret. Reluctantly, I marked my page with a bookmark. Because people who dog-eared books were monsters. Things were heating up again between Sophia Leonides and Charles Hayward and providing an excellent distraction to the dumpster fire that was my life right now. "Come in," I called.

Mom was carrying two mugs of her lavender chamomile tea. Handing one to me, she settled on the corner of my bed, the soft glow of the lamp catching the auburn of her hair, tucked away in a perfectly executed chignon. "Thought you could use some of this."

"Thanks," I said, taking a small sip of the fragrant tea. I didn't love chamomile, but the lavender and the undercurrent of hibiscus offset the earthy taste of what always amounted to sawdust for me.

Mom reached out, patting my foot. "I'm sorry about dinner."

"It's okay. The news is upsetting and unexpected."

"I don't understand—" She broke off as she started to build steam again. Taking an audible breath, she tried again. "Portia, what's happening with Will's Island—you did everything you could."

"No, I didn't," I said matter-of-factly. "I could have done more. I'm sure of it."

"This isn't your fault. It's not like there was more money to offer."

"It was my job to sell Archie on it."

"One could argue that we should have kept better track of our town's assets," Mom said, with a slight smile. "Isn't that what my daughter the lawyer would say?"

"Not within earshot, no."

"It's shocking to me that Will would have left the island to such a mouth breather, but maybe he thought Archie would do the right thing."

"Maybe he never met Archie?" I offered.

Mom snorted delicately. "This will be very hard on all of us, but your sisters are right. Bard's will go on; the festival will go on. We'll find another venue for the mainstages."

"I know that."

"I know you know that in that marvelously complex brain of yours," my mother hummed. "But do you really believe it?"

"Working on it," I said. "I let you down."

"You didn't let me down. More importantly, this has no bearing on my health whatsoever."

That landed. I opened my mouth to speak, but she shushed me with a single elegant flick of her hand. "I'm your mother. I know things."

I glanced out the window, unable to meet her gaze, my eyes lighting on the dock that overlooked the pond. Cloaked in shadows and illuminated only by moonlight and the occasional flicker of a firefly, it looked like the loneliest place on earth right now. I desperately wanted to be there instead of here where one of the people I loved best was trying to put on a brave face, just for me.

"There's a whole world outside Bard's," Mom continued. "We all need to get out of our comfort zones once in a while. See who and what else is out there waiting for us." She tapped the paperback. "Instead of cooping yourself up here and excoriating yourself for something that wasn't your fault."

"I had considered going for a run," I admitted, "but Miranda mentioned something recently about the uptick in the fisher cat population."

"Fearsome creatures," she agreed.

"What time is that new gelato place open till?" I asked.

"Ten in the summer, I believe." She looked at her watch. "If you left now, you'd make it with twenty minutes to spare." She frowned. "We have regular ice cream downstairs in the freezer."

I made a face.

"I know, I know. They are not one and the same." She held her hands up. "My daughter the frozen treat purist."

"That would be like me saying Shakespeare and Marlowe are one and the same."

"My daughter the heretic," she amended.

I barked out a surprised laugh.

"Would you like some company, or is this an exercise in solitude?" she asked.

"Would you be offended if I said solitude? It's been a day."

She shook her head. "Of course not. I like to be alone when I'm working through something."

"Want me to bring you anything back?"

She shook her head. "Cordy baked a Sacher torte. You should get a move on though."

"Thanks, Mom," I said, setting aside the paperback and reaching for my trainers.

MOM WAS RIGHT, of course—I made it with exactly twenty minutes to spare.

Parting Is Such Sweet Gelato was a more recent development in

Bard's, popping up in the spring of that year, and like most things in Bard's, it was thoughtful and charming, if not a bit overrun with Shakespearean decor.

Under a cheerfully blue-and-green-striped awning and perfectly situated in the large glass window, a case full of eye-popping flavors awaited me. I wove around the outdoor bistro tables, where couples sat chatting and trading tastes of gelato on brightly colored spoons. I pushed away the thought that Ben and I would never be one of these couples.

Inside I studied the handwritten labels, my eyes sliding over Et Tu, Brûlée and Twelfth Scoop and pausing for one fleeting instant on Montague's Mint Chip before deciding that last one was a hard pass. I settled on the Cherry Wives of Windsor, a promising-looking vanilla bean swirled through with chocolate chunks and cherries.

"And for you, ma'am?" the second server asked the patron behind me.

"Petruchio's Pistachio," came the swift reply. I didn't need to turn around to know who the voice belonged to. But I did anyway, because it seemed the polite thing to do.

"A classic," I said to Emmeline McGandry, who was looking rather fabulous in some sort of lightweight trench coat, her hair twisted neatly at the nape of her neck.

"I'm certain I'm the only one under eighty ordering it these days, but it seems like the right thing to do. To keep it in circulation."

I thought pointing out that gelato wasn't like a library book would be unwise. Our peace was a delicate one. "Sound plan."

We moved down to the register, where I accepted my scoop in its dish and nodded to Emmeline's. "Both, please," I said to the young girl behind the counter.

"Thank you, dear," Emmeline said, nodding.

"My pleasure."

"Do you have a minute to sit?"

The girl at the register flinched, but the place was still two-thirds full, so they were going to have to flick the lights at close anyway, I was guessing. I jammed a twenty into the tip jar.

"Sure," I said. It's not like I was in any rush to get home. "Lead on."

Emmeline wove her way across the parquet-tiled floor to a two-top in the back that was free of sprinkles and ice cream drips. She didn't waste any time. "I'm not surprised that little snipe didn't see the value in what the town was offering him."

Oh great, it was round two of disappointing intimidating women I admired. I didn't even ask how she knew. Gossip moved fast here, and news like this would be occupying primo airtime wherever it landed. So I schooled my face into my polite, listening mask and prepared for the deluge.

But it didn't come.

Instead, Emmeline licked her spoon. "It's times like these, Portia, that tart women have to take action."

Oh god, did she want to whack Archie? Did she want me to be her murder buddy? I was half-horrified but also a little flattered she was considering me for the job.

"I thought we were pretty creative with our profit-sharing suggestion," I said carefully to pressure check that we were not actually going to discuss whacking Archie in the middle of a cheerfully lit gelato parlor. That seemed more like a parking lot conversation.

"That island has a rich and storied history, Portia," Emmeline said firmly. "Do you know much about its history?"

"Other than every mainstage since the town's founding has been held there?"

"Yes, yes," she said impatiently, "but did you know that over the years the island served as the site for early political debates, the settling of locals' concerns before the town hall was constructed and a community forum? Who knows? Maybe if you dig deep enough, you'll find something worth protecting."

"Do you mean literal digging?" I tried not to make a face. I really did. "Is that what you're saying?"

"I'm saying the person with the fancy law degree should think a little more broadly about all the protections under the law that one might seek when protecting a piece of property," she said, stabbing her gelato spoon at the air in exasperation.

The bulb flickered to life in my head, painful and bright.

"You think there's another way to protect Bard's?"

"I'm not saying there is, but if there were, where do you think it would be?"

"The title?" I suggested.

"I've seen it," Emmeline said, shaking her head. "It's clean."

Now, I might have questioned that kind of analysis from a non-title lawyer, but Emmeline was no mere mortal.

"So if not the title, the will?" I regarded her. "Have you seen William Douglas' will?"

"Stop thinking so literally. Forget the paper."

I blinked. "The island? You think there's something on the island?"

"What I'm saying, dear, is that there's a lot of history on that island if you know where to look."

I sat back in my seat, blowing out a deep breath. "You up for a little B and E, Emmeline?"

I'd meant it as a joke.

But Emmeline just tittered and reached across the table to pat my hand. "That's young-people work, dear. But you be sure to come and tell me if you find anything."

The Bowels of Hell

Two days later, Emmeline's words still plagued me. The island. What could be on the island? I wondered. As far as I could remember (and I hated to keep harping on this), there were a lot of rocks, a lot of trees, an outdoor stage, a costume cabin and a storage shed where the props were kept. None of those seemed particularly promising. Nor did traipsing around an island that would soon belong to the guy whose porch I'd stormed off in a huff.

Slipping out of my workout clothes, I stepped beneath the warm stream of the shower. Even the run hadn't helped me escape the internal hamster wheel I seemed to be on. I could understand why Ben was so angry at me for interfering in his work. I'd be upset too if our roles were reversed. That all made sense. But what stuck out was the weird Gerald tangent. Those rants about Gerald going after Dane Development did not seem Ben's speed. He was too levelheaded for that kind of rabbit hole. Or maybe I wanted to focus on this because I didn't want to face the larger issue that Ben and I were done.

Against my better judgment, I'd spent the better part of an hour last night scouring our firm's electronic document management system for anything we had on Dane Development in any of our offices. Nothing. Then I'd tried several combinations of Internet searches looking for a link between Gerald and Dane Development. Other than some rather flattering references to Dane Development as an upcoming shop to watch and, of course, lawyerly accolades for the great Gerald Cutler, I found nothing that linked them. This should have filled me with some sense of relief, but it only made me think I was missing something. And that made me antsy.

Still full of nervous energy that should have been alleviated by my run, I made a quick pit stop at Mercutio's Mercantile—they really did have the best deli in town—and then drove over to the workshop, the unassuming and un-air-conditioned subbasement of the high school, where my father spent a good chunk of the summer working on the sets for the mainstages.

Clutching a white paper bag in one hand and two water bottles in the other, I descended into the bowels of the building, the air smelling dry and sweet like sawdust.

"Dad?" I called out, not wanting to startle him if he was mid–power tool use.

After a beat, Dad stepped out from behind some sort of half-painted scaffolding. He propped his safety glasses on top of his silvery hair, his face breaking into a broad smile.

"Lambkin."

I held up the bag. "I thought we could lunch together. Pastrami on rye?"

"You spoil me," he said, wiping his brow. "I have a box fan set up over by the workbench. Or we could eat on the practice field?"

"Workbench works for me," I said, following him deeper into the workshop, walking past painted thrones and wine barrels and a vine-covered trellis. "What are you working on?"

He pointed to a half-finished table standing in a pile of wood shavings. "Your sister wanted a more imposing table for the family to do battle around for *Shrew*."

I cocked my head at it. "It looks a little like . . ." I hesitated. "Our kitchen table."

"No, that's not—" Dad stopped and then laughed, the sound of it booming through the otherwise still workshop. "You're right."

"I usually am," I said, preening. "Looks great though. Besides, what better table to model battle-ready dining off of than ours? Remember the time Cordelia tried to flip it?"

His face lit up with glee at the memory. "What were we playing? Trouble?"

I shook my head. "Candy Land."

"That's right," he said, and I could practically see him recalling it. Cordelia had been the fiercest six-year-old I'd ever known, with striking dark pigtails, bottomless blue eyes and no social filter. Really, the only things that had changed over the years were those pigtails.

Pigtailed Cordelia had drawn a character card that necessitated her going back to the beginning of the game, and she wasn't having it. Lucky for all of us though, a six-year-old trying to flip that massive wooden table was more hilarious than anything else.

"She was concentrating so hard," Dad said, "sticking her tongue out and everything."

"She was so mad," I agreed. "More mad that she couldn't flip the table than she'd been about drawing that stupid card in the first place."

We laughed some more as I handed Dad his sandwich and unwrapped my own turkey on whole grain with the barest swipe of stoneground mustard. Even with that small respite of joy, something that had been decidedly lacking in my landscape the last couple days, I couldn't will myself to be hungry. I tried to savor the taste of fresh turkey and my favorite condiment, but I couldn't rally. The sandwich tasted like sand in my mouth, and my stomach clenched in protest as I swallowed. It was Berlin all over again. With a sigh, I pushed the sandwich aside and commenced peeling one of the two oranges I'd brought.

"Something wrong?" Dad asked, lifting a brow.

I stared down at the work table, battered and battle-scarred.

"You can't blame yourself for Will's Island."

"I don't think you know how guilt works," I said, with a shaky smile.

"You're talking to the guy whose soulmate tried to pull a fast one on him last year with her health and would have gotten away with it had it not been for you girls. I think I know a thing or two about misplaced guilt."

"I should have closed Archie when I had the chance," I said, shaking my head. "I didn't press hard enough. I got cocky. I left him too much time to think and talk to that wild card of an attorney instead of leaning on him to sign the papers right there. And here we are. Short an island."

Dad pressed his lips into a firm line, but the bottom one trembled and his eyes were doing that crinkly thing at the corners.

"It's not funny."

"It's a little funny. It's not like you lost an actual island, lambkin."

"I kind of did," I fired back, but even I was starting to see the humor in it. "Could you please stop? I'm trying to wallow here."

"I thought we were having lunch."

"Yes, of course," I said, resuming my half-hearted orange peeling. "Back to lunching in the bowels of hell."

"Oh come on, it's not that hot."

"My fingers are sweating from the act of peeling fruit."

"When you were little and we'd go out to the car in the summer, you used to beg me not to turn on the air-conditioning in a hot car," he said, his eyes taking on that faraway quality of someone who was remembering a long-ago you. "You'd say, 'Daddy, I like the way the heat tickles my skin.'"

"Yes, well. I also used to wear a lot of pink and gingham. With age comes taste. For most people." I smiled at him, popping a segment of orange into my mouth. "Speaking of good taste, tell me about this Scotland trip you have planned."

"Your mother taught a fellowship in Edinburgh. She's wanted to go back ever since, and who am I to say no to misty moors and legendary lochs?" He looked at me from over the top of his sandwich. "Also, the opportunity to golf and sample whisky are pretty appealing."

I snickered. "Mom can go shopping that day."

"As long as she saves McNaughtan's to do with me, she can buy the whole of Scotland."

"McNaughtan's?"

"Oldest secondhand bookstore in Scotland. Located in the basement of an eighteen-hundreds tenement building, they sell rare and hard-to-find books. Real antiques. When you go in, it's like stepping into the study of an old friend. The smell of the books—that paper and lignin smell, like vanilla but not as sharp. The sensation of something both fragile and enduring in your hands. Your mother and I visited one afternoon and didn't leave until it was dark outside."

Even as I smiled at him, something clenched in my chest. I could see him, a younger version of himself, leaning against a bookshelf, his eyes intently scanning an old copy of Yeats. The moment he looked up to find my mother engrossed in her own work, their eyes meeting, that shared, knowing smile of love and familiarity.

It hurt. That chest-twisting, heel-to-the-heart kind of hurt. Because in that split second, I'd stopped imagining my parents as younger versions of themselves; I saw Ben and me. Or Ben and me as I imagined we could be. The two of us, clinking wineglasses and digging into an expertly prepared meal out at some cramped, candle-lit South End restaurant. Ben talking animatedly about a deal he'd closed, me leaning over, peppering him with a million questions to better understand it. Ben and me, walking past the New England Aquarium, Hamlet on a leash between us, the little furry prince pausing at the outside exhibit, peering at the alien blubbery seal bobbing in the water.

"Portia, are you all right?" Dad asked.

"Yes," I said hurriedly. "I was thinking about . . . Scotland. You and Mom in Scotland," I finished lamely.

"Thought I lost you to the heat for a second."

"It would take more than the heat to fell me," I scoffed, then admitted, "I'm a bit out of sorts."

"This Will's Island thing will pass, I promise," he assured me.

Except I wasn't thinking about the island. I'd been thinking about something else I'd lost.

"When I'm out of sorts, I like to do something I'm good at."

"Recite random ballads from *The Lord of the Rings* verbatim?" I asked.

"Well, that's certainly in the rotation, but I was thinking, when nothing else will do the trick, I like to work with my hands, make something clean and useful from raw material."

"So you're saying I can use the table saw?" I teased.

"Any Barnes is welcome to use my table saw. Except Miranda, of course."

"Of course."

"You're welcome to hang out in the bowels of hell this afternoon and help me with sets, but I was thinking something more cerebral might suit you."

My face split into a wide grin. "I have festival business to finish."

"Exactly."

Standing up, I swung around the table and pecked him on the cheek. "You're a genius. I'm going to head to the café for an afternoon of caffeine and problem-solving."

"That's my girl," he said. "Although recitation of 'The Song of Nimrodel' would have been nice too."

"I love that you think I know what that is," I said, giving his shoulder a quick squeeze.

"*The Lord of the Rings* makes for a great listen on audio," he called after me.

"So does Michael Lewis, but you don't see me pushing 'how to break the federal government' podcasts on you," I fired back.

"That's why you're my favorite daughter."

"You say that to all of us," I retorted in the wake of his familiar chuckle. Taking a steadying breath, I pushed open the doors and stepped out into the blistering sunlight. Caffeine and contracts it was.

DAD HAD BEEN right. After several hours at my preferred bistro table in the back of Much Ado About Pastry, making my way through several last-minute plans and permit requests and multiple flat whites—okay, two flat whites before Cordelia cut me off—I was more myself again.

That was until my least favorite developer and crusher of small-town traditions walked in. All my earlier Ben-based wistful fantasies of the two of us walking a dog we didn't own and dining at places I'd never make it to because I worked all the time fizzled and gave way to squaring off on Ben's porch, neither of us willing to back down.

For his part, when Ben sighted me, his eyes narrowed, but he didn't falter in his step. Inadvisable. But point for bravery. "What are you doing here?" he asked, his tone sullen.

"What am *I* doing here? My parents own this café, remember?"

"I meant you're not normally here in the afternoons."

"Oh, is this your regular afternoon place to set up camp and wreck our town?" I smiled, acidic and sharper than the flat whites Cordelia had served me. "Will you try and buy this place too? Well, I'm sorry to tell you—not for sale."

"I know you're upset—" Ben began, trying another tack.

"Could you kindly leave my family's establishment? I'm pretty sure I speak for all of us when I say nobody wants you here."

"I'm sorry about the way we left things. Can we talk? This is a huge strategic play for Dane. I have investors counting on this. I can't pull out of something over personal reasons. Surely you can understand that."

"Don't make me complicit in this."

"I'm not making you—"

"You're about to take a wrecking ball to a town's identity, history and income stream."

"Would you sit down with me for a second? I'll show you the revised plans for what I'm thinking. You'll see they're not tacky at all. They may even benefit the town—"

I held up a hand. Was he still trying to sway me to his side? Did he have any idea who he was dealing with? "Do your plans involve knocking down the amphitheater?" This was a slightly unfair question, since I knew that to build anything on that heap of rocks, the amphitheater had to come down.

"Yes, but—"

"I'm good. As much as I'd love to sit around and be gaslit—"

"I'm not trying to gaslight you," he insisted. "I want you to hear me out."

"How about you hear me out?" I hissed. "You can still withdraw the offer. I'll personally pay whatever damages are owed for breaking it."

"Are you serious right now?" Ben asked.

"As serious as you are."

"I thought maybe you might see reason—"

"Not 'reason,'" I corrected him. "You mean your way of thinking. There's no reason here, Ben. No facts. You have a narrative. I have a narrative. They don't match up."

"That's because you're not hearing me."

"I heard you fine. I've listened to your narrative. I'm just unimpressed by it."

"Ben, can I get you something, or were you leaving?" Cordelia said pointedly as she emerged from the kitchen. Gone was the sunny warmth of her smile and the light of her eyes. In their place stood a steely-eyed, unwavering pillar of support—albeit, sporting some flour smudges.

"My apologies, Cordelia. I'll be on my way," Ben said, his cheeks coloring.

To me, he said, "I'll text you."

"Don't bother," I shot back. "We're done."

We both waited until Ben had cleared out.

"And you," she said, whirling on me. "Please kindly stop polluting my sacred space with your negative relationship energy."

"It's hardly sacred space," I scoffed. "Everybody in town and every tourist that's ever read a sonnet comes in here for their caffeine or sugar fix."

"Keep it up and I'll restrict your fruit tart privileges."

I flinched. "I withdraw my previous comment."

She came around the table and plopped into the chair across from me. I could smell cinnamon and cloves on her. I would never, ever admit this to her, but I loved that she smelled like her baking. That was probably a weird thing to tell someone. Even to Cordelia, who had a pretty high bar for weirdness.

"What is going on with you two?" she asked. "I thought it was all meeting of the minds and loins."

"Gross." I made a face. "No, I didn't sleep with him. I wanted to, but then this whole thing went down with Will's Island."

"So you're letting this Will's Island sale get between you?"

"Whose side are you on?" I hissed. "He can develop property anywhere. I will personally help him find other waterfront property and negotiate the deal free of charge. He just can't have Will's Island."

Cordelia regarded me, searching my face. "Oh wow. You're invested."

"I am completely invested. I am invested in Mom, Dad and Miranda. Tillie, Alice, Aaron and Dan. Candace and Byron. Something like this is going to affect everyone in town. You too."

"So it's not a matter of beating Ben? That's a relief."

"Are you joking?" I asked, confused.

"Portia, your prior track record speaks for itself. You don't lose. I can't see a scenario where you'd be happy losing to someone you're in a relationship with, or whatever you're calling what's between Ben and you." Cordelia stood and walked over to the doors, flipping the sign to "Closed." She repeated this with the adjoining door to the bookstore. Then she dimmed the lights and disappeared behind the counter, reappearing with a fruit tart. "Tell me everything."

I plunged my spoon into the shiny, glazed kiwi. "I don't even know where to start." But I found that, after wolfing down the entire tart, I was able to tell my sister everything, from the moment I'd decided to represent the merchant association to realizing that there was a distinct possibility I might more than just like Ben. Well, up until two nights ago, anyway. And every bit of good and bad in between.

"Well, shit," she said when I'd finished, covering my hand with hers.

"I've never had strong feelings like this about anyone."

"You do seem to be skating dangerously close to the L-word on this one."

"But I've also never felt so strongly about anything like this thing with Bard's. Except maybe that time with Tillie and Opal."

"That was one hundred percent the right thing to do."

"Of course it was. Just like it is now."

"Yeah, so Opal's life forever being altered by a piece-of-shit dead-beat dad is a lot different than the town losing Will's Island," she said in her "I know you're going to hate this, but I'm saying it anyway" voice. Then she looked furtively around. "You can never tell Mom or Miranda I said that, but it's different. The town would go on from this. You could let it go, Portia. I'm just saying."

I shook my head. "No, I don't think I can."

"Financially, I think the town will still be okay."

"I'm not talking about the financial health of Bard's."

"I know that," Cordelia sighed, "and it's freaking me out. This level of personal growth, I don't know what to do with it. But Bard's is more than just some island. Who's to say change wouldn't be better for Bard's and the festival in the long run? We could still buy Peaseblossom's and rebuild."

"That's . . . not the worst idea I've ever heard. But not ideal."

"Thanks." Cordelia touched her heart. "So effusive."

I offered her a half smile. "But why should the town have to take the hit? There are years and years of traditions steeped in that island. Why should some meaningless development go up there when I can do something?"

She smiled back, but it was a little sad. "I can't answer that. Given my druthers, I'd rather we keep Will's Island because it means so much to Mom, Dad and Miranda and so many others. That and the locals-only party is so lit on an island."

I stared at her.

"Sorry," she muttered.

The island, I thought. That other conundrum that had been per-colating in the deep recesses of my mind. Emmeline's hypothesis. If the contracts couldn't save the island, maybe the island could save itself.

"You could walk away here," she continued. "No one is forcing you to take up that fight. And nobody would fault you for whatever the outcome is."

"I know that." But the question still begged to be answered. What if the island could save itself?

"Do you? It's not your lot in life to rescue us."

"I know that." But I was still thinking about the island. What if it was my lot in life to rescue the island?

Then it hit me. I knew exactly what I needed to do. Not about Ben—no, that would have been too convenient—but the island? I knew exactly what needed to be done.

"Do you though?" She smiled slightly. "Is there also a possibility that you're hurt Ben's not willing to put aside work for you?" She held up her hands. "Because that would be reasonable."

"What if neither of us can put the other above work?" I asked. The dreaded question hung in the air. "It doesn't matter if it's Ben winning or me winning. What if neither of us can ever yield? Is it the kind of relationship I'd want to be in if I can't put him above work, or vice versa?"

Cordelia closed her eyes tight and nodded. "I think that's the right question, sis."

I stared grimly at the empty plate. "Yeah." I blew out a breath. "Unfortunately, I think I already know the answer." I sipped at the dregs of the green tea Cordelia had downgraded me to. "Hey, speaking of questions, what are you doing Friday night?" I asked, sounding bolder than I actually felt.

"General mayhem with my big sis?" she guessed.

A slow smile spread across my face. "You have no idea how right you are."

....

Will's Island

A re we sure this is a good idea?" Byron asked, his fingers white and tight on the steering wheel of the *G.L.O.A.T.*—aka the *Greatest Lawyer of All Time*, aka the worst boat name in the history of bad boat names. To his credit though, he slid right alongside the dock without crashing into it.

"It's a terrible idea," I assured him, patting his arm.

"The first rule of not getting caught is actually believing you won't get caught," Cordelia called over her shoulder, leaping onto the rickety dock.

"That's not a thing," I yelled back.

She looked up from where she was deftly tying the knots, raising an eyebrow. "Wanna bet?"

"Could we focus on the task at hand, please?" Miranda interjected.

"Which is breaking and entering," Ian gleefully finished for her. Ian Grant, Miranda's best friend and co-owner of Valhalla Lit, had arrived in town that morning. So naturally, Miranda had recruited him to break the law. No sense in letting him settle in or anything. For his part, Ian cheerfully leapt off the boat alongside Cordelia and helped tie up the lines.

"Actually, it's trespassing," I corrected him, as I grabbed our go bags and stepped gingerly onto the dock.

"Much better," he called over his shoulder, his chestnut hair peeking out from beneath a black knit *Valhalla Lit* cap. "That'll look better on my rap sheet."

"You have a rap sheet?" Adam asked. Coincidentally, he was wearing a black zip-up fleece with *The Winters' Tail* embroidered over his chest. I was committing a felony with people who weren't smart enough to wear non-identifiable gear. I wasn't sure how to feel about that.

"You don't?" Ian called back in a stage whisper.

"Children." Candace's voice was as calm and cool as the night air. "Flashlights on."

Obediently, we all clicked our flashlights on.

"Excellent. That decreases the likelihood of me having to splint and carry one of you down the hill and back to the boat," she muttered.

"What exactly are we looking for again?" Ian asked. "I came for the snacks."

"Samesies," Miranda chimed in, then, with a glance in my direction, added, "And sisterly solidarity, obviously."

"Emmeline McGandry told me we'd find what we need on the island," I repeated for them, as I had on the boat and when I'd called each and every one of them—except for Ian. I hadn't called him. But wherever Miranda was, he generally showed up.

"The same woman who banned you from the town hall?" Cordelia said. "That Emmeline?"

"We've moved past that," I insisted. "Besides, she's invested in this."

"Or maybe she's invested in setting you up to fail," Byron muttered, pulling his socks up over his pants.

"What are you doing?" Ian asked, eyeing Byron with interest.

"Ever dig a tick out of your leg hair before?" Byron asked.

"I can't say I have," Ian said, a mild look of horror on his face as he bent down and started tugging on his socks.

"I did have a look around after rehearsals for the mainstages today," Miranda noted, watching Ian nearly topple over in his sock-tugging zeal. "I didn't see anything in the amphitheater itself or costume cabin that would point to the town owning the island. That is what we're looking for, right?"

"I'm not sure what we're looking for," I admitted. "But maybe if we all look together, our hive mind will come up with something."

"I love this plan. I'm excited to be a part of it!" Ian clapped his hands together. "Should we split up? Cover more ground that way?"

"Only if we want to get picked off one by one, slasher flick style," Candace pointed out.

We all looked at one another and nodded in silent agreement. So, with that, we set off into the woods, the underbrush crackling beneath our feet and the whine of the mosquitos rising up in our ears. Even with flashlights, the trek was tortuous. When I'd described the island as a pile of rocks, I hadn't been engaging in hyperbole.

We hiked first to the amphitheater, where I'd watched Miranda act in the mainstages over the years. "Spread out," I said. "Look for anything that might help us. Something that might indicate Archie doesn't own the property or, alternatively, something that might definitely prove the town does. Or, I don't know, something out of the ordinary?"

"Like a giant 'Property of Bard's Rest' burned into a bench or something?" Byron asked.

I shot him a withering glance, which I'm sure lost potency in the dark. "We have to look. We owe it to the town."

My ragtag bunch of family and friends—and it was weird to think that I had friends close enough to sneak onto an island with under the cover of darkness—might not have had any idea of what we were looking for, but we worked as a team, checking the stages and benches, looking for inscriptions or anything that might be out of the ordinary for a seldom-used theater out in the woods. But other than what seemed like an excessive amount of spiders, the amphitheater revealed no secrets.

Still, I could sense the undercurrent of determination as we worked our way over to the costume cabin, where shimmery gowns floated like headless ghosts on the rack and an assortment of crowns hung along one wall before giving way to weapons. Miranda split us up into three groups, one for each of the rooms contained therein. The room that I found myself in with Candace and Cordelia was full of neatly labeled bins—shoes, gloves, undershirts, collars—and a four-wall collection of wigs that I was sure would fuel my night-mares for decades to come.

"Something doesn't seem right," Candace murmured beside me as she pushed aside a bin of those over-the-top ruff collars. "This stuff is all new stuff. Theater stuff. This couldn't have been what Emmeline meant."

Setting aside a bin of my own, I stood and wiped my brow. "You're right, but what then?"

She shook her head. "I'm not sure."

"Maybe we should pry up the floorboards or check the walls for secret compartments?" Cordelia suggested.

"I think someone would notice if we pried up all the floorboards." I hesitated. "But maybe we could tap on the floorboards and walls and see if any of them sound different from the others."

"Good plan," Candace said.

"You take walls, I'll take floorboards," Cordelia said, with a fe-rocity that made me want to hug her.

What felt like twenty minutes of tapping the walls didn't yield anything other than sore knuckles, although Ian did find a secret compartment of sorts in one of the desks. It was full of expired condoms still in the package. Of course it would be Ian to find the drawer full of condoms.

After an hour or so, we all reconvened in the largest room, but other than the condoms and an envelope of promising-looking doc-uments Adam found that turned out to be prop maps of Mantua, we came up empty. Worse, everyone was looking at me expectantly while my mind tried to frame this ill-fated excursion as anything other than a complete failure.

"Is that everything?" Byron finally asked.

"There's a storage shed up by the ball field where the locals-only party is held," Miranda said. "That's where we store old or broken sets and props that are too big to be down here in the way, but that we don't have the heart to throw away yet. We could check there."

I looked at each member of our group, everyone sporting slightly sweaty expressions and even more tragic hair. "It's probably not worth the additional hassle," I said, not wanting to put them through more than I already had.

"Nonsense," said Ian. "We've come this far. I say we do it."

I glanced at Candace, who shrugged. "My tetanus shot is current. I'm game."

My sisters nodded in agreement, as did Adam and Byron. This strange tightness that had nothing to do with costume cabin dust lodged right in the middle of my throat and stayed there, making it hard for me to string words together. "Okay, let's do this."

We worked our way up the rest of the hill, muttering and swearing as feet collided with rock and branch, until we stood in front of the storage shed. I wouldn't have called the costume cabin luxurious by any stretch of that word, but the old shed, listing to one side and sporting a roof that could best be described as sagging, was certainly elevating the cabin by comparison.

Eyeing the roof, I stepped forward and jiggled the handle. It didn't come off in my hand, which seemed like a promising start. Stepping over the threshold, we moved gingerly inside. There wasn't much in the way of room. Miranda hadn't been kidding. Every spare inch seemed to be occupied by musty wooden sets, broken things like a cracked-down-the-middle cauldron and a treasure chest whose top had been torn off and now lay beside it. When I looked in the treasure chest, I saw that someone had tossed in a bunch of dolls.

"Nope, nope, nope," Byron whispered beside me.

Adding that to the list of mental images that could never be unseen, I shone my flashlight over the walls. There were bookshelves that sloped and leaned, their contents in such bad shape that I hesitated to still call them books. On the bottom shelves were ancient-looking cardboard boxes, the only things that seemed to be keeping the shelves upright. Against the wall was a desk that looked like it might collapse under the weight of all the loose paper scattered over it.

"Well, this seems promising," Adam said softly, flicking his flashlight over the desk.

"You're right," Byron agreed. "We're definitely going to be murdered in this room. I can feel it."

"It's hard to tell where the props begin and whatever else is in here begins," Ian said, boldly stepping forward. He maneuvered his way around something that I think might have been a ship mast to reach the desk. He riffled through a stack of papers, a mushroom cloud of gray dust billowing up and into his face. He coughed into his sleeve and continued flipping through the stack. "Sexy stuff over here."

"Yeah?" Byron asked, a note of interest creeping into his voice.

"Do you want to know how much women's hosiery cost in 1973?" He waved a paper in our direction. "Because I now know the answer, thanks to what I think might be fifty years' worth of receipts here."

"This is going to take hours," Miranda murmured to Adam. "Aren't you glad I brought snacks?"

I made a frustrated sound in the back of my throat. "It has to be something here. It has to be. What else could it be?"

"I'd call it trespassing," a familiar and thoroughly unimpressed voice said from behind me. I whirled around to find Ben glowering at me, his face lit by the harshness of his flashlight. "Motion-sensor cameras," he said. "Pretty low-fi, given the weak signal, but they pick up enough. Care to explain what you're doing here?"

We filed out of the shed into the blessedly particle-free night air. However, the absence of mildew and the influx of moonlight only illuminated the situation. Which was dire.

"I'll ask again," Ben said, his arms crossed over his chest. "What are you doing here?"

I glanced at my sisters and friends, who all gazed back at me with wide, frozen eyes. Right. This was my show. Think, Portia. Think.

The dust must have been eating away at my brain, because nothing promising immediately sprang to mind. In the absence of rational thought and logic, I turned to my very favorite coping mechanism. I decided to brazen my way through it.

"We're saying goodbye to the island," I said, letting a note that bordered on haughtiness creep into my tone. "This place holds a lot of memories for us."

"Miranda was actually born here on the island," Cordelia said, jumping in.

"It's true," Miranda admitted, and I could practically hear her eye roll in the dark. "My mother didn't want to miss that year's *Tempest*. I was born during intermission."

"That still doesn't give you the right to come onto my property," Ben said.

"It's not technically your property yet," I noted.

Ben scowled fiercely at me.

"Not helping," Candace breathed.

"How about we call Archie?" Ben offered, his voice as unperturbed as mine had been. "Let him know the Scooby-Doo gang is crawling over his island."

"There's no need to do that," I said smoothly. "I'd ask you give us a few minutes to let us say goodbye to this place properly. You can at least do that, can't you?"

"Right," Adam said hurriedly. "There's something we need to do. To close the book on this chapter of our lives."

"What would that be?" Ben asked, exasperated. He took out his phone. "Forget it, this is ridiculous. I'm calling Archie. He can decide whether he wants to call the sheriff or not."

"Wait." The color drained from Adam's face. He licked his lips, and then he looked over at Miranda and his expression transformed into one of both determination and adoration. "Portia's been covering for me. I've been stalling all night, but I wanted to do it here on the island."

I realized in horrifying clarity what Adam meant to do. "You don't have to do this," I said quickly.

"I want to. But over there." He gestured with his hands to the clearing where the locals-only party was held. "Please?" he asked Ben. "Because I'm the guy who saved Hamlet?"

"She saved Hamlet," Ben said, jerking his thumb at me.

"Yes, but I'm the one who deticked him."

"Fine," Ben grumbled. "But make it quick."

There were a lot of glances and shoulder shrugs as we walked the approximate ninety seconds to the clearing. Once we'd cleared the tree line though, Adam wasted no time, dropping to one knee in front of Miranda backlit by the gloriously full moon. His hand, shaking in the moonlight, reached for his pocket and withdrew a dark blue velvet box.

"I remember the first time I ever saw you at a mainstage. You were all freckles and flower crowns," he began, the words spilling out of him. "I thought to myself, 'I'm going to marry that girl.' I was only seven at the time, but it still counts," he said, his eyes never leaving her face. "I have loved you since we were kids and all the years in between. I loved you and I lost you here in Bard's. But this place, this island brought us back together."

He flipped open the box to reveal an emerald solitaire that caught the light of the moon and burned eerily bright. "I think we were meant to find each other again." He licked his lips, his hair falling in his face. "Miranda Hathaway Barnes, will you walk through this life beside me? Ride the highs and lows with me, adopt an unreasonable number of pets and, when the situation calls for it, hunker down in the trenches with me?" Adam blinked rapidly, his eyes suddenly suspiciously wet. "Would you be my wife and partner in all things?"

"Yes," Miranda cried. She stared down at her finger as Adam slid the ring on. "Yes, you ass, I had no idea you were going to do this," she cried as he rose and swept her into a fierce kiss.

When she came up for air, Cordelia rushed her, and I followed suit. There was hugging—so much hugging—and happy tears. Our sisterly pretzel knot was further fortified by a literary agent, an event planner and the town attorney. Cue more hugging and tears.

I felt a momentary pang of guilt for Ben, who was standing alone. An outsider to these proceedings. But I was so excited for my sister. Eventually though, like all human pretzel knots, we loosened and more or less regained control of ourselves. Except Miranda and Adam, who had their arms wound around each other, grinning at each other like loons.

I felt this strange catch in my throat at having witnessed this moment, this shared intimacy between them. Wiping at dust in my eyes (yes, it was an island full of rocks, of course there was dust in my eyes), I found my voice. "Will you let them go, and you and me can settle up here?" I asked Ben. "If you want to call Archie or the cops, you can call them on me. But let my friends go celebrate."

Ben nodded. "Okay," he said, that one word strangely thick with emotion. It seemed that although he'd not been included in the human pretzel knot, he'd felt some of the aftereffects of the proposal as well.

"I'm staying," Candace said.

"I go where she goes," Byron said, crossing his arms.

"I have no idea what's going on," Ian said, still misty. "But I'm in."

"Samesies," said Cordelia, while Miranda and Adam nodded enthusiastically.

I bit my lip. I was not looking forward to the words Ben and I were going to have. But damn if I didn't have more dust in my eye at that moment. "Byron, I'm not going to let my sister celebrate her engagement on some pile of overly expensive rocks." I glared pointedly at Ben when I said that. "You have to drive the boat. Candace has to make sure you don't hit the dock when you park."

"Hey!" Byron called. "I know how to park my boat."

"The scuff marks would suggest otherwise," Candace muttered under her breath, even as she smiled at him.

"Besides, Ian can't spend his first night here in jail," I added.

"It's definitely a second-night kind of thing," he agreed.

I turned to my sisters. "I'm fine. I will take care of this," I said, gesturing to Ben in a none-too-flattering way. "I got this."

My friends and family exchanged glances with one another.

"Go," I insisted. "Drink all the champagne for me."

Finally, Candace nodded, collecting the troops and heading down to the boat. I stopped Miranda and Adam, giving them each one last hug, and waved goodbye until the *G.L.O.A.T.* disappeared into the night.

Swallowing hard, I turned to face Ben, who looked as grim as I felt. Wordlessly, I followed him onto a much smaller boat and settled into the seat at the bow, as far away from him as I could get without waterskiing behind the boat. Ben turned on the motor and I gave myself over to the drone of it. As we drove, I leaned into the spray of the wake on my face, closing my eyes tight.

Come what may, I thought, channeling the wretched Bard.

....

The Temporary Offices of
Dane Development

W here are we going?" I asked when we reached the dock and
Ben tied up his boat.

"I figured we could discuss this like adults back at the Folly, unless you'd like to go straight to the sheriff's office and explain what
you were doing trespassing."

I didn't point out that Eddie was likely at the Tavern enjoying
wings. He'd be on call for sure, and although I liked my chances—
daughter of beloved local family and occasional dispenser of town-
friend legal advice against upstart outsider developer—it would be
a shame to ruin Eddie's night over this.

"The Folly is fine," I said, shrugging a careless shoulder.

"We could also go to your place," he offered. "If you'd feel more
comfortable."

"I think I'll spare my parents a sparring match. But thanks."

Much like the boat ride, the drive over to the Folly was silent and
frosty. Only there was no drone of the boat motor to chew up the
silence. We pulled into the driveway of the Folly. He hesitated.
"When I undo the locks, are you going to bolt on me like a coward
without talking this through?"

"I'm not going to bolt on you," I protested. "First, because I never run from a fight. And second, because I really need to use the bathroom."

Ben made an exasperated noise.

We stepped out of the car and climbed up onto the porch, where Ben opened the door for me, pausing to turn on the light. I stared around the lavishly furnished living room, dominated by a stone fireplace, an emerald couch that assaulted the eye and an oversized painting of Shakespeare looking down on us. To the right was a small alcove with a magnificent wooden desk that would have been truly impressive had it not been for the weird bust of the Bard himself in the corner, perched like one of those owls that farmers used to scare other animals off their crops. "Wow," I breathed.

"Wait until you see the bathroom," he muttered. "It's down there on the right."

Nymphs. There were a lot of nymphs in the bathroom. Watercolor nymphs in the wallpaper, nymph soap dispenser, nymphs embroidered into the towels; and when I looked up, the ceiling was like the Sistine Chapel's but with—you guessed it—topless nymphs.

"That's a lot of nymphs," I remarked when I came out. "I don't know what a group of nymphs is called. But that one would definitely be categorized as a plethora of nymphs."

"I don't like to use that bathroom," Ben said, standing in the doorway of the study and looking slightly less angry now. "Their creepy little eyes follow my every movement."

"Fair."

Ben dug his hands into his pockets and blew out a long breath. "It hurts that you stooped to trespassing to sabotage me."

"I told you we wanted to say goodbye to the island."

"I don't believe that for a second."

"Yes, but it will make for such a good story," I countered. "A proposal and everything. Just some quasi adults having a little fun."

"Like anyone is going to believe that."

"I'm quite certain Eddie will believe it."

"I'm not going to call Eddie," he huffed. "Can we cut the shit? What were you thinking?"

I hadn't been thinking. I'd been acting like a self-destructive vigilante. If Kim were here, I was sure she'd make some insightful comment about me subconsciously not wanting to commit to Ben and self-sabotaging by attempting to rescue the town instead of confronting the real issue. Except the real issue wasn't that I didn't want to commit to Ben. I wanted Ben to commit to me.

"I had a card left to play, and I played it," I said instead.

From the way his mouth twisted, he didn't like that answer. Nor should he. It wasn't the truth. "You have to let this go."

He was right, of course. But hell if I was going to tell him that. "Oh, because you can let it go, Ben? Let's face it, neither one of us is walking away from this."

"Are we still talking about the island?" Ben asked, his voice dangerously quiet.

I swallowed hard. "What else would we be talking about? It's always work first for people like us. Fun second."

He took a step toward me. "Bullshit."

I held my ground. Even when he took another step.

"Is that all I am to you, a bit of fun?" he growled.

"I'm not even sure you're that." I leaned in. "All that fun, I mean."

"Then by all means, don't let me keep you." He stepped aside so I had a clearly communicated pathway to the door.

"What if I don't want to leave?"

"That would pair nicely with my own feelings on the subject," he murmured, dragging his gaze down my body. "There are so many things I'd like to do to you right now given half the chance."

I spun on my heel, sauntering away from him. But not toward the door. I unpinned my hair and shook the cool coils loose as I headed down the darkened hallway and toward what I thought was an office. Glancing over my shoulder, I called, "Here's your chance."

Ben's footsteps sounded behind me, but I was faster. I spun around to meet him, surging forward, crushing my mouth to his and pressing him back against the wall with the full weight of my body. Not wanting to argue with words any longer, I presented my case with my lips, tongue and teeth.

Ben's counterarguments were as persuasive as they were devastating. Even though I may have had him pinned against the wall, it was he who held me in place with that hot, insistent stroke of his tongue.

I ground against him, reveling in the growing bulge in his jeans. Jeans. That's right, why did we need clothes at this juncture in the evening?

Without breaking our kiss, I trailed my hands down his T-shirt. Palming his pecs and abs, I twisted my fingers in the soft fabric and yanked it up to his sternum, and only then did I momentarily pull away from Ben's mouth to slip the shirt over his head.

"Come back," he mumbled, reclaiming my mouth. His hands slipped under my black zip-up, the only all-black gear appropriate for espionage in the woods. His fingers froze on my stomach and I giggled against his lips as he figured out how easy it would be to relieve me of my top. Triumphantly switching tactics, he made quick work of the zipper, encircling my now bare waist with his large hands and hauling me against him. One hand snaked purposefully up my spine as Ben unhooked my bra. It dropped to the floor with a soft but decisive thud.

"Impressive," I whispered, pulling away from his lips to press kisses all along his jawline and down his throat. Wriggling out of my dark wash jeans, I swept them to the side and reached for the top of Ben's. Working the button loose, I dipped my hand into the slit in his boxers and curled my hand around his length. Ben inhaled sharply.

"You like that?" I withdrew my hand, warm from where I'd touched him, and I placed my palm flat against his chest. I dropped to my knees, dragging my palm down his bare chest until I reached the top of his jeans, yanking them down with both hands. Using deliberately delicate motions, my fingers slid his boxers to the floor. "How about now?" Tickling his ankles up through his inner thighs, I rested my hands on his hips, paused and took him into my mouth, tracing the curve of him with my tongue.

"Portia," Ben groaned in reluctant warning. He bent down,

scooping me up and onto his desk. Burying his face in my neck, he nipped and kissed along my collarbone, up to my ear and back to my mouth. His hands were cold as he found the warm swell of my breasts, and I hissed at the sudden shift in temperature.

His mouth latching back onto mine, he swept his hand across the desk, and all manner of folders, documents and pens clattered to the floor. He clumsily grabbed for the bust of the Bard and dropped it out of sight on the floor. Good man. Then he laid me back on the desk, climbing on top of me and pausing to admire the view.

"Like what you see?" I teased.

"That position suits you," he retorted as he dipped down to catch one breast in his mouth, while his hand worked the other. I moaned, running my fingers over the muscles in his back. He was so smooth and taut beneath my hands, I could have spent hours exploring every inch of his skin. At some point I would, I swore, but I had a more urgent situation pooling between my thighs, sending out waves of ache and need like a homing beacon.

Never the shy one, I reached for Ben's hand and guided him under the band of my silk underwear, my only surviving pair of clothing. But not for long, as Ben lifted me up and freed me of them. Between my legs, he stroked me experimentally once, twice, and finding me wet, he slipped a finger inside of me, making slow, deliberate circles that had me arching up off the desk. "What's the matter, Portia?" he whispered against my neck, smiling against the delicate skin there. "You in some kind of hurry?" he asked as several other fingers joined the first. He spun them slowly to the left, then, picking up the pace, he turned right as if he were a master safe-cracker and I was his prized vault. I whimpered, unable to bite back the noise or remember my name as I grew slicker by the second.

Wait. To hell with that. I was Portia freaking Barnes and I too had a pair of talented hands. I reached for him, entwining my fingers around him and sliding up and down his shaft before curling my grip around him more firmly and settling back into that quick and hard rhythm he seemed to enjoy. "Were you saying something?"

I asked as I expertly reduced him to a panting, quivering puddle of man in my hands.

Ben made a noise somewhere between a hum and a moan as he worked me in tighter, more frantic circles. "That's what I thought," I said as I playfully bit down on his earlobe.

"Tease," Ben murmured before circling that sensitive spot within and tweaking it. I cried out in surprise. Most men couldn't find that spot. Hell, sometimes I had trouble getting it right, and Ben had just hit the exact spot and that first thrum of reverberating pleasure shuddered through me.

"I need you inside of me, right now," I demanded. "Do you have—"

Ben's free hand came up with a foil packet. "I didn't want to assume anything, but—"

"Oh my god, Ben. So impressed by your foresight, but just put it on," I half growled, half moaned. "I can't wait."

Ben obliged, and once he was ready to go, he slid his hands under my ass, cupping them and pulling me up to him. I guided him in, hissing when he filled every inch of me.

Once he'd settled in, I extricated my legs, twining them around his back and locking my ankles together. We moved slowly together at first—maddeningly slowly—until we found that pace, that delicious rhythmic beat of being one and I lost myself there, in the rise and fall against him, with him, the two of us in tune and in time with nothing else but each other.

I don't know how long we moved with each other, but as the speed picked up, that urgency climbing and twining inside of me, I rocked and bucked beneath Ben until I could stand it no longer. Arching up against him, I held his eyes and gently pushed him up so that I could climb on top.

With a wild, delighted grin, he stretched out beneath me as I positioned my knees on either side of his thighs. I slid myself down onto his length and very slowly I rose onto my knees until he was nearly out of me, then I twisted myself down around him and came down fast and hard.

Ben cried out and gripped my hips. "So that's how it's going to be?"

"You don't know the half of it," I promised. And we were off again, rocking against each other, him thrusting me upward and me pressing him down again and again. I twisted this way and that, varying the pace and depth at which I descended on him and keeping him guessing as to my next move.

Our bodies grew slick with sweat as we rode together, our rhythm increasing to frantic heights until I couldn't wait a second more. I shouted Ben's name and he gripped me so tight as I came in big shuddering waves against him, my whole being clenching all at once around him and sending him over the edge as well with a cry of his own.

Panting hard, I stared down at him. He looked as undone as I felt. Gloriously so. I couldn't help but feel satisfied that I'd been the one to leave him with that dazed, contented expression.

He gazed up at me through unfocused eyes and smiled. "As much as I want to stay like this for eternity—" he began.

"You're as sore as I am from having sex on the world's most unforgiving desk?" I supplied helpfully.

"Something like that," he said with a slight groan as I slid gently off him and pulled him up with me, both of us sitting on the edge of the desk, our legs swinging over the side. I surveyed the carnage of our clothes and the contents of the desk on the floor.

"I think there's a pair of robes upstairs in the bathroom," he noted, following my gaze.

I weighed the wisdom of donning a robe from Falstaff's Folly against having to crouch down on the floor to figure out where I'd tossed my jeans. That sounded like work, actually, and I wasn't sure I had the leg strength for that yet. I appreciated Ben for offering to go upstairs, because I wasn't sure I'd be able to manage that either.

"Thanks," I said. "I'd appreciate it."

"You know, there's a perfectly comfy king-sized bed upstairs," he said hopefully. "You could stay over," he offered, almost shyly. "If you wanted."

"Is this your idea of house arrest?" I teased.

"I wish I had a snappy retort to that, something about the break-in on the island," he said with a slightly sheepish expression, "but mostly, I don't want you to leave. I want to get you upstairs and under the covers and hold that glorious body of yours against mine until I pass out."

I caught my bottom lip in my teeth, trying not to giggle.

"I promise we don't have to talk about anything else tonight. We'll sort it all out in the morning." He turned my face toward his and kissed me gently. "Please?"

"Oh, did you actually think I was going to do the walk of shame out of Falstaff's Folly? My sisters would never let me live that down if they found out. You know this place was a notorious swingers' sex pad, right?"

"I don't think the listing mentioned that."

"Well, in any event, yes. Let's go upstairs, I'm freezing. We'll deal with whatever we have to in the morning," I said, tracing his lips with my fingers. "But only if you promise we start the morning off right. Just not on this desk."

"Cease-fire, then?"

"Cease-fire," I agreed.

ACT THREE

August

....

The Festival

The hundred and first Bard's Rest Shakespearean Festival opened on a bright, sunny Monday without a cloud in the sky overhead. Sitting on the back porch of the Folly, which overlooked a surprisingly demure garden with soft pink roses and only one satyr-themed fountain, I sipped the mug of steaming English breakfast that Ben had brought me. We'd both forgone the Folly's robes in the name of hygiene, and I was wearing a pair of Ben's navy sweatpants, which were so soft and broken in that Ben was in serious danger of me not returning them. We were also sporting matching white T-shirts, Ben's indecently formfitting, of course, while I was swimming in mine. Still, it beat the robes and last night's covert island break-in gear, still bunched up on the floor of the study. Best of all, these clothes smelled of Ben, like he was still curled around me, holding me.

I'd never been much for morning-after lingering. Not because I was an unfeeling robot or anything. But I always needed to go home, brush my teeth, take a shower, answer my email, pop into the office. The tasks of the day couldn't wait. Except today. Other than a looming Talk we needed to have, I didn't need to be anywhere or do anything. It was glorious.

Stretching my legs out in front of me, the morning sun warming my toes, I looked over at Ben, who looked as content as I felt. Last night—last night had been all urgent need. But this morning—this morning had been slow and deliberate, Ben working my body from head to toe until I felt loose and completely Zen. Like a really good yoga retreat, but with more orgasms.

"So," Ben said from behind his own mug.

"So," I said, unable to do anything but smile. "I very much liked your idea of a cease-fire."

"Last night was the cease-fire," he noted. "Today, I thought we'd work on a go-forward plan for a truce."

"A truce, huh?"

His face grew serious, his dark brows knitting together. "Is there a scenario where we don't let this business with Will's Island get between us? I'm going to be here through September. You're going to be here through September. I, for one, would very much like to see where this goes, you and me." Ben stole a sideways glance at me. "If you're up for it. Because I am falling for you, Portia Barnes. The more time I spend with you, the more I know there's something more for me out there than just the job. Something worth getting up for other than the bottom line. Someone I can wake up next to every morning. Someone who goes toe-to-toe with me but who I know I can trust with the most vulnerable pieces of me." He looked out over the garden.

I closed my eyes, the warm morning air tickling my bare arms, breathing in the faint sweetness of honeysuckle on the breeze. Ben's words wrapped around me and held me fast. Ben, who was all granite and polish on the outside, but inside was so thoughtful and generous. Ben, who didn't shy away from hard work or hard decisions. Ben, who'd seen a far less sanitized version of me than most and hadn't made any noise about me needing to be a softer, kinder human. Ben, who made me happy in a way I'd long suspected wasn't a possibility for someone like me.

This was one of those moments—those growth opportunities that Kim liked to harp on. I had a chance to move forward in a relationship with someone who meant something to me. But to do so, I'd need to get comfortable with putting aside my need to win and my fear of disappointing others, mainly my family. I needed to believe them when they said they weren't blaming me for what happened. I'd taken that burden on alone. If my family could find a way to make peace with Will's, to embrace the inevitable change that came for us all, maybe I could too. I didn't have to win here, to charge in and save the day.

Ben cleared his throat. "Where'd you go?" he asked, a soft smile playing across his lips. Lips that had done some thrillingly and thoroughly filthy things last night.

"I'm here," I answered. "I want to be here. With you."

"Yeah?"

"Yeah," I repeated, emphatically. "I can park Will's Island outside of whatever this is. This means so much more to me." I neglected to mention that I was exceptional at compartmentalizing things but figured that might be an off-putting thing to say to one's romantic partner.

Ben sat back in his chair. "That's a relief." He looked over at me, grinning. "Have I mentioned how much I like the way you look in my clothes?"

"Oh yeah?" I surveyed the garden, the high wooden fence, the trees providing a perfect canopy of privacy. I set down my mug, rose from the chair and padded over to where he sat on the all-weather outdoor couch. He watched me with interest, setting down his own mug without taking his eyes off me. I lowered myself onto his lap, my knees on either side of his thighs. "What do you like more, the way I look in them or out of them?"

"Is that a trick question?"

Giggling, I grasped the soft white T-shirt, yanking it up and over my head, and tossed it at him. Shrugging out of my bra, shivering slightly as the air rolled over previously unexposed skin, I tossed my hair. "If it's all right with you, I thought we might enjoy the great outdoors."

Ben's eyes widened. "Why, Portia Barnes. You're full of surprises," he said as his hands slid up to cup my breasts.

"Oh, did you think because I was such a corporate badass, I must be this frigid, sex-starved creature?"

"The thought had crossed my mind," Ben said with a wicked gleam in his eyes.

"You are so in so much trouble," I purred as I bent down to claim his mouth.

"WHAT HAVE YOU been up to today?" Miranda asked, shaking her crimson hair out behind her and smoothing down her cobalt dress that, despite not having a corset, somehow still looked very Elizabethan without trying to. I suspected she'd gone easy on the dress-up for me, and I appreciated it. Not one for costumes, I'd opted for a simple black sundress. Besides, for every Bardolator sporting one of those weird neck ruffs, there was a person kicking around in boat shoes looking just as delighted to be here.

"I took advantage of the weather," I said, my voice mild, even as the blood rushed to my cheeks. I'd enjoyed myself multiple times in the great outdoors this morning, but who was counting? Pushing down the rising smile that cropped up when I thought of Ben, I surveyed the cordoned-off street lined with rows upon rows of food booths and vendors hawking everything from Elizabethan gowns to full turkey legs you could eat right off the bone. If you were gross like that.

"You feeling any better about stuff?" she asked, her voice low.

"Much better, thanks." Nothing that a little perspective and about a half dozen orgasms couldn't fix.

"We'll figure it all out," she said, squeezing my hand. "Now come on, I want to eat my way down the left side of Main Street now, catch the minstrel show and work my way up the right side. Candy apples first?" She pointed to a booth in the shape of a turret with red and white flags fluttering in the breeze. "That's sort of like a fruit course."

I eyed the shiny, sugary surface of the apples peeking out from beneath a layer of smooth caramel dotted with chopped nuts. "Sort of."

"You want crushed Oreos, chopped nuts or the boring plain one?"

"Is that a serious question?"

"One with nuts and a boring plain one, please," she said to the damsel behind the counter. No, really—she had one of those conical hats with pink streamers coming out of the top.

"Thanks," I said, biting into the apple. "Where's Adam? I thought I was getting a twofer tonight?"

"He'll be along shortly," she said, her grin mischievous.

"He's coming in a doublet, isn't he?" I groaned.

"One can only hope," she said dreamily, batting her eyelashes at me.

"Is it weird that he's your fiancé now?"

"It really is," Miranda said. "That word is so pretentious." She held up her ring finger. "I've scratched myself about half a dozen times with this thing." She laughed.

"I'm sorry," I started, not sure how to position it, "that your proposal, uh . . ."

"Are you kidding? That was so us. I wouldn't have wanted it any other way. In one of my favorite places with all my favorite people around." She squeezed my arm. "I had a lot of fun with you that night."

"Yes, we'll have to engage in B and E more often," I said dryly.

"I meant it was so fun to be with you all spontaneous like that. Bonus, you're not behind bars in Eddie's one-room jail cell. So clearly things must have worked out okay between you and Ben."

My mind flashed to straddling Ben this morning, my thighs on either side of his on that outdoor couch, his hands guiding me up and down as I rode him. The way he'd come, yelling my name again and burying his face in my breasts. "Yeah, sometimes you have to get everything out in the open."

We munched on our apples, stopping at a stall called the Barest Bodkin that sold daggers. Seriously, that's all they sold. I pointed to a delicate silver blade with an elaborate amethyst jewel in the hilt; its neighbor, a similar pattern on it, had a garnet. "Which one for your registry?"

Miranda swatted my arm but laughed. "My luck, I'd probably trip and impale myself on it. Then Adam would have to take me to Mount Auburn and I'd have to explain how I fell on a ceremonial blade."

"That's . . . yeah, no, that's not that far-fetched," I said, thinking about the time Miranda had given herself a black eye with an exercise band. "Let's skip the knives." We walked toward a much safer-looking booth, where a pair of women were selling perfume in ornate glass bottles. "How's the book going?"

"Great," she said enthusiastically. "There's something about being back here. It shakes the words loose. That and I don't feel this enormous pressure anymore like I did when I was Hathaway. If this book sucks—"

"Which it won't, because you're a fantastic writer," I interjected.

"Thanks, sis. But if it does suck, then I'll write it off as a botched foray into adult fiction and I'll go back to writing YA."

"I like it. Good to have a backup plan."

Just then, I heard a small, familiar yip. I looked up and saw Adam walking toward us, and on the leash he held, straining for all he was worth in his efforts to get to us, was Hamlet. I quickly closed the distance between us as I knelt to the ground and a small ball of wriggling, yipping and licking puppy crashed into me.

"He remembers me," I managed between tongue baths. Hamlet was trying to crawl into my lap, using my knee as leverage to tuck his head up under my chin. "Oh wow, he smells good," I said, giving the little guy the leg up he needed and snuggling him into my chest.

"Special proprietary shampoo." Adam winked. "I brushed his teeth too."

I hugged Hamlet to me. "Hello, little man. I missed you."

"He missed you too," Miranda said. "He doesn't greet anybody else that way."

As I stood, Hamlet planted his bulk—such that it was—directly on my feet. He looked up at me, tail thumping.

"Here," Adam said, "you take his leash while we walk around.

Now that you're here I don't think he's going to let anyone else walk him."

"Sure," I said, taking the leash, not sure how that was going to work. But Hamlet was a natural. "Any luck in finding him a good home?"

"We've had a few inquiries," Adam said, looking at Miranda. "But nobody we're in love with. Hamlet needs someone special. But we do have some exciting news. His DNA results are back."

"Oh yeah? What is he?"

"He's around sixty percent cane corso, about thirty percent Labrador and ten percent super mutt, meaning they have no idea."

"Cane corso." I frowned. "What's that?"

"It's an Italian breed of mastiff," Adam supplied helpfully. "A highly intelligent breed, very protective of and attached to the people they decide to call their own."

"How did an Italian breed of mastiff end up in the woods of New Hampshire? Do you or your father have any patients that are cane corso?"

"Nope. My guess is somebody's Labby got out and met up for a late-night rendezvous with some summer person's prized companion, and these puppies were the result. I even hiked up to the Look Out and searched for any sign of Mom or other puppies, but nothing. I mean, it's a big wooded area out there. Maybe he was separated from Mom and he was lucky that you found him before someone could snack on him. But as you can see, he's a perfectly happy puppy now." Hamlet barked in agreement.

"Adam thought it might be good to get him out and socialize him a bit. Hold on to his leash and be prepared to stop every fifty feet, because everyone is going to want to pet him," Miranda said with a laugh.

She wasn't kidding. Despite the presence of people walking around with actual falcons on their arms, Hamlet was a huge draw. Kids in particular wanted to pet him, and Hamlet was only too happy to oblige them, dropping to the ground and mugging for belly rubs. Clearly, he'd picked up a thing or two from his doggy mentor, Puck.

We walked like this, the four of us, down Main Street, taking in the bright colors of the tents, little children in fairy crowns, their ribbons streaming down their back, weaving in and out, people laughing and consuming their weight in meat pies.

Hamlet gave a resounding yip and I looked down at him and then up at the approaching figure. Turned out I wasn't the only one he recognized.

"Ben," I called and then turned down my megawatt smile. Otherwise, Miranda would know I'd slept with him.

To my surprise, Ben had a woman with him. She was tall and slender with sable hair that fell to her shoulders and was wearing a magenta wrap dress that I was dying to ask about, but I figured we should be introduced first.

"Portia," he called back, his own grin breaking wide open as he saw Hamlet. He dropped down to one knee as I had and commenced telling the puppy what a good boy he was. His sudden drop in altitude meant that I was now staring at his stunning companion.

"Portia Barnes." I offered her my hand, reaching over Ben to extend it.

"Sam Maeda," she said, taking my hand and squeezing it. So this was Ben's business partner, the one he talked about in almost reverent tones. "The infamous Portia Barnes I've heard so much about."

"I've been called a lot worse," I admitted. "So you're the mysterious Sam."

Sam's lips quirked upward. "Well, I've certainly been called worse."

"It's a pleasure to meet you. Sam, this is my sister Miranda and her boy . . . err . . . fiancé, Adam Winters," I corrected mid-sentence. "Sorry, Adam."

"Not at all, it's new," he said, shaking Sam's hand. "Besides, I've always wanted to be a boy-fiancé," he deadpanned.

Sam laughed. It was a good laugh, a confident laugh. I could tell I was going to like this woman. Especially when she added, "Ben, are you going to get up off the ground anytime soon? I'd like a go too, you know."

"Sorry, Sam," he said, rising. "Sam's a big dog fan," he explained, as Sam commenced with her bent-knee greeting of Hamlet. "Two rescues at home and a bit of a Shakespeare buff."

"Oh, then Adam is your person for dogs and Miranda's your person for the Bard," I said.

"And what are you my person for?" Sam said, quirking a perfectly plucked brow.

"Cutthroat business tactics not for the squeamish." Ben smiled, putting his arm around me. "And pointers on how to tackle an alpaca in three moves or less."

There was a general round of laughter over that one (it had been two moves or less, thank you very much) and like that, our group of three and a half (counting Hamlet) became five and a half. Sure, there were a few raised eyebrows here and there in Ben's direction as we strolled down Main Street, but for the most part the townsfolk either didn't know his connection to Dane Development or were using their best "the Bardolators are here" manners. Also, walking beside Miranda, the golden child of all things Shakespeare, probably bought us some additional goodwill.

Our little group wandered together until Adam, Ben and Miranda came upon a stall selling those loaded poutine fries. Sam, who confessed she couldn't do cheese, was eyeing the soup in a bread bowl thing on the other side of the street. "Count me in," I told her as Hamlet trotted between us, confident that he'd be able to scam something off the two of us.

After placing our orders, we stepped off to the side to wait, admiring a rather impressive display of the Bard's work in a variety of shapes and sizes and covers that ran the gamut from those that looked like actual wood cuttings with gilt lettering to modern buttery soft pastel leather with the name of the work scrawled in cursive across the front.

Sam picked up a copy of *The Tempest*, turning it over in her hand. "I think I'm going to like you, but this is the obligatory part of the conversation where I need to tell you that I care very much about Ben."

"You'll break all the parts I hold dear if I break his heart?"

"Exactly." She looked up at me. "Why should male BFFs have all the fun?"

"My thoughts exactly. Ben's lucky to have someone so forward-thinking in his life." I picked up a collection of sonnets so I had something to do with my hands for this next part. "I think it's possible I like Ben very much too. So we're perfectly aligned, I think."

"Good. He's not had an easy go of it," she said. "I know he looks indestructible, but he's a big marshmallow on the inside."

"I'm starting to see that," I said. "He's lucky to have you."

"He is," she laughed.

"How long have you been partners?"

"We were roommates first," she explained. "My last year of law school, the friend I had lined up flaked on me, and Ben's housing situation had fallen through as well, so we found each other on one of those Craigslist posts that shouldn't have worked, but did and we moved in together." She raised an eyebrow. "Ben's like a brother," she added. "So don't go down that path."

"Wouldn't dream of it," I said. "Ben didn't mention you're a lawyer."

"I'm not practicing," she said, and for the first time her expression seemed to lock down into one of guarded neutrality. "I'm on the business side of the house now." Her answer didn't invite any questions, so I didn't press. Instead, we chatted about Hamlet, Sam nodding along and laughing as I recounted our rescue of him in the woods and extolled the virtues of having a future brother-in-law as a vet.

"Was that the night you took Ben to a local make-out spot?"

"Oh come on," I cried. "Is that how he's positioning it?"

Sam quirked an eyebrow.

"I'm going to withdraw that last comment," I said archly.

"Probably for the best."

Our names were called and, sloshing bread bowls obtained, we rejoined our group over by the picnic tables that overlooked the town square, where the minstrels were warming up. Ben leaned over. "What did you two talk about?"

"You, of course," I said, smiling at Sam.

"Don't worry. I'll wait a bit before telling her all the good stuff," Sam told Ben.

"She's like a female Ian," Miranda whispered to Adam.

"If Ian were an adult, sure," Adam agreed.

"Where is Ian?" I asked.

"Apparently, he and Cordy made some sort of bet at Christmas and she lost. She's teaching him the secret of her mousse cake," Miranda said.

"We need to get that recipe," Adam breathed.

"We need to get some of that mousse cake," Ben said to me, squeezing my hand, a gleam in his eyes. "Sam, you in too?"

"Who says no to mousse cake?" Sam scoffed.

Beneath the table, Hamlet settled on my feet and promptly started snoring. All in all, it had been the best opening night of the festival I'd ever been to.

The Mainstages

Although I was not much for Shakespeare or bugs, even I had to admit there was something special about sitting beneath the stars on pine benches. That or I was preemptively mourning the loss of this next year. No, I told myself firmly. No, we were not going there.

I sat with Ben and Sam to my left and Chris, Callie and the twins, Alyssa and Kayla, to my right. I wasn't sure how much of the gender-flipped *The Taming of the Shrew* they were clocking, but given they were Chris and Callie's progeny, my guess was not much got by them.

As good an actress as Miranda had been growing up, she was an even better director. There was something so alive about her plays, the way she coached her cast into bringing Shakespeare to vivid reality, that made me sit up and pay attention and forget for a few hours that I was not, in fact, a fan of William Shakespeare.

Shrew was no different. Cat Jackson, the chestnut-haired dynamo who owned Comedy of Eros, the local sex shop, was apparently double-dipping this year in the mainstages and dinner theater. Playing the traditionally male Petruchio role, Cat was all swagger and charm. Frankly, I abhorred the problematic sexism of *Shrew*, but by gender-flipping the roles and positioning it as more of a battle of the sexes and less a dark meditation on power, control and marriage, Miranda had won the day again for a modern audience.

Beside me, Ben absently stroked my hand, his eyes on the brightly lit stage and his leg pressed against mine. He'd already made it through an admirable grilling by Chris and Callie, Callie being the far tougher of the two, and seemed to have earned at least provisionary approval from the Rogerses. Maybe, if he ever earned more permanent status, we could do dinner with them in Boston when they visited.

Boston. Boston loomed large in my mind, as it was now mid-August, the beginning of the second and final week of the festival. The thing was, the prospect of being in Boston in the charming brownstone condo I'd purchased on a quiet street in Back Bay wasn't the problem; if anything, the idea of living in Boston had increased in attractiveness since I met Ben. No, it was the thought of returning to the FrancisPearl fifteen-hour-a-day grind with weekend work that was not a welcome one. Not because I didn't like to work hard. But because there was now something—no, someone—in my life who warranted my time and attention.

I wasn't sure how that was going to work. I just knew it was going to have to work somehow, because I was not going to compromise on Ben. He was going to be a part of my life in Boston. A rather large part of my life, if things kept going the way they were.

Then there was the matter of Gerald. I had not appreciated his heavy-handed insinuation that I needed to reconsider representing the merchant association. He said he trusted me, so why did it seem like I was more under his thumb than ever?

I juxtaposed that with my inability to reconcile what Ben had said about Gerald. It wasn't that I didn't believe Ben; it's that I knew that everybody had their own narrative and perception of events. Sure, Gerald was a "win at any cost, just not at any price" kind of attorney, but that didn't mean he'd stooped to doing something underhanded.

During intermission, Ben surprised us all by gallantly offering to take the twins over to the candy apple booth so Callie and Chris could have a few stolen moments at the outdoor bar.

"Would you like some backup?" I offered.

"I'm pretty sure I can manage twins for fifteen minutes," he said with a self-deprecating grin. "But you ladies are welcome to join me if you like."

"I may tag along for the sheer entertainment value," Sam said, her smile wicked.

"He's adding sugar to an already volatile equation," I breathed.

"Come along, girls," Ben said to Alyssa and Kayla, blithely ignoring us. The two giggling girls followed Ben toward the smell of cinnamon and sugar, while Sam and I trailed behind.

"What did you think of the performance so far?" I asked.

"He's doomed," Sam said, her eyes on Ben.

I snorted. "I meant the mainstage."

Her brown eyes danced with amusement. "You know, I never cared much for *The Taming of the Shrew*. But I rather like what your sister has done by gender-flipping it. It's significantly less offensive."

"Wholeheartedly agree."

Ahead of us, Ben and the girls had reached the candy apple line and were in deep negotiation.

"I think he's losing," I sighed.

"He's got a soft spot for kids," Sam said. "One of the guys at work has a daughter a little older than these two, and Ben's her honorary uncle. He actually instituted a bring-your-kid-to-work day. We're a pretty young team, so only one of us has a kid. It made for a very entertaining Friday—eleven adults taking one child out to a very fancy Boston lunch."

"I bet she loved it."

"She completely loved it," Sam agreed.

I squinted at Ben, who was bent over the girls and gesturing to the sign. From the booming sound of his laugh, I could tell they were haggling. "It certainly helps explain why he's getting his ass handed to him."

"I promise you he's much better on the Boston development scene."

"I would hope so," I laughed. "I hear it's among the most cut-throat of the markets."

"It is, but you wouldn't know it from the way Ben runs Dane. He's very focused on his employees and keeping everyone gainfully employed. Even in the leanest times when we were just scraping by, he never cut benefits or hours."

"That can't be great for the bottom line," I observed, though I was secretly pleased Ben cared so much for his people. It fit.

"Tell me about it. Sometimes I wish my partner was less of an exemplary human being," she grumbled. "Then I remind myself that part of the reason I love what I do is that everyone around our place is generally happy, and turnover is low, so we don't have to hire incompetent jerk wads."

"Incompetent jerk wads can be a real drag on morale."

"You have no idea. In this business you have to be especially careful who you hire. Employees who thrive in the Boston development scene aren't always the most scrupulous bunch. You really have to pick through some garbage to find the gems."

"Oh yeah?" On sabbatical and off duty or not, I knew industry gossip when I heard it.

"It's a vicious ecosystem," Sam confided, dropping her voice and leaning into me. Her perfume smelled of orchids with something calm beneath the floral—maybe ylang-ylang? How long did you have to be in someone's acquaintance before you could tell them they platonically smelled delicious? "Opportunities are scarce and the choice bites go to the bigger predators," she continued. "We smaller, independent fish, the best of us anyway, are trying to stay out of the muck, if you catch my drift."

I stared at her a long moment. Her eyes didn't waver on mine. "You're referring to Boston's rampant corruption problem, I assume?" I said in a low voice.

She dipped her head once. "I am. Dane does not wallow in the muck, if that's what you're wondering."

"It never occurred to me you did. Having met Ben and now you, neither of you seem up for . . . muckraking."

Her smile was sharp. "You know, when Ben told me who you were and I looked you up, I wasn't sure I was going to like you. But I do like you. You don't mince."

"I don't mince," I agreed. I suspected a *but* was coming and I was curious how she thought I figured into this small, vicious ecosystem. "Nor do you strike me as a mincer either."

"I'm not. Which is why I know you'll appreciate my bluntness when I say I can't understand why you still work for Gerald Cutler."

"Well, this isn't the first time my working with Gerald Cutler has come up in the context of Dane Development. Something you want to talk about?"

"Woman to woman? Yeah," Sam said, her dark eyes gleaming. "Your boss is a real problem for me. I don't find his tactics to be very ethical."

"Gerald Cutler is a lot of things, mostly an overbearing pain in my ass these days, but I've never found him to be unethical."

"That's because you've never had to sit across the table from him," Sam said evenly. "As much as he's a New York partner, the idea for your Boston satellite office was his play. He's kept his hand in the development scene there, and I'm guessing he wanted to put someone he trusts, someone he's groomed to be as ruthless as he is, in place to keep an eye on things."

"That's . . ." I didn't have the words I wanted. I appreciated Sam's directness but didn't love the implication that I was somehow Gerald's puppet. So I settled on, "That's a rather serious thing to say. Can I ask where you're coming from on that?"

"When I was still practicing, I represented a developer on a bid by the Pru. After work one night, I was in the Financial District having a drink with friends when a man approached me at the bar. This guy wanted to offer my client cash to step out of a bid. Not knowing who he was, I treated him to a lecture on ethics and the rules of the bid process in general. The Boston development bid scene might be a tad shady, but I am not," Sam said firmly.

"Anyway, when that didn't work, this guy found me again, this time at my office after hours. He barged into my office and showed me a bunch of photos of my client snorting an"—she paused delicately—"an illicit substance. Threatened to send it around to the guy's wife and everyone he worked with if we didn't back out of the bid. Then he pulled out some pictures of me from college, smoking weed." Her eyes flashed. "As a woman of color, Portia, I don't need to explain to you what a tight leash I'm on. Moreover, I have two very conservative Japanese parents. Those pictures were the last thing I wanted them to see."

"That is so inappropriate," I hissed between my teeth.

"You're telling me. So I had a long heart-to-heart with my client, and while I wanted to report this creep, damn the consequences, my client ultimately backed out of the bid."

"Sam, are you telling me Gerald Cutler intimidated your client to back out of a bid?" My voice was deadly quiet. "Because I don't care who he is to me, I will file a complaint with the New York State Board of Law Examiners and email firm leadership tonight. This kind of behavior is unacceptable."

"No," she said. "Gerald didn't do it directly. Your boss is too smart for that. But I did hire a private investigator to investigate the charmer who approached my client. His name is Richard Kerrigan, aka Dickie K."

"Dickie K?"

"Right?" Her magenta-glossed lips twisted. "Tacky, but that's the Boston underbelly for you. You ever hear Gerald mention him?"

"No," I said emphatically.

Sam looked disappointed, but unsurprised.

"How do you know this"—I couldn't say *Dickie K* again—"this individual is tied to Gerald?"

"I don't. The investigator couldn't find a direct paper trail to Gerald, but he did discover several other incidents involving bid intimidation and Dickie K. Every single one of these incidents involved a bid that a FrancisPearl client was participating in."

"That's not exactly what I'd call a strong causal link." I held my hands up. "I'm not defending Gerald." I didn't mention that I was actually trying to quiet the rising gorge slicking its way up the back of my throat.

"I know," she said, shaking her glossy hair in frustration. "But I can't shake this feeling that Dickie Kerrigan is your boss's fixer."

This was not *Michael Clayton*; lawyers did not go around hiring fixers. Especially well-respected, well-tenured partners of big law firms.

Or did they? A wave of uncertainty washed cold and unwelcome over me. Gerald was a dogged fighter, a win-at-any-cost kind of bruiser. Could I have missed something in our decade-long partnership? Or had he concealed it from me? And if he had, was it because he didn't trust me, or did he think (and rightly so) that I wouldn't have gone along with it? God, I was hoping it was the latter.

"I don't know, Sam. I believe what you're saying and what your PI found, but this—it's not enough." And it wasn't. I did believe Sam. Boston was a small ecosystem and an important market for FrancisPearl. Even before the plans were set in motion for me to launch the Boston office, the firm had had a strong foothold there. In fact, that was part of the pitch for a satellite office. Gerald's pitch, I remembered with vivid recall. I'd been at the partners presentation when he'd rolled it out.

"Will you send me what you have on this? You have my word I won't share it with Gerald, though if you're okay with it, I may employ some resources of my own to corroborate what you've found. I can assure you I'll be very discreet. You can trust me."

Sam's eyes lingered on my face. "Ben was right. You're one of the good ones, aren't you?"

For some reason, that kindled something warm inside me, chasing away the cold cringe of doubt. "Thanks for telling me," I said. "You took a risk."

"Sometimes you have to take a calculated risk. Otherwise, you're just a complicit cog in a broken system."

I was genuinely starting to like Sam, despite the fact that she'd just saddled me with knowledge that could potentially derail my entire career. What if she was right? If so, I couldn't work for Gerald anymore, that was clear. But what if it wasn't just Gerald—what if it was FrancisPearl? Sensing the dangerous direction of that line of thinking, I steered myself back on course. At least for now. "Can I ask you something?"

"You can always ask," she said with a half smile.

"Did these experiences lead to your decision to not practice law anymore?" I asked.

Sam thought about this for a long moment. "Was it a contributing factor? Yes. I was tired of being on the back foot like that. To know that your colleagues aren't playing by the same rules is infuriating. But was it the main reason? No. Being a lawyer didn't light my fire the way I thought it would. Leaving practice was a huge deal with my parents. It wasn't so much that I wasn't going to be a lawyer anymore but that I'd appear weak by pivoting to something different.

"I'm glad I did it though. I love what I do now. I'm much more suited for the business side of the house. I can't imagine doing anything different, and I certainly can't imagine not having Ben as my partner. Has he told you much about the early days of Dane?"

"Not much," I admitted.

"When I tell you Ben built Dane from nothing, I mean literally nothing. He hustled and scraped to find investors and loans in those early days and worked nights, weekends, holidays, double shifts, sometimes even triple shifts. I don't know how he did it, pushing himself to the physical and mental brink like that, but you know what the first thing he did when we could afford to start hiring people was? He gave them everything he never had—benefits, perks, a sense of security. Ben has this knack for seeing what a person really needs and giving it to them. In my case, I wanted a challenge, more variety and greater scope over what I was working on. Ben gave me that chance." She held up her hands. "I'm not knocking the legal profession; it just wasn't for me. I know Ben said you were all in on being a lawyer?"

"I am." I considered her, not sure I wanted to say the words out loud, because then I'd have to own them, to know they were out there. But here was another professional woman, one who I thought would understand me. Palms a little sweaty, I forged ahead. "Lately, I've felt conflicted about the lifestyle. I'm not saying I want to lie around all day on some aimless quest to find myself, but I've started to wonder if maybe there's a way to do the work I enjoy that doesn't cost the balance of my whole life." I frowned. "What is it with you Dane Development people? Why are you so easy to talk to?"

Sam laughed. "Take it from someone who's been where you are, Portia. There is no shame in a pivot."

"What's a pivot?" Kayla asked, wedging her way between us, her hand closed around the candy apple stick like it was a sticky mace.

"It's a change in course," I told her.

"Like when my dad gets lost and the voice on his phone tells him to make a U-turn?" Alyssa chimed in. Her mouth was already glistening with caramel. I sincerely hoped Callie had brought wet wipes with her.

Ben's laugh rose up into the night air, curling like campfire smoke. He offered me a shiny red candy apple. "You strike me as a purist." To Sam, he handed one loaded down with M&M's and Oreos. "Some utter chaos for you."

Thanking him, I regarded the shiny surface of the apple and saw a smiling reflection of myself with slightly windblown hair. Unguarded and, if I was being honest, maybe a little uncertain—but utterly happy. Somehow it looked right on me.

I slipped my hand into Ben's and kissed his cheek. "Thank you."

"For the candy apple?"

I shook my head. I wasn't going to be so trite as to say "For being you," because I'd throw up in my mouth. So I settled on "For everything" and kissed him again.

THE NEXT MORNING, I walked into the café, a smile on my face and that clean wintry smell of Ben still clinging to my skin. I ordered a red-eye from my sister and settled down at my usual bistro table. Had I been here long enough to have a usual table? I wasn't sure, but

I was rather covetous of this particular one in the back, flanking an exposed brick wall with a photo of a sun-drenched Ponte Vecchio hanging over it.

Turning to the task at hand, I opened my personal laptop, and as expected, there was an email from Sam in my inbox with several attachments. Taking a deep breath, I prepared to perch upon the slipperiest slope of my professional career and prayed that I wouldn't slide down it.

I hadn't called Chris for advice. Not because I didn't trust him, but because I didn't want to put him in the same position I was in. On the one hand, I was taking actions that could be construed as acting against the interests of the firm of which I was a partner. On the other hand, if it turned out Gerald had committed professional misconduct and I reported it, I'd be doing the firm a favor. I hoped.

First, I reviewed the carefully prepared report of Sam's investigator, Dion Hill. The report was methodical and thorough, detailing the ask, the research performed and the actions taken. There was photographic evidence of Richard Kerrigan appearing to converse with several individuals, all of whom were identified by their company affiliation. Each one of the companies represented had confirmed participation and later withdrawn from a bid. While none of the individuals Kerrigan was photographed with were clients of FrancisPearl, all of the bids had one thing in common: at least one participant, though not always the ultimate winner of the bid, was a FrancisPearl client. In fact, more than half of the clients in question were Gerald's clients.

Swearing under my breath, I drained the rest of my red-eye. Although I had connected the dots to Gerald's clients, the evidence against him still wasn't conclusive. At best, there was a pattern that could be explained away by Gerald's prominence in development and the rather small sample size of deals. There was certainly nothing in anything the PI had found connecting Gerald to Richard Kerrigan. In short, I had only a growing suspicion that my longtime mentor might not be as by the book as I had originally thought.

Running my hands through my hair, I exhaled and slumped in

my seat. Immediately straightening, I reminded myself that personal turmoil was no excuse for poor posture. Scanning the now busy café, I spotted a familiar face lounging across a bistro chair and savoring a bite of oatmeal, looking for all the world like a hipster lumberjack.

Ian lifted his spoon in greeting and wove his way over to my table. "I was wondering when you would look up and notice me. How is the Queen of Air and Darkness this fine morning?"

One of the many things I admired about Ian was his ability to be discreet. Last Christmas, when I'd come to visit Miranda for the holidays, she and Adam had called it a night, while Ian wanted to visit a new wine bar. One thing led to another and I ended up sharing both a bottle of wine and a bed with him. He'd never said a word. Never made it weird. Acted like a perfect gentleman the next day and reverted to his pet nicknames for me, like always. I could appreciate a man who kept to the unwritten rules of the one-night stand.

In fact, the only person who knew about it was Candace, because it had been too good not to share the details. Someday somewhere somebody was going to have the wherewithal and inner thigh strength to lock that man down for good.

"Flying hard and fast as always," I told him. "What are you up to?"

"Trying to find a date to the dinner theater, actually. I have an extra seat for tonight's performance. You available?"

"Sadly, no. Because I'm in the dinner theater, remember?" I said dryly.

"I know, but you're an expert multitasker. You could come sit with me for the scenes you're not in."

I snorted. "I'm sure that wouldn't be disruptive. How did you end up with an extra ticket?"

"Ask your sister," he said with a wink. "The chef. Your sister the chef," he added by way of clarification. "Not your sister the newly engaged."

That wasn't like Cordelia to bail on dinner theater, but there were two more performances left, and I was sure Candace could scratch up an extra ticket for her, if she wanted one. The more interesting question was why she would be bailing on the dinner theater.

"How you doing with this whole engagement thing?" I asked.

"I vacillate between giddiness at planning the best bachelorette party ever and abject terror that Miranda and Adam are fully committed to adulting and I'll be left behind."

"That is surprisingly insightful."

"I'm more than just a pretty face, you know." He smiled at me from beneath lashes that most women would die for. "Speaking of pretty faces—"

"Miranda's right. You're terrible at segues."

"Are you going to deny me details about the hot developer? That hardly seems fair. You're practically taunting me with your sex hair."

"I do not have sex hair," I said archly, and made a show of tossing my hair. And then smoothed it to make sure I did not, in fact, have sex hair.

"I never thought I'd see the day that Portia Barnes was mooning after someone."

"It's hardly mooning," I protested.

"Well, I grant you that committing B and E is a strange method of foreplay, but hey, I'm not judging you corporate types."

"You're a corporate type," I pointed out.

"No, I'm a *creative* type," he corrected.

"The salient difference being?" I asked.

"I make my own fun." He winked. "Now, in that vein, you'll need to excuse me. I have a costume shop to raid." He stood up, hiking his bike-messenger-bag-turned-man-purse over his shoulder.

"Ian, wait."

Ian, who was already tall and now had the advantage of standing while I was seated, peered down at me. "You want to come?"

"Could you sit down a minute? I was hoping to ask you something. If you don't mind."

He sat down, all traces of his earlier playfulness gone. That was another thing I liked about him. He knew when the wind had shifted. "Sure, what's up?"

"What I'm about to ask you needs to stay between us. No Miranda. Can you do that?"

Ian's nostrils flared as he considered it. "Can I ask a question before I answer?"

I nodded.

"What you're about to ask me wouldn't put me in an awkward position with your sister, right? You're not about to tell me something horrible you found out about Adam, like he's secretly an avid collector of lampshades made of human skin or something, right?"

"I . . . no. That's horrible," I replied, wrinkling my nose. "Is that really where your mind goes?"

"Portia, your 'This is Sparta' game face right now is freaking me out."

Sighing, I tried to relax the muscles in my face, which was easier said than done. "This has nothing to do with Miranda or Adam or anybody you care about."

"Okay, lay it on me."

"Have you ever used a PI before? In Boston."

"Oh." Ian's shoulders slumped in comical relief. "No, but I've dated a few." His face broke into a grin. "Wait, I've got a gym buddy who's a PI."

"Is he any good?"

"He benches like a bull and never name-drops, but I get the sense he does all right."

"Can you send me his contact information?"

"Sure," Ian said slowly. He opened his mouth to speak and then shut it. I knew without a doubt that he had just stopped himself from asking me for further details. Instead, he asked, "Are you okay?"

"I am. It's a work thing, not a personal thing. I need someone local."

While I hadn't doubted Miranda's sincerity when she extolled Ian's many virtues over the years, I was now basking in the full sun of his humanity. She was right. It was glorious.

"I'll get you his information today," Ian said. "If something changes and you need any help, you let me know."

"Thanks, Ian. I will."

Sensing we were done, he stood. "My queen," he said, dipping his head to me, and then louder, "Cordy, my love. I'll see you soon, my culinary muse," he called in the direction of the kitchen.

Once he'd left, I slipped behind the counter and made my way to the kitchen. By the sounds of it, Cordelia was beating on some dough. At least, I hoped it was dough. With Cordelia you could never be too sure. "Bailing on dinner theater tonight?"

Cordelia spun around, a rolling pin in her hand. "Warn a woman when you come into her space like that."

"Well, it's not like there's a door to knock on," I said. "Can we discuss why you're skipping dinner theater tonight? Who's doing the desserts?"

"Oh, that. Candace co-opted one of the pastry chefs to help out. Second-string, I know," she teased. "But something came up and I need to drive to Boston for something early tomorrow morning. I'll catch your turn on the stage on closing night, don't worry."

"I'm not worried about that. Is everything okay with you? Are you . . . well?"

"Oh yes, nothing medical," she said quickly, but didn't elaborate further. I leveled my big-sister gaze on her and waited—one second, two seconds, three seconds . . .

"I have a job interview."

"In Boston? That's great."

"Not exactly in Boston. The company is in Boston. The role is . . . abroad."

"That's cryptic."

"There's this group of—I don't want to say elite pastry chefs, but that's kind of what they are, and judging by the way you're biting your lip right now, I'm so glad you don't have Miranda's power of the pun, because I know it's ripe for it."

"Go on," I said, sighing and desperately trying to think of something funny to say involving elite pastry chefs.

"They cook for exclusive functions all over Europe—castles in Scotland, rooftop villas in Florence, private parties in the gardens of Versailles. It would be a six-month gig to start."

"Wow," I breathed.

"Yeah," Cordelia sighed dreamily. "I'm talking next-level pastry technique. But"—I could see the exact moment she came crashing down to earth—"there's the café and Mom and Dad to think about."

"Slow down," I said, coming to stand beside her. "Mom and Dad would want you to be happy. If that means finding someone to manage the café while you're gone or even permanently, that can be arranged."

Cordelia twisted her fingers nervously. "It's not just the café. I mean, that's a huge part of it, but we don't know where Mom's going to be with . . . stuff." She looked immediately guilty. "You can't ever tell her I said that. She would be royally pissed if she thought I was giving something up to stay here and help. But I can't leave Dad on his own." Hastily, she added, "I didn't mean it like that. You and Miranda are helping out too."

"But you've been shouldering the brunt of it. That's not fair to you. You should be able to take this opportunity. With Miranda and me both in Boston, we can cover Mom. That's assuming she even needs more treatments. Dr. Wu thinks she has a good shot at being done after this round."

"Look at you being all optimistic," Cordelia noted.

"You should take the opportunity if you love it," I said. "We'll all be here to support you. I can help Mom and Dad find your temporary replacement—somebody who can make a halfway decent fruit tart, of course—and do all the paperwork. Not to get all hokey, but Mom said something to me recently about there being a whole wide world out there begging to be explored. I'm sure that motherly advice applies to you as well. You don't have to stay in Bard's. You can"—the words felt strange on my tongue—"you can pivot."

My sister took a deep, shuddering breath. "Thanks, I needed that. I love Bard's, but . . . but I think it may be time for a change."

"I hear that," I said. I didn't want to make the moment all about me, but wow, did that resonate for me too. I leaned in, hugging her. "Tomorrow after your interview, I want to hear about this elite pastry task force you're considering joining. Maybe you can brush up on your pate a choux hand-to-hand combat?"

"Yeah no, you're still terrible at jokes," she said, her voice muffled against me. "But I do like this new life-affirming big-sister routine."

Falstaff's Folly

The sunlight filtered across my face, coaxing me into consciousness.

"Good morning," Ben murmured into my neck. From behind me, his arms wrapped around me. God, I loved the way that felt, like an extra dose of sunshine, warm and skin tingling.

"Good morning to you too," I said.

"Sleep okay?"

"More than okay," I murmured, torn between wanting to turn around and face him and reluctant to break this embrace, even if only for a brief moment. "I slept great. Didn't even think about the host of disturbing things that have likely transpired in this bed before us."

Ben's mouth curved into a smile at the base of my neck. "I was going to say, I had an incredible couple of days with you. I know you're not the biggest Shakespeare fan, but there is something incredibly fun about the festival."

"Mmm," I agreed, though my mind flashed to *The Taming of the Shrew* beneath the night sky, knowing that even if the town or merchant association decided to buy Peaseblossom's and turn the driving range into some sort of outdoor theater, it wouldn't be the same.

There was something magic about the experience of being on the island, the sound of water lapping on rocks in the distance, the occasional eerie hoot in the trees. *Stop,* I told myself. I needed to let this go. *Move forward, Portia,* I told myself.

All the while I'd been thinking, Ben was tracing lazy patterns up and down my back, making me shiver in anticipation. Until his fingers touched the scarred patch below my left shoulder blade in just the wrong way. I involuntarily flinched and turned over onto my back.

He sat up quickly. "Did I hurt you? Portia, if I—"

"No," I said just as quickly. "Most of the time I forget they're even there, and other times they're . . ." I trailed off. *Burning* wasn't the right word anymore. "Sensitive," I finished.

Ben was looking down at me, the question in his eyes, but no words on his lips. Giving me the space if I wanted to talk about it. I appreciated that. Did I want to talk about Berlin? Other than my therapist, I hadn't told anyone about it. But staring up at Ben, I had this one driving thought. I wanted him to see all of me. Even the ugly part.

"I was heading up this project. Project Berlin. It was a highly complicated, highly confidential restructuring that had to occur over a two-week period while I had a half dozen other deals going off. The project was inadequately staffed—we were suffering from low retention of associates, like everyone else in the industry—and after a three-night bender sleeping on a chair in my office, I may have collapsed in a very public manner on a call with half a dozen I-bankers, my client and the rest of the deal team.

"An ambulance was called and I was admitted to the hospital with a severe kidney infection. Once that was under control, the doctors discovered that I had a painful case of shingles on the left side of my back and two gastric ulcers that eventually required surgical repair."

"That's horrible."

"It wasn't that bad," I insisted. "No." I shook my head. "That's not right. It was horrible. I knew something was wrong that whole week, but I couldn't stop. The worse I felt, the harder I pushed through it. Right before the deal call that was heard around the office, I could see things creeping in at the edges of my vision, because my fever had spiked so high I was hallucinating, apparently. But I thought it was something that could wait until the deal closed. I was wrong."

"I'm so sorry," he said, settling in beside me again and holding me close.

"Don't be," I said. "It was my fault."

"Getting sick is hardly your fault."

"No," I corrected him. "It was my fault because it was preventable."

"Possible you're being a little hard on yourself?"

I hadn't told him the worst part, which hadn't been physical at all. Sure, the shingles had burned and the ulcers had made eating an unpalatable and dicey proposition for months. But what had killed me was how disappointed Gerald was with me that I'd let myself get into this condition in the first place. It became this rallying cry of "I won't have another Berlin on my hands."

I'd been mortified, embarrassed and completely crestfallen at how I'd failed Gerald, broken our unspoken pact of professionalism by literally breaking down on the job.

But when I thought about it now, it struck me how callous Gerald had been about the entire thing. Rather than care about my personal well-being in the face of a serious physical setback, he'd been more concerned about my reputation—and, by association, how it reflected on him.

Maybe that was slightly revisionist of me, but the more I thought about it, the less I liked how he'd acted. I supposed I'd been thinking a lot about Gerald and our past interactions in a different light these days. The shine was off the proverbial apple. And I was starting to truly believe the apple was rotten to its core.

"What was the fallout like at work from something like that?" Ben asked.

"Besides attaining urban legend status as the partner who nearly died trying to close a deal?"

"Yes, besides that."

"Let's just say I promptly hired a nutritionist and a therapist."

"Did they help? I find seeing a therapist to be very helpful."

I smiled warmly at him, grateful that he'd entrusted me with another piece of him.

"The nutritionist has helped me so I can eat again without discomfort or fear. For the most part. There are still some times that I eat something and it's like literal fire inside of me. Other times, I feel fine but food tastes like nothing. Unclear if it's still my body rebounding from the ulcers or something psychological left over from that period in my life. Either way, I'm working on it."

Ben winced. "That sucks."

"Beyond the telling of it," I agreed. "But it is so much better than it was." I looked down to where I'd apparently ensnared one of his hands, twining my fingers in his as I'd told him about the lowest lowlight of my life. "Therapy has taught me I need to listen for signs and symptoms in my body and not ignore them in favor of billable hours." Therapy was so much more than that, of course. But I couldn't open up the floodgates more than I already had, and I could tell from the way he was slowly nodding that Ben got it.

"It was bad timing more than anything else. Berlin hit, and right on the heels of it, I found out a few months later that my mother had cancer. It drove home the concept of mortality and prioritizing one's health."

"You don't say?"

I swatted him with my hand. "Oh, don't pretend you were born with an innate sense of your own mortality."

"Never," he said, his voice all mock solemnity. "Where did Berlin fit in the timeline of going out for managing partner?"

"The opportunity surfaced in the back half of that year," I admitted. I waited for him to comment or condemn me for what amounted to doubling down on work after a serious illness instead of taking a step back.

Instead, he said softly, "Sometimes when opportunity knocks, it's the least opportune time." And I was grateful for it.

"If I hadn't, I'd always be wondering, looking back on it."

"If you could do it all over again, would you?"

I opened my mouth to reply yes, of course. But the words disintegrated in my throat. It was such a complicated question. On the one hand, it was like I learned nothing from being seriously ill. On the other hand, by the time the opportunity came up, I was doing better physically and mentally, and I had wanted this position like I'd never wanted anything in my whole life. But now? After what I'd learned about Gerald? I wasn't so sure. Maybe being in two separate offices and my new managing responsibilities would create enough distance between us. Maybe he'd stop micromanaging and keeping tabs on my every move. Maybe not.

"I don't know," I admitted. "Being in Bard's this summer has given me a lot to think about." Tucking a piece of hair behind my ear, I added, "I know how it sounds. I'm not normally this indecisive, but the timing . . ." I trailed off.

"Sometimes timing is everything," Ben said, his thumb tracing circles over my skin. "Right after Danny died, I wasn't sleeping or eating well. The whole world was gray. An investment opportunity came up, and it was just big enough to introduce some real risk into Dane Development. It was one of those 'here on Friday, gone on Monday' kind of deals, of course. And I went for it. Even though I wasn't in the best state of mind—and I knew that—I had to go for it."

"Did it pay off?"

"It did. But it was touch-and-go for a while, and there were moments when I doubted myself, wondering if I was doing something so risky to distract myself from my grief."

"And?"

"And the deal paid off, but I don't look back on it as a success. I did it for the wrong reasons."

"But it helped you with your grief over losing Danny."

Ben was thoughtful for a long moment. "It certainly distracted me for a time. But it was a temporary fix. It wasn't until I started to see a therapist that I learned to live with my grief and address my anger at having such shit parents."

"You're pretty up-front about therapy, huh?" I asked, a little surprised. I didn't want to make a broad generalization here, but most of the men I worked alongside, Chris included, wouldn't have copped to seeing a therapist. As good as we all were getting at bringing our quasi-authentic selves to work, therapy was still a taboo subject at the upper levels.

"It's not something I widely publicize with external clients," Ben said, "but I certainly don't hide it either. Sam knows, as does my whole leadership team. Asking for help is not something I'm ashamed of. I needed it and found the means to do it. Not everyone is so lucky."

I blew out a long breath. I'd never felt like I'd been lacking in the confidence department, but damn if I didn't admire how frank he was about seeking help. I could barely bring myself to talk about it with any of my family or what few friends I had. It certainly wasn't because I didn't trust my parents or sisters, or Candace or even Chris; I'd always wanted to spare them my problems, not burden them. But had it been more than that? Had I fallen into that shame trap of not wanting to admit that I'd needed help at various points in my life?

"Hey, where'd you go?" he teased, his breath tickling my ear. "Come back to me."

"I'm right here," I breathed. "Not going anywhere until you kick me out."

"I was hoping you'd say that, because I would so love for you to be my breakfast buddy. I'm oddly famished this morning." He gave me a rakish grin. "But sadly, the coffee maker downstairs is on the fritz. I'm pretty sure it saw its best years during the Obama administration. I was thinking I should pop out to the café and return with coffee and sustenance."

"Would you like me to go with you?" I offered.

"Nah, why don't you log a bit more sleep?" he said, his gray eyes tender. "Also, it reduces the likelihood of your sister mocking us when we both stumble into the café with bedhead."

"It's like you already know her," I said, biting my lip to keep from laughing.

Ben swung out of bed and shrugged on some jeans. Although it was far sexier to see him taking his pants off, there was still something alluring about the way the jeans molded around his lean frame and—*Down, girl*, I told myself. Let the man get some breakfast first.

I tried to snooze while Ben was gone. My body still seemed to be in this mode where it snatched every available hour it could to sleep. As if it had been starved for so long. I pushed away thoughts of what would happen in a few weeks when I returned to Boston and started managing. While I might still have Ben, it wouldn't be like this anymore. No admiring him as he slid into his jeans while I lazily looked on. I'd likely be halfway out the door, stealing a quick kiss—if I was lucky.

Stop, I told myself, pulling a pillow over my head. *Take the sleep while you still can.*

But even with the sex marathon last night, I couldn't fall back to sleep, so I decided to wander around downstairs and raid the fruit bowl on the counter. Padding downstairs in nothing but Ben's T-shirt and bare legs, I fully owned that I was a walking cliché, but at least I had hot sex hair.

Pausing at the open door to the office, remembering our first encounter on that desk, I noted that Ben had restored the desk to actual working order—neatly stacked papers, file folders and—drawings. These looked similar to the ones Ben had showed me on his phone, only they were printed out and . . . different. The condos had a different architectural look now, less modern, more salty New England and a little more set back from the water's edge. I still didn't like them, but even I had to admit they were more in line with other houses in Bard's Rest.

Behind the desk I spied dusty boxes and recognized them as the ones from the storage shed. They were unopened and stacked in a corner. Ben must have had them moved here after our clandestine outing to the island.

Staring at them in the light of day, they looked even more wilted and faded. They'd seemed so important the other night on the island. But given that they were more than likely stuffed to their carboard gills with old theater receipts and things with Ben were . . . progressing, the smart play was to ignore them.

But then I caught sight of something. Peeking out through the space cut out for the handle of one of the boxes, I could make out an old black-and-white photo of what had to be a performance— maybe a mainstage.

I was reminded of one of those twisted fairy tales Miranda used to read. The tale of Bluebeard's wife. The woman who was given keys to all the rooms in the castle and was told by her much older mansplaining husband she could go anywhere except the creepy underground chamber. So of course our girl went to investigate and discovered a room full of bodies for her trouble.

Swallowing hard, I took one barefoot step forward, and another, until I was standing directly in front of the boxes. No, I was not going to snoop. With an unsteady breath, I forcibly turned away from the boxes and headed for the kitchen, where I found a bowl of apples and helped myself.

Ben returned a few minutes later with Cordelia's still-warm croissants and heavenly coffee. We tore into the pastries, Ben watching me intently as I licked gooey chocolate off my fingers.

"I thought I'd find you sleeping. I'm a little sad you're not still in bed."

"I came downstairs for some fruit and couldn't resist exploring a bit more," I confessed. "You are staying in a notorious swingers' hideaway and all."

Ben's eyes widened. "So that's what those rings are over the bed?"

"What?"

He laughed. "I'm kidding, but one of the smaller guest bedrooms does have some oddly placed mirrors."

I waggled my eyebrows at him. "You did promise me a second act later."

"My, my, we're full of surprises this morning." Ben cupped my face in his hands, kissing me, his lips tasting of chocolate and coffee. He backed me against the wall and hoisted me up, my hands braced against the cabinet on one side and the doorjamb on the other. I locked my legs around him, grinding against him. "Keep that up and we won't make it upstairs."

We didn't make it upstairs. We wound up in the office on the desk again—what was it with this man and desks? But I couldn't say I minded.

"Thank god I bought four croissants," Ben panted when we'd finished. "It could be hours before I'm fully functional again."

"I'll reheat the coffee," I said, kissing his nose. "Regroup in the living room?"

"That's giving my limbs an awful lot of credit right now," he said, his expression doubtful.

I snickered, pulling Ben's T-shirt back over my head. Out of the corner of my eye, I caught sight of the boxes again. I looked between Ben and the boxes and decided I was going for it. "Those are the boxes from the island, right?"

"I had them moved here in a fit of pique after a mob of vigilantes broke into a storage shed," he said dryly.

I shot him a withering glance. "We were hardly vigilantes."

"They do smell a bit like campfire smoke and mothballs, don't they?" Ben asked. "I should move them out to the garage."

"Or I could take them to the town hall," I offered. "If you don't want them, maybe Emmeline would. It looks like at least one of the boxes has some old photos in it. She could make a display at the town hall or file them or something." *A small consolation,* I thought. But something in me told me Emmeline would be horrified if we threw away any of the town's history without so much as a glance.

Ben weighed me with his eyes. "This isn't some ploy to thwart the sale of Will's Island?"

I shook my head. "If my family can move on, so can I," I said. I meant it. I wanted to see where things went with Ben. I needed to let go of this thing with the island. "I saw your plans for the condos on your desk. I hope you don't mind."

"Not at all. What did you think?" Ben asked, his voice suspiciously casual.

"Better."

He clutched his chest. "My heart brimmeth over."

"More thoughtful and in keeping with Bard's Rest culture. Don't get me wrong—I still think the locals will burn you in effigy wherever they decide to hold the mainstages. But I think you're moving in the right direction."

"Glad to hear it. Maybe donating those boxes will curry additional favor. Emmeline's welcome to anything in there, unless there's any bullion. I call dibs on any recovered bullion."

"This is a town of Shakespearean enthusiasts, not pirates. You get that distinction, right?"

"Hamlet was kidnapped by pirates. Shakespeare had a thing about pirates."

"Right, yes. I can see how you could make the logical leap between Shakespeare, pirates and the town of Bard's Rest, which is thoroughly landlocked from any salty body of water and which the Bard never set foot in." I shook my head at him fondly as I headed for the kitchen. "I highly doubt there's any treasure buried in there."

Emmeline's Office

Emmeline frowned down at the dusty boxes I'd lugged to her door. "I preferred the lemon scones."

"Don't worry, those are in the car. I didn't think balancing them on top of mildewed boxes was a particularly sanitary move on my part."

"You're not wrong," she said dryly. "Where did you say you found these?"

"I didn't." I smiled beatifically.

Her brows rose sharply, but she let it go. "Here," she said, "you get the scones, I'll get some tea going."

When I sent a questioning look her way, she added, "Where else do you have to be today?"

As usual, she had my number. Today was the final day of the festival. I'd be performing in the closing performance of the dinner theater tonight, but otherwise, I had nowhere else to be until late afternoon. Unlike the last few days, which had been a flurry of putting out small festival fires during the day, dinner theater performances in the early evening and nights in Ben's bed.

Then there'd been the business with Reese Hill, Ian's surprisingly solid PI buddy, who I'd finally decided to call. I wasn't sure what I'd been expecting—maybe someone slightly shady, relentlessly charming, sipping booze in a dive bar and sporting a seedy mustache. But Reese had been a total professional, even a bit bland, outlining his services and asking me all the right questions until I'd eventually offered him employment and he'd accepted. I'd had more titillating conversations with my accountant.

After some stomach-churning indecision, I had eventually turned over everything Sam had sent me, as well as my own suggestions and avenues that he might explore based on my own dealings with Gerald. In any event, there was no going back now. I needed to see it through.

"Besides." Emmeline startled me out of my thoughts about Gerald, her lips curling into one of her rare smiles. "Don't you want to know what's in there?"

I was torn. There was a part of me that wanted to move on. Whatever was in those boxes was from a bygone era and had no practical application in this time and place. But there was another part of me, like Bluebeard's wife, that was dying to know what was in the box.

When I returned with the scones, Emmeline's sunny office smelled of strong English breakfast. She served it to me in a white mug with "Bard's Rest Shakespearean Festival—1973" emblazoned on it. Despite being older than I was, this mug was in pristine condition with nary a chip or speck of paint missing from its cheerful, cartoonish comedy and tragedy masks. This wasn't terribly surprising. Emmeline seemed like the kind of person who took care of things.

During my trip back out to the car for the pastry, Emmeline had stacked the boxes and divided them into two equal piles, one by her desk and one by a small card table. I assumed my position at the table, appreciating how she'd angled it so I'd catch a bit of the breeze coming in through the window.

I don't know why, but I found myself a little nervous as I lifted the lid of the first box. Not that I expected to find any bullion or anything, but as a lifelong history nerd, there was something alluring about taking a peek into the past like this. I hoped it didn't turn out to be a bunch of old receipts. But I had seen that photo peeking out of the top of one of them.

While there were some loose photos on the top, the rest of the contents were thick, oversized envelopes with the year and the name of the mainstage on them. The most recent ones, including last summer's, were on top and looked professionally done. I quickly dug through the envelopes and found the years that Miranda had been in high school, the peak of her mainstage career, and located her turns as Hero, Juliet, Beatrice and, my favorite, as her namesake from *The Tempest*. She looked so young and a little wild-eyed and uneasy. Or maybe I was projecting that onto a younger Miranda who I knew was less comfortable in her skin than the Miranda I knew today.

I proudly showed the pictures of my sister to Emmeline. "Can I make copies of these? I'd like to get them framed for her." They'd make a great shower or wedding gift.

"Wait until you find the ones of your mother. I know the photographer from just looking at those. She started the year before your mother took the stage. I bet they're in there as well."

"Which years?"

"Check the seventies."

I nearly knocked over a chair in my haste to return to the box, tearing through it until I found the relevant dates on the envelopes. I quickly flipped through some truly terrible polyester and regrettable hair choices until I found her. "Oh my god," I breathed. There was Mom, decked out in this white lace ensemble that would have made Stevie Nicks jealous, a crown of flowers entwined in her hair. My mother was a beautiful woman today, but then she'd been a beautiful girl, her mouth mischievous like Cordelia's, her hair wild and defiant like Miranda's, and there—in the way she stared at the camera dead-on—I saw me. My throat tightened unexpectedly.

"She was a formidable Titania," Emmeline said from over my shoulder. "I thought you'd want to know."

"Thanks," I said, dabbing at my eyes. "I think the dust is getting to me."

"That must be it," Emmeline said, but her voice wasn't unkind.

I found several other photos of my mother and Miranda and some candid ones of Dad, Tillie, Alice, Dan and Aaron. There was a particularly hilarious one of my parents in matching terry short shorts that I thought would make for a great gag holiday gift. I made a list on my phone of each picture I took and what envelope I'd taken it from. Sentimentality was no excuse to be an agent of chaos.

The second box contained more photos, but much older, as they were all black-and-white, all posed photos of the cast. "Am I going to find you in any of these?" I asked Emmeline.

When she didn't answer, I made it my personal mission to dig through every single photo until I eventually found a photo of a young Emmeline. I didn't know the play right off, but given that it was a man onstage with three women, Emmeline being the youngest, I felt reasonably confident that it was *King Lear*. I slipped that one into my pile without a word. I'd be framing that one as well.

The third and fourth boxes were an accountant's nightmare—or nirvana, I supposed, depending on the accountant. I marveled at the old receipts and painstaking accounts of wardrobe budgets but didn't spend much time on these.

After some vigorous handwashing and a tea break, I moved on to the fifth box. No photos in this one, and it looked to be much older than the others, even from the outside; the brown box had faded to the color of underdone overnight oats. This one was full of handwritten meeting notes. I picked up a sheaf of paper, and it was so delicate that I was afraid if I breathed on it, it would go to pieces in my hands. I squinted at the faded ink, noting that the dates across the pages ranged from the 1860s to the 1940s.

I carefully paged through the notes, not sure what I was looking at until something from 1876 called out to my inner lawyer. A draft amendment providing for two-year terms for governors, councillors and legislators—my pulse began to race.

"Emmeline," I called out, my voice and hands shaky.

New Hampshire was the first of the colonies to enact its own state constitution and formally rebuff British rule. I was pretty sure that I was holding an original amendment to the oldest state constitution in the United States.

"Let me wipe my glasses, dear," she replied.

Oh god, were my hands getting sweaty? Was I sweating on a piece of history? I hastily set it down while I waited for Emmeline. And just then, from one of my piles, a piece of paper slipped to the floor, delicate as tissue. Gingerly, I picked it up, the roar of blood in my ears nearly overwhelming me as I bent over to retrieve it.

This paper wasn't like the meeting notes, which were on thin but sturdier paper stock. No, this looked like personal correspondence. The handwriting was neat, if a bit flowery, but my eyes skipped to the signature.

A signature that was as deliberate and straightforward as the man it belonged to. Josiah Bartlett. I dropped it to the desk, pushed my chair back and stood. My pulse was banging its insistent fists against my rib cage.

Emmeline was suddenly hovering beside me. "That," I said, pointing to the amendment, "and this." I offered her the correspondence like it was a holy relic. I held my breath as she scanned the documents.

Her eyes still on the letter, she said, "Josiah Bartlett had a summer residence here in the early days of Bard's Rest. But it was a little before even my time, dear," she added dryly. Still, there was a scratch in her tone, the slightest sign of—bullshit. I knew bullshit when I heard it.

I shook my head firmly. "Don't hold out on me now, Emmeline. There's a portrait of him in one of the photos on display in the hall. You wrote out the label for it. He's also in your New Hampshire Notables hall of fame. You sent me to the island to look for this."

Emmeline looked down her glasses at me imperiously. "I suspected from some of the land maps and older records in my office that somewhere on the island may actually have been the first town meeting place, which would have been rather pivotal in terms of the New Hampshire general assembly. Potentially. I had no concrete proof, of course. Until now. But I had my suspicions. And my hopes."

I studied her for a long moment. "All of this would need to be vetted, of course, but I think . . ." I faltered, not wanting to provide false hope. "I'm not a hundred percent sure, but one might argue that that structure, maybe the whole island, might qualify for a historical landmark, or some sort of special protection at least."

"You think?" She cackled.

I glared at her. "Why didn't you tell me earlier in the summer you suspected this?"

"Would you have believed me? More importantly, would you have done anything about it?"

I opened my mouth. Closed it. Opened it again.

"Point for you," I grumped. "But why didn't you say anything to anyone else? You know, when the whole town was in turmoil over Will's."

"Because I wasn't sure there was actually anything out there. So I pointed the person in the best position to do something about it in the right direction. And trusted the rest to fate."

I blew out a frustrated breath. "You people put too much faith in the concept of fate. I blame Shakespeare."

Emmeline preened. "And yet, here we are."

"Here we are."

"It would seem to me you have all you need in that box if you wanted to do something about Will's Island."

She was right. I held in my hands what I suspected would be enough to prove that the storage shed—I had to stop thinking of it as the storage shed—that Will's Island could possibly be declared a historical site.

A historical site that would sink Ben's plans for waterfront development on Will's.

Ben, I thought, my throat tight with guilt. Ben, who handed over these documents to me without a second thought. Ben, who thought I'd use them for some local-interest display. Ben who would never forgive me for this.

"Wait, what do you mean if I *want* to do something about Will's Island?" I asked, my hand resting protectively on the box.

"These records, in and of themselves, are a once-in-a-lifetime discovery. Who's to say where they came from? I could say someone left them outside the town hall for us to discover."

Was she giving me an out here? I stared at Emmeline for a long moment and decided she was. I considered it. We could pretend we hadn't looked at these until long after that shed was a pile of timber and—I shook my head. "I couldn't."

Emmeline nodded slowly. "Or I could let people know in a few days that you dropped off these boxes, but that I made this discovery myself. I could run it through the Perkins and Townsend gossip express. If that would be easier for you." Emmeline's smile was knowing and a little sad.

Well, it wasn't like Ben and I'd been keeping a low profile at the mainstages. Of course Emmeline could have seen me out with him and put it together. I swallowed hard. I was generally not quick to cry, but somehow the decency in that gesture, her offer to surface this discovery without implicating me, brought the threat of tears to my eyes.

I shut my eyes tight, willing those tears to go wherever unshed tears went. "No, that's not right either." That wasn't how I wanted Ben to find out. I couldn't keep my part in all this from him, any more than I could hide this discovery from Bard's at large. I had lied to him once. I wouldn't do it again.

Emmeline gripped my arm with her cold hand in a bracing moment of solidarity. The woman had a grip on her. Though I appreciated she didn't feed me some platitude about doing the right thing or any line like that. "I knew you were a fighter, Portia Barnes."

I acknowledged that with a tight nod.

"Go fight, and when the dust clears, make sure you have ahold of what you were fighting for."

Braveheart it was not, but nevertheless, my spine stiffened, and my resolve returned. I turned to Emmeline. "I will," I said. Even if I wasn't sure what I could possibly be holding when the dust cleared, I did have an idea of who I wanted to be holding when the dust had cleared.

....

The Kitchen of Falstaff's Folly

Ben had left the front door of the Folly open for me. But I still called out to him as I stepped over the threshold. I didn't want to startle him, especially not before I rocked his world, and not in the fun way.

"In here," his voice rang out from the kitchen.

Ben was putting the finishing touches on a cheese board that was bursting with what I guessed to be both cow and goat varieties, marcona almonds, honeycomb, pita crisps and even cornichons. Yes, the man had added tiny pickles. He was a keeper. Even more so, I thought as he headed to the fridge and handed me a chilled glass of Beaujolais.

"You do know I'm performing in the dinner theater in a few hours and you're sitting in the audience, yes? If you're unfamiliar of the protocols I can walk you through them, but they boil down into components: watching theater and eating as many courses as there are scenes." At least, I sincerely hoped we'd still be attending the dinner theater this evening.

"It's a late lunch for you. It's not like you'll be eating onstage. C'mon, we can take this out to the back porch."

Was it better form to introduce bad news into the conversation before or after the cheese course? But knowing Ben as I did, I knew he'd want to know sooner rather than later. I reached for his hand, covering it with my own. "I need to talk to you first."

"You okay?" he asked, looking up at me with his full attention.

"I'm fine. But I need to talk to you about Will's Island."

He frowned, though his face didn't entirely shutter. "I thought we agreed not to talk about that," he said in a measured tone.

"I know we did. But those boxes I took over to the town hall, I looked through them with Emmeline so we could catalog them for records. We found something." I handed him the file of photocopied pages of Josiah Bartlett's correspondence as well as some of the older meeting notes and the amendment. "The storage shed on the island may actually be the former town meeting hall of Bard's Rest. If these meeting notes are accurate, it's potentially one of the oldest meeting sites in New Hampshire." I pointed to Bartlett's letter. "We also know from records that Josiah Bartlett spent several summers in Bard's. He may have even drafted the amendments to the New Hampshire constitution here. In that building. Since we found a draft of it in the boxes."

"I don't understand," Ben said, flipping through the papers. "What am I looking at here?"

"I'm not a historian, and these records would need to be vetted. But potentially I think it may be some sort of historic site. I think."

Ben's head snapped up, his gaze locking on mine.

"Emmeline believes it's the original building. She's compared it against some old drawings in the archives at the town hall. There are no records to suggest it's ever been rebuilt or altered. Obviously, this will all need to be confirmed by some sort of expert. I'm not expecting you to take my word for it."

"How did nobody know this?" Ben demanded. "How did this not come up during due diligence?"

"I'm not sure. At some point, the town expanded and moved into a bigger meeting space and then, like a lot of things, the significance of the island was lost."

"Is there any way Archie knew about this?"

I shook my head. "I doubt it. Unless he examined all those boxes and put it together with what was left in the archives, there's no way he could have known. Also, it's Archie. I refuse to give that man any undeserved credit."

"What does this mean?" He looked at me, bewildered. "That we can't build there?"

"I haven't worked out all the details," I confessed. "I'm not an expert on historic sites and the process to qualify them as such, but I don't think you can demolish the building."

"You mean the storage shed that nobody has cared about for several hundreds of years and currently contains old costumes and props," Ben said dryly.

"Just because something has been forgotten doesn't mean it's not important," I said carefully.

"Who would miss it?" He raked his hands through his hair.

"I don't think that's for you or me to decide," I noted quietly.

"That's not what I meant—I have to call Sam. Then our lawyer."

"Yes," I said. "You should get your own legal counsel and advice here. I just wanted to give you a heads-up."

"A heads-up about what exactly?"

"The town will likely take some sort of action to prevent the sale of the property from going through, as well as put in place a temporary ban on any kind of construction activity while it undertakes the process to qualify the island as a landmark."

"It can do that?"

"I'd imagine whomever they hire for counsel can ask a judge to do that, yes. Again"—I shifted uncomfortably—"you're going to want to talk to your own lawyer about this."

"Instead of taking my girlfriend's word for it? Yeah, I think I'll do that," he said mirthlessly.

Girlfriend. How had he infused so much bitterness into that word? He'd never used that word in relation to me before. Why did the first time have to be now, with so much sting behind it?

"Why?" he asked, his expression more crestfallen than angry.

"Why did you have to keep digging, keep looking for an angle here? To prove you were right all along?"

"I didn't mean to," I sputtered. "I thought it would be doing right by the town to preserve some of its history. I didn't expect to find what I found."

"I'm sure," Ben snorted.

"I didn't do this to screw you over."

"Except that now Dane Development is going to take a bath on development costs and materials and—"

"Are you saying I should have ignored it?"

"Don't pretend you give a shit about that building as some sort of historic site. You'll do anything to keep me from building on that island," he snapped.

"Who's making it personal now?" I shot back. "It's not about you."

"You expect me to believe it's all some big coincidence you stumbled upon and you just happened to find a loophole. Win at any cost, right? Don't stop until you've scraped the bottom of the barrel? Is that what Gerald taught you?"

"Stop bringing him into it," I fired back. "I'm not Gerald. I'm not his lackey. I wouldn't stoop to the level you've accused him of and I don't appreciate the implication I would. The irony isn't lost on me how ready you are to excoriate him for bid tampering but here you are suggesting I should have covered up this development with the island? That doesn't exactly smack of being on the up-and-up."

"It's not the same thing."

"No, it most certainly isn't." Before I could stop myself, the words, angry and hot and indignant, spilled right out of me: "Do you think this is how Danny would have behaved if he'd found out something like this about something he'd purchased?"

"Don't bring him into this," Ben growled. "You didn't even know him."

"But from everything you've described of him, you think he'd be proud of you right now?"

"I guess when your mentor is Gerald Cutler, you don't have to worry about whether he's proud of your actions or not, huh? As long as you win," he barked back.

"It isn't about winning," I spat. I tried to slow my breathing, to pull my body back to center. It was so difficult when every instinct within wanted to go in for the kill. It took everything I had ever learned in therapy to pull back. This was not some deal; this was Ben. Ben. "Look, I like you. I more than like you. But we can't black box a major obstacle that's in our way. It isn't working."

"It was working fine."

"No." I shook my head. "I didn't set off to torpedo you. But that doesn't change the fact that we are where we are. We can't ignore it. Will's Island is back on the table, and we need to discuss it."

"How convenient of a conclusion," he muttered. "Now that you have the upper hand."

I stopped, my blood as cold as sleet, and stared at Ben. His angry posture. The betrayed look in his eyes. He truly believed that I had screwed him over.

My frustration rose cold and howling like a desolate December gale. We were never going to get past this. We were always going to be those people who put their jobs above all else. People who had things that were on- and off-limits.

My shoulders sank with the weight of that. "Where do we go from here?" I asked, not sure I wanted to hear his answer.

"It's not like you've left me any choice."

Of course there was a choice. We could stop this right now and get on the same team. "We could pivot. We'll figure something out. Some other play. I can help. We can do this. I know we can. But we do this together or not at all."

Ben was looking at me like I was a stranger. No, not a stranger. An unwelcome intruder in his life. He shook his head vehemently, crossing his arms over his chest. "No, we can't."

"Can't do what exactly?"

"I don't think we can move forward together. Not when you've done everything you can to undercut me. How can I ever trust you to be in my corner?"

The pressure in my throat and behind my eyes built to a fever pitch. I turned to go, thought better of it and took a deep breath. "For the record, I knew that by coming here with this, I was running the risk that this could happen. But I didn't veer from it; I didn't try to hide or pass it off like someone else found it. I didn't undercut you. I met you on the level, Ben. Because I care about you. I want to be with you. But I can't pretend I didn't find something like this. I can't bury it. That's not who I am, nor would I want to be with someone who'd want me to do something like that."

"And I can't be with someone who can't ever let anything go," he fired back.

"If that's the way you see it, Ben, then you're right. We're done here." The words had come unbidden and acidic but rang true in the air all the same. I stalked out of the kitchen and made it to the car without a backward glance. To hell with Benjamin Dane.

Scene Twenty-Seven

···········

The Dinner Theater

Chris sat beside me, a brave smile plastered on his face as he tucked into a plate of Tavern wings. "You sure you don't want Callie here instead?"

Poor Chris had been on his way to what I'm sure would have been a very enjoyable afternoon of mini-golf and ice cream at Peaseblossom's if it hadn't been for my texts. I'd repeatedly told him he didn't need to come; I was filling him in on what had gone down over at Will's Island. But Chris had shown up anyway.

"With you here, there's less of a chance of having to have a meaningful discussion about feelings," I quipped.

Chris sighed and took a mighty pull off his beer. "Nope, we're going to talk about feelings. If I have to sit through Shakespeare this evening at the dinner theater, we are going to talk about why, in the near decade we've known each other, this is the first time you've ever looked beaten. It's freaking me out. More so than the prospect of Shakespeare."

I tried for a smile, but it was wobbly. In halting tones, I told Chris everything that had happened with Ben and the island, even the stuff about Gerald. He listened quietly as I word-vomited the whole tale. When I finished, he nodded. "I agree with you that you did the right thing with the island. I don't think you could have ethically sat on something like that. If that's of any comfort."

"I know," I said glumly. I nibbled on a celery stick. "Out with the *but* that I know is coming."

"I'm not here to opine," he said. "We are not issue-spotting each other's deals here."

"I can take it," I insisted. "Please? I want your opinion."

Chris weighed me with his eyes. "At the risk of being a pedantic mansplainer or that smugly superior married guy who thinks he knows it all, because I'm the first to admit that marriage is damn hard—"

"Your disclaimer is acknowledged and appreciated," I told him and made a "hurry up" gesture with my hand. Chris snorted.

"—I think you might be glossing over something here. Relationships are a constant rebalancing of the ecosystem between you and your partner. I think you rightly identified that carving big issues out of your ecosystem with Ben wouldn't work in the long term."

"But?"

"Portia, you gave up too easy when it got hard."

"Ouch," I said. "That's surprisingly . . . hurtful."

"You asked for my opinion. I'm not giving it to hurt you."

"I know that," I acknowledged. "But I'm not so sure you're right. Ben and I are both married to our careers, and we're going to be circling around each other in the Boston development scene. The island might have been the first roadblock, but I'm sure there will be others. How do you know when to dig in and fight for a relationship and when to cut your losses?"

"There's no easy answer to that, and I'm pretty sure you're going to stab me with a fork if I tell you that you just know when you know. So I'll say it this way. Even early on, when I was fighting with Callie, I realized that unlike my previous relationships, I was fighting *with* Callie, but not against her. We were fighting, sure, and sometimes it felt like the whole world was going down and us with it, but we were fighting for the same thing. We were fighting to stay in it together. That's how I knew when to dig in and fight *with* Callie."

I nodded slowly. "That makes a lot of sense. But I'm not sure that's what we have here. Ben and me."

Chris looked at me for a long a moment. "You're the only one who can answer that." He took a fortifying sip of his beer. "Permission to play devil's advocate here?"

I rolled my eyes. "Of course."

"Why was it so important you had to be the one to tell Ben about the island? You told me you had an out. Emmeline could have kept you out of it."

"Because I owed it to him."

"Mmm," Chris said. "Say more on that."

"That's really annoying," I informed him.

"So I'm told all the time by the three ladies I share my life with. But I'm a firm believer in examining why we feel compelled to take certain actions but not others. Why some stories we hear and tell ourselves ring true and others don't. What sticks out for me here in what you've told me is why was it so important for you to tell Ben the truth about the island? When doing the exact opposite would have yielded a more favorable outcome?"

Because I love him, I thought. *Because I love Ben.* The answer was so obvious and yet it still rocked me back in my seat. My mind immediately tried to reconcile that with the image of walking out on Ben. But when it had gotten hard, I'd folded and walked out. I looked up at Chris. "I didn't walk out because I didn't love him. I walked out because I was scared."

Chris reached over and patted my hand. "Good chat."

"I owe you one."

"We owe each other so many I'm not sure we'll ever get the tally right. How about, you keep me flush in drinks tonight at the dinner theater and drive me home. I don't think I can face Shakespeare sober."

"Of course," I agreed. "Thanks." My voice was barely a whisper, but I knew from the way he smiled down at his plate that he'd heard the real thank-you. Who was I kidding? Chris had always heard me, always seen me. He knew when to let me be and when to offer me his ear. Why hadn't I taken him up on that more over the years? Probably for the same reason I hadn't told my family about Berlin. In wanting to spare the people closest to me of the burden of my emotions, I'd cut myself off from letting them be there for me and me for them. Just like I'd cut Ben off the first time things got hard.

Speaking of hard things, I wasn't quite done ruining Chris' night. There was something else I very much needed to get off my chest. "You should probably order another drink, because I have something else to tell you." I winced.

"Something worse than Shakespeare and relationship problems?" His eyes widened. "You're right. I'd like another beer."

After we'd ordered Chris another round, I told him the rest of it: Ben and Sam's suspicions; what their PI had found; my decision to hire my own PI, who had so far corroborated what Sam's PI had uncovered.

"Wow," he said heavily.

"I know."

Chris stared down into his beer as if the foam might contain the answer. "I don't think what you have is conclusive."

"I know."

"If you're wrong . . ."

"If I'm wrong, I've just ruined my entire career."

"Looks like it," Chris agreed.

"If I'm right, I may still have ruined my career. At FrancisPearl anyway."

He steepled his fingers. "What are you going to do?"

"Have Reese keep digging. Then make a decision based on the information I do have."

Chris closed his eyes. He didn't try to talk me out of it. Didn't warn me to be careful. Or try to sway me either way. He accepted it for what it was: my call.

HOURS LATER, I sat in front of the dressing room mirror in the basement of Titania's. My face was serene, my makeup perfect, with not a hair out of place. But inside, my stomach roiled, and the coil of anxiety lodged tight in my throat. And for once it had nothing to do with stage fright.

Stage fright I had learned to acknowledge and ignore last summer, when I'd been persuaded into breaking my "no stages, no Shakespeare" rule. Back then, my body would tense up about thirty minutes prior to each show, my skin would prickle, my pulse would race and my palms would sweat. Now I'd name it for what it was and remind myself that I'd yet to drop a single line onstage as Dame Jan.

This was different. The stress I experienced now felt insurmountable. I'd expected that Ben would have at least acknowledged my text from earlier asking if we could talk. But I'd been met with a wall of silence.

I checked my phone one more time. Just in case. Nothing from Ben, but there was a text from Cordelia indicating her interview had gone well. At least, I think that's what that string of emojis meant.

Smiling, I texted, Of course you killed it. Can't wait to hear more details. I slipped the phone into my bag and returned to examining my face.

"Hey," Candace said softly, appearing behind me in the reflection of the mirror. One look at her tightly drawn expression told me all I needed to know.

"He's not here," I said.

"His seat is still empty with ten minutes to curtains up."

I bit down hard on my bottom lip, tasting the waxy matte of the lipstick I'd applied for the performance. "Thanks for checking."

Candace sat beside me on the bench. "Listen, this is still fresh for him and for you. He may need some time to process his anger."

"I blew it," I said miserably.

Candace said nothing, but her eyes told a different story. She placed a cool hand on my arm. "I think you did what you had to do. Now he needs to decide if he can live with it."

I nodded. Chris and Candace were saying all the sensible things. So what was it about that empty chair that made it feel so final?

"He'll get there," she assured me. "Now come on. I hate to be a prima donna here, but we're five from opening."

Wordlessly, I followed Candace up the stairs and backstage. If nothing else, I was someone who could be counted on to perform.

Glimpsing through the cracks in the curtain, I spotted Chris, Callie and the twins at the table I'd reserved for them. There should have been an empty seat. Instead though, it was occupied, and not by Ben.

Sam looked up from her phone just then, staring right at the curtain as if she could see me. She couldn't. Logically, I knew that. But what was she doing here? I had no time to think about what her presence might mean as Candace stepped onstage to introduce the dinner theater.

The performance was a blur, but they all were. Acting was like an out-of-body experience. I usually remembered walking out onto the stage and off it, but all the lines, motions and pauses were lost to me. I'd forgone the cliché of experimenting with mind-altering substances in college and law school. But I'd have to imagine this was similar.

After the final curtain call, Chris, Callie and the girls were waiting to shower me with compliments and bouquets from Sweet Williams. I appreciated that my sister had forgone her threat to give me a bouquet of condoms from Comedy of Eros. I was all for supporting local business but didn't want to face the wrath of Callie by introducing contraception into an otherwise pleasant evening for the girls. That, and Chris had gone pretty easy on me during our relationship chat earlier, so I owed him.

What I hadn't expected was that Sam waited for me while I said my thank-yous and good-nights to everyone. Looking like a bolt of lightning in an electrifying white wrap dress, she reclined against the bar, sizing up the room with an unhurried air.

As much as I desperately wanted to change out of my stage clothes and cleanse the rather ridiculous amount of makeup from my face, I made my way over to her.

"Thanks for coming," I said.

"I didn't want to miss what must have been a stretch performance for you, playing a lawyer and all," she replied, her tone playful.

"I'll admit I'm a little surprised to see you here."

She tucked a swath of her shiny black hair behind one ear. "As much as I'd like to pretend that dinner theater was on my Bard's bucket list, I was hoping for a word with you. Is there someplace we can go that's more private?"

Of course she'd want someplace more private to eviscerate me for what I'd done to Ben and their company. I could respect that.

"We could take our drinks into the gardens?" I offered.

"That works," she said, sipping her drink as I ordered a glass of chenin blanc and led her out the back door into the twinkle-light-illuminated paradise of fountains and statuary. If she had trouble maneuvering in her ankle-strap Louboutins, she said nothing.

I steered us toward a pair of bistro chairs set around a little table with ornate wrought-iron vines for legs and fairies in its top. It wasn't the most ridiculous deal table I'd ever sat across a potential hostile party from, but it was up there.

Sam swirled the contents of her martini glass and fixed me with eyes that were as dark as ocean floors and giving just as little away. "I find myself vacillating between the urge to applaud your actions with the Will's Island transaction or destroy you for what you did to Ben. In either event, you have made my life rather difficult."

"I respect that," I said, bracing myself for what was to come. "I'm not sure it's any consolation, but I didn't go looking for it. Once I found it though, I couldn't sit on it." I stared down into my glass, watching the bubbles ascend and break. "As much as I might have wanted to," I said in a quiet voice.

Sam nodded slowly. "I know that. I think he does too. But I'm not here for something so pedestrian as to play go-between."

"Of course not," I said with a slight frown. "That would be beneath you."

"Agreed." Her lips twitched.

"So why are you here?" I hadn't told Sam that I'd hired a PI, so that wasn't it. I was playing this close to the chest for now. Especially if Reese's searches came up blank.

"I wanted to give you this." She slid a gleaming, white business card across the little table.

I examined it, surprised it wasn't hers. It was for Collins, O'Brien and O'Berg LLP, a boutique corporate firm in Boston with an excellent reputation that I recognized from a reconnaissance report that FrancisPearl's tactical research team had prepared for me. "What is this?"

"An opportunity to pivot."

I stared at the card.

"You'll find Rajani's personal cell on the back. She's the current managing partner, but all industry intel suggests she's looking to transition, and there's no viable internal succession plan." Sam shrugged delicately. "No pressure, but if you do call, she's expecting you."

"Why?" I probed. "Not to put too fine a point on it, but I've taken direct action against Dane Development, and we both know you have strong opinions about Gerald Cutler."

Sam stared at me; her eyes glittering chips of onyx set against the shadow-dappled gardens. "I can respect the play and hate the result. For what it's worth, I don't think you're anything like him." She sipped her martini. "Women of intelligence and influence are still depressingly rare commodities in our line of work. Let's say you're someone I could see myself potentially partnering with in the future. Under a different set of circumstances."

I nodded, appreciating her angle and the lack of heavy-handedness in her playing it. Sam Maeda might indeed make a strong partner. Under a different set of circumstances.

Courtroom Number One

Five days. Five days and Ben hadn't so much as called or texted or acknowledged my voice mail. Life had crawled by slowly as I said goodbye to Chris, Callie and the girls on that Saturday morning after the festival. I'd worked alongside Miranda and Cordelia, helping pack up the festival for the following year. Sunday, I'd holed up with Candace and Byron, putting together an emergency request for an injunction that Byron was planning to file on Monday.

I'd done all the idiot things. Restarted my phone several times. Obsessively checked my personal email even though Ben and I hadn't used email much. But maybe he'd lost his phone and was trying to get in contact with me? And then, in the lowest of low moments, I allowed myself one detour past Falstaff's Folly on my way into town. His car hadn't been in the driveway. I had this unshakable sinking feeling that not only was Ben ghosting me, he'd left Bard's.

Day three had been the real low point. That had been the day Gerald called again. This time his tone had been brusque and not altogether friendly.

"What's this I hear about you filing to appear in district court?"

With a chill that squirmed down my spine, I realized that I'd been right—Gerald had been keeping close tabs on me. But I was hardly going to give him the satisfaction of asking how he knew. You play the hand you're dealt. Aces or deuces, you front just as hard.

"I thought you had dropped this sentimental foolishness with the merchant association."

The words built up in my throat and broke like an inadvisable dam. "And I thought I was afforded the respect of a managing partner who can select my own pro bono cases, Gerald. Without your oversight."

"This is hardly just any pro bono case, Portia. I'm concerned about what the board will think."

"You went to the board on this?"

"I can hardly keep this from them."

He was trying to intimidate me. Old dog, same tricks. I closed my eyes and took three sips of breath. "I hardly see how this is a board matter," I said in as cool a tone as I could muster. "Or why you felt the need to bring it to the board without discussing it with me first."

Gerald saw right through my bravado. "I'm afraid that it must be brought to the board's attention. We can't have our new managing partner sending conflicted messages to the Boston development community about who we represent. Surely you can understand." He waited a beat. "Of course, if you were to drop this matter, I think we could avoid the board entirely."

If a silence could be pregnant, this one was carrying triplets.

Sitting in the now cooling air-conditioned car, I stared at the boxy brick courthouse, the US and New Hampshire flags standing at attention on either side of the stairs leading up to its entrance, while I considered my options. Backing down wasn't one of them.

I briefly thought about confronting Gerald here and now. But I wasn't ready. When I'd spoken with Reese a few days ago, he had told me he was going to try another avenue. This time he'd follow the money, certain he would find something. The more I thought about it, the more I shared his certainty. When I confronted Gerald, I'd come at him with everything I had.

I decided my best course of action was to parry. Serenely, I said, "You do what you need to do, Gerald. I am more than happy to answer any questions the board may have."

"It will be a closed session, Portia. Since it goes to your fitness as managing partner."

The words stung like a physical slap to the face. Just as he'd meant them to. For one brief moment, I considered caving. Texting Byron that he'd have to go it alone. Terminating my representation of the merchant association. Obtaining a final invoice from Reese and paying it. Getting back in Gerald's good graces.

That lasted only a moment, as I righted myself, drawing on my hard-fought experience and banishing the doubt that had been my shadow for as long as I could remember. Screw this. He was good, but I was better. "Well, if I'm the board, I'm sure I'll be thinking about your fitness as well, Gerald. Since you're the one who championed me for this opportunity."

"I think you're making a very serious mistake," he said, stepping on the end of my words. I'd rattled him.

"And I think you're overstepping," I said, coating my words with hoarfrost. "If there's nothing else, Gerald, I'll speak with you in September." Not waiting for his dismissal of me, I hit end.

I stepped out of the car into the languid afternoon air. Pearls of sweat broke out on my brow. It was the third week of August, after all. What had I expected? My palms were sweaty and clammy. Running them over my navy skirt suit wasn't helping matters. Nor was giving this Gerald thing another thought. The chips would fall and we'd see—Gerald and I—where we stacked up. In the meantime, I had something I actually cared about to attend to.

Chin up. Shoulders back, I told myself. *Time to shine.* I crossed the parking lot to where Tillie was waiting for me. She took one look at me and patted my shoulder reassuringly. "No need to kill anyone today. You've got this, sugar pie."

"I'm about as far from 'sugar pie' as you can get."

"Yes, but 'Teflon-coated titanium knuckle sandwich' doesn't quite roll off the tongue like 'sugar pie.'"

"Fair enough. That was nice of you to wait for me."

Somehow it was fitting that it was Tillie here beside me. My first-ever court appearance had been on her behalf and now here we stood once more.

"Alice is saving me a seat," she said, as if reading my thoughts. "I wouldn't miss this for anything. Just like old times, my girl."

"Like old times," I agreed. I squared my shoulders and walked alongside her into the first court building I'd ever made an official appearance in. Together, we walked down the echoing corridor, bathed in late-afternoon sun, toward courtroom number one—the largest of the courtrooms, if memory served me correctly.

A familiar and most welcome face waited at the end of that corridor.

"Hey, partner," Byron said, drawing himself up from his cross-armed slouch against the doors. He gave off this oddly reassuring air of utmost competence mixed with boredom. Like he'd seen and done it all. "You got the memo on matchy-matchy, I see," he said, nodding to his own navy suit and then over at mine. "Black is for funerals. We're not going to ours today."

I gave Byron a fierce smile. "Of course not."

He glanced at Tillie. "Can I walk you in, or do you know where you're going?"

"I know how to find a peanut gallery, thank you very much. I also know when I'm being dismissed. It's a good thing you're cute," she said to Byron, cuffing him on the back of the head as she strode past him with the air of a conquering queen, pushing on the swinging doors and disappearing within.

"Someday people will take me seriously."

I cast him a sideways glance.

"You're right, I'll probably have to move." He loosened his shoulders, rolling them backward like we were going for a run and not going before the judge seeking an injunction. "You ready?"

"Let's do this." I squared my shoulders, smoothing down my suit one more time and giving my hair a confident flick. "If you have to walk into hell, you might as well act like you own the joint."

"Amen," Byron snickered.

Inside, Byron and I stood at the oak table on the right, with the town at our back: Tillie, Alice, Dan, Aaron, Candace, my entire family, Emmeline, Del, Cat Jackson—to name a few. I almost felt bad that every available seat behind me was filled and people were standing in the aisles, while exactly four people occupied the table to our left: Archie; the dubious Ted Stinson, who I continued to suspect was just some really bad actor Archie had hired; and two men in expensive suits, who I guessed had to be representing Dane Development. Nobody sat in the rows behind these two men, both of whom I placed in their late fifties, both carrying themselves with the easy grace of lifelong litigators.

I'd half hoped to see Sam or Ben or at least some other member of the business team. But I knew that in light of Ben's five-day communications ghost op, it was unlikely he'd be here. Still, now knowing that to be true hurt more than I'd expected. We were well and truly done.

The court officer snapped me back from my Ben-based thoughts by calling the room to order and asking us to rise for the honorable Coraline Rhodes, a statuesque Black woman in her sixties with a tight smile and a no-nonsense air about her. I liked her immediately.

"Your honor," I began, when it was our turn to speak, "my name is Portia Barnes. I am here on behalf of the Bard's Rest Merchant Association, and I am joined by my colleague and co-counsel, Byron Greene, representing the town of Bard's Rest on its request for an emergency temporary injunction against Archibald Douglas and Dane Development in the matter of the property known as Will's Island."

"On what grounds do you seek a protective injunction?" Judge Rhodes asked.

"We seek to enjoin the sale of the property because Dane Development is in the business of construction and intends to convert the structures currently located there into condos. We believe the site that Dane Development seeks to purchase from Archibald Douglas may be a historical one. The paperwork and process to qualify it as such is currently underway."

"I see. On what grounds do you believe this property to be a historical one?"

"We believe based on documentation recently recovered from Will's Island that the structure located there may have been the original town meeting site of Bard's Rest. Pending authentication of the records, we believe this could be one of New Hampshire's oldest town meeting sites and, further, that amendments to the New Hampshire Constitution may have been drafted or reviewed in this building by Josiah Bartlett." I looked over at Byron. He was up.

"Moreover, your honor, we would like it to be noted that the town of Bard's Rest, in partnership with the Bard's Rest Merchant Association, has offered to compensate Mr. Douglas at the appraised value of the property in accordance with the current property assessment that Mr. Douglas himself had performed this summer at the sum of two point four million dollars."

"Thank you, Counselor Barnes and Counselor Greene. I have reviewed your petition. At this time, I would like to hear from Mr. Douglas and Dane Development." I had to hand it to Judge Rhodes, who sat there like a sphinx in her robes. I had no idea if she was leaning one way or another or whether she'd already made her mind up.

I mentally readied myself for the onslaught and the counterpoints that Byron and I had worked on late into the night last night. It wasn't like I had been planning on sleeping anyway. My subconscious didn't want to deal with the loss of Ben any more than my waking self did.

"Your honor, if it pleases the court, Dane Development has withdrawn from the purchase and sale of the property located at Will's Island," said one of the suits with that ease of tone, the mark of one who'd spent his whole career on his feet in front of judges. "We don't speak for Mr. Douglas, of course," he said with a somewhat dubious glance at Archie and his lawyer.

Now, this would have been the moment in that barely realistic, nothing-like-real-life courtroom drama where the room let out a collective gasp. Instead though, I stood there in stunned silence, along with a bunch of my nearest and dearest.

"To confirm, Counselor. Dane Development does not intend to proceed with the purchase and sale of the property known as Will's Island?" Judge Rhodes clarified.

"Confirmed. Neither Dane Development, nor any of its affiliates, will be purchasing any property in Bard's Rest at the present time."

I scanned the faces of Dane Development's lawyers, but of course, these two were pros and gave nothing away.

"Mr. Douglas. Do you understand what an injunction is?"

Archie nodded. "Yes, your honor. My lawyer—" He gestured to Ted. The man looked like he was in need of a shave, but at least he'd worn a suit. It was mint green. But it was a suit. "My lawyer has explained it to me."

"Do I need to issue one against you to enjoin you from selling the property located at Will's Island to anyone other than the town of Bard's Rest?"

Archie shook his head. "No, your honor. If Bard's Rest will pay me the full appraised value of the property of two point four million, then I will gladly sell it to the town so it can proceed with its historical . . . venture."

"Magnanimous as the day is long," Tillie snorted.

Archie was not going to be a popular man around town, but I suspected that once he had Bard's money, he wasn't long for the town anyway.

Dane Development's attorneys, wearing twin blank expressions, filed out of the courtroom with no fanfare. I waited a respectable number of beats before following them out to see if they were calling someone from the hall or, I dared hope—meeting somebody out there.

But the pair walked without stopping toward the exit. I resisted the urge to follow after them any farther, because there was a limit to my creepiness.

Quick footsteps sounded behind me. I spun around, but it was only Byron. "Well, that was all sorts of weird. Not how I saw things going at all. I can't believe Dane isn't putting up a fight. I was ready for one."

"Yes," I agreed woodenly. Had it been Ben? Sam? Clearly one or both of them had pulled the plug. Had they just not wanted what might have amounted to an ugly and potentially public legal battle? Or was it something else? "That was unexpected," I said, shaking myself. "This is what we wanted. Who cares how we got here?"

I plastered a bright smile on my face as the courtroom door opened and everyone who'd ever known me in town spilled out. Hugging—so much hugging—and thanking ensued. I tried to deflect as much of the attention as I could on Byron, but it didn't hold. It wasn't until Emmeline McGandry put her arms around me and whispered in my ear that this outcome was "thanks to tart women doing the hard thing" that it felt real.

The Dock

W ell, who the hell wanted to date a developer anyway?" I asked.

Hamlet cocked his head at me, pausing mid-chew of his antler, his mouth hanging open.

"We're better off without him," I assured my dog. My dog. I had signed the adoption papers, paid the fee and bought him a ridiculous bespoke collar from Royal Ruffs, the new pet store in town, the owner assuring me that it was the ultimate luxury item and wouldn't make Hamlet's neck chafe, even in the most humid of weather. It wasn't lost on me that this dog drank from the toilet every chance he got and rolled in dead things.

I took a pull off the bottle of champagne I'd popped and nibbled on a chocolate strawberry as the sky burned hot pink and orange, the brilliant golden sun sinking over the pond. The count was up to nine days. Tomorrow would be double digits that I'd been completely Ben-less. And it sucked beyond the telling.

"She looks like an L.L.Bean ad," Miranda whispered from behind me.

"That champagne is far too expensive for L.L.Bean," Cordelia insisted. "But Hamlet looks just right for the Bean target demographic."

I thought that was unfair, given I was drinking straight out of the bottle.

"There's plenty more in the fridge," I called over my shoulder to the incoming cavalry making their way down the rickety dock. They plopped down on either side of me, Cordelia's sparkly flask flashing in the setting sun.

"Your post-breakup moping session is not like other people's post-breakup moping," Miranda said under her breath.

I handed her the champagne bottle and a plate of chocolate-dipped strawberries. "I'm not moping. I'm ruminating. There's a difference."

"What's the difference?"

"For starters, I don't have raccoon mascara eyes, nor am I eating cake with my fingers," I offered.

Miranda made an indignant noise while Cordelia did a poor job of covering her guffaw.

"We all process differently. Although, I have to say, adopting a dog post-breakup is a total power move."

"I'd decided to adopt him a while ago," I insisted. "I was just getting around to formalizing it."

"Welcome to the life of luxury, kid," Cordelia whispered to Hamlet, leaning over me to rub behind his ears. "So many Puppuccinos in your future."

"If we're done with the sisterly mocking portion of these proceedings, what can I do for you two?"

"It's more like, what can we do for you, sis?" Miranda asked.

"I'm fine," I insisted.

"Mom says you're leaving this weekend."

"Tying up the festival and putting the papers to right for next year isn't taking that long." I left the part out about not wanting to be in Bard's without Ben.

"But think of all the free drinks and food you're missing out on by leaving early," Cordelia insisted. "You're the town hero. I would milk that as long as you can."

"As fun as that sounds," I said dryly, "I have a condo to furnish and puppy proof. A dog walker to hire. A canine camera to install."

"And the new role, of course," Miranda chimed in.

"Mmm-hmm."

At first I'd resolved not to mention recent developments to my sisters. Like the email I received two days ago from the board that my position as managing partner was under review. Normally, something like that would have sent me into some sort of existential tailspin, but I didn't think Gerald actually had the grounds or the juice to have me removed. This was a display of power on his part, but we both knew his power wasn't unlimited. It was more likely I was going to be put on some sort of double-secret probation. If I stayed at FrancisPearl, which was a big if.

Gerald wasn't the only one with cards to play. I had received my final report from Reese, and while there wasn't definitive evidence there, there was enough. There was no doubt in my mind my former mentor was dirty. The only thing I was still mulling over was what to do with the information I did have.

But as I sat there on the dock between my sisters and thought about how each of them had shown up for me—not only this summer, but time and time again—I realized I didn't have to spare them. They could handle it. More importantly, they deserved to hear what was really going on with me. So I took a deep swig of champagne and told them everything, watching their eyes widen as I unfurled the entire sordid tale, beginning with Berlin and ending with the offer from Collins, O'Brien and O'Berg currently sitting in my inbox.

When I'd finished, blissfully uninterrupted except for a few clarifying questions posed here and there, Cordelia was the first to speak. "Shit, Portia."

"What are you going to do?" Miranda asked.

"I'm honestly not sure," I admitted.

The two exchanged loaded glances, and it took everything I had to keep from smiling.

"And you're okay with that?" Miranda pressed.

"I think I have to be," I said slowly. "I have a lot to think about, and I think I should take the time to think about it and figure it out."

"Okay, who are you and what have you done with Portia?" Cordelia demanded. "Ow," she cried as Miranda reached around me to shove her. The motion on the dock woke Hamlet, who eyed the three of us disapprovingly. He stood, yawning and shaking himself, before deciding my lap was the superior place to continue his nap.

"My entire professional career has been with FrancisPearl. I don't know anything else other than that life. For years, I rode the high of deal after deal, spending my nights hammering out drafts, achieving the impossible for my clients and making a name for myself. Berlin came along and knocked me down. That should have been a wake-up call that the job was killing me. Literally killing me."

My sisters were twin studies in stillness, watching me and waiting for me to say it.

"But what did I do? I doubled down. I went after managing partner. It wasn't until I was back in Bard's this summer that I realized that all of the things I was doing here—sleeping more than four hours at a clip, eating normal meals instead of inhaling granola bars at my desk because I didn't have time for anything else, hanging out with you two, doing dinner theater with Candace and Byron, gardening with Mom, lunching with Dad, adopting the world's most objectively perfect dog, and okay, even breaking and entering, made me realize that I don't want to work fifteen-hour days and sacrifice my nights, weekends, holidays, health and family. I want a life that's sustainable, something that's still fulfilling from a career perspective, but a balanced one where I can have normal interests and interactions like everybody else."

"I was with you right up until you included breaking and entering as a normal interest and interaction. I know you're relatively new to this whole concept of free time, but you may need to find less destructive ways of filling yours," Miranda said, patting my shoulder. "Might I recommend the dog park?"

"Nonsense. I'll be your B and E buddy whenever you want," Cordelia chimed in. "Just say the word."

"Really?" I said dryly. "That's what you zero in on?"

"In our defense, I think most people would zero in on B and E when the other choices are gardening or the performing arts," Miranda quipped.

"Well, you two can rest easy—there are no immediate plans for B and E in my future. Even if I take this offer, I'd still be a managing partner. A boutique firm in a new city with established market players won't exactly be a stroll through the Boston Common, but from my conversations with Rajani, the firm prides itself on work-life integration, which means I'd work a sixty-hour week instead of an eighty-hour one and be able to take vacations and enjoy the dog park on the weekends." I rubbed Hamlet behind the ears, just where he liked it. "Like I said, lots to think about."

"I noticed that nowhere in that 'come to Portia' moment did you mention Ben," Cordelia noted. "Intentional?"

"What do you want me to say? I made my choice, and he made his. If we couldn't get past Will's Island, we weren't going to work anyway."

"So that's it?" Cordelia asked. "You turn the page?"

"I turn the page," I agreed. "I did what I thought was right for me and mine. I don't regret that."

"I'm not saying he was right to do so, but one could see how he might have reacted if he felt he wasn't one of yours, Portia," Cordelia said, then frowned. "Why do we sound like upscale mobsters?"

"Because 'me and mine' is a very weird expression," Miranda offered. "Even for Portia."

"You two were great at the life-affirming piece, but you suck at the post-breakup portion of this pity party."

"You mean rumination," Cordelia said slyly.

Ignoring her, I continued, "I don't fault Ben for the decision he made. His business is his purpose. I might have reacted the same way in his position. But I think that gets to the heart of the issue. People like Ben and me, we're not people who prioritize relationships the way you'd need to for a lasting partnership."

"Yeah, that logic would work, except you prioritized all of us above what was best for you," Cordelia said.

I shook my head. "It's irrelevant now."

"Not if you love him," Miranda insisted.

"I think we all know that sometimes love isn't what wins the day."

"What are you talking about? Look at our unrealistic adult role models and half this town. Imperfect people all over the place, making it work. Relationships don't—and by their nature can't—be perfect," Miranda pointed out. "They're a constant work in progress. Sure, they're hard and frustrating and sometimes somebody surprising the ever-loving shit out of you with a proposal, but they're also freaking exhilarating and worthwhile."

"Way to sell it, sis." Cordelia winked.

"Oh, shut up. We can't all be sex pirates pillaging the entire Northeast. Some of us just want someone to love us in our ratty pajamas and eat pasta in bed with us."

"You eat pasta in bed?" I asked, wrinkling my nose.

"Eating pasta in bed is a total perk in the colder months. Particularly when you're not the one making it."

"You have me there," Cordelia said wistfully. "I wish I had someone to make me complex carbs in cold months."

"Cordelia, you're a pastry chef."

"Yes, but the dishes," she sighed wistfully.

"Are we actually talking about this?" I asked.

"No, we're sort of dancing around it, because feelings are hard for you," Miranda said, patting my hand. Cordelia nodded.

"Feelings are not hard. They're inconvenient," I shot back. "I appreciate that you found your person, Miranda, and I respect your sex pirate plundering, Cordelia. But in that same vein, you should respect my judgment here that I don't need Ben to be happy." It would have been a brilliant shot across the bow if my voice hadn't quavered on his name. "I mean, yes, he made me so happy and I felt like he's the guy who really sees me for who I am and doesn't try to make me nicer or more palatable to others. He liked my sharp edges, my drive, my competitive streak. And I liked his unwavering commitment to the business he built from nothing, his sense of fair play and the way he treated the people in his life. Because in business, you sometimes have to hide your humanity. He didn't." I sighed. "But I can't force something he doesn't want. I have to accept it and move on."

"Right, because you're so the person who settles for no," Cordelia snorted. "You counsel your clients that's the best they can do and advise them to take the deal. You definitely don't go to the mat for what you think is best and turn a problem over in your head until you can see a solution."

"Normally, I'd say I feel so seen, but I don't think this characterization is going to end well for me."

"The problem here isn't that it's high stakes. You live, breathe and eat high stakes. It's that these are your personal high stakes and you're afraid to push it all in."

"I did push all in. He ghosted me, remember?"

"So that's it? You're done? After one rebuff?" Miranda asked.

"It was a major rebuff," I protested.

She snorted. "Cordy, the flask please."

Cordelia handed over the sparkly flask.

Miranda uncorked it and took her first sip, coughing. "The hell?"

"It's Portia's pity party."

"Liquor should not burn on the way down," Miranda insisted.

"No, liquor should not taste like the juice at the bottom of a cafeteria fruit cup," I retorted. I accepted the flask and took a long pull. "What would I even say to him that I haven't already said?" I asked.

"'I love you and miss you even though you're being an ass' isn't a bad place to start," Miranda offered.

"I'll take it under advisement," I snickered.

"This is much nicer with champagne and warm blankets." Cordelia sighed and rested her head on my shoulder.

Miranda followed suit. "This is nice," she agreed.

"So, as much as I've thoroughly enjoyed being under the sisterly microscope, did you make any progress on the whole—" I waggled my eyebrows at Cordelia.

"Are we talking about the sex pirate thing or the elite pastry chef thing?" Miranda asked.

"Is that how she characterized it to you too?" I asked. "Did you come up with a good pun?"

"It doesn't need a pun. It's hilarious by itself," Miranda said, in all her infinite snark-based wisdom.

"I received an offer," Cordelia said, almost shyly. I threw one arm around her, careful not to displace Hamlet, but squeezing her hard enough that I hoped she heard how happy I was for her. "Thank you, thank you."

"Are you going to take it?" Miranda asked.

"I think so? Like Portia, I have some time to mull it over. The hard part will be telling Mom and Dad."

"Bring snacks," Miranda offered. "You make the best snacks."

"I cannot believe we're considered adults by any standard," I muttered.

Cordelia snickered. "What are you talking about? Miranda's getting married. She's the most adult of all of us. You've adopted a dog. I'm joining an international elite pastry squad. What could be more adult?"

"I would like the flask again," I said. "Maybe if I keep drinking, that will make some semblance of sense."

We sat there watching the sunset as Hamlet snoozed on my lap. As the sun was sinking over the pond, I snapped a picture of the deep pink and purple sky, managing to capture most of Hamlet and some of my feet. I typed: Even though you're a complete jerk for ghosting me, I still miss you and hit send.

Modern love at its finest. Take that, Shakespeare.

......

Titania's Bower

"Oban 18, neat?" Rowan asked.

"You have any more of that Barrell Bourbon Gray Label 15?"

"In the mood for scorched earth, are ya?" Rowan's smile was knowing, not unkind.

"Seems to be all I'm capable of these days," I said, trying for self-deprecating.

"Candace is in a catering meeting. But she'll be out in a bit."

"Thanks," I said, even though I already knew that from texting with her. I could have waited longer before driving over, but with my parents on a date night and Hamlet in full-on puppy pass-out mode, the house had seemed unbearably empty.

Rowan slid the drink in front of me. "On the house. For the town hero."

"Thanks, Rowan." I took a sip, savoring the burn on the back of my tongue. *Blood orange. Scorched earth. And an undercurrent of finality.* I squeezed my eyes shut for a moment, savoring it. *Time to turn the page, Portia.*

Tomorrow, I'd drive back to the city to resolve my remaining relocation details and make my final decision on whether to remain at FrancisPearl or accept the offer at Collins, O'Brien and O'Berg LLP. I was definitely leaning in one direction. But first, I would say a proper goodbye. This morning, I'd brunched with Byron, and I would soon have my last dinner here with Candace. An early-morning breakfast tomorrow with my family, and then Hamlet and I would be off.

Someone sidled up to the stool next to me, and I thought about sliding down a seat, but it was a Friday night and the bar was certain to fill up, so what did it matter?

Rowan turned around from the bar, where he'd been reaching for a bottle. His customer-bright smile ratcheted up a tick. "May I help you, sir?"

"Oban 18, neat, please."

My head swiveled right. Ben stood there, looking like the first time I'd ever seen him—in charcoal slacks and a white button-down open at the neck and rolled up at the elbows—only that trademark confidence had been dialed down to a subdued smile.

"Hey," I sputtered. Brilliant conversationalist that I was at the moment.

"Hey, yourself. May I join you?"

I nodded. "Sure. I didn't realize you were back in Bard's."

"I drove up today."

"Ah," I noted as Rowan slid Ben's drink between us. "Are you meeting someone here?"

"You, I hope."

"How did you know I'd be here?"

"Cordy. I stopped into the café this afternoon."

Afternoon, I noted, which would have given my sister several hours to warn me. I would take time to be put out about that later. For now, I planned to brazen through this current awkwardness with grace and dignity. Or at least dignified indifference. "How's Boston?"

"Humid, gritty, full of Massholes."

"You're really selling it." I sipped my drink. "How's work?"

"Truth be told, I'm the most engaged I've ever been."

"That's good to hear," I said, but it somehow sounded like it felt—hollow. "Any particular reason?"

"Sam and I have decided to pivot the business to focus on eco-friendly plays and special historical restoration projects."

"Special historical restoration projects?"

"Any chance you're familiar with the Liberty Hotel project?"

I tipped my hand back and forth. "Remind me?"

"Developers rehabbed the Charles Street jail in downtown Boston and transformed it into a hotel while still preserving much of its original architecture. Stuff like that. Apparently, when you gracefully bow out of a project because of your moral objection over razing a treasured local landmark—"

I raised an eyebrow.

"—a treasured local landmark such as the Bard's Rest original town meeting house, word gets around and it buys you all sorts of do-gooder cred. That, and Sam's been after me for years to get in on eco-friendly."

"Oh, I see. Well, that's a lovely windfall for you both."

"Sam and I have already booked several projects. Fascinating stuff too, figuring out how to work within the metes and bounds of new regulations, et cetera, and making sure what we're doing fits with the landscape and culture. It's both challenging and maddening. I love it."

"I can imagine."

"Don't know if you've heard yet, but Dane is in the running to be considered for the restoration of the oldest town meeting space in Bard's Rest. It's on Will's Island—perhaps you've heard of it?"

I barked out a surprised laugh. "You don't say."

"Apparently, we understand some of the unique challenges in restoring a landmark that abuts a treasured amphitheater better than some of the other applicants."

"Shameless," I noted. "I'm meeting Candace soon. Did you need something?" I hadn't meant for it to sound as harsh as it did, but it twisted my stomach to sit here and listen to Ben talk about pivoting his business and being in the running for the Bard's restoration. I wanted to be happy for Ben, but I couldn't help that bitter twinge I felt that the very thing that had driven us apart—a literal island—was apparently now a nonissue. All's well that ends well for Ben. Not so much for Portia.

Ben set down his drink. "I have a deal I'd like to pitch you."

"I'm not representing Bard's on the restoration matter. You'll have to talk to Byron."

"Different deal. This one's a long-term play. Tons of upside, manageable risk."

"Not interested. I think we've established I've no interest in representing you."

"I don't want you to represent me. I want you to be my partner in this deal."

"With you and Sam?"

His lips twitched. "Definitely not."

"All right, pitch me."

"Like I said, this deal is a long-term play. There are some preexisting challenges I need to clear to make it work."

"Like what?"

"For starters, I'd like to apologize for a serious lapse in judgment. Specifically, for not responding to your texts and failing to show up for the hearing."

"I ruined your business deal; you didn't owe me anything," I said wearily. Ben hadn't come here to see me. Not really. He'd driven three hours to absolve himself of his guilt.

"No, I behaved like a petulant frat boy, and you deserved better, Portia."

"It's all in the rearview now."

"I'm sorry I didn't fight for us," he said in a quiet voice. "When things got hard and I'd framed it in my head as you choosing the island over us, it broke me. I reacted in the worst possible way. I withdrew. Went underground. Wrote us off."

"Eh, we both had unclean hands here. It's water under the

bridge," I said and tried to mean that second platitude. If he didn't stop, he was going to be treated to my entire arsenal of them. *Just take the easy out, Ben. I'm offering it.*

"Yes and that would be a fine thing to say if we were two business associates who couldn't see eye to eye on a deal. But this is different."

"Not really." I shrugged, still determined to escape here with my dignity intact. Mostly intact.

"I love you, Portia."

"What?" My mouth sort of fell open. Well, there went my dignity.

"I love the way you attack each day like it's a personal challenge. Watching you pick it apart and distill it down into its best parts has been the highlight of my summer. I love how fiercely you care about your family and friends, even when that meant I was on the receiving end of your defense of them. I love that you're unapologetic about how much you enjoy your work. I love that when we're together I have someone who not only listens to me and makes me feel whole but would literally fend off a backwoods attacker with nothing but an umbrella or take down a goat if the situation called for it."

"I do have a very particular set of skills. Backwoods fisticuffs and farm animal management being two of my more in-demand ones," I quipped, still hoping to brazen my way through this without bursting into tears. Crying prettily was not in my skill set.

"I'm hoping that begging your forgiveness and convincing you that even though I acted like a jackass, I love you and want to make things right is in my skill set."

"Mine are better," I pointed out, trying to buy enough time to make sure I'd gathered my thoughts in a coherent way so I could say what I needed to.

"Have I mentioned that your competitive streak is one of the things I find most attractive about you?" He smiled, but it was a shaky thing and utterly unconvincing.

"I appreciate you coming here to apologize. But if you're looking for a reciprocal apology, I can't give it to you. I don't regret my decision. I'm sorry that I lost you and I ache that you're not in my life anymore," I said, my eyes flicking to his. "But I want to be clear. I didn't choose the island over us because I needed to win, to prove that I was the best. I did what I thought was best for Bard's, and I had to do it, because once I'd discovered those papers, I couldn't hide them. If there was any other way I could have done it without hurting you, I would have. But you weren't wrong when you said I chose the island over us.

"What you failed to mention is that you did the same thing. If I hadn't found those papers, you'd be drawing up plans for the island. You chose the island over us too. Neither one of us could set aside something so important to who we are at our core. I protected my family and friends, their way of life and the town's history. You protected your business and the people who work for you and who count on you. We're uncompromising people that way."

Ben's eyebrows knit together, and he was silent while he thought it over. I'd sweated some deals in my life, but nothing like this. I was sure I'd blown it. He'd offered me an olive branch and I'd taken a blowtorch to it. "Is that the worst thing?" he finally said.

"Not necessarily." I shrugged. "It didn't end well for us though."

"Maybe that's more a symptom of how we tried to resolve it. Trying to maneuver around what proved to be a major obstacle instead of hitting it head-on with everything we had and working together on a solution that, while not perfect for either of us individually, would have netted a better result for both of us."

I wrinkled my nose. "What would that have even looked like?"

"I should have listened to you when you asked me to walk away from the deal."

"Okay," I said, trying to think. "I shouldn't have gone behind your back and brokered a counter-deal."

Ben bit his lip, trying to hold back a smile. "Really?"

"Okay, fine. It was a brilliant counter-maneuver. What I should have said is, when I realized how much the development of the island bothered me even after we agreed to carve it out of our relationship, I should have told you and trusted you with my feelings."

"And I should have heard you and respected your feelings. We should have gone after it together instead of going underground on each other."

"Agreed."

"See, that wasn't so bad."

"There's one other thing I need to tell you," I said.

Ben groaned. "We were doing so well. What is it?"

"I love you too." I twisted my fingers in my lap. "I'm not much for big declarations. But I love you the way I love deals."

He blinked. "Wow. You are bad at this."

I held up a hand. "I bet you practiced your speech in the parking lot."

"Maybe," he admitted, the corner of his lips tugging upward.

"Well, I didn't. So you can just put your understanding-boyfriend face on while I bumble through this."

He grinned and pointed to his face. "Like this?"

"It'll have to do," I sniffed, although my own smile was now bending my lips to mirror his. "Ben, you spark a curiosity in me that never fades and you challenge me to give you my all. I want to spend each day trying to better understand you because from every angle I examine you, I love you. You're confident but vulnerable about who you are and where you've come from. You're competitive but never petty about it. You're kind when you could be cutthroat. Normally, I'd tally that as a weakness, but it's working for you. In short, I think you're the world's sexiest Rubik's cube."

Ben burst out laughing, taking my face between his hands and kissing me. And it was like coming home.

"Okay, where do we go from here?" I finally asked when we broke apart. "I hate to be a downer, but you know how I need a plan."

"We go forward. We do more of the dating thing. We're great at this dating thing. I hear there's this axe-throwing place downtown. Want to try for a hat trick of victories over me in the 'sports that aren't really sports' category? Unleash the ruthless competitor within again?"

"Oh, so now I'm ruthless?"

"You're a big softie. But your secret is safe with me. So what do you say, will you give this high-upside, manageable-risk, long-term deal with me a try, Portia?"

"Your annoyingly cheerful optimism is one of the things I love most about you."

"Uh-huh."

"We'll figure it out," I said, encircling my arms around his neck. "You and me against the world. Well, not exactly—it would be you, me and Hamlet against the world."

"You adopted Hamlet?" A delighted grin lit up his face.

"Of course I adopted Hamlet. I now spend my Sunday mornings staring at the treats in the trendy pet store wondering whether a previously feral dog prefers chicken apple sausage bites to moo tubes."

"Just curious . . . what is the preference of previously feral dogs?"

"Moo tubes," I said.

"What's a moo tube?" Rowan piped in from behind us.

"I'm not entirely sure," I admitted. "But I think it has something to do with the small intestine of a bovine."

"Well, that's revolting, I'm sorry I asked," Rowan said. "But in any event, you may not kiss against my bar. You two will need to take that and your talk of moo tubes outside."

"Exactly what I was thinking," Ben said.

"You can use the back exit," Rowan offered.

"I'm hardly a back exit kind of girl," I protested and stopped, groaning, when both men stared at me. "That's not what I meant."

"All class, this one," Ben teased and he led me out a side door to the back gardens.

"Candace is not going to love us wandering the grounds like this."

"Who do you think helped me set this up?" he said as he took me down a path to a burbling pond where koi fish swam in lazy circles. A table for two had been set up, and fairy lights hung between the trees.

As if conjured by the mere speaking of her name, Candace stepped out from behind one of the trees. "You like?"

"What's all this?" I demanded.

"I owe you a tasting menu dinner at Titania's. I always make good on my bets," Ben said. "This lovely woman was kind enough to set me up for success."

"What can I say, I'm a sucker for a pretty face. Yours, of course," she said to me.

"This is so beautiful," I told her. "You didn't have to go to all this trouble."

"Yes, well. You're worth the trouble. Except, can we maybe put a moratorium on B and E for the foreseeable future?"

"Fine, tie my hands," I grumbled.

"Another time," Ben whispered under his breath. I elbowed him with a laugh. Then I studied Candace for a beat, taking in the sleek dinner sheath of fiery red gold. "Where are you off to?"

"A lady never divulges her secrets," she scoffed.

"Treachery," I teased.

"If you must know, I'm having dinner with a friend."

"That is not a dinner-with-a-friend dress," I pointed out.

"Well, I'm keeping an open mind about his current status."

My eyes must have been bugging out of my head at this point, because both Candace and Ben were laughing at me.

Candace picked her way gracefully down the path. "Enjoy your dinner, you two."

"I want details later," I called after her.

I turned back to Ben. "Just curious," I said, "but what if I'd turned you down at the bar?"

"I'm sure Rowan would have made for a fine dinner companion out here. He has lovely taste in bourbon."

I slapped at his arm. "Well, I'm glad I said yes."

"Me too," he said, pulling me to his side and kissing the top of my head. "Because I have one more offer I'd like you to consider."

"I was serious about the back exit thing," I deadpanned.

"Oh, I think you're going to want to hear me out."

....

The (Now Thoroughly Deadheaded) Back Gardens

Portia, dear. I have cherished having you home this summer to help in the garden. But Bard help me, if you start deadheading the healthy blooms, we are going to have a problem, daughter of mine," Mom said, her voice serene as she stood, her gardening hat in one hand and a pair of shears in the other, with her back to the sinking afternoon sun.

"Sorry," I said, hastily wiping my hands on my leggings. I hadn't intended to deadhead, otherwise I'd have grabbed gloves, but then I'd seen that wilted Cosmo and I'd been unable to resist. Besides, they were black leggings. A little dirt wasn't going to kill me. But my mother might, if I overdid it in her flower beds.

"Maybe you should join a community garden in Boston. Now that you've made your decision."

"I think it's more likely I'd pull a Miranda, move out to the burbs with a backyard for Hamlet and attempt some raised beds."

At the sound of his name, Hamlet thumped his tail happily from his full-sprawl snooze in the grass beneath my mother's favorite wicker chair.

"That might be a lot of change in a short amount of time," Mom observed.

"You're right. I'll have to ease into the idea of moving to the burbs. For now, I'll plan to drive up here on the weekends and wreak havoc in your gardens."

"You wouldn't," she said. Was I mistaken, or had her grip on her shears just tightened?

"Oh please, with Cordelia jet-setting around the globe and Miranda planning her wedding, you're going to have your hands full finding a backfill for the café and talking Miranda out of Puck being the ring bearer. You know that dog has none of Hamlet's common sense. Puck will eat that ring on his way down the aisle."

My mother tried so hard to stifle a laugh. But even a classic French upbringing will only get you so far. "You know you're welcome here whenever you like. Just keep your hands off my roses."

"I can come up in three weeks for your appointment," I offered.

She shook her head, not a hair coming loose from that elegant bun. "It's only lab work and a check-in with Dr. Wu." She smiled, taking my hands. "I wanted to tell you first because I know how deeply you feel these things. But it's confirmed. It doesn't appear I'll be needing any more chemo anytime soon. I'll still be monitored, of course, but for now, I'm done with treatments."

"That is the best news of all," I said, throwing my arms around her and hugging her tight. "The best news, Mom." She was going to be okay. My mother was going to be okay. I tried to hold back my tears but a few stealthy ones slipped out anyway. Relief apparently tasted salty.

"Well, I would say it's certainly on par with Cordelia pursuing an opportunity outside of Bard's, Miranda marrying the person who makes her happiest and you," she said, pulling away, but still holding me by the wrists in that warm "like you're still hugging" way that only mothers can pull off, "pivoting."

"You don't think I'm throwing my life away?" I asked, unable to meet her eyes.

"I don't. But I think the more important question is what you think. Yours is the opinion that counts."

I nodded. "Well, if I crash and burn in this new role, I can always fall back on being a successful mini-golf entrepreneur. Maybe branch out and franchise?"

"I cannot believe you bought Peaseblossom's," she chuckled. "You think you finally reach an age in life where you can no longer be surprised, and then you're delighted to be proven wrong."

"I bought Peaseblossom's as a purely strategic play because I didn't trust Archie not to sell it to some skeevy developer."

"You should probably stop referring to developers as skeevy. Since you're dating one."

"I didn't say *Ben* was a skeevy developer," I corrected. "That would be rather shabby of me to disparage my minority silent partner in this venture," I said, smiling at the memory of Ben's pitch for us to buy Peaseblossom's to not only keep the only other development-eligible parcel of land in Bard's out of reach from less-than-community-minded interests, but as our forever date night spot, pointing out that as owners we could play whenever we liked. "In any event, Byron and Candace have offered to help us hire someone to run it, and they'll keep an eye on it. Nobody will even notice ownership has changed hands, unless it's to remark on the leveling up in maintenance." I didn't mention that someday I dreamed of building a third course onto Peaseblossom's for people who were allergic to Shakespeare. It would have classic windmills, a loop-the-loop and an utter dearth of water hazards.

"Maybe you can deadhead the gardens over there," Mom deadpanned. "Some of those beds are criminally leggy."

"I should probably get settled first, but I'll be up here before you know it to do just that. Don't tell Candace, but gardening might be better than yoga."

"I won't," Mom promised. "Now, on to more important topics," she said, leading me toward the house and away from her gardens. "What are your father and I making tonight for you and Ben's last night in Bard's?"

"Good question. Whatever it is, we're pairing it with bubbly. We have to celebrate this milestone in your treatment journey."

"I'm afraid you'll be disappointed, my darling. I know that you're accustomed to a higher standard of champagne in the city, but you'll be lucky to find anything over twenty dollars at Mercutio's."

"That's cute," I said, patting Mom's hand. "I have several bottles stashed in the basement. Remember when we celebrated you coming home from your surgery last summer? I figured we'd have more occasions to celebrate you in the future. That and I didn't feel like lugging that crate home to New York."

"There is three-hundred-dollar champagne stashed in our basement?"

"And you thought Cordelia was the reckless one."

....

The Office of Gerald Cutler

The Monday after Labor Day in New York was gloriously sunny, one of those still-warm days where all the outdoor cafés by Central Park would be packed by eleven. I stood in the reflective glare of the glass panels of FrancisPearl, allowing the sun to wash over me, and pushed through the revolving door into the building.

Chris waited in the lobby, nonchalantly sipping his coffee and scrolling through his phone. He rose when he saw me, sauntering over.

"Thanks for coming."

"I wouldn't miss this for the world. Even though I hate what it means."

I glanced at the elevator bank. "Ride up with me?" I asked. "One last time?"

He nodded. "For old times."

"For old times," I agreed.

When the door opened and we were about to part ways, Chris back to his partner's office and me to Gerald's, instead we stood there staring at each other. "Give him hell" is what he said, but what I heard in his words was "I'll miss you."

"I will," I said, clutching the manila envelope, now creased and slightly damp from the tight grip of my fingers. "You're the best friend I ever had here."

"I hardly think the 'had here' is necessary. How about, I share the honor with Candace? I'm secure enough to be one of your two best friends. As long as when in conversation, I am to be mentioned first, since I've known you longer. 'Chris and Candace, the best friends I don't deserve' . . . that kind of thing."

I knew what he was doing, trying to loosen me up with humor. I loved him for it. "Thank you. For everything."

He stepped forward, hugging me tightly. "Good luck."

I watched him turn and go, retreating into the belly of the corporate beast. "Good luck," I whispered under my breath and reminded myself that just because he was a partner here now didn't mean he would be a partner here forever. People could pivot, I reminded myself with a smile. Then I squared my shoulders and headed for Gerald's office.

I could tell from the way Gerald gripped his tablet as he scrolled through the *Times* that it had not gone unnoticed that I was nearly ten minutes late for our meeting. Rather than apologize, because I was thoroughly done apologizing to Gerald, I said in a bright tone, "Thanks for waiting for me."

Gerald looked up from his tablet, a flash of annoyance glinting in his eyes before he tamped it down. Ever the performer. "You're looking well rested."

"I am," I agreed. "Full of fresh perspective."

"Well, I for one am glad to hear it," the old gladiator said. "You've given us a lot to think about these last few months. I'm glad you're back on track. It was no easy feat talking the board into not withdrawing its offer."

As much as I wanted to point out that that was a problem of his own creation, that if he hadn't questioned my judgment at the board level in the first place, he wouldn't have had to walk it back, I remained silent, a serene smile anchored in place.

As I suspected, that threw Gerald. He'd been expecting me to say something. I wasn't following my usual playbook of strike first, ask questions later.

He stood, clearing his throat. "I'm afraid you've left us no choice after your little stunt in Bard's Rest. Consider the first six months of your management as probationary. Rex in HR will walk you through the profit-share implications and impact to your equity." He watched me, waiting for the impact of his blow. But I didn't even flinch. Instead, I notched up the wattage of my smile.

"That's too bad. I think it's a real shame I wasn't given an opportunity to present to the board on the matter of Bard's Rest. I rather considered it a coup from a pro bono perspective that FrancisPearl was able to be so instrumental in the discovery and protection of a previously undiscovered historical landmark."

"Yes." Gerald's face grew pinched like a prune. "That would certainly be a coup if we were in the business of defending against outside development. But since a large part of our practice is representing developers, you can see what a confusing message that sends to our clients. Our paying clients," he added, his voice souring on the last two words for emphasis. "As I've always said, pro bono is great for the complexion and all, but it doesn't pay the bills. Lucky for you I was able to frame this to the board as a one-time lapse in judgment brought on by misguided sentimentality." His eyes turned hard. "But I would certainly never expect such an error in judgment from you again. We have to have trust between us for this to work."

"By 'trust,' you mean I should follow your lead and take your direction without question. Stay out of your way and do as I'm told."

The sharpness of Gerald's gaze could have cut glass. "I expect you to continue to run all major decisions by me. In fact, the terms of your probation require senior management partner oversight, and I volunteered to be your mentor in this regard."

"I bet you did," I said softly, almost a purr. "So you can keep an eye on me, make sure I'm in your pocket and under your thumb at all times. Your eyes in Boston." I turned my back on Gerald to look out over the city. "I'm going to miss this view," I told him.

"Portia, I don't think you understand the seriousness of the board's decisions and the implications here—"

"Oh, I think I understand what you're implying. The gloss you're missing here is I just don't give a shit." I turned back to Gerald, crossing my arms over my chest. "Did you think you were the only person who has eyes and ears at the firm? Did you think during my sabbatical I would actually unplug?" I tsked. "Come on, Gerald, I learned from you to never take my finger off the pulse. I know you called the board meeting to discuss my fitness. I also know you called every single one of them in advance to convince them I'd gone rogue. How you alone could bring me back in line. You discredited me from the start and then made sure I wouldn't have a chance to speak at the meeting. Predictable and brutish, but effective. Just like you, Gerald."

"Watch your tone," he growled.

I lifted an eyebrow. "What's next, 'know your place'?"

"You're not going to have a place here if you don't stop this insolence. As managing partner, I expect you to exercise prudent judgment and act in the best interest of this firm."

"No you don't," I said tartly. "You expect me to do whatever you tell me and act in your best interest. The question is, what are you going to do, Gerald, when I don't? When I decide that the best course of action for the firm doesn't align with yours?"

"Do you hear yourself right now? What has gotten into you?"

"Fresh perspective," I deadpanned. "Maybe you should rethink your sabbatical requirements. I'm done being your hatchet. I'm not going to put my head down and do whatever you tell me. That's not what this firm needs. This firm needs someone who thinks for themself and questions the status quo when the situation calls for it. Because if I'd done that sooner, maybe we wouldn't be here."

"And where is 'here' exactly?"

"This is the part where I tell you I'm unwilling to accept your offer of probationary status as managing partner."

"Ah," he said, settling down a bit because he thought he'd figured out what I wanted. "Well, I'm afraid that won't be possible until you earn back our trust."

"*Your* trust," I corrected. "Go back to being your yes person." I shook my head. "That's not in the cards for us. I'm afraid you've lost my trust as well. Unfortunately for you though, there's no earning it back. Not when you've crossed an ethical line."

"I'm certain I don't know what you're talking about," he said, his voice stiff as his beloved two-finger pours.

"I'm talking about intimidating the competition, Gerald." I tossed the file onto the desk between us. It landed with a soft thud, but it was nevertheless the most satisfying thing I'd done in this office in a long time.

"What's this?" he asked, looking down his nose at the file.

"The account activities for RK Consulting, Inc. and DK Associates LLP. Clever of you to pay Dickie K out of your own pocket and off the FrancisPearl books. Audit will love you for that. Paying him out of Gillian's account was particularly devious. My PI might not have found it if I hadn't asked him to also run down not only your information, but hers. I know how much you value family."

Gerald stared at me with an almost bored expression. But for the way his fingers tightened around his Montblanc, I would never have known that I'd struck a blow. The benefit and curse of having worked together with someone so long was that you noticed tics like that. "I'm sure I don't know what you mean."

"Oh, is this the point where we play coy?" I smiled, and it was a vicious thing. A killing thing. "Let's just say I can now link several of those large payments to bids in Boston involving your clients, Gerald. Financed by your archivist wife. Doesn't seem like she'd run into much construction bidding in her day-to-day at the Cloisters."

"Leave her out of this," he growled.

"Why? You didn't."

"You have no proof of wrongdoing."

"I don't have to prove wrongdoing, Gerald. Remember? I just

have to call your judgment into question. Like you did mine. The appearance of impropriety here alone will do that. Well, those records and signed affidavits by Samantha Maeda of Dane Development, Trinity Johnson of Sage Associates and Hernando Serrano of Serrano and Sons, all attesting to intimidation tactics at the hands of a Richard Kerrigan. Known to his friends—and by 'friends,' I mean other lowlifes living under rocks—as none other than Dickie K."

"Circumstantial conjecture." He smirked.

"You say 'circumstantial conjecture'; I'm saying 'the appearance of impropriety and some unusual banking activity involving your wife's account.' I guess we'll let the board decide."

"You will not go to the board with this, Portia," he commanded, his voice a low roll of thunder now.

"It's too late for that, Gerald."

"I will ruin you," he hissed. "Do you hear me?"

"What, you'll try and have me fired from FrancisPearl?" I took a step closer. "You'll discredit me? Make sure you leverage all of your contacts to ensure I never find work at a reputable firm again? Engage in street-level intimidation tactics?" I smiled nastily. "You really are just a common thug in a nice suit, aren't you?"

"You'll never work as an attorney again when I'm done with you. Not even the ambulance chasers will take you on."

"I love that you think I didn't anticipate that."

I shook my head with a dramatic sigh, took out my phone, opened my Outlook browser, clicked on my saved drafts folder and hit send on the only email in there. A moment later the computer on Gerald's desktop dinged. "I wanted to give you a chance to be a better man here, but I'll be honest—I knew you weren't going to play fair. That's not your MO, is it?"

"What have you done?"

"Everything I've amassed on your interference with bids and Dickie K has been sent to the board with a detailed explanation of its contents. Oh, and lots of pictures."

Gerald snorted. "This will look like retaliation against me."

"It could," I agreed. "But I think when we tally up all the facts and circumstances and the reaction of several board members who were surprised you would call a board meeting to vote on my fitness without so much as a response from me, well, I think it's going to look more like a pattern of retaliation on your part."

"This won't save you."

"I don't need saving," I retorted, fixing him with the deadliest smile of all. "I sent my resignation to the board this morning. Thanking them for the opportunity here but declining for obvious ethical reasons." I'd also called Gillian this morning and given her a heads-up on what I'd discovered. But that bit I kept to myself. Because I liked Gillian and I wanted her to have the element of surprise on her side when she confronted Gerald. If the impressive swath of swears she used as I told her what her husband had done with her bank accounts was any indication, Gerald was a dead man.

"Cutting off your nose to spite your face, then?"

"I'm a big believer in winning at any cost. This is the cost. In the end, we're lawyers, Gerald. We can live in the gray, but we're not supposed to swing in the dirt; we're better than that. Our profession demands it."

"Such a Girl Scout," he spat.

"You're an embarrassment to the profession. I'm only sorry it took me so long to see that." I walked toward the door, my head as high as it had ever been in this office.

"Where are you going?" he shouted. "I'm not done with you."

"Oh, but I'm done with you, Gerald." I exited his office and the firm of FrancisPearl and never looked back.

Epilogue

....

Because I've Been Told All the Best Shakespearean Plays Have Them

The sun still shone brightly as I stepped outside the offices of FrancisPearl for the last time.

Ben leaned against the side of his car. Illegally parked, I might add. But strangely, I couldn't find it in me to care.

"How'd it go?" But before I could answer, Ben licked his finger and held it up, as if testing the wind. "Do I detect scorched earth?"

"He'll never get the smell out of his office," I assured him. "Not that I think it will be his office for much longer."

"Bravo." Ben clapped. "So, what's it feel like to be unemployed?"

"I'm not unemployed. I'm on vacation for the next three weeks," I amended. Three weeks, and then I'd assume the managing partner role at Collins, O'Brien and O'Berg LLP, the number one corporate and real estate boutique in Boston. Not only that, I'd convinced Riki to come with me. No more shark tank for her. I'd scored her an office with a window, a hefty signing bonus, a relocation stipend and a firm that had made meaningful strides to prioritize work-life integration over the churn-and-burn mentality of FrancisPearl. I think we both knew that life at a boutique would of course be challenging and fast-paced, but we had a chance to establish more meaningful boundaries. Especially me, not only for myself, but for the entire firm. I could model the change the legal profession so desperately needed. And when I fell short, I would have the world's sexiest life partner and a highly pettable dog to pull me back to balance.

"So what is this? A mini-sabbatical, then?" the aforementioned life partner teased.

"Something like that," I said as I drew him against me and kissed him long and thorough. "Any chance you can take an early lunch?"

"It's nine forty."

I snickered. "You know I didn't actually mean lunch, right?" I lightly ran my fingers down his chest, letting them rest on the top of his belt buckle.

"Actually, it so happens that I asked Sam to cover for me. I'm taking a few weeks off. Starting right now."

I grinned. "Sam must have loved that."

"Sam loves you," he corrected. "I'm in the doghouse for the next quarter, but it's worth it." He bent down, brushing his lips against my ear. "Let's go on an adventure. Where shall we go?"

"Other than back to my condo and its luxurious bedroom accommodations?" I said, a little breathless at the prospect.

"I was thinking somewhere that involves the airport and our passports."

I pulled back from him. "What about Hamlet?"

"He's crashing at Miranda and Adam's. Lucille's already his biggest fan."

"Of course she is. She's a pig of discerning taste," I sniffed.

"The problem will be getting him back from Miranda and Adam."

"Future Portia and Ben problems."

"Agreed, though I'd put my money on you in an animal-related brawl any day," he laughed. "So, where we going?"

"Mmm, Paris?" I suggested.

He waggled his hand back and forth. "I prefer Paris in the spring. How about Barcelona?" he countered. "Topless sunbathing? My tan lines are getting outrageous."

"Too hot right now. Italy?"

"Who says no to pasta and sun-drenched villas?"

We both looked at each other.

"Florence," we said in unison, laughing as we wound our arms around each other and kissed.

Acknowledgments

....

Now that I'm practically an expert on writing (two whole books out in the wild—watch out, world), I've come to realize it takes a special kind of person to get down in the book trenches with you. That person has to be willing to reassure you that your book is great, your sex scenes aren't gross and readers will find you. To that end, Maggie Cooper, thank you for always getting down in the book trenches with me. You are the best agent a word nerd could ask for and I'm so lucky to work with you.

To my talented and dedicated team at Berkley. Kate Seaver, thank you for giving me this opportunity and allowing me to take risks. Your margin comments are the highlight of the editorial process. Chelsea Pascoe and Jessica Plummer, I don't know how you do it, but thanks for making sure the whole world knows about Bard's. Amanda Maurer, thanks for keeping me on track.

Gilli Messer, I ugly cried the first time I heard you read my dedication to Em. Thank you for bringing the characters of Bard's to life through your narration. I hear your voice in my head when I write now, which is frankly far superior to listening to my own. Especially when it involves bowers.

Nikki Terry, you're insanely talented. Random words come out of my mouth and somehow you translate these into a gorgeous website that showcases all my best book angles.

Flor Fuertes, your work always thrills me. Thank you for another stunning cover.

Christy, it's always hard to write yours because thanking someone for their unconditional love and tireless, invaluable support sounds cheesy. So I'll just say, you're my best everything.

Pete, if you'd asked me the first day of Colby who I'd still be in deep platonic like with all these years later . . . yeah, I wouldn't have picked you. But here we are, friend. Thank you for always being in my corner, listening to me whenever I need you and reading my books and gushing about them. Yes, you totally gushed.

You really want to know what the best part of writing a book is? How the people in your life love your book like it's their own. Whether that's showing up at your book signings, hyping your book on social media, strong-arming their book clubs that only read thrillers into reading it or even accosting the occasional random stranger in a bookstore and demanding they read it, I am so appreciative to call you all friends (and some of you family). Thank you, Allison, Amanda, Anna, Auntie Winnie and Bella, Britt, Carolyn, Cheryl, Hilary, Jess, Karli, Katelyn, Melissa (yes, you, law school buddy), Melissa (yes, you, neighbor), Michelle, Rachel, Sofia, Val, my Little Elephant yoga crew (Julie, Michele, Karen) and the N-O-K-O-M-I-S girls (Alice, Jamie, Jane, Julie and Meredith).

Big, Boom, Brougham, Goose, Huff, if you're reading and thinking to yourself, *Wow, this partner buddy of Portia's is a damn delight,* he really is. I have the best guy friends to model him after.

Barb, thank you for keeping the cheese from sliding right off my cracker.

Amy and Amena, you are remarkable women. Thank you for showing me how to grab life and shake the joy from it.

Thank you to my team at work, Jenai and Tom. You are the best of colleagues (even if your collective checkered pasts have involved grand theft auto and the misappropriation of public pool facilities). Nobody's perfect, but you two are close.

Thanks to the entire [corporate name withheld to protect our illustrious brand] legal team for embracing this side hustle of mine.

Thank you to Ben, Betsy, Conboy, Harry, Jess, Jodi, Juliana, Kathleen, Kevin, Lance, Nancy (the original lambkin), Rich and Rick for being the kind of coworkers you never need to duck in the hallway.

Thank you to Whitelam Books, my local indie bookstore. Liz, your store and staff are magic. Whitelam was the first place we visited when the world opened up. Em and I sat down in your kids' nook and cracked open a chapter book, and all felt right again.

To Austin Tichenor of the Reduced Shakespeare Company. You're a true delight. Anytime you want to dish Shakespeare, you know where to find me.

To the crew at Barnacle Billy's and The Sparhawk. I'm not joking when I tell people I do my best writing on the porch. They just so happen to be your porches. And while I'm waxing poetic about Ogunquit, John and John at the Perkins Cove Pottery Shop, thank you for adopting me as your local author and bringing books to the Cove.

I am never going to stop thanking the dog people in my life who brought Phee home to us and opened my eyes to what it takes to rescue a dog. Susan, Mindy and Molly, you're forever on my list of favorite people. You too, Kerri Hark, you really are the cheese. As is Moneypenny, my furry firstborn. And finally, a special shout-out to Charlotte, Gracie and Riley, the dogs who started it all.

To the Sons of Larry. If you had asked me who my most die-hard supporters would turn out to be, I would not have necessarily pegged you golf-loving, hip-breaking, authority-challenging rap-scallions, but I am grateful for all of your help in getting the word out, especially you, Dad. 43.6334° N, 71.3860° W.

Justin, thanks for helping me carve out spaces and places to write.

John and Janelle, thanks for the love and support. Stay weird.

To my beautiful mother, Edna. Thank you for coming to all my book signings and acknowledging my book is actually funny. (I told you it was funny!) This one's for you.

Finally, to my daughter, Em. Thanks for always barging in while I'm trying to write and demanding to know what happens when animals poop underwater at the zoo. You're the best part of my day. Stay salty, kiddo.

The

DANE

of My

EXISTENCE

JESSICA MARTIN

READERS GUIDE

Questions for Discussion

....

1. Prior to assuming her role as managing partner, Portia is required to take a three-month sabbatical. How would you feel about taking a sabbatical? If you had the opportunity to take one, how would you spend that time?

2. Portia and Ben go toe-to-toe at Peaseblossom's mini-golf, a quintessential New England mini-golf course. If you could design a themed mini-golf course, what would it be? For the record, this author is pulling hard for a "Classic Literary Scenes" course. Holes would include Dracula's castle, Moby Dick taking down the Pequod, Daisy's dock (complete with a green light) and a gorgeously manicured Pemberley.

3. Like Portia, Ben is a tough nut to crack. He's unapologetically driven and thriving in the savage ecosystem that is the Boston development scene. But he's able to be vulnerable and authentic with Portia. Terrible taste in music aside, what do you make of him as a leading man?

4. If you've read *For the Love of the Bard*, the first book in this series, you'll recognize a lot of recurring characters coming back for a second helping of Shakespearean fun. Who were you most excited to see return? Or, if you're new to Bard's, who's your favorite character?

5. Portia, who's not exactly known for making fast friends, nevertheless forms a bond with the indomitable Emmeline McGandry. What did you make of this intergenerational relationship? Are there any particular hard-fought relationships you're grateful for in your life?

6. Portia feels like an outsider in her hometown of Bard's Rest. Despite this, she has continued to help out her hometown from afar. What do you think drives her decision to do so? What is your own relationship to your hometown like? Do you relate to Portia?

7. Let's talk about dogs, specifically Hamlet. One might say this author uses the plucky pup as a chance for Portia to step into the role of a badass, umbrella-wielding protector. Have you ever gone above and beyond to rescue an animal? (Hint: this would be an excellent time to steer the conversation to your undying love for your pets and acts of bravery in their name.)

8. Throughout this book, several characters contemplate the concept of pivoting—whether it's their careers or their relationships with others. What are the risks and rewards of their pivots? Have you ever been in a situation where you had to pivot, and if so, how did your experience compare with the experiences of the characters in the book?

9. Shenanigans abound in Bard's Rest, sometimes manifesting themselves in the form of farm animals wreaking havoc in the downtown area or covert island break-ins under the cover of darkness. Of the characters Adam, Byron, Candace, Cordelia, Ian and Miranda, who would you want by your side? Defend your answer.

10. On a scale of one to the Cliffs of Despair, how disappointed are you that Bard's Rest isn't a real place? If you could add a business or character to this thriving hamlet, what or who would it be? (My favorite reader suggestion so far is "Out Damned Spot Dry Cleaning.")

Author photo by Sarah Jordan McCaffery

Jessica Martin is a lawyer by trade, a writer by choice and a complete smart-ass by all accounts. Based in the suburban wilds of Boston, Jess shares her life with a finance geek, a small sass-based human and a pair of dogs named after Bond characters.

Ready to find
your next great read?

Let us help.

Visit prh.com/nextread

Penguin
Random
House